THE ART OF NOIR

THE ART OF NOIR

DELUXE ENTERTAINMENT BUNDLE

FOREWORD BY

RICHARD SMOLEY

Published 2025 by Maple Spring Publishing

Front cover design by Tom McKeveny
Interior design by Jason Snyder

Library of Congress Cataloging-in-Publication Data is available upon request

ISBN: 979-8-3505-0181-0

10 9 8 7 6 5 4 3 2 1

December 4, 2024

FOREWORD

BY RICHARD SMOLEY

The name *film noir* comes from the French for "black film." It is a term applied to a genre of films, chiefly from Hollywood in the 1940s and '50s. As often happens, it is easier to point to examples of film noir than to spell out a definition that can apply to all of them.

The term was originally applied by French critics in the aftermath of the Second World War. When the German occupation of France was over, they were able to see American films that had been made in the meantime, such as *The Maltese Falcon, Double Indemnity,* and *Laura*. And *noir* was the theme they had in common—both in mood and photographic style.

As the noir films in this collection show, similar elements recur in many. They often feature an antihero—the drifter Sam Masterson in *The Strange Love of Martha Ivers,* and the drug-addicted jazz drummer played by Frank Sinatra in *The Man with the Golden Arm*. On the other hand, *The Stranger* offers us a straight hero—the war crimes investigator played by Edward G. Robinson—as well as a conventional villain, a perpetrator of Nazi atrocities on the run, played by Orson Welles (who directed the film).

Another frequent figure in noir is the femme fatale, played by actresses such as Barbara Stanwyck, whom we see in *The Strange Love of Martha Ivers* and who had a similar role in 1944's *Double Indemnity*—acclaimed as one of the greatest noir films of all time. In *The Man with the Golden Arm,* the femme fatale is, bizarrely, the hero's wife, who plays invalid to make sure he feels guilty enough to stay with her. Stranger still is *Rebecca,* whose eponymous femme fatale never actually appears in the film, having died before the action begins.

Other characteristics of the noir genre include what critic Joan Copjec calls "the deep-focus photography and the chiaroscuro, 'expressionistic' lighting that pervade this cycle of films." These were developed in the film industry of Weimar Germany (1919–33). The famed *Cabinet of Dr. Caligari* (1920), with its bizarrely angled sets, was no doubt the first and greatest exemplar. Although *Caligari,* about a sinister hypnotist, fits better into the horror than the noir genre, we can see it as a precursor. This is also true of Fritz Lang's 1922 film *Dr. Mabuse Der Spieler* ("Dr. Mabuse, the Player") whose villain, again a sinister hypnotist, is capable of escaping prison with his mystical powers and inserting himself into the bodies of others. A 1931 film by Lang, *M*, which starred Peter Lorre as a serial killer, has even more elements that could be recognized as noir.

When the Third Reich came to power in 1933, many German filmmakers and actors—particularly the most creative ones—had to flee the country. Many ended up in Hollywood, which put their talents to good use. Lang, for example, directed the noir classic *Scarlet Street*, from 1945, and Lorre appeared in what sometimes seems to be the quintessential film noir, *The Maltese Falcon* of 1941. It did not exactly launch the noir genre (that honor generally goes to the mostly forgotten *Stranger on the Third Floor* from 1940, which also starred Lorre) but brought it into full view.

Hollywood did not come up with the name *film noir*. Nor, at least in the original period, did it ever apply it; hence it has been called "the genre that never was." (The term was only thought up by French critic Nino Frank in 1946.) Probably the best reply to this claim came from Billy Wilder, director of noir films including *Double Indemnity* and *Sunset Boulevard*: "I do not imagine Monet painting the landscapes and telling himself, 'Now, wait a minute. I'm an Impressionist. Therefore I must do it this way.' He didn't think. He painted.... If you have any kind of style, the discerning ones will detect it."

To see the noir genre as a whole, we can start with the feature that gave it its name. It alludes to the chiaroscuro—sharply contrasted black-and-white—style in which the films were shot, and which, again, go back to the German Expressionist films of the Weimar period.

The mood of many if not most noir films arises partly from the photographic style, which, as Copjec observes, creates "the empty, private spaces that compose the primary territory of *film noir*. Through the use of wide-angle lenses and low-key lighting these spaces are represented as deep and deceptive, as spaces in which all sorts of unknown entities may hide."

Hence noir films are characterized by a sense of dread, unease, and often inevitable disaster. In "Paint It Black: The Family Tree of the *Film Noir*," an influential essay from 1970, the English critic Raymond Durgnat observes, "Black is as ubiquitous as shadow, and if the term *film noir* has a slightly exotic ring it's no doubt because it appears as figure against the rosy ground of Anglo-Saxon middle-class, and especially Hollywoodian, optimism and puritanism."

But the mood is also generated by the action—crime, usually murder—which in turn arises from the motivation of the characters, who frequently feel desperate and cornered. This is patently true with Meinike, the fugitive war criminal of *The Stranger*. But it is also the case with Martha Ivers, who is raised in the upper class and has flourished in her hometown as an industrialist. At one point, her husband, Walter O'Neil (played by Kirk Douglas in an early role), tells her that she is "a little girl in a cage waiting for someone to let her out."

This desperation in turn stems from an underlying major theme: isolation, a theme that permeates American film and literature. There are few major American novels that do not center on the theme of isolation: crazy Ahab on the *Pequod*; Huck and Jim, the fugitive slave, drifting alone down the Mississippi; Gatsby, pining away in his ostentatious mansion. Even in novels where the main character is firmly installed in his niche of society—like the Boston Brahmin George Apley in John P. Marquand's eponymous novel—he is isolated, often because of some longing that his social niche does not allow him to fulfill. Indeed there are direct links between major literary novels and noir: 1951's *A Place in the Sun,* starring Robert Mitchum, is based on Theodore Dreiser's classic *An American Tragedy,* which in turn was based on a notorious 1906 murder.

In film noir as in American fiction, isolation plays an ambiguous role. It is not necessarily seen as negative: Sam Masterson, the drifting gambler in *Martha Ivers,* seems to relish his freedom, only returning to his hometown by accident. He does not end up alone—going off with Toni Marachek—but now they are in isolation as a couple. This is accounted a (more or less) happy ending. Note the contrast to the isolation of Martha Ivers and her husband, who are imprisoned in social roles that stifle them and drive Walter to drink.

In their study *The Moment They Met It Was Murder: "Double Indemnity" and the Rise of Film Noir,* Alain Silver and James Ursini, authorities on the genre, point to another central theme: obsession. It features prominently in all four of the films here: The deceased Rebecca (whom we never see) is the obsession of Mrs. Danvers, the sinister major domo who is the single most evil figure in any of these films. Martha Ivers remains haunted by Sam Masterson, her childhood love. In *The Stranger,* Mr. Wilson (played by Edward G. Robinson, another frequent actor in noir films) is obsessed with tracking down war criminal Franz Kindler—with good reason, since Kindler is portrayed as an architect of the Holocaust. Indeed *The Stranger,* released in 1946, provided one of the first public showings of footage from the newly liberated concentration camps. As for Frankie "Dealer" Machine in *The Man with the Golden Arm,* a heroin addiction is obsession enough for anyone.

Anyone looking for influences on film noir can find many sources: German Expressionism; the Hollywood gangster films of the 1930s; and perhaps most importantly, the persistent American fascination with crime, which has not only brought generations of moviegoers to theaters but has furnished rich material for true crime stories as well as their fictional developments (as we have seen with *An American Tragedy*).

But there is one influence above all that needs to be taken into account, even though it is the background. In fact it was in the background of every Hollywood movie made from the early 1930s to the mid-1960s: the Production Code Administration, which functioned as a de facto censor for that entire period.

Anyone who watches old silent films—I am thinking here of D.W. Griffiths' 1916 epic *Intolerance*—will notice that they had much more leeway in, for example, showing women's breasts (either naked or under diaphanous garments) than films would have for another fifty years. In the first couple of decades of Hollywood, decency codes amounted to what the studios could get away with. Since sexually provocative material is always a draw, they permitted themselves a lot.

This attitude began to change in the 1920s, when Hollywood was hit with a series of sex scandals, notoriously the Fatty Arbuckle case, in which Fatty, the lovable star of Mack Sennett comedies, was arraigned for the rape and manslaughter of actress Virginia Rappe in a San Francisco hotel in 1921. (For a salacious picture of the scandal, including the charge that Arbuckle raped her with a champagne bottle, see Kenneth Anger's *Hollywood Babylon*.) The ensuing trials acquitted Arbuckle, but apart from ruining his career, they aroused a call for greater "decency" in films.

Consequently, the Motion Picture Producers and Distributors Association (MPPDA) engaged the services of former postmaster general Will Hays to write a code of conduct for the industry. But the code was not enforced until the early 1930s, when the advent of violent and sexually provocative films such as *Scarface* and *Baby Face* provoked a number of powerful figures—many of them Catholics—to call for a sterner attitude.

In 1934, Joseph Breen was appointed to head the Production Code Association (PCA; known informally as the Hays Office), which was tasked with enforcing the code. Although adherence to the code was voluntary, most film exhibitors would not show a film without the PCA seal of approval.

The strictures of the Hays Office shaped what could and could not be done in movies. One provision: "The sanctity of marriage and the home shall be upheld." Hence adultery, excessive passion, and seduction or rape could never be more than hinted at. Categorically forbidden were sexual perversion, white slavery, miscegenation, sexual hygiene, vulgarity, obscenity, profanity, nudity, indecent exposure, as well as hangings, gruesomeness, branding of people or animals, apparent cruelty to children or animals, the sale of women, and even surgical operations, according to Robert L. McLaughlin and Sally E. Parry in their book *We'll Always Have the Movies: American Cinema during World War II*.

Perhaps the single most crucial provision of the Hays Code for the noir genre was this: "No picture shall be produced which will lower the moral standards of those who see it. Hence the sympathy of the audience shall never be thrown to the side of crime, wrong-doing, evil or sin."

This provision dictated the endings of noir films. A number of them arouse a certain sympathy for criminals and criminal elements, but they can never be vindicated. Happy endings (although loved by Hollywood and for that matter Americans) were not required, but justice was. Characters have to pay for their wrongs.

Note how this plays out in *The Strange Love of Martha Ivers*. Toni Marachek (played by Lizabeth Scott) is in trouble with the law; in fact, she is jumping parole. She has been charged with the theft of a fur coat. Here is her account:

> "Where'd you get the fur coat, Toni?" the judge asked me. "I met a guy," I told him. "He said he was in love with me. He gave me the coat." "A likely story," he said. I said, "But it's true, every word of it. I tried to pawn it because I needed the money." "Where is the man?" he asked. "I don't know." I said. "He took a powder. He blew, he flew to the moon." "You don't fly, Toni," the judge says. The charge is theft; you do one to five."

We are led to understand that Toni is telling the truth. The Hays Code did not dictate, or at any rate enforce, any requirement that the law or the legal system be shown as pure. In this film, Sam Masterson gets the charges against Toni dropped by what we may as well call blackmailing Walter O'Neil. But as we have seen, Toni has a happy ending with Sam. Why is she entitled to it? Because she is not a criminal: she did not steal the coat; she was framed. But Martha, who has killed her aunt and covered it up, pressures Walter into becoming a district attorney so that he can frame an innocent hoodlum for the murder. No happy ending can be assigned to Martha Ivers.

The law in *The Man with the Golden Arm* appears in an even worse light. Frankie's sidekick, Sparrow, gets him a new suit by questionable means: "A new thing by Brax department store!" says Sparrow. "No salesgirls. Just help yourself. It's what they call a honor system." Unfortunately gambling bigwig Zero Schwiefka overhears this and tells the police, who drag Frankie into jail for theft. It is all a setup: Schwiefka frames Frankie so that he can pressure him to going back to dealing cards in return for his release.

Durgnat calls this "The Sombre Cross-Section. A crime takes us through a variety of settings and types and implies an anguished view of society as a whole." The two instances above display the same corruption in lowlife Chicago and in the upper stratum of respectable American society.

As we have seen, the classic noir genre is dated to the 1940s and '50s. Sometimes Orson Welles' classic *A Touch of Evil*, released in 1958, is reckoned as the last film of the true noir genre. Certainly it features many recognizable themes: a seedy setting in a Mexican border town, corruption and crime (drug smuggling), and an antihero in the form of the degenerate and crooked police captain Hank Quinlan (played by Welles himself). At one point Marlene Dietrich, playing an aging post–femme fatale, tells him, "Your future's all used up."

So it turned out for Quinlan, but such was not the fate of the noir genre, whose themes have been used and reused ever since to the point where they have become hackneyed. Yet there is some truth to the claim that the late fifties marked the end of the classic period of the genre. *Out of the Past,* from 1947, is invariably classed as a noir film. But its 1984 remake, *Against All Odds,* is not, even though it is similar and in many ways a better film (certainly the plot is clearer). Why? Because of the photography. *Against All Odds* is shot in color, and the setting is bright and sunny Southern California, so it lacks the characteristic noir mood. The same is true for Roman Polanski's 1974 film *Chinatown,* despite its countless genre themes, including a jaded detective (played by Jack Nicholson), a femme fatale (Faye Dunaway), and corruption high and low (shady dealings over the Los Angeles water supply: Durgnat's "Sombre Cross-Section"). Because it was shot in color, it is regarded as a "neo-noir" film. *Noir* means *black*—and black in this case means black-and-white. Indeed some scenes from these films—like the refugee ship at the beginning of *The Stranger*—are so dark that it is hard (for the YouTube viewer at least) to see what is going on.

Neo-noir films have surfaced constantly in the American cinematic in the sixty years that have passed since the end of the classic phase of the era. Examples that come to mind are *The Grifters* from 1990, which features Annette Bening and John Cusack as a mother-son team of swindlers; Quentin Tarantino's 1998 film *Jackie Brown,* in which Pam Grier plays an airline stewardess caught up in drug smuggling and murder; and Tarantino's 1994 post-noir *Pulp Fiction,* which self-consciously plays with the genre (as, for example, in its title). The masterful *Nightmare Alley* of 2021, outlining the rise and fall of a seedy carnival barker, is a remake of a 1947 film of the same title, which, unlike many noir films, had an A-list budget and cast, with Tyrone Power and Joan Blondell.

The demise of the Hays Office in the 1960s led to a major change in the noir genre. Now it was no longer obligatory for criminals to come to justice. Today they are often the objects of the audience's sympathy, as in the case of numerous heist movies, such as 1999's *Heist,* directed by David Mamet and starring Gene Hackman and Danny DeVito. Indeed the heist film constitutes a genre of its own.

As much as the cinematography and moral backdrop of the noir genre have changed, its prime concerns—notably the isolation and alienation of American life, which can easily lead to desperate crimes—remain with us. They continue to serve as sources of entertainment in the cinema and of disquiet in the national psyche.

RICHARD SMOLEY, a graduate of Harvard and Oxford universities, is the author of fourteen books, including *The Dice Game of Shiva: How Consciousness Creates the Universe*; *Forbidden Faith: The Secret History of Gnosticism*; and *Seven Games of Life and How to Play.*

THE STRANGER

Screenplay by ANTHONY VEILLER
(ORSON WELLES and JOHN HUSTON, uncredited)
Adapted by VICTOR TRIVAS and DECLA DUNNING
Story by VICTOR TRIVAS

CAST

Orson Welles .... Franz Kindler/Professor Charles Rankin
Edward G. Robinson .... Mr. Wilson
Loretta Young .... Mary Longstreet Rankin
Philip Merivale .... Judge Adam Longstreet
Richard Long.................................. Noah Longstreet
Konstantin Shayne .... Konrad Meinike
Byron Keith .... Dr. Jeffrey Lawrence
Billy House.. Mr. Potter
Martha Wentworth...Sara
Isabel O'Madigan.................................... Mrs. Lawrence
Pietro Sosso ....Mr. Peabody
Erskine Sanford .... Party Guest

The film begins with a SECRETARY exiting a door with the sign "Allied War Crimes Commission, Dept. 12." She carries some files.

FADE IN: BLUE SKY—DAY

Close-up of WILSON, with prison gates behind him. He is smoking a pipe. His face is grim as he listens to men's voices off scene.

WILSON

Leave the cell door open, that's all there is to it. Let him escape.

The CAMERA pulls back to reveal several MEMBERS of the War Crimes Commssion.

FIRST VOICE

(an English accent)

In my view, it's all very irregular. It might entail the most embarrassing repercussions—

SECOND VOICE

(French accented)

***Exactement.* Certainly. It is a responsibility of the first magnitude.**

FIRST VOICE

I'm sorry, Mr. Wilson, but you must see . . .

Suddenly, without warning, WILSON turns on them. His voice is sharp with suddenly released rage.

WILSON

Blast all this discussion. What good are words . . .

(gesturing with his pipe)

I'm sick of words . . . Hang the repercussions and the responsibility. If I fail . . . I'm responsible. Leave the cell door open! Let him escape! Let him! It's our only chance! You can threaten me with the bottom pits of hell . . . and still I insist.

(he pounds on the desk for emphasis, the pipe still in his hand)

This obscenity must be destroyed. You hear me? Destroyed!

WILSON slams his pipe down on the table, breaking it.

FADE OUT

FADE IN: EXT. DECK—NIGHT (CRANE SHOT)

MEINIKE, in shadow, is walking on the deck of a passenger ship, muttering to himself.

VOICE OF ANNOUNCEMENT

Todos pasajeros disembarcen! All passengers ready to disembark!

MEINIKE

(muttering to himself)

I am traveling for my health . . . I am traveling for my health . . .

MEINIKE turns around; we see WILSON, with his back turned to us, identified by his now repaired pipe, on which he is puffing. MEINIKE does not see him.

VOICE OF ANNOUNCEMENT

Tenga vistas y passaportes! Get your passports ready!

MEINIKE

(muttering to himself)

I am traveling for my health . . .

EXT. LOWER LEVEL OF DOCK SHED—NIGHT

MEINIKE approaches the immigration desk, behind which an IMMIGRATION OFFICIAL and the Ship's PURSER sit side by side. Opposite them are lined up the ship's PASSENGERS. An AMERICAN LADY, MRS. DEVRIES is talking to the OFFICER.

As the OFFICIAL examines the next person, the CAMERA SWINGS SLIGHTLY to focus on MEINIKE, the next in line. His lips move in a soundless rhythm of "I am traveling for my health . . . I am traveling for my health . . ."

MADAME DE VRIES

I'm afraid I don't understand.

OFFICIAL

Your business in this country, Senora?

MADAME DE VRIES

I am joining my husband.

OFFICIAL

(stamping the passport)

Next, please.

MEINIKE shuffles the necessary step forward and extends his passport with trembling fingers; his lips continue to move.

OFFICIAL

(with same casualness as he opens the passport)

Stefan Polowski.

As he pronounces the name, he hands the passport to the PURSER.

PURSER

(looking up at MOINIKE*)*

Your business in this country, Señor?

MEINIKE once again completes his silent repetition of the phrase, then speaks it aloud.

MEINIKE

I am traveling for my health.

OFFICIAL

Health?

MEINIKE

I am traveling for my health.

OFFICIAL

Oh. You are a native of what country?

MEINIKE

Poland.

CAMERA CRANES UP to WILSON, standing on the upper level of the dock. He is leaning against a pillar, but we do not see his face; only his pipe. As we watch him, he removes his dead pipe from between his lips and raps the inverted bowl twice against the pillar. SENORA MARVALES is standing next to him. But we do not see their faces. We hear the sound of a passport being stamped and the OFFICIAL's voice.

OFFICIAL'S VOICE

(Over Scene)

Next, please.

SENORA MARVALES descends from the upper deck and follows MEINIKE on the main deck. He continues on, but she turns and goes down a flight of stairs, where a MAN is waiting in a vehicle.

MAN

Que paso?

SENORA MARVALES
(says something in Spanish)

MARVALES
Bien.

He drives off.

STONE BRIDGE—NIGHT SKY

This DISSOLVE is almost a FADE OUT, the CAMERA being focused on the limitless darkness of a night sky.

We see MRS. MARVALES as she follows MEINIKE, who walks across a rustic bridge. There is the sound of a slow, sad tango and the faint murmur of voices. MEINIKE is passing a cheap nightclub.

As MEINIKE moves out of scene, CAMERA remains stationary, still tilted up. MARVALES is standing in the recess of the window, his face half hidden, as he watches MEINIKE in the street below. In his room, MARVALES picks up a phone.

MARVALES
(into phone)
Hotel Nacionale? Siete, siete, cero, dos . . .

We hear the ringing of a telephone.

We see the shadow of a cradle telephone as a hand reaches for it and picks it up. Next to the phone are a couple of books, one open. WILSON's hand closes one. We see its title: The Old Clock Book. Under it is The Clock Book by Wallace Nutting. WILSON's hand sets down his pipe on top of it.

WILSON
Hello? Yes.
(pause)
You haven't lost him? You're sure you know where he's going?

MARVALES—AT WINDOW—NIGHT

MARVALES
(into phone)
My wife is following him; he is going to the photographer's, probably to get a new passport—and new instructions.

***DISSOLVE TO: INT. PHOTOGRAPHER'S STUDIO—
CLOSE SHOT—MEINIKE EARLY DAWN***

We see MEINIKE's face in a mirror. The PHOTOGRAPHER, next to the mirror, takes a shot of him.

MEINIKE
(in a loud voice)
I wish to know the whereabouts of Franz Kindler. Franz Kindler.

The PHOTOGRAPHER starts.

PHOTOGRAPHER
(slowly)
There is no Franz Kindler. Franz Kindler is dead . . . and cremated.

MEINIKE comes into the shot, his face shadowed in quarter view.

MEINIKE
(shouting)
It's a command!
(his voice lowers but its intensity remains)
I have a message for Franz Kindler. From the All Highest.

PHOTOGRAPHER
(uncertainly)
It is forbidden.

MEINIKE
(his voice high and piercing)
I command you in the name of that authority!

Invoking this power intimidates the PHOTOGRAPHER. He moves across the shabby room. He pauses at a small table on which there is a large album, then hesitates, glances back at MEINIKE.

The PHOTOGRAPHER begins to leaf through the album, turning pages slowly. He stops, turns to stare at MEINIKE. The PHOTOGRAPHER, with a doubtful sigh, turns a few more pages in the album, and removes a picture postcard.

PHOTOGRAPHER
You know the name he's using?

MEINIKE does not answer but reaches for the card.

INSERT—CLOSE SHOT—
PICTURE POSTCARD HARPER TOWN SQUARE

On the postcard is a photograph of the Harper Square: main street, shops, and church. We can see the clock in the church tower, but it is inconspicuous. Written on the bottom of the card are the numerals "23478-678901," and "Harper, Connecticut."

MEINIKE

Con-nec-ti-cut. In the United States. The town of Harper.

FADE IN: EXT. HARPER CLOCK TOWER—DAY

The scene turns to the main square of Harper. We see the church with the clock tower, identical to the picture on the postcard. Camera now swings and pans down to disclose the Harper town square, fronting a green, around which the township itself is clustered.

A bus pulls up in front of Potter's Drugs. Inside the bus, the DRIVER calls out:

DRIVER

Harper!

MEINIKE gets up to take down his bag. As he does, WILSON is already taking down his own bag. His repaired pipe falls on the floor. WILSON picks it up.

WILSON

Oh. Excuse me.

MEINIKE looks at WILSON with apprehension, then hastily takes his bag and leaves the bus. WILSON takes his bag and follows him.

MEINIKE goes into Potter's Drugstore, looking uneasy.

POTTER is seated at an open window, laughing at a radio broadcast.

WILSON comes up to the window.

POTTER

Good afternoon. Have a nice trip?

WILSON

Yes, thank you.

MEINIKE looks at them both with extreme apprehension.

WILSON

Quite a fine store you have here, Mr. Potter.

POTTER

That's me. We sell about everything here.

At the phone booth, MEINIKE rifles panickily through the phone book. WILSON takes a look at him and leaves. MEINIKE finds a number and memorizes it.

POTTER is still chuckling at the radio broadcast. MEINIKE comes up to the counter and puts his bag down on it.

MEINIKE

This suitcase—I could leave it here?

POTTER

I don't assume no responsibility. Just put it up on that shelf. It'll be there when you want it.

MEINIKE puts his bag on the shelf and leaves. WILSON reappears in the window, with a magazine.

WILSON

I'll buy this magazine. What's the best hotel in town?

POTTER

The best place to stay is Mrs. Peabody's. It's just down the road here a piece.

On the street, WILSON sees MEINIKE and follows after him—in the opposite direction to the one that POTTER has indicated.

POTTER

This way, Mister.

WILSON

Yes, thank you.

But WILSON continues to follow MEINIKE. MEINIKE knows that he is being followed and quickens his pace. He dashes across the street and is almost hit by an oncoming car. The car halts and honks. MEINIKE goes on, followed by WILSON.

On another street, MEINIKE looks around in panic for a place to run to. We see a concrete post with the sign "Harper School for Boys." MEINIKE goes up the stairs to an unlocked door at the top, opens it, and goes in, closing the door behind him.

WILSON, below, has missed MEINIKE but looks up at the door and goes up the stairs too. He closes the door behind him.

Inside the school, MEINIKE goes into a gym, followed by WILSON. MEINIKE stops in front of a couple of fire extinguishers; an axe is hung in the middle. MEINIKE goes to take down the axe but thinks better of it and moves on.

WILSON enters the gymnasium. Above, on a mezzanine, we see MEINIKE. Two gymnastics rings are hanging on chains near him. MEINIKE swings one down and hits WILSON on the head. WILSON falls down unconscious. MEINIKE flees through a mezzanine door.

The scene changes to a street with a house in front of it. MARY is standing in the window, hanging curtains. MEINIKE goes up to the house and knocks. MARY opens. MEINIKE barges in and closes the door while saying:

MEINIKE

Can I come in?

MARY

Yes, of course!

MEINIKE peers apprehensively through the curtain on the door. He goes into the hallway.

MEINIKE

Does Mr. Charles Rankin live here?

MARY

Yes, he does, but he isn't here right now.

MEINIKE

Are you expecting him?

MARY

Yes, in a few minutes.

MEINIKE

How soon?

MARY

A few minutes.

MEINIKE

How soon?

MARY

A few minutes.

MEINIKE takes off his hat.

MEINIKE

I may wait here?

MARY

Yes, if you like. Would you like to sit down?

MEINIKE

Thank you.

MEINIKE sits down in a chair in the corner. MARY picks up the curtains she was hanging.

MARY

Are you a friend of Mr. Rankin?

MEINIKE

Yes, a friend.

MARY

I'm Mary Longstreet. How do you do?

MEINIKE

How do you do?

MARY sets down the curtains on the ladder she was standing on.

MARY

Mr. Rankin ought to be here now. Sometimes he stays after class, but he'll be coming straight home today, I'm sure. This is our wedding day.

MEINIKE

You are getting married?

MARY

Yes, at six o'clock. I know it's most unconventional, my being here today, but I want to get these curtains up.

MEINIKE gets up uneasily and puts on his hat.

MEINIKE

When he comes, which way does he come?

MARY

From Webster Hall. It's the big building right over there, see?

MARY opens the curtains to show him.

MEINIKE

Thank you.

He goes out.

MARY

But who should I say—?

But MEINIKE has left before she can finish.

We now see RANKIN walking down a school sidewalk in front of the chapel. As he passes, MEINIKE accosts him from behind a bush.

MEINIKE

Franz! It's me, Franz!

RANKIN

Meinike! We mustn't be seen talking together. Go back into the church—into the woods! Follow the path; I'll meet you there.

MEINIKE obediently goes off. Four STUDENTS come up to RANKIN from behind.

STUDENT #1

Hello, Professor Rankin!

RANKIN

Hello, men. What are you up to?

STUDENT #1

Paper chase. I go ahead and lay the trail.

STUDENT #2

You oughta have Jerry's job, Professor Rankin. Take a little off that waistline.

STUDENT #3

You ought to go with us, Mr. Rankin.

RANKIN

Where to?

STUDENT #2

The woods.

An attractive BLONDE goes by in the background. The STUDENTS whistle.

RANKIN

The woods? I'd like to, but I'm afraid I have a couple of other things to attend to.

STUDENT #1

Join us later. We'll be out till dark.

RANKIN

All right.

STUDENT #1

We'll catch up with you.

In the woods, STUDENT #1 is throwing paper; the other STUDENTS are following him.

Elsewhere in the woods, MEINIKE comes up to RANKIN, who embraces him.

RANKIN

Meinike!

MEINIKE

Yes, Meinike.

RANKIN

I thought—

MEINIKE

I had been hanged—the others, but not I.

RANKIN

You haven't much changed—put you back in your old uniform, you'd look very much the same.

MEINIKE

Franz, I'm a different man from before.

RANKIN

I too. I too am different. I've changed a lot, Conrad. You know I gathered and destroyed every single item in Germany and Poland that might provide a clue to my identity. Guess what I'll be doing at six o'clock tonight? Standing before a minister of the Gospel, with a woman standing by me—the daughter of a justice of the United States Supreme Court, a famous liberal. The girl is even good to look at. Yes, the camouflage is perfect. Who would think that I was the notorious Franz Kindler in the sacred precincts of the Harper School, surrounded by the scions of America's first families? I'll stay hidden until the day we strike again.

MEINIKE

Franz! There will be another war?

RANKIN

Of course.

MEINIKE

War is an abomination. That is why I am here. That is why they released me. They set me free so that I could come . . .

RANKIN

Who set you free?

MEINIKE

The Almighty.

RANKIN

You don't mean . . .

MEINIKE

I mean God!

RANKIN clutches him by the arm and laughs.

RANKIN

Come!

MEINIKE

Franz, I'm a new man since I—

RANKIN

You, Conrad, religious!

MEINIKE

Franz, all doors were open to me! All the doors! It was one of God's miracles!

RANKIN

Mm . . . hmm.

RANKIN pauses as he realizes the truth.

RANKIN

They freed you so you could lead them to me. Have you been followed? Were you followed here?

MEINIKE

Yes!

RANKIN

Who followed you?

MEINIKE

The evil one! He looked like any other man. He was dressed just like any other man. He even smoked a pipe! I recognized him. And I killed him. I hit him. God's will be done.

RANKIN

You killed him—the man with the pipe?

MEINIKE

Yes.

RANKIN

The man who followed you? No one else followed you?

They walk on.

RANKIN

Mm-hm. Mm-hm.

MEINIKE

You must be brought to salvation, Franz. Confess your sins, as I have. Proclaim your guilt! Only thus you can obtain salvation.

RANKIN

You really think so, Conrad?

MEINIKE

The strength can only come from God.

RANKIN

Mm-hmm.

MEINIKE

Kneel, my new friend, and together we will pray to him to give you strength.

But they do not kneel. MEINIKE removes his hat.

MEINIKE

(praying)

I have sinned against heaven, and before Thee. I am not worthy to be called Thy son. Say these words after me: I despair of my sins.

RANKIN

I despair of my sins.

MEINIKE

O God of all holiness, how could I have ever offended thee?

RANKIN takes MEINIKE by the neck.

RANKIN

. . . of all goodness . . .

RANKIN strangles MEINIKE.

STUDENT'S VOICE

This way, fellas! And don't let him get away!

RANKIN runs off.

The STUDENT runs past the bush where MEINIKE's body lies and goes on.

RANKIN drags MEINIKE's body off the path and covers it hastily with dirt. He runs off in panic to the site where he and MEINIKE stood talking and cover the tracks with dirt as well. He picks up some of the paper chase papers and strews them in another direction.

STUDENT'S VOICE

Hey, fellas!

Two other STUDENTS run after the first one, past MEINIKE's body, which they do not notice. RANKIN runs off.

STUDENT

This way, fellas!

The scene shifts to a church, where RANKIN and MARY are standing before a CLERGYMAN. JUDGE LONGFELLOW is at MARY's right; LAWRENCE is at RANKIN's left.

CLERGYMAN

Dearly beloved, we are gathered in the sight of God and in the face of this company to join together this man and this woman in holy matrimony.

The scene now shifts back to the gym, where WILSON is lying, recovering consciousness. His pipe is lying before him. He picks it up distractedly and stumbles to his feet.

Back in the church:

CLERGYMAN

. . . And forsaking all others, be faithful to her alone, as long as ye both shall live?

RANKIN

I will.

CLERGYMAN

Mary, wilt thou have this man for thy husband to live together after God's ordinance in the holy estate of matrimony? Wilt thou love him, honor him, comfort him, keep him, in sickness and in health, forsaking all others, keeping only unto him, so long as ye both shall live?

MARY

I will.

In the main square of Harper, WILSON walks along, touching his head, which is still in pain. He goes into the drugstore. POTTER is at the counter.

WILSON

Afternoon.

POTTER

Afternoon.

Through the window, across the green, WILSON sees the wedding party.

WILSON

Wedding?

POTTER

Yeah. Judge Longstreet's daughter. He's a Supreme Court justice, you know.

WILSON goes to the counter.

WILSON

Bottle of aspirin, please.

POTTER

(pointing)

Right back there, third shelf down from the top. You'll see the big one's on the left, the economy size. You've got to get it yourself, Mister. Right back there.

WILSON goes toward the aspirin.

POTTER

All your needs are on our shelves. Just look around and help yourself. Right, down that shelf. That's it.

WILSON reaches onto a shelf and removes a bottle.

POTTER

Living down at Mrs. Peabody's?

WILSON

Just for a few days only.

WILSON approaches the counter.

WILSON

Coffee too, please. Or should I get it myself?

CUSTOMER AT COUNTER

Cafeteria style around here.

POTTER

That's right: self-service. Three dollars even.

WILSON

What about the cream?

POTTER

Folks around here take it black.

WILSON goes to a coffee urn.

CUSTOMER

The one on the right.

WILSON pours himself a cup.

WILSON

Thank you.

(now behind counter, drawing a cup of coffee)

Who's Miss Longstreet marrying?

MR. POTTER

One of the teachers down at the school.

FEMALE CUSTOMER

Stranger in town.

POTTER

I issued the license.

WILSON

(interestedly, coming around opposite POTTER*, carrying cup)*

Oh?

MR. POTTER

Yeah. I'm town clerk.

WILSON comes up to the counter, where there is a checkerboard.

POTTER

Checkers?

WILSON

All right.

WILSON sits down in front of the counter to play.

WILSON

Town clerk, huh? Well, must be quite a responsibility!

POTTER

(making move)

Town clerk runs the town, you might say . . . We usually make it for 15, 20—we often play as high as 25¢ a game.

WILSON

Kind of stiff for me, but I'll take a fire. Make a million, lose a million.

POTTER

That's the way it goes. My move.

WILSON

All right . . . You must know just about everybody in town here?

POTTER

Not just about. Know everybody.

(his tone changing)

Are you here on business?

(WILSON *nods)*

WILSON

Uh-huh.

POTTER

School business?

WILSON shakes his aching head.

POTTER

Sellin' somethin'?

Again WILSON shakes his head.

Buyin'?

WILSON's eyes search the room. They see a sign. It announces a sale of antiques. WILSON points to it.

MR. POTTER

Oh . . . antique dealer. They all come to Harper.

(WILSON *nods)*

Judge Longstreet's got the best collection in these parts. Won't do you no good, though.

WILSON

No. I don't suppose he'd sell.

(casually)

Happen to know if there are any other out-of-town buyers here?

MR. POTTER

Come to think of it, there was a fella come in this morning. He came on the same bus with you. Left his suitcase here, never did come back for it. He might be one of them. But no . . . no, he was more of a missionary type. Wasn't in here but a minute. Just looked in the phone book. Tiny little fella, he was. Thinnish. Unfortunate-looking.

WILSON takes off his hat and rubs his head painfully.

POTTER

Hurt your head, Mister?

WILSON

No, nothing serious.

WILSON makes a bad move on the checkerboard.

POTTER

That's too bad.

POTTER triumphantly jumps five men. WILSON looks startled.

MR. POTTER

(with great unction and satisfaction)

In this game, you gotta keep your mind going. 25 cents, please.

DISSOLVE TO: INT. LONGSTREET HOME—NIGHT

The wedding reception is in progress. Most of Harper is present, both school and town.

CAMERA, on crane, moves through the crowd with MARY, who still carries her bridal bouquet. She stops by old MRS. LAWRENCE.

MRS. LAWRENCE

I won't pretend I'm not disappointed . . .

Mary comes to a group surrounding JUDGE LONGSTREET, which includes NOAH.

MARY

Has anyone seen my brand-new husband?

JUDGE LONGSTREET

Don't tell me he's deserted you already.

MARY

(pushing back his lock of hair)

Looks as if. The brute.

She turns to find her Irish setter, RED, at her heels.

Red . . . where's Charles? Go find Charles! Go on! Hurry up!

The dog runs off obediently.

DISSOLVE TO: EXT. WOODS—NIGHT—CLOSE SHOT

RANKIN is finishing filling up a grave with MEINIKE's body. He covers it with leaves. Realizing that he still has MEINIKE's hat, he hastily covers it with some leaves and dirt.

DISSOLVE TO: INT. LONGSTREET HOME—NIGHT

NOAH is reporting to MARY, who stands beside JUDGE LONGSTREET.

NOAH

I've looked everywhere for him, Mary And I can't find him.

MARY

But where could he be? I'm getting worried.

RANKIN'S VOICE

(over scene)

Are you, darling? What about?

Camera pulls back to include RANKIN as he reaches her side. He wears a slack suit.

MARY

Oh . . . you've changed.

RANKIN

Don't you think you'd better? Weren't we supposed to go on a honeymoon or something?

MARY

Just give me five minutes.

MARY rushes out of the room.

INSERT—A PAGE

It is headed "Arrivals in Harper last 12 months." Beneath this are six names, through the top four of which a thin line has been drawn. The fifth and sixth names on the page are SAUNDERS SCUDDER and CHARLES RANKIN. Entries after the names establish their occupations as teachers at the Harper School.

INT. WILSON'S ROOM—DAY

WILSON tilts back in his chair, frowning thoughtfully. His eyes wander out the window. What he sees jerks him upright.

THE VILLAGE SQUARE

WILSON is looking straight across at the clock tower. The hands of the clock move . . . stop . . . move again . . . and stop.

INT. WILSON'S ROOM

WILSON whirls from the window, shoves the papers on table into his pocket, snatches up his hat, and exits.

INT. CHURCH

WILSON, removing hat, enters, crosses the length of the church and starts up the stairs leading into the belfry . . . CAMERA following.

INT. BELFRY

WILSON ascends and goes up two flights. He sees NOAH above him.

INT. CLOCK TOWER

WILSON sees NOAH, back turned, wiping the clock's works with a cloth. WILSON comes forward as NOAH, surprised at the interruption, faces him.

WILSON

Hello there.

NOAH

(politely)

Hello.

WILSON

(examining the works)

Is that you working upon there on the clock?

NOAH

No, sir. I'm just cleaning around it.

WILSON

Beautiful clock, beautiful, from what I could see out front!

(casually)

Oh, by the way, my name's Wilson.

NOAH

I'm Longstreet, Noah Longstreet.

WILSON

(he and NOAH *shake hands)*

Glad to know you. I couldn't tell from out front, but I would say that it was late 16th century. Probably by Hobrecht of Strasbourg. You know, the clock.

NOAH

I wouldn't know. My brother-in-law is going to work on it.

WILSON

Oh. Is he up there now?

NOAH

No, he's on his honeymoon. He plans to work on it when he gets back.

WILSON

Oh. Is he an expert?

NOAH

(shrugging)

Yes, but it's really more of a hobby with him.

WILSON

Really? It is with me too. Honeymoon?

NOAH

Yes. He and my sister . . . He has to be back on Friday because of examinations. He's one of the teachers at the school. His name is Rankin.

WILSON

Oh?

DISSOLVE TO: INT. LONGSTREET LIVING ROOM—NIGHT

WILSON is examining a silver inkstand, with JUDGE LONGSTREET and NOAH standing next to him.

JUDGE LONGSTREET

It's nice to show it to somebody who knows what Revere silver's all about. But, personally, my specialty is pewter.

WILSON

(a little absently—not wanting to get caught on a subject he's not boned up on)

Yes . . . pewter.

(then, brightening, as he remembers a quote from the book he's been studying)

The Revere workmanship, although sometimes heavy in design, almost invariably shows the sign of a master craftsman. This is beautiful.

MARY and RANKIN come in. MARY comes up to NOAH and embraces him.

MARY

Noah.

She kisses her father.

MARY

Adam.

JUDGE LONGSTREET

Mr. Wilson, my daughter Mary. My son-in-law, Charles Rankin.

WILSON shakes MARY's and RANKIN's hands.

MARY

How do you do.

WILSON

How do you do. I hope you won't mind my intruding on your homecoming.

SARA and LAWRENCE enter.

LAWRENCE

Good evening, Mary.

MARY

Jeff, how are you! You're looking good.

LAWRENCE and MARY hug.

SARA

Welcome home, Miss Mary. Dinner is served.

To SARA's embarrassed delight, MARY embraces her.

MARY

Hello, Sara.

SARA

(squirming)

If you don't set down, it'll get cold!

JUDGE LONGSTREET

Well, sister, how were the mountains?

MARY

They were perfectly marvelous!

TRAVELING SHOT

Camera moves ahead of them as they move into the dining room, where a table is set. MARY sits at one head of the table, facing JUDGE LONGSTREET.

MARY

Mr. Wilson, will you come sit here on my right? Jeff, in your usual place, and darling, you're right there.

They all sit down.

MARY

You ought to see Charles on skis. He's absolutely wonderful!

RANKIN

No . . .

MARY

Yes, darling, you are. And I'm pretty good too, aren't I?

RANKIN

Very.

MARY

Well, for a beginner.

LAWRENCE

Did you remember to keep your knees together and your apparatus in?

MARY

Yes, Jeff, I did.

JUDGE LONGSTREET

Mr. Wilson here is compiling a catalogue of Paul Revere silver.

NOAH

(to Rankin)

Mr. Wilson is also an authority on clocks.

RANKIN, sipping his soup, pauses momentarily.

MARY

Really! Why, that's Charles's hobby.

WILSON

Yes, so your brother tells me.

(turning to RANKIN*)*

I understand you're going to fix the one in the church tower?

RANKIN

I may try.

WILSON

Quite an undertaking.

MARY

To show the kind of wife I am, I hope he fails. I like Harper just that way is . . . even to the clock that doesn't run.

As the scene progresses, SARA moves around the table, serving dinner. RED, the setter dog, has followed them into the room and settled himself beside MARY.

RANKIN

How long have you been in Harper, Mr. Wilson?

WILSON

Since Friday, a week ago.

LAWRENCE

(looking up quickly)

You've lost a day. I patched you up on Friday. By the way, how's the head?

WILSON

Very much improved, thanks to you, Doctor.

LAWRENCE

You were hurt on Thursday. The day of the wedding.

RANKIN's fork poises midway to its destination.

WILSON

Yes, that's right. Wednesday I left Bangor.

RANKIN

You were hurt, Mr. Wilson?

WILSON

Oh, nothing serious.

LAWRENCE

Serious enough to raise a bump on his head the size of a billiard ball.

RANKIN's last doubts are removed. This is the Devil that pursued MEINIKE to Harper.

WILSON
(to the table at large)
The usual door.

RED raises up on his haunches and puts his head on MARY's lap.

JUDGE LONGSTREET
Good thing you're back, Sister. That dog of yours has been inconsolable.

MARY
(lifting a scrap of meat from her plate)
That's for missing me, Red.
(she turns to her father)
There's a good boy. How was your meeting, Adam?

JUDGE LONGSTREET
Irritating . . .
(explaining to WILSON*)*
The Foreign Policy Association.

NOAH
I read that fellow's report.

JUDGE LONGSTREET
Yes, Standish.

NOAH
I think he's full of prunes.

JUDGE LONGSTREET
That's the way we used to talk in the 1930s, Noah.

LAWRENCE
Standish?

WILSON
The *London Times* man in Berlin.

JUDGE LONGSTREET
Of course he was quoting rumors, mostly. Men drilling by night . . . underground meeting places . . . pagan rituals.

NOAH
Do you believe them, Pop?

JUDGE LONGSTREET

Anything's possible.

LAWRENCE

I'm sorry, sir, but I think it's ridiculous. There may be some fanatics, but no German in his right mind could still have any taste for war.

WILSON

Do you know Germany, Mr. Rankin?

RANKIN

(easily)

I'm sorry. I have a way of making enemies on that subject. It's pretty unpopular.

WILSON

We shall consider it the objective opinion of an objective historian.

RANKIN

A historian? A psychiatrist could explain it better. The German sees himself as the innocent victim of world envy and hatred . . . conspired against, set upon by inferior peoples, inferior nations.

*(*WILSON *is fascinated;* MARY *and* HER FATHER*, surprised;* LAWRENCE *skeptical; only* NOAH *continues his dinner)*

RANKIN

He cannot admit to error, much less to wrongdoing. Not the German. We chose to ignore Ethiopia and Spain. But we learned from our casualty lists the price of looking the other way . . .

. . . Men of truth everywhere have come to know for whom the bell tolled. But not the German. He still follows his warrior gods, marching to Wagnerian strains, his eyes still fixed upon the fiery sword of Siegfried.

(he pauses, glances from one face to the other, ending on WILSON*)*

In those subterranean meeting places . . . that you don't believe in . . . the German's dream world comes alive, and he takes his place in shining armor beneath the banners of the Teutonic Knights. Mankind is waiting for the Messiah. But for the German, the Messiah is not the Prince of Peace. He's another Barbarossa, another Hitler.

WILSON

Then you have no faith in the reforms that are being effected in Germany.

RANKIN

I don't know, Mr. Wilson. I can't believe that people can be reformed except from within. The basic principles of equality and freedom never have and never will take root in Germany.

(continuing eagerly)

The will to freedom has been voiced in every other tongue . . . "All men are created equal." "Liberté, égalité, fraternité . . . " In German . . .

NOAH

(interrupting quietly)

There's Marx: "Proletarians, unite. You have nothing to lose but your chains."

RANKIN

But Marx wasn't a German. Marx was a Jew.

JUDGE LONGSTREET

My dear Charles . . . if we concede your argument . . . there is no solution.

RANKIN

Once again, I differ.

WILSON

What is it then?

RANKIN

Annihilation . . . down to the last babe in arms.

MARY

(disturbed . . . a little worried)

Charles . . . I can't imagine you're advocating a Carthaginian peace.

RANKIN

(smiling)

Well, as an historian, I must remind you the world hasn't had much trouble with Carthage in the past two thousand years.

WILSON looks extremely disturbed.

JUDGE LONGSTREET

There speaks our pedagogue . . .

MARY

(brightening)

Speaking of teachers, Mr. Wilson, the faculty is coming to tea next Tuesday. If you have nothing better to do, would you like to join us?

WILSON
I'd like to, but my work here is finished. I'm leaving Harper tomorrow.

DISSOLVE TO: INT. RANKIN HOUSE—NIGHT

MARY and RANKIN enter. RANKIN closes the door and turns on the lights as MARY says:

MARY
Extraordinary, isn't it . . . clocks being Mr. Wilson's hobby too?

RANKIN
Yes, isn't it?

RED comes up to them.

MARY
Well, Red, how do you like your new home?
(RED *wags his tail)*

RANKIN
He loves it. Come on, Red, I'll take you for a walk.

MARY
You don't have to walk him. Just let him out. He won't run off.

RANKIN
I'm restless. I need the walk. Come along, Red.

MARY turns and starts up the stairs. RANKIN snaps his fingers for RED and goes out the door.

INT. WILSON'S BEDROOM—NIGHT

He is sitting at the phone in his shirtsleeves.

WILSON
(into telephone)
I'll be in Washington tomorrow afternoon. You were right about Rankin. He's above suspicion.

DISSOLVE: EXT. THE RANKIN HOUSE—NIGHT

RANKIN comes out, closing the door behind him. Then, with long, hurried strides, he moves unhesitatingly towards the woods. RED follows him.

DISSOLVE TO: EXT. THE WOODS—NIGHT

Rankin enters and, as he finds MEINIKE's grave undisturbed, his face lights up with relief. Then, CAMERA MOVING AHEAD OF HIM, he turns and starts for home. After a few paces, he realizes that RED is not at his heels. He turns and snaps his fingers. When RED fails to appear, he whistles. Then:

RANKIN

Here, Red . . . Red, come here . . .

He waits a moment. RED does not appear. He starts back whence he came.

Beside MEINIKE's grave, RANKIN reenters and looks towards the grave. His eyes narrow.

RANKIN sees RED, his forepaws industriously digging into the earth, the leaves scattered in all directions. RED continues his digging as RANKIN watches him. RANKIN tries to chase him off, but RED keeps going back to the grave. RANKIN kicks out with all his strength, hitting RED in the ribs, and falling down himself. At the moment of contact:

INT. WILSON'S ROOM—NIGHT

WILSON, lying in bed, suddenly sits bolt upright as though awakened by RANKIN's kick.

He switches on a light and gets to his feet. Then hurries to the desk, seats himself, and picks up the phone.

WILSON

(into phone)

Uh . . . Get me long distance . . . I want Washington, D. C. . . .

EXT. WOODS—NIGHT

RANKIN is having a cigarette to calm himself.

INT. WILSON'S ROOM—NIGHT

WILSON is continuing his telephone conversation.

WILSON

(into phone)

. . . Well . . . who but a Nazi would deny that Karl Marx was a German because he was a Jew . . . I think I'll stick around for a while.

(hangs up receiver and sits staring out the window thoughtfully)

DISSOLVE TO: INT. RANKIN BEDROOM—NIGHT

RANKIN, in pajamas and dressing gown, emerges from the dressing room, casting a long shadow on the sleeping MARY. He stands for a second, looking down at the sleeping figure of his wife. The lights, from the room beside him shine across her bed. In her sleep, she stirs fitfully and whimpers, childlike. Suddenly her body jerks spasmodically and she is awake. She stares up at her husband, frightened.

RANKIN

What is it, dear?

MARY

(dazedly)

I'm sorry, I was dreaming.

(brushing her hand across her eyes)

About that little man.

RANKIN

(sitting beside her)

What little man?

MARY

I told you about him . . . he came here . . . the day we were married.

(she shakes her head)

Light me a cigarette, honey.

RANKIN

(lighting one for her)

Oh . . . yes. I remember.

He hands her the lighted cigarette. She puffs on it gratefully.

MARY

I never had a dream like that before. It frightened me. The little man was walking, all by himself, across a deserted city square. Wherever he moved, he threw a shadow. But when he moved, Charles, the shadow stayed behind him, and spread out just like a carpet.

(she stops, takes another puff on the cigarette . . . then, with an abrupt change of tone)

I wish you could think who he might have been.

RANKIN

You're overtired.

MARY

Perhaps.

(smiling at him, handing him her cigarette.)

Here, put this out, will you?

There is the whimpering bark of a dog. She starts in surprise.

MARY

What was that?

RANKIN doesn't answer. The howl is heard again.

MARY

Why, that sounded like Red, Charles.

(she starts getting out of bed)

What in the world is the matter with him?

RANKIN

(quietly)

I have put him in the cellar.

MARY

(startled)

No wonder he's howling. He's never been locked up in his entire life.

RANKIN

But if he's to live with us, he must be trained. At night, he will sleep in the cellar. In the daytime, he will be kept on a leash.

RED howls again, the sound dying away in a moan.

MARY

(facing him)

Charles, I don't believe in dogs being treated like prisoners. And he's *my* dog.

RANKIN

(gently)

Please, Mary . . . I know what's best . . .

Their eyes stay met for a long moment. Finally, a decision reached, MARY lies down. RANKIN kisses her and leaves. MARY lies awake, looking worried.

FADE OUT

FADE IN: EXT.

NOAH is sitting in a boat in front of a tackle shop. WILSON comes up to him, RED running in front of him.

WILSON
Hi there, Red! I thought you'd gone to live with your mistress!

NOAH
Mary brought him home. Said he howls all night.

WILSON
Ah. Fishing any good in these parts?

NOAH
Pretty fair. Like to come along?

WILSON
Well, I'm afraid I've got the wrong clothes on, but the fish probably won't mind. Thank you.

WILSON and NOAH are in the boat. NOAH has his fishing line out. Then he reels it in and puts the rod away in the boat.

NOAH
I'm just not lucky today, that's all.

NOAH holds out a candy bar.

NOAH
Would you like a candy bar?

WILSON
I don't mind if I do. Thank you.

WILSON
All your folks like fishing?

NOAH
Oh, my dad's great. He always brings in something.

WILSON
What about Charles?

NOAH
(hesitates for a moment)
Charles? Oh! I have to call him Mr. Rankin in school. I get a little mixed up sometimes. He spends most of his time on the clock.

WILSON
Why don't you like him, Noah?

NOAH
What do you mean?

WILSON

You don't like your brother-in-law. It's none of my business, but I wish you'd tell me why.

NOAH

I like him well enough. No reason why I shouldn't.

WILSON

Don't tell me I'm butting in, because I know I am, but I can't help myself. It's my business. I hate bringing you into this, Noah, but you're the only one I can turn to. I need your help very badly.

NOAH

What is it?

WILSON

Your sister may be in great trouble. I know that you're man enough for what I'm going to ask you to do for her. The truth is, I'm not really an antique dealer. I'm sort of a detective.

WILSON and NOAH are getting out of the boat.

NOAH

What do you want me to do, Mr. Wilson?

WILSON

It would help me a lot if I knew every move Charles Rankin made on the day of his wedding. Right up to the ceremony itself.

NOAH

(frowning)

I should be able . . .

(a new thought)

. . . unless Charles realizes what I'm doing.

WILSON

I'll keep him busy.

They walk along the dock.

NOAH

(incredulity reasserting itself)

Gee, Mr. Wilson, you must be wrong. Mary wouldn't fall in love with that kind of a man.

WILSON

I hope I am wrong, Noah. But that's the way it is. People can't help who they fall in love with.

WILSON walks off. NOAH follows him uneasily with his eyes.

INT. POTTER'S—NIGHT

WILSON enters POTTER's drugstore.

Four HARPER BOYS enjoy their sodas at a table in the rear. WILSON goes around behind counter and fixes himself some coffee. POTTER sets up the checkers.

WILSON

Evening, Mr. Potter.

POTTER

Evening, Mr. Wilson.

One of the HARPER BOYS goes to POTTER to pay.

POTTER

Eighty-five cents.

WILSON sits down across from POTTER for a game of checkers.

POTTER

Hear you and Perfessor Rankin aim to fix the clock.

WILSON

That's right.

POTTER

Figure it'll tell time rightly?

(another nod)

And will the angel circle round the belfry?

(another nod)

Is that a man or a woman angel, Mr. Wilson?

WILSON

I don't know.

MR. POTTER

Well . . . reckon it don't make much difference 'mongst angels.

WILSON makes a move, enabling POTTER to take several of his men on the board.

POTTER

Give up?

WILSON

No, no, we'll play it out. That's my privilege: 25 cents. By the way, has Mr. Rankin picked up his supper this evening?

MR. POTTER

No. He kind of gets through up there about now.

WILSON

Yes . . . I know.

POTTER

Gets dark earlier these days.

WILSON looks at the shelf behind POTTER and sees MEINIKE's suitcase.

WILSON

Our little man never did pick up his suitcase, did he?

MR. POTTER

Nope.

WILSON

Strange.

MR. POTTER

Ain't it, though?

(he pauses, then:)

I've been tempted once or twice to look and see what's inside of it.

(he looks hopefully at WILSON*)*

It isn't even locked.

WILSON

Seems to me that, under the circumstances, you have a perfect right.

MR. POTTER

You do? I wouldn't want to do it without a witness.

WILSON

That's me.

MR. POTTER

It is?

WILSON nods. POTTER reaches down, takes out the bag, and places it on the counter. He rubs his palms together. He opens the lid. As he does so, WILSON strikes a match and puts it to his pipe. He does not look at the suitcase as POTTER fishes through it.

POTTER

Wonder what's in it?

WILSON

Soiled linen . . . a sweater . . . soap and a razor wrapped in a towel with "S. S. Cristobal" written across it . . . a pair of old shoes . . . Nothing but religious pamphlets.

POTTER is too intent on what he is doing to note that WILSON is not looking into the suitcase.

MR. POTTER

Yep . . . that's all.

The door opens, and MARY and RANKIN enter.

MARY

Good evening, Mr. Wilson . . . Mr. Potter.

WILSON

Good evening. Mr. Potter and I have been poking our noses into somebody else's business. That suitcase. That little chap left it here and never did call back.

MR. POTTER

That was more than two weeks ago.

RANKIN now knows this is MEINIKE's suitcase. He moves over to stand on the opposite side of MARY from WILSON.

MARY

(with normal interest)

Did he say what he was doing there?

MR. POTTER

Nope. Looked in the phone book but didn't telephone. Kind of scrawny-looking, with starey big blue eyes. Weird walk . . . like any second he might break into a run.

MARY

(with sudden excitement)

Did he have a foreign accent?

Beneath the counter, RANKIN's hand closes like a vise on her wrist. She turns to face him as POTTER replies. Their eyes meet, warning in RANKIN's. Wilson observes this.

MR. POTTER

Why, yes, he did. Not so much of an accent . . . as a foreign way of talking.

RANKIN's eyes, fixed on MARY's, glare briefly. Then, conscious of WILSON's interest, RANKIN looks down at the counter. But his hand on her wrist increases its pressure.

WILSON

Do you happen to know who he could be, Mrs. Rankin?

MARY

(forces a laugh)

Why, no . . . I was just trying to complete your mystery. Don't all foreign . . . strangers have foreign accents?

RANKIN looses his grip. They all turn towards the door as NOAH comes in.

NOAH

Mary, have you seen Red?

MARY

Why, no. Not since I took him home to you a couple of days ago.

NOAH

He's spending all his time out in the woods. Doesn't even come home for meals.

RANKIN

I thought you told me he never ran away.

NOAH

(answering for MARY*)*

He never did.

MARY

That's why Noah's so anxious.

(slips down from her stool)

Good night, Mr. Wilson, good night, Noah.

MARY leads the way out, RANKIN at her heels.

EXT. POTTER'S—NIGHT

WILSON and NOAH come out and see RANKIN and MARY go into the church.

NOAH

Were you able to find out anything?

WILSON

(nodding)

Meinike did go to Rankin's house. And your sister did see him.

They move down the street.

NOAH

Did Mary say so?

WILSON

She started to. Your sister is a fine woman, Noah. But she must find out what kind of man she's married to.

NOAH

You don't know Mary. She wouldn't listen to anything against him . . . much less believe.

WILSON

Noah, we must arrange it so that she finds out for herself. Do you understand?

NOAH nods.

One thing's certain, she knows nothing now . . . nothing at all . . . except that he didn't want her to admit having seen someone she did see. I'd give something to know what explanation he's making right now.

DISSOLVE TO: INT. CHURCH—NIGHT

RANKIN and MARY are sitting in a pew.

RANKIN

I was a student at Geneva. There was a girl . . . The night before I was to leave, we went out on the lake together. She told me that unless I promised to marry her, she'd never return to shore. I thought she was joking, naturally. But she wasn't. Before I could stop her, she stood up in the boat and—well—I dived in after her, but it was too late: she was gone.

RANKIN

(he pauses)

Only one person knew we were out on that lake together. Her brother. He knew I hadn't murdered her, but he told me he was willing to call it an accident, for—compensation. I gave him what I had. As the years went by, I allowed myself to believe that the dead past really was dead.

(again he pauses)

Then, on our wedding day, Mary, he appeared again. Her brother was the little man. I gave him all the money I had in the world . . . and he went away again.

MARY

You should have told me... not carried this awful thing around by yourself.

RANKIN

You're a very wonderful person, Mary.

(He kisses her tenderly.)

And I love you very much.

MARY

Charles...

(he looks at her inquiringly)

... Why—why didn't he go back for his things?

RANKIN

(after a pause)

Well, I suppose, once he had money, he could afford better. Darling, I'm extremely nervous... I think I'll work alone on the clock. By myself. It will calm me... You understand, don't you?

MARY

(rising)

Of course I understand.

RANKIN

Shall I walk you home?

MARY

No, dear, there's no need of that.

RANKIN

(tenderly)

It's really late...

MARY

That's all right... In Harper, there's nothing to be afraid of.

He kisses her again.

RANKIN

I love you.

She goes off. RANKIN looks after her apprehensively.

EXT. OUTSIDE DR. LIVINGSTON'S HOUSE

The next day, NOAH is holding the dead body of RED. WILSON is there, smoking his pipe.

NOAH

Poor old Red . . . He heard my whistle, I'll bet, but he couldn't bark or anything. He just crawled this far and died.

(His lips tremble threateningly. To cover his emotion, he bends over, and pats the dead dog's head very gently)

. . . Why do you think he died?

WILSON

Let's go and find out.

DISSOLVE TO: EXT. DR. LAWRENCE'S OFFICE—HARPER SQUARE

WILSON and NOAH, still carrying RED, go into LAWRENCE's office, which is next to POTTER's drugstore.

RANKIN goes into POTTER's drugstore. POTTER is sitting at the counter. He is looking out the window and sees NOAH and WILSON. RANKIN opens a bottle of Coke and pours it into a glass.

POTTER

That's young Longstreet's dog. Looks like he's dead to me. They're taking him up to Dr. Lawrence's office. Do you know anything about it?

RANKIN makes an indistinguishable noise and guzzles the rest of his Coke.

POTTER

Checkers?

RANKIN

No.

RANKIN makes to leave.

POTTER

Hey! Coke's a nickel!

RANKIN goes back to the counter and pays him.

POTTER

Thank you, Mr. Rankin.

Outside, CAMERA, on CRANE, moves in on an office window. The lettering on it says, "Jeffrey Lawrence. Office hours . . . "

Through the window, we see WILSON, NOAH, and LAWRENCE looking at RED's body. LAWRENCE is holding a test tube. WILSON is holding a crumb of dried mud.

WILSON

Oh, doctor? How long could the dog have lived with that amount of poison in him?

LAWRENCE

Not more than a minute or so.

WILSON

Well, then, Red must have been poisoned within a few hundred yards of where you found him, Noah. And the latter part of the distance he must have been moving slower and slower.

(abruptly)

Thank you very much, Doctor.

NOAH

Yes . . . Thanks, Jeff.

They leave. LAWRENCE pulls a sheet over the dead dog.

EXT. POTTER'S—AFTERNOON

POTTER is leaning out over the counter of his newstand, directing his assistant, PEABODY, at work.

MR. POTTER

Mr. Peabody, would you please get that magazine rack in and hurry up about it!

PEABODY

Yes, Mr. Potter.

POTTER sees WILSON and NOAH come out of LAWRENCE's office next door.

POTTER

Afternoon, Mr. Wilson. Afternoon, Noah.

EXT. SQUARE—NOAH AND WILSON

NOAH

(absently)

Evenin', Mr. Potter.

CAMERA, on CRANE, precedes NOAH and WILSON as they move across the square, walking toward the Harper Inn.

NOAH

What does the law say about this kind of murder? Is it the same as killing a man? It ought to be. It's just as bad.

WILSON

(showing NOAH *the piece of dried mud in his hand)*

Forepaws muddy . . . No mud on hind.

(he crumbles it and looks at it)

Dry leaves mixed with the mud. Red must have been digging somewhere in the woods.

NOAH

Have you got any idea what for, Mr. Wilson?

WILSON

(nodding)

A body, I think . . . Meineke's.

NOAH

(in horror)

The little man . . .

(WILSON *nods)*

Then . . .

(the thought is too monstrous for words)

INT. POTTER'S—EVENING

The shop is dark. POTTER is unlocking the door, letting in RANKIN, who rushes in distractedly. POTTER turns on the lights in the shop.

POTTER

You just caught me.

RANKIN

Anything wrong?

POTTER

Wrong? Oh, you mean, closin' up like this?

(RANKIN *nods)*

Just goin' on the search. What were you after?

RANKIN

A can of machine oil . . . What search?

MR. POTTER

For the body.

(RANKIN *stiffens)*

State police've deputized half the town . . . Just reach up there—Fourth shelf . . .

RANKIN

(forcing himself to be casual as he crosses to shelf)

One misses the news . . . up in the clock tower. What body are they searching for?

POTTER

My bet is it's the feller that left his bag here. Scrawny little duck. Unhappy looking. I knew he'd come to a bad end. That oil'll be 15 cents, mister . . . or I'll just put it on your account.

RANKIN hurries out.

DISSOLVE TO: RANKIN BEDROOM—NIGHT

On the bed, RANKIN is packing an open suitcase. MARY comes into the room.

MARY

(entering)

Sara told me you were up here . . .

(she breaks off, seeing him packing)

Why are you packing? Are we going somewhere?

RANKIN

***We* aren't, my dearest . . . I am.**

MARY

What are you talking about?

RANKIN

As a rule, men leave their wives because they don't love them, but I . . . I must leave you because I do. Oh, you won't object once you know the kind of man you married.

MARY

But you *are* the man I married, and that's all that matters. I meant what I said . . . for better . . . for worse.

RANKIN

(harshly)

Even to killing Red?

MARY recoils instantly. RANKIN watches narrowly for her reaction.

MARY

(aghast)

You couldn't.

RANKIN doesn't answer.

MARY

It was an accident.

RANKIN

No, I meant to kill him. Murder can be a chain, Mary. One link leading to another until it circles your neck. Red was digging at the grave of the man I killed. Yes . . . your little man . . .

MARY

(in a whisper)

You killed him?

RANKIN

With these hands.

(he holds them out to her)

The same hands that have held you close to me.

(again harshly)

Now are you satisfied to let me go?

MARY

(in an agonized voice)

Why? Why did you do it?

RANKIN

I'd have given him all I had . . . but his dreams were far grander. He knew that your father was well-to-do . . . He knew that Justice Longstreet would be glad to protect his daughter from any scandal by paying a few thousand dollars.

(turns back to face her)

Oh, Mary, I should have gone away and lost myself in a world where he could never find me. But . . .

(He looks at her for a long moment)

I loved you, and I was weak.

MARY

(she comes to his side, then softly)

Darling . . . if one of us goes, we both go. You would have shared half my trouble, if I'd had any. Charles, what is there to connect you with that man?

RANKIN

Nothing, actually. You're the only one that knows I knew him.

MARY

Then you have no need of fear . . . if I'm the only one who can speak.

RANKIN

But Mary, in failing to speak, you've become a part of the crime.

MARY

But I'm already a part of it, because I'm a part of you.

For the first time, RANKIN feels completely secure. He starts to sweep her into his arms. She yields herself willingly to him. Then some instinctive reaction that she herself doesn't understand makes her body tremble. RANKIN instantly pulls back . . . only his hands remaining on her arms.

RANKIN

And yet you shudder at the first touch of my hands, as though it is the touch of death.

MARY

(shaking her head)

It's nerves.

(forcing herself)

Hold me close, Charles. Hold me close.

She raises her lips to him. Watching her intently, he kisses her.

EXT. THE WOODS—NIGHT

Several cars have been driven in near the grave, their powerful headlights stabbing across the scene. A row of lanterns lines the area around MEINIKE's grave, which has been opened. A rope has been strung on stakes around it to keep the crowd from trampling around it. The exhumed body lies, under canvas, beside the grave. Uniformed state patrolmen are getting pictures of the scene.

POTTER is standing there in a checked flannel shirt.

POTTER

Mr. Peabody, go back to the town with the sheriff and open the coroner's office.

PEABODY

Yes, sir.

POTTER

I knew durn well it was the same feller. Of course, he's changed some—being buried in the earth does it. Evenin', Mr. Wilson. Evenin', Noah. A mess, ain't it?

WILSON and NOAH are on a little knoll, looking down at the scene. NOAH turns to WILSON.

NOAH

What'll we do about Mary? We can't leave her alone with him . . . now that we know.

WILSON

(smokes his pipe in silence, then:)

She realizes now that whatever story he told her about Meinike was false.

(he pauses)

Noah, I think your sister should be ready to hear the truth.

INT. RANKIN LIVING ROOM—NIGHT

MARY and RANKIN are sitting at a table; she is holding a cup of coffee.

MARY

Charles . . . will they make me look at the body?

RANKIN

I shouldn't think so.

MARY

Because I couldn't do it. I mean, I don't think I could. You seen, I've never seen a dead person. I . . .

She breaks off as SARA enters, vegetable dish in hand.

RANKIN

How many are you having to tea, Mary?

MARY

Twenty-eight, all together.

SARA

(glancing at MARY*'s coffee)*

You didn't eat nothin' at dinner. You'll be fainting again, Miss Mary.

RANKIN

(to MARY*)*

Isn't that rather a lot? Twenty-eight for just you two?

SARA

No, we'll manage all right.

She exits into the kitchen.

MARY

I suppose I should . . .

RANKIN

Should what?

MARY

(numbly)

I don't know. I only know that I'm terrified of seeing anybody . . . of being seen.

RANKIN

(voice level)

Mary, you must get tight hold of yourself. If you're determine to go through with this thing, you must know what you are going to say at all times. Perfect naturalness at all times. Darling, really, listen to me. Darling, I am prepared to go to the police.

SARA comes in.

SARA

It's your father, Miss Mary. He wants to talk to you.

MARY

Yes, thank you, Sara.

MARY slips from her chair and goes to the telephone in the hall just outside dining room. At the telephone:

MARY

(into phone)

Hello.

(pause)

Yes, I think so . . .

(again a pause)

Just a minute, and I'll see.

She holds her hand over the mouthpiece of the phone.

MARY

He wants me to come over.

RANKIN

(levelly)

Did he ask me too?

MARY

(shaking her head)

He said he wanted to see me alone.

RANKIN

There's nothing unusual about a father wanting to see his daughter, is there? *Is there?*

MARY

No!

(into the phone)

All right, Adam. I'll be right over.

She hangs up and looks at her husband.

(to RANKIN*)*

Don't you think that's rather strange?

RANKIN

Strange? No, not strange at all.

(reassuringly)

Tell you what I'll do I'll go to the church and work on the clock while you're with your father. When you're through, you can come by and pick me up later.

MARY

Charles . . . I'm so afraid. It was so pointed . . . his wanting to see me alone. And his voice sounded so different.

RANKIN

(his hand on her hair)

You know what you're going to say?

Looking up at him, she nods slowly.

DISSOLVE TO: INT. JUDGE LONGSTREET'S STUDY—NIGHT

MARY enters JUDGE LONGSTREET's study. WILSON is at the door and closes it behind her. The room is dark; a film is running. WILSON shuts off the projector and turns on the lights. JUDGE LONGSTREET has been standing at his desk but comes over to her.

JUDGE LONGSTREET

(gravely)

Come in, Mary.

(he closes the door behind her, smiles at her reassuringly)

Sit down, my dear.

MARY

(looks from her father to WILSON *and back to her father again)*

Is something wrong?

JUDGE LONGSTREET

Mary . . . Mr. Wilson is here on a very serious matter and we must try to help him in every way possible. He wants to ask a few questions of you.

MARY

What do you want to know, Mr. Wilson?

WILSON

You know about the body that was discovered yesterday, Mrs. Rankin?

(MARY *nods)*

Did you ever meet the deceased?

MARY

No, no, I never met him.

WILSON

Have you seen the body, Mrs. Rankin?

MARY

No . . .

WILSON

Then how can you be sure you never met him?

MARY

(hesitates)

Of course I can't be certain . . .

(masking fear with a show of anger)

Mr. Wilson, do you suspect me of something. If so, what?

WILSON

Of shielding a murderer.

(he pauses, then with apparent irrelevance)

WILSON

Perhaps this picture will refresh your memory, Mrs. Rankin . . .

CLOSEUP—PHOTO OF MEINIKE IN CIVILIAN CLOTHING.

WILSON

(over scene)

Do you recognize this man? That is Conrad Meinike. Commander in charge of one of the more efficient concentration camps. You know him, don't you? You *have* met him here in Harper . . .

MARY

No, no, I've never seen that man, Mr. Wilson.

JUDGE LONGSTREET has an extremely grave look on his face.

WILSON

Judge, would you mind turning out the lights?

JUDGE LONGSTREET goes to shut them off.

WILSON

I've been showing your father some films, Mrs. Rankin, and I'd like you to see them too. I'm on the Allied Commission for the Punishment of War Criminals. It's my job to bring escaped Nazis to justice. It's that job that brought me to Harper.

The screen shows a pile of exterminated bodies.

MARY

Surely you don't think . . . Mr. Wilson, I've never so much as even seen a Nazi.

WILSON

You might, without realizing it. They look like other people and act like other people—when it's to their benefit.

Mary doesn't answer.

We now see the film on the screen, of an empty gas chamber.

WILSON'S VOICE

(over scene)

. . . A gas chamber, Mrs. Rankin . . . the candidates were first given hot showers so that their pores would be open and the gas would act that much more quickly.

BACK TO SCENE

MARY looks up, the flickering of the screen reflected on her face, then back to screen.

We now see a shot of some GIs standing at the entrance to a lime pit. WILSON is silhouetted against the screen.

That is a lime pit in which hundreds of men, women, and children were buried alive.

MARY

(unable to take her eyes from the screen)

Why do you wish me to look at these horrors?

WILSON

All this you've seen: it's all the product of one mind... the mind of a man named Franz Kindler.

MARY

(trying to identify the name)

Franz Kindler...

WILSON

Yes, he was one of the most brilliant of the younger minds of the Nazi party. It was Kindler who conceived the theory of genocide—mass depopulation of conquered countries, so that regardless of who won the war, Germany would emerge the strongest nation in Western Europe, biologically speaking.

He pauses. Her eyes go back to the screen.

WILSON

Unlike Goebbels and Himmler and the rest of them, Kindler had a passion for anonymity. The newspapers carried no picture of him. Oh, no. And, just before he disappeared, he destroyed every evidence that might link him with his past, down to the last fingerprint. There is no clue to the identity of Franz Kindler... except one little thing... He has a hobby that almost amounts to a mania... clocks.

MARY

So have lots of people... you... yourself.

WILSON

(ignoring her question)

Well, I'm not quite finished, Mrs. Rankin. In prison in Czechoslovakia, a war criminal was awaiting execution. This was Conrad Meinike, one-time executive officer of Franz Kindler. He was an obscenity on the face of the earth. The stench of burning flesh was in his clothes. But we gave him his freedom on the chance that he might lead me to Kindler. He led me here, Mrs. Rankin. And here, I lost him... until yesterday. Your dog, Red, found him for me. But unfortunately Meinike was dead and buried... Now, in all the world, there is only one person who can identify Franz Kindler. That person is the one who knows... knows definitely... who Meinike came to Harper to see.

The last frames of film run through the projector and the loose end flaps monotonously against the still turning reel. The bright light shines full on the screen. WILSON ignores it.

MARY

(finally . . . almost moaning)

No! . . . He's not a Nazi! My Charles is not a Nazi!

Now WILSON snaps on the room lights and turns off the projector.

MARY has risen and opened the door to the second-floor porch, WILSON and JUDGE LONGSTREET following.

INT. SECOND FLOOR PORCH—NIGHT

WILSON

(pounding at her)

You were at Rankin's house during the afternoon of the day you were married?

MARY

Where?

WILSON

Rankin's house.

MARY

(gasping)

Yes, yes.

WILSON

Did anyone come while you were there?

MARY

Not that I remember.

WILSON

Try to remember. It was not so long ago—only two weeks. You were hanging curtains.

MARY

No one came.

WILSON

Were you alone all the time?

MARY

No.

WILSON

Who else was there?

MARY

Charles.

(with a great effort of will she composes herself, then continues)

He came right after his last class, and we were together for more than an hour. You have nothing to link my husband with this man . . . Kindler . . . except a wild suspicion. It's a ridiculous suspicion. You're trying to use me to implicate him. You can't. You can't involve me in a lie . . . That's all it is . . . a lie!

MARY dashes into the room from the porch and out the door.

JUDGE LONGSTREET

Mary, Mary! Wait a minute! Mary!

We then see her running out of the front door of the house. JUDGE LONGSTREET follows her.

JUDGE LONGSTREET

Mary!

MARY keeps running.

JUDGE LONGSTREET

(calling to her from doorway)

Wait a minute, sister!

The use of the old term of affection stops her; she pauses, irresolute, then turns to face him. She runs into his arms, and he hugs her.

JUDGE LONGSTREET

That's better.

(he turns her to face him)

They walk along together. MARY is sobbing.

JUDGE LONGSTREET

You know that your welfare and Noah's means more to me than anything, don't you?

MARY

(her voice a little unsteady)

Yes, yes.

JUDGE LONGSTREET

We've got to face this thing with complete honesty, sister. Your entire happiness may well depend on your telling me the absolute truth.

(Mary begins to cry silently)

If Mr. Wilson is right and you have innocently married a criminal . . . then there is no marriage, and there is no call upon your loyalty as a wife.

MARY

He's good. He's good. Charles wouldn't hurt anybody . . . except to protect somebody he loves.

JUDGE LONGSTREET

In that case, the truth can't hurt him.

(she looks up at him. His voice is very gentle.)

Charles was not with you that afternoon, sister. I remember your saying so when you came home.

MARY

(suddenly flying out)

You're against him too, Adam, yes you are! You've never liked him! That's why you won't believe me! Leave us alone, Adam! . . . He's my husband . . . He's not a Nazi! He's not one of those people . . . He's not! Leave us alone!

She runs away, her footsteps sounding on the graveled walk. JUDGE LONGSTREET looks after her sadly. Then the JUDGE hears WILSON's footsteps as he comes slowly down the graveled path. The JUDGE turns to face him. WILSON carries a case holding the projector.

WILSON

Well, she has the facts now, but she won't accept them. They're too horrible for her to acknowledge. Not so much that Rankin could be Kindler . . . as that she could ever have given her love to such a creature.

He starts walking, LONGSTREET moving too.

Camera precedes them to follow action.

WILSON

But we have one ally.

(JUDGE LONGSTREET *looks at him, not understanding)*

Her subconscious. It knows what the truth is and is struggling to be heard. The will to truth within your daughter is much too strong to be denied.

JUDGE LONGSTREET

(thoughtfully)

Look here, Wilson . . . if he's not Charles Rankin, we should be able to expose him without too much difficulty.

WILSON

I'm not interested in proving that he isn't Charles Rankin. I'm only interested in proving that he *is* Franz Kindler.

JUDGE LONGSTREET

How do you propose to do that?

As they walk, they come under a street light, their faces bright, then they pass by light and move off into darkness.

WILSON

Through your daughter.

(he hesitates)

Unless I'm mistaken, she's headed for a breakdown. That's the usual result of a person being inwardly divided. Rankin will recognize this, and that's what I'm banking on.

JUDGE LONGSTREET

What do you mean?

WILSON

He can't afford to trust a person approaching hysteria. He won't. He'll have to act.

(dispassionately)

He may try to escape before she collapses. Which would be only an admission of guilt. Or . . .

JUDGE LONGSTREET

(impatiently)

Go on.

WILSON

(calmly)

He may kill her. You're shocked at my cold-bloodedness. That's quite natural. You're her father. It's because you are her father, Judge Longstreet, that I'm talking like this.

(he pauses)

Naturally, I shall try to prevent murder being done.

In the far background, the silhouette of the clock tower comes into view.

WILSON

However, the proof that murder is his aim would be the strongest evidence your daughter could have . . .

We now see the clock in the tower. It is telling the correct time—11:00—and two bronze figures—an angel and a devil—-move mechanically around in front of it.

DISSOLVE TO: INT. CLOCK TOWER—NIGHT

MARY is climbing up the ladder to the belfry. As she approaches the top, we see RANKIN above her, looking down. The clock is striking.

MARY

Charles!

RANKIN

Listen. It's striking! After a hundred years . . .

MARY

It was a trap . . . just like you said. Mr. Wilson was there. He tried to tell me that you were a Nazi . . . and I was supposed to believe it! Imagine . . . you . . . being an escaped Nazi. Oh, he thinks he's very clever, that Wilson. His idea was to horrify me into telling him about the little man.

RANKIN

Who did he say he thought I was?

MARY

A Nazi. Franz Kindler. He made it all up . . . just to trick me . . . but I didn't tell him anything. And I didn't tell Father anything. I outfaced them both of them, Charles. It'll be simple enough to prove you're not that . . . (she hesitates over the name) . . . that Nazi. We'll just find someone who was in your class at college. He'll identify you . . . and that's all there'll be to it.

RANKIN

If what you say is true, he can't touch me. I'm quite safe . . . if you say nothing.

RANKIN is now hovering directly over MARY's head.

MARY

I won't, Charles . . . I promise I won't. They can torture me, and I won't tell them anything.

OVERSCENE the sound of voices. Calls from the distance. Below we see the citizens of Harper flocking to the church.

RANKIN

The chimes have awakened Harper. We must go down and greet them. We must act naturally, smile at them—you understand? Are you all right?

MARY

Yes, I'm all right. We'll face them, darling.

They start down the ladder.

DISSOLVE TO: EXT. CHURCH—NIGHT

Six or eight townspeople have been called out by the chiming of the clock. Some are fully dressed, but most have hastily pulled on whatever was handiest. POTTER, overcoat over pyjamas, occupies the forefront.

MR. POTTER

. . . and when she struck, that angel started marching. It was a sight to behold.

RANKIN and MARY emerge from the church. They are instantly surrounded.

FIRST MAN

Professor, you sure knocked it off. My hat's off to you.

SECOND MAN

Congratulations, Mr. Rankin.

WOMAN

Won't the Rector be delighted?

POTTER

What I want to know is, if it's going to chime all night long, how's a body going to get any sleep?

MARY

(*to* RANKIN)

We'll face them, darling . . . all of them.

POTTER

Them chickens is going to be off their roosts every fifteen minutes!

FADE OUT

FADE INTO: INT. RANKIN LIVING ROOM

It is now daytime. MARY rushes to draw the curtains.

MARY

Sara . . . I've told you, I want these curtains drawn. I don't like the sunlight streaming in.

(finishing closing them)

It's bad for them.

SARA

Miss Mary, that's rubbish and you know it. Up at the other house, we never drew a curtain in our lives.

MARY

That has nothing to do with it. This is my house, and I want them drawn.

SARA

(starting out)

Suit yourself. But it's certainly going to look mighty gloomy for the party.

MARY

(a momentary panic is in her eyes)

Is it that time already?

For answer, the doorbell rings.

SARA opens the door to admit two GUESTS, MRS. TINSDALL and MR. RANDALL, who enter.

MRS. TEASDALE

Did you see when they opened the grave, Mr. Randall? Was it too horrible?

MR. RANDALL

Well, not the most pleasant sight.

MRS. TEASDALE

There's Mary! Hello, Mary!

MARY smiles wanly and advances to greet her guests.

INT. POTTER'S—AFTERNOON

POTTER is handing RANKIN a bottle of prescription medicine.

MR. POTTER

Fillin' out prescriptions, that's one part of this business I hate; sleeping pills, that's another. $1.65. Want 'em wrapped?

RANKIN

No.

POTTER

Sleeping pills—don't approve of 'em. Man does a day's work, man gets a night's sleep.

Across the square, the clock strikes the quarter hour.

POTTER

Leastways, he could until that clock started bonging every few minutes.

RANKIN pockets the pills. He starts out. Then remembers something. Stops.

Oh . . . I believe Mrs. Rankin ordered some ice cream.

POTTER

Ice cream? Already gone.

RANKIN looks at him in surprise.

POTTER

A man said was he was goin' on to your house, so I gave it to him.

RANKIN

A man?

POTTER

Mr. Wilson!

RANKIN stiffens inwardly. Then, without a word, he hurries out of the store. POTTER looks after him in surprise.

INT. RANKIN LIVING ROOM—AFTERNOON

The living room is crowded with GUESTS. WILSON is at the door, holding two bags of ice cream. SARA lets him in. WILSON hands her his hat.

WILSON

Mrs. Rankin.

Across the room, MARY sees WILSON and is startled as she stares at him. He walks across the room towards her.

MRS. TINSDALL

I'm absolutely terrified. I wouldn't dream of setting foot outside the house, unless Fred were along. Who knows . . . he might be anywhere . . . the murderer, I mean . . . waiting for a new victim.

WILSON comes forward easily to MARY. DR. HIBBARD is standing next to her.

WILSON
(taking her hand)
I hope you haven't forgotten you were kind enough to invite me, Mrs. Rankin.

MARY
(staring at him in disbelief)
No . . . No of course not, Mr. Wilson.

WILSON
(holding up the bags of ice cream)
Mr. Potter asked me to deliver this.

Before MARY can answer, NOAH appears beside them.

NOAH
Oh, the ice cream. Sara's waiting for it.

WILSON
I hope it hasn't melted.

NOAH takes the ice cream away.

WILSON
I won't detain you any longer.

LAWRENCE and DR. HIBBARD advance toward WILSON.

LAWRENCE
I have a drink for you.

WILSON
Oh, thank you!

LAWRENCE hands WILSON a drink.

LAWRENCE
Do you know Dr. Hibbard?

WILSON
Oh, yes, of course. How are you, Doctor?

CAMERA moves with MARY as she nears a large chair in which old MRS. LAWRENCE is seated.

MARY
Grandma Lawrence, can I get you something?

GRANDA LAWRENCE

Nothing more, I'm fine, thank you.

MARY passes a MALE GUEST, whose back is to us.

GUEST

Where's Dr. Rankin?

MARY

He'll be here in just a few minutes.

MALE GUEST

I want to have a word with him about that clock.

MARY goes over to MR. LUNDSTRUM, who, standing, is addressing a couple of other GUESTS, including MRS. RAND, who are seated.

MRS. RAND

And what was that Frenchman's name?

(*to* MARY)

Oh, hello, dear.

MR. LUNDSTRUM

Landru. There may well be ten . . . or a dozen . . . graves out there in those woods.

MRS. RAND

The autopsy showed that the murder to be committed just three weeks ago.

MARY moves away from the group toward an ELDERLY MALE GUEST. She attempts to take his teacup.

MARY

Can I get you some?

MALE GUEST

No, thank you.

LAWRENCE approaches.

MARY

Jeff, can I get you another drink?

WILSON advances toward MARY. The door opens, and RANKIN enters.

DR. HIBBARD

What does Emerson say about crime? Oh, there's Rankin; he may know.

RANKIN advances into the room.

RANKIN
(to MARY)
Sorry to be late.

HIBBARD
Oh, hello there, Rankin. Do you know that quote? "Commit a crime, and the earth is made of glass."

RANKIN
No, I don't.

WILSON
(quoting)
"Commit a crime, and the earth is made of glass. Commit a crime, and it seems as if a coat of snow fell on the ground, such as reveals in the woods the track of every partridge and fox and squirrel and mole. You cannot recall the spoken word, you cannot wipe out the foot-track, you cannot draw up the ladder, so as to leave no inlet or clew."

MRS. LAWRENCE approaches.

MRS. LAWRENCE
You're Mr. Wilson, aren't you? D'you know you are the number one suspect in our murder case?

WILSON
Oh?

MRS. LAWRENCE
So far, you're the only suspect. Potter put the finger on you. He thinks you committed the crime to get possession of some priceless antique.

RANKIN takes MARY by the arm, indicating that they should go elsewhere. As they pass through the crowd, they hear the voice of a FEMALE GUEST:

THE VOICE OF A FEMALE GUEST
Charles Rankin . . . I wish you'd left that clock alone. Harper was a nice quiet place until it started banging.

MARY and RANKIN go into another room.

RANKIN
Mary, what's Wilson doing here?

MARY
I don't know.

RANKIN

You invited him, didn't you? What's he up to?

MARY

I don't know.

RANKIN

Are you all right?

MARY

Yes, quite all right.

DISSOLVE TO: INT. HALLWAY—LATE AFTERNOON

MARY, RANKIN at her elbow, stands in the doorway, speeds the last guests.

MARY

Good night!

She closes the door and turns, hard and composed. As she faces RANKIN, their eyes meet and hold. Her hand goes to her throat, and she runs one finger around the inside of the pearl necklace she is wearing, as though it were suddenly too tight for her.

RANKIN

Can I help you, dear?

He takes a step towards her. Then she raises both hands and attempts to unfasten the necklace. The catch sticks. She jerks at it. It still sticks.

MARY

No!

The string breaks, and the pearls fall. MARY suddenly breaks into a wild sobbing.

MARY

No! No!

SARA enters and watches them apprehensively.

RANKIN

Mary, Mary, Mary. It's all right, it's all right.

DISSOLVE TO: INT. JUDGE LONGSTREET'S STUDY—NIGHT

JUDGE LONGSTREET, NOAH, DR. LAWRENCE, and SARA are present with WILSON, to whom SARA is speaking. All eyes are fixed on her. She is sobbing.

SARA

It broke, and the beads fell all over the floor. He took her upstairs. When I left, I could still hear her crying.

WILSON

The floodgates have opened. Her subconscious has almost won.

(pause)

From now on, we must know every move Mrs. Rankin makes. She's never to leave the house, unless I know where she's going. If, for any reason, I can't be found . . . she's to be detained . . . no matter on what pretext. Do you understand, Sara?

JUDGE LONGSTREET

(his voice tortured)

When she snapped those beads, she signed her death warrant. We're carrying her life in our hands. Every time she walks on a slippery sidewalk . . . is near somehing that can fall . . . drives an automobile . . . anything that could result in accidental death . . . her life is in danger.

SARA

(grimly)

Don't worry. She won't get by me.

DISSOLVE TO: INT. BELFRY—NIGHT

A thin wedge of moonlight stabs down from above onto the foot of the ladder. RANKIN is near the top, sawing through one of the rungs.

Outside, the clock in the tower strikes midnight. The mechanical angel passes in front of its face.

INT. WILSON'S ROOM—NIGHT

WILSON, in pajamas and dressing gown, stands at the window, smoking his pipe. The striking of the hour continues.

EXT. TOWN SQUARE—NIGHT

Through the window, WILSON sees the clock, the angel making his march as the hour chimes.

INT. MARY'S BEDROOM—NIGHT

The chiming of the clock has not ceased.

MARY lies in bed, moving around uneasily. She brings her hand to her forehead, then turns and goes back to sleep.

DISSOLVE TO: INT. BELFRY—NIGHT

From the bottom of the ladder, we see RANKIN at the top, sawing.

INSERT:

Timetable on RANKIN'S desk. It reads:

3:25 PHONE MARY
3:30 Go to POTTER'S DRUG STORE
ESTABLISH TIME
4:00 LEAVE POTTER'S

RANKIN's hand adds the last entry:

4:05 HOME

In a Harper classroom, over scene, there is the sound of footsteps and boys' voices as the class assembles. Camera pulls back to full shot as RANKIN, rising from his desk, slips the paper into his pocket and faces the class. The wall clock indicates half past two. RANKIN's manner is relaxed. All strain has fallen from him.

RANKIN

Good afternoon, gentlemen.

BOYS

Good afternoon, sir.

RANKIN

(glancing at clock on wall behind him, comparing it with his watch)
Today we will attempt to finish with the career of Friedrich der Grosse, König von Preussen, Kurfurst von Brandenberg, Prinz von Polen . . . Frederick the Great, to you . . .

DISSOLVE TO: INT. POTTER'S DRUG STORE—DAY

RANKIN is in a phone booth. He puts a coin into the phone and dials. There is a sign that says, "Gentlemen, do not deface walls! Use pad for your convenience." Below is a notepad of paper, on which he draws a swastika as the phone rings.

In her house, MARY answers the phone.

MARY

Hello?

Back at the phone booth, RANKIN crosses out the swastika.

RANKIN

Mary, this is Charles. Can you hear me, dear? I can't speak very loud where I am, but I want you to understand this . . . something very important has come up. You must come to the church immediately. The church tower. You understand?

MARY

(on the phone)

Yes, I understand.

CHARLES

I don't want anybody to know that you're going there. Mary, don't tell anybody you're going. Go to the church. Leave your car in the rear, and come in through the back door. OK. Bye.

He hangs up and pulls open the door to the booth, tearing off the paper with the crossed-out swastika. As he does so, we hear POTTER's voice.

POTTER'S VOICE

Peabody!

PEABODY'S VOICE

I'm coming! I'm coming!

PEABODY comes in, carrying a load of firewood.

POTTER

Put that back there along with the rest of 'em, then get back to work.

PEABODY

Yes, sir.

RANKIN seats himself in the checker player's chair. POTTER is already on his comfortable throne. PEABODY lets the load of firewood tumble noisily down.

MR. POTTER

Watch that, Mr. Peabody . . . Your move, perfessor.

INT. RANKIN HOME

MARY, hatted and gloved, is coming down the stairs. She sits down to put on her shoes. SARA appears at the living room door, broom in hand.

SARA

Goin' someplace? Where to?

(Mary pretends not to hear the question. Starts on)

I asked you where you were goin', Miss Mary.

MARY
(stops)
I heard.

SARA
Well?

MARY
Sara, you seem to forget, I'm not a child any longer but a married woman.

SARA
You ain't been married very long . . .

MARY glances at her, surprised. Then decides to ignore SARA's behavior, starts on.

SARA
Wait, Mrs. Rankin.

MARY
(sharply)
What is it? I'm in a hurry.

MARY has opened the door to leave.

SARA
(aggrieved)
Well, you don't need to go bitin' my head off.

MARY slams the door shut.

MARY
What is it, Sara?

SARA sobs. MARY grabs hold of her.

MARY
If you've got something to say, say it. What is it?

SARA
I don't know what's got into you lately, indeed I don't. You was never mean to me like this, back at the old house.

MARY
(resignedly)
Sara . . .

SARA

(raises the corner of her apron, dabs at her eyes)

Maybe I've outworn my usefulness. I know I ain't as young as I used to be. Maybe you don't want me around anymore.

MARY

In heaven's name, stop talking such nonsense.

SARA

Well, it's true, and you know it. I'm going to pack my things and leave here, indeed I am.

SARA sits down, sobbing.

MARY

Sara, I'm sorry if I hurt your feelings. I didn't mean to, really I didn't. Sara, now I couldn't get along without you, and you know that, don't you? Well, don't you?

SARA

(through her tears)

Honestly?

MARY

(crossing her heart)

Honestly, honestly. You shan't ever leave me, Sara.

SARA clutches MARY to her, still sobbing.

SARA

You know the way I feel about you, like you was my own daughter, my own little girl.

MARY hugs her. Kisses her on the cheek.

MARY

Sara, I've got to go. I promised to be somewhere.

SARA

Where to, Miss Mary?

MARY

Stop fussing, Sara.

(smiling)

It's a secret.

MARY is at the front door, which she opens. SARA collapses. MARY rushes over.

SARA

Oh, Miss Mary!

MARY

What's the matter, Sara?

SARA

(gasping)

My heart . . . I can't breathe . . . the pain . . .

MARY puts a cushion under SARA's head.

MARY

Lie flat and keep quiet. Don't stir.

SARA obeys.

SARA

Don't leave me, Miss Mary. Maybe I'm dying.

MARY

No . . . I won't leave you.

She runs to the telephone, picks it up.

SARA

Stay with me!

MARY

(into the phone)

One three O, please . . .

NOAH answers the phone in the Longstreet house.

(after a pause)

MARY

Hello, Noah . . . I was supposed to meet Charles in the clock tower, but I can't get there. Will you go there and tell him to please wait for me? And, Noah . . . no one's to know where or why you're going or why. It's important.

NOAH

All right.

He hangs up the phone, troubled. Then he picks it up again.

NOAH

(into the phone)

Two three eight, please. Hello, may I speak to Mr. Wilson?

DISSOLVE TO: INT. POTTER'S DAY

RANKIN and POTTER are sitting at the checkerboard.

POTTER

Looks like it's coming up for snow.

RANKIN makes a move and jumps several of POTTER's men. POTTER glares at RANKIN, determined to vanquish him.

We then see NOAH and WILSON walking briskly outside toward the church.

MRS. RAND and MRS. LUNDSTRUM come into the drugstore. RANKIN turns to greet the ladies.

RANKIN

Mrs. Rand . . . Mrs. Lundstrum . . . Isn't it after hours? You ladies are working too hard at the library . . .

MRS. LUNDSTRUM

Why, no, Mr. Rankin. We closed at 3:30 . . . as per usual.

RANKIN

You're perfectly right . . . I dismissed class 10 minutes early

(glances at the clock in the tower)

Three forty-four . . .

TRAVELING SHOT

As he speaks, the CAMERA begins to move slowly toward the window. We glimpse RANKIN, speaking to the ladies, as CAMERA CONTINUES TO MOVE until it seems to press against the pane. Across from Potter's we see NOAH and WILSON climbing the church steps.

RANKIN

. . . I've been playing checkers all this time with Mr. Potter and I didn't realize it.

MRS. RAND

You know what you are, Mr. Rankin? You're the absent-minded professor . . .

This bit of wit convulses her: she is in a state of mild hysteria as she and MRS. LUNDGARD move off and sit down at a nearby table.

DISSOLVE TO: INT. BELFRY—AFTERNOON

The camera looks down from the belfry to the foot of the ladder. WILSON has begun climbing, followed by NOAH. The camera focuses on his hands as they grasp the rungs of the ladder. Finally WILSON's hand grasps one of the rungs RANKIN has sabotaged and then the other. The rungs snap, leaving WILSON dangling in midair.

Back at the drugstore, POTTER and RANKIN are still playing checkers.

POTTER

You sure are lucky today.

RANKIN

I am?

POTTER

You sure are.

VOICE OF MR. HILL

Evening, Mr. Potter.

POTTER

Evening, Mr. Hill.

VOICE OF HILL

Mr. Potter, I can't find them! The earmuffs!

POTTER

Right over there by the mittens!

(*to* RANKIN)

Be right back.

POTTER leaves the checkerboard.

RANKIN looks at his note, which says, "4:00 leave Potter's. 4:05 home."

POTTER

(off camera)

Right there in that box, where I told you they was.

VOICE OF MR. HILL

How much you want for them?

POTTER

Eighty-five cents.

VOICE OF MR. HILL

That's an awful lot!

POTTER

They come high this year.

POTTER comes back to the checkerboard and picks up a piece of crumpled-up paper. He sees RANKIN's note.

POTTER

You want this thing?

RANKIN

I'll keep it.

POTTER throws his own trash in the pot-bellied stove.

RANKIN

You know, Mr. Potter, you're a bad influence. I intended only to stay a couple of minutes; you've made me stay the whole afternoon. Look what time it is!

POTTER

I'd like to get even.

RANKIN

Your move.

Back at the church, WILSON is climbing down the bottom of the stairs. NOAH is already down.

WILSON

He really had the wind up. You can still smell the glue where he joined it.

INT. POTTER'S—DAY

POTTER and RANKIN are still playing checkers. They look out the window.

POTTER

It's like I told you, Professor. It's like we're coming up for snow.

RANKIN gets up and goes to the stove. He puts his own note into the stove, makes sure that it is burning, and throws it in.

POTTER makes a move that he thinks is brilliant.

POTTER

Look here, Professor. Double or nothing?

Without sitting back down, RANKIN makes a couple of moves on the checkerboard. He makes to leave.

RANKIN

Good afternoon, Mr. Potter.

POTTER

Afternoon, Mr. Rankin.

We now see the clock in the tower striking 4.

Light, feathery snow is now falling fast outside POTTER's window. RANKIN is walking outdoors.

At the RANKIN house, RANKIN comes in and closes the door. We see the silhouetted shadow of MARY in the background.

MARY

Charles?

RANKIN looks around him, startled and furious. He sees her and advances toward her in the living room.

RANKIN

You didn't go to the church?

MARY

Sara...

RANKIN

Sara? What about Sara?

MARY

Just as I was leaving, Sara had some kind of an attack. She's resting. Jeff said it wasn't very serious, but said I should stay with her.

RANKIN

Mm-hm.

RANKIN turns and distractedly begins to wind a grandfather clock.

MARY

(coming forward)

What's the matter, Charles?

RANKIN

(sharply)

Nothing's the matter.

MARY

Then why did you want me to go to the church? You said it was important!

RANKIN

Nothing's important, nothing actually. It's my sense of proportion, failing me these days.

MARY grasps him by the shoulders from behind.

MARY

Please, Charles, what is it?

RANKIN starts and slams the door of the grandfather clock. MARY recoils.

RANKIN

I'm sorry. I've just begun to feel the strain.

(He smiles, trying for the old charm)

You see, I have my weak moments too. I'll tell you in my own good time.

MARY

(tonelessly)

Have they found out anything more?

RANKIN

No, nothing. There's nothing to find out. Unless you . . .

MARY

No, I haven't seen anybody all day. I've been in my room.

RANKIN sits down.

RANKIN

(his self-control restored)

There's a rumor going around that there's an arrest to be made.

(rubs his right temple with the heel of his hand)

My head . . . The incident of the beads, yesterday, it made me doubt your strength. I thought perhaps you'd gone to your father and told him something. If you had . . .

MARY

You didn't have to be afraid . . . What did you tell Noah?

RANKIN

(without turning)

Mm. What—what about?

MARY

(looking up quickly)

Didn't you see him?

RANKIN

(not knowing what she is talking about)

Why should I have seen him?

MARY

Did you come here directly from the church?

RANKIN

(turning to her)

Am I being cross-examined?

MARY

No, but when I found I couldn't leave Sara, I called Noah and told him to go there and tell you I was detained.

RANKIN

(furiously)

I told you not to call anybody.

MARY

But surely Noah . . .

RANKIN

(imperiously)

Call him and tell him not to go.

MARY

I can't. I talked to him over half an hour ago.

RANKIN

(suddenly shouting)

Call him, I say!

MARY

(all control gone)

He's gone!

RANKIN

If he dies, his blood will be on your hands.

MARY

(coming to her feet)

What are you saying . . .

RANKIN

(ranting)

It's your meddling that's done this. It would have been all right if it hadn't been for you. But you had to be here . . . on that day . . . hanging your stupid curtains . . . Calling Noah! . . .

MARY

(sharply)

Charles . . . have you killed Noah?

RANKIN

Yes, if he goes to the church and climbs up that ladder!

MARY

It was I you intented to kill.

RANKIN

No!

MARY

Why wasn't it I? Franz Kindler!

At the mention of his name, all expression leaves RANKIN's face. His eyes are dull, his mouth hanging slightly open.

MARY

Kill me. Kill me. I want you to. I couldn't face life knowing what I've been to you . . . and what I've done to Noah. When you kill me, don't put your hands on me. Here . . . use this . . .

She picks up a poker and holds it out to him.

EXT. RANKIN HOUSE—DAY

JUDGE LONGSTREET drives his big sedan towards the house at high speed. In it are WILSON, DR. LAWRENCE, and NOAH. The car skids to a stop in front of the house.

INT. RANKIN LIVING ROOM—AFTERNOON

Close-up of the poker being thrown to the floor.

The men rush into the RANKIN house. A door is swinging, indicating that RANKIN has fled. MARY stands dazed while NOAH comes up to her.

NOAH

Mary!

MARY

Oh!

MARY faints into NOAH's arms. From her point of view, we see NOAH's face close up and blurred as we hear WILSON on the phone.

WILSON

(tapping on the phone)

Operator? Operator! Get me the state police!

We see the clock in the tower striking ominously.

WILSON

(on the phone)

Yes . . . the roadblocks are up. We're watching the railroad station, and he isn't hiding in the woods . . .

MARY is lying in her bed in her room. She comes to full awakening. She gets up; we see her through the mirror in her nightgown. She picks up her coat, puts it on, and leaves.

Outside, we see her walking from her house.

In MARY's bedroom, SARA looks in to find her missing.

SARA

Judge Longstreet! Judge Longstreet!

We see MARY walking through a cemetery in the snow.

The men rush outside of RANKIN's house.

JUDGE LONGSTREET

Get Wilson, Noah! I'll go for the police!

JUDGE LONGSTREET and NOAH run off in different directions.

Outside the church, MARY walks in through the back door.

NOAH rushes into the RANKIN living room, where WILSON is still on the phone.

NOAH

Mr. Wilson!

WILSON

If he's where I think he is, it's going to be easy. We'll do everything possible to get him alive.

NOAH

She's gone, Mr. Wilson! She's not in the house!

WILSON

(throws the receiver on the hook and turns to Noah, his voice quiet but his eyes full of anxiety)

The clock tower?

NOAH

I don't know.

WILSON

(grimly)

If that's where he's hiding, and she gets there before us . . .

NOAH

(in a small voice)

What will we do?

WILSON

(rushing out of the room, shouting after him)

Call Captain Samuels, and the deputies! Get all the help you can!

NOAH

Where?

WILSON takes a fall on the stairs and cries out in pain. NOAH reacts and dashes down the stairway toward him.

NOAH

Mr. Wilson!

With NOAH helping him, WILSON gets painfully to his feet.

WILSON

(gasping through his teeth)

The church . . . the church . . .

NOAH

But what about you, Mr. Wilson?

WILSON

(breathing hard as he starts to move)

Hurry up now! While your sister may be still alive!

With a worried look at WILSON, NOAH hurries off scene. WILSON hobbles after him.

WILSON

(grimly)

I'll get there . . .

DISSOLVE TO: INT. VESTIBULE—NIGHT

MARY, a package under her arm, begins mounting towards the belfry. She sees the ladder with its missing section. Clutching a package under one arm, with her free hand she grasps the one still standing upright and mounts up to the top.

RANKIN'S VOICE comes out of the darkness.

RANKIN'S VOICE

Don't move. I have a gun.

CLOSE SHOT—MARY

She stands rigid on the ladder.

MARY
(quietly)
You don't need it. I'm alone.

RANKIN
(incredulously)
What are you doing here?

MARY
(levelly)
Lift me up.

RANKIN hoists her up.

RANKIN

You're telling the truth?

MARY

Why should I lie?

RANKIN

Were you followed here?

MARY

I came by our way. Through the cemetery. No one saw me.

INT. BELFRY—NIGHT INT. LANDING—NIGHT

RANKIN throws open the door to the clock room, and he and MARY go in. She still carries her package. Silently, she hands him the package. She watches him as he tears the paper, revealing a shoebox. He jerks off the lid. He is staring down at emptiness. He looks up at her slowly.

MARY
(quietly)
I needed the excuse. I was afraid you wouldn't let me up.

RANKIN

What do you want?

MARY

I came to kill you.

RANKIN

No, Mary, it's you that are going to die. You were meant to fall through that ladder. You're going to fall.

MARY

I don't mind. If I take you with me.

RANKIN

You are a fool. They've searched the woods. I watched them like God looking at little ants . . . They've sure they've done such a fine search they won't search it again. A day or two and they'll be sure I've gotten out of town.

MARY

Not when they find me. They'll know you're still here.

RANKIN

But darling, you're on the verge of a breakdown. Now, you've cracked. Why else would you leave your bed . . . come to an empty church tower in the dead of night . . . ? Any child could see you'd wind up killing yourself.

He is interrupted by the sudden slamming of the clock tower door. WILSON stands before him. RANKIN draws a gun out of his pocket.

WILSON

(sweating with pain, but his tone cool and final)

Killing is what led you here. It won't help you now.

RANKIN draws the gun on WILSON. MARY grabs at RANKIN's arm for it. He pushes her aside and lunges for WILSON.

WILSON

Look out the window! Look!

RANKIN

That's on old trick, Wilson! And a very poor trick!

WILSON

Tricks! That's all you know is tricks! I don't need any tricks! No matter what happens to me, tricks won't do you any good! You're finished, Herr Franz Kindler!

VOICES are heard. We see a crowd of CITIZENS rushing toward the church. RANKIN looks through a window, sees them, is alarmed.

WILSON

The citizens of Harper. They've come after you. The plain little ordinary people, the ones you've been laughing at, have friends, Franz Kindler. Well, you can't fool them anymore.

RANKIN rushes toward WILSON but halts.

WILSON

Oh, sure, you can kill me . . . Mary . . . half of the people down there. There's no escape. You had a world and it closed in on you till there was only Harper. That closed in on you and there was only this room. And this room, too, is closing in on you. . .

RANKIN's face has again been stripped of all expression; the eyes are dull, the mouth hanging open. As WILSON's indictment sinks into him, a faint moistness appears on his lips. His eyes come alive, crazed, frenetic. Suddenly he is slobbering.

RANKIN

It's not true, the things they said I did. It was not my idea. I followed orders.

WILSON

You gave the orders.

RANKIN

I only did my duty.

(pleading)

Don't send me back. I can't face them. I'm not a criminal.

MARY

You *are*.

RANKIN turns to face her. This is the moment WILSON has waited for. He strikes out at RANKIN's wrist. The gun flies across the room. It lands at MARY's feet. She snatches it up. Her hand is steady as she faces him.

RANKIN rushes up the belfry, into the works of the clock, which he causes to go haywire. From below, MARY fires at RANKIN, hitting him in the arm. RANKIN falls onto a platform.

WILSON

Give me that gun!

WILSON takes the gun from MARY and fires, but it is empty. RANKIN rushes out to the window ledge and plunges out. He falls onto the outside platform of the clock, where the angel and devil are moving. He makes his way past the devil, but the outstretched sword in the hand of the angel skewers RANKIN. When it stops moving, he frees himself and pushes the angel down on the CROWD, who flee back. The clockworks go haywire, the hands rushing wildly around the dial. RANKIN falls to the ground. The crowd is screaming. The clock's hands swing round and round furiously.

The scene turns to the interior of the church. We, and WILSON, are looking down at the CROWD. MARY is descending the ladder and reaches the bottom. POTTER is at the foot of the stairs.

POTTER

OK, let me give you a hand, Mr. Wilson!

WILSON

No, no, no, thanks!

POTTER

What happened?

WILSON

V-E Day in Harper.

POTTER

I don't get that. Come on down!

WILSON

No, no. Not until you get me a new ladder. I've had my ankle busted and my head conked. From here on in, I'm taking it easy!

POTTER

Well, I'll get you another ladder, Mr. Wilson. You've had enough trouble.

MARY looks up at WILSON, who is puffing on his pipe.

WILSON

Good night, Mary. Pleasant dreams.

FADE OUT

ABOUT THE FILM

The Stranger (1946), the third film directed by the legendary Orson Welles, is a film noir thriller of the highest order.

In the wake of World War II, Mr. Wilson, an official with the Allied War Crimes Commission (played by the legendary Edward G. Robinson), is on the trail of Franz Kindler, an escaped Nazi who was the chief architect of the regime's mass genocide. Wilson allows a concentration camp commandant, Conrad Meinike, to escape in the hope that he will lead him to the elusive Kindler. The trail takes them to the quiet Connecticut town of Harper, where Kindler (played by Welles) has taken on the guise of Charles Rankin, a history teacher at a boys' school.

Kindler, as Rankin, is about to marry Mary Longstreet (Loretta Young), the daughter of an eminent Supreme Court justice, Adam Longstreet (Philip Merivale). Wilson has to establish Rankin's identity as Kindler and overcome Mary's disbelief.

The drama centers around a Gothic clock in a church at the center of Harper, which has not worked for many years. Rankin undertakes to restore the clock—thereby providing a clue to his identity with the Nazi Kindler, who has a mania for clocks.

The Stranger has the plot and pacing of a thriller, contrasting the profound evil of Kindler and Meinike with the naivete of a small New England town. Its sharp characterizations include the relentless Wilson, the suave Rankin, the earnest and devoted Mary, her loyal and vigilant brother Noah (played by Richard Long), and the grave but affectionate Judge Longstreet.

In an attempt to convince Mary of Rankin's true identity, Wilson shows her then-recent newsreel footage of the Holocaust. The Stranger is the first Hollywood film to show this shocking but authentic footage.

In addition to the dramatic and tightly paced story, *The Stranger* features many characteristics of Welles' masterful directorial hand: the use of shadows to create stark chiaroscuro effects; unusual and startling camera angles; and trailing camera shots that move individual scenes across locations.

The Stranger is a classic example of the Hollywood film noir genre. It will enthrall not only aficionados but anyone who appreciates the power of a compelling, tightly paced thriller.

THE MAN WITH THE GOLDEN ARM

• • •

Based on a novel by NELSON ALGREN
Screenplay by WALTER NEWMAN and LEWIS MELTZER
A film by OTTO PREMINGER

CAST

Frank Sinatra .... Frankie "Dealer" Machine
Eleanor Parker .... Sophia "Zosh" Machine
Kim Novak .... Molly Novotny
Arnold Stang .... Sparrow
Darren McGavin .... "Nifty Louie" Fomorowski
Robert Strauss .... Zero Schwiefka
John Conte .... Drunkie John
Doro Merande Vi
George E. Stone .... Sam Markette
George Mathews .... Williams
Leonid Kinskey .... Dominowski
Emile Meyer .... Captain Bednar
Shorty Rogers .... himself (bandleader at audition)
Ralph Peña .... himself (bassist at audition)
Shelly Manne .... himself (drummer at audition)

We see a busy Chicago street in the 1950s. A bus pulls up to a stop. FRANKIE "DEALER" MACHINE gets out, carrying a suitcase and a drum in a case, played by Frank Sinatra. He goes down the street. The neighborhood is seedy. He passes a strip club. He then passes in front of a building. Two attractive women, undoubtedly prostitutes, are looking out the windows. One of them says:

PROSTITUTE

Hi, Frankie.

FRANKIE "DEALER" MACHINE

Hello.

FRANKIE walks on, past a pool hall. He looks inside. Then past a policeman, who is hauling a suspect out of a pawnshop into a police car.

POLICEMAN

Get in there.

FRANKIE passes a sign on a window: BEER. He looks inside and sees several men taunting a paraplegic, who is missing one arm and one leg. NIFTY LOUIE Fomorowski, a sharply dressed but shifty-looking man with a small mustache, is holding a glass of whiskey to the man's nose.

"NIFTY LOUIE" FOMOROWSKI

Nothing like that first drink of the day. Come on, drink up, enjoy it. Hey, they tell me you're some dancer.

The paraplegic man shakes his head.

"NIFTY LOUIE" FOMOROWSKI

Well, how about a little dance anyway?

The paraplegic shakes his head.

"NIFTY LOUIE" FOMOROWSKI

No?

NIFTY LOUIE makes as if to pour the glass of whiskey on the floor. The paraplegic hops around pathetically, to the men's laughter. We see FRANKIE, looking inside the window. He seems a bit saddened by the prank, but then he has an affectionate smile: these men are his friends.

FRANKIE goes into the bar, where SPARROW is in a booth, combing a schnauzer. SPARROW is a young man, unshaven, with black-rimmed glasses and a baseball cap. He is of the type that used to be called a punk. FRANKIE pulls off his glasses.

SPARROW
Hey, give me back . . . Don't horse around . . . What's a big idea?

SPARROW looks up and recognizes FRANKIE, who puts the glasses back on SPARROW.

SPARROW
Frankie? Frankie! Frankie, when did you get back?

SPARROW hugs FRANKIE.

SPARROW
How are you? You all right? You know . . .

FRANKIE "DEALER" MACHINE
The monkey's gone.

SPARROW
Let me look at you. Let me look at you. Not even a posty card.

FRANKIE "DEALER" MACHINE
You can't read anyway.

SPARROW
Well, you could have drawn pictures.

FRANKIE "DEALER" MACHINE
There you go, punk. How's the lost dog business?

SPARROW
Yeah. As soon as they see me hanging around, people start locking up their mutts. I tell you folks just don't have that trust in their fellow man anymore. You know what I mean?

Laughter behind FRANKIE and SPARROW as the barflies continue to taunt the paraplegic, who is still hopping around.

SPARROW
Hey, Yantek, look who's out!

YANTEK, the middle-aged bar proprietor, comes over and shakes FRANKIE's hand enthusiastically.

YANTEK

Frankie, you are all right? Clean?

FRANKIE "DEALER" MACHINE

Yep.

YANTEK

Good kid.

FRANKIE "DEALER" MACHINE

Enough already. Buy me a drink.

YANTEK

Sure.

FRANKIE goes over to the bar, where he greets a number of barflies, all of whom know him well. One of them is VANGIE, a middle-aged woman. NIFTY LOUIE is also there.

MALE SPEAKER

Look what the cat dragged in.

VANGIE

Frankie, honey.

MALE BARFLY 1

You was gone so long, I thought maybe you was made warden.

MALE BARFLY 2

Hey, you're looking good, Dealer.

FRANKIE "DEALER" MACHINE

Put on six pounds.

BARFLY 3

Wow! Six pounds.

BARFLY 1

He's gone so long I thought maybe he was made warden.

VANGIE

How was it down there? Frankie?

FRANKIE "DEALER" MACHINE

Greatest place you ever see, Vangie.

BARFLY 2

He means Lexington.

FRANKIE "DEALER" MACHINE
I'm telling you, ball games, great food. I even learned how to play the drums.

BARFLY 2
You make it sound as if I missed something by not going to jail years ago. It's a prison, no?

FRANKIE "DEALER" MACHINE
More of a hospital kind. Let me show you something.

BARFLY 3
Ah, federal pens is always best, ask anybody.

VANGIE
Well, I know . . .

BARFLY 1
He's gone so long, I think he's made warden.

FRANKIE produces a large drum out of his case.

FRANKIE "DEALER" MACHINE
Have you seen anything so pretty?

SPARROW raps on the drum.

FRANKIE "DEALER" MACHINE
Don't touch.

SPARROW
Hey, how'd you sneak them out, Frankie?

FRANKIE "DEALER" MACHINE
The guys give me them up there in the band.

BARFLY 2
They let you have a band?

FRANKIE "DEALER" MACHINE
Yeah, I was in it. They chipped in and bought me these when I left.

SPARROW
Wow.

NIFTY LOUIE is standing by the doorway.

"NIFTY LOUIE" FOMOROWSKI
Long time, dealer. How was it there? Bad?

FRANKIE "DEALER" MACHINE

It was all right.

"NIFTY LOUIE" FOMOROWSKI

Six months. You can hardly wait, I bet. Come over to my place.

FRANKIE "DEALER" MACHINE

No thanks, Louie.

"NIFTY LOUIE" FOMOROWSKI

You broke? Now ain't you being stupid? It's for free.

FRANKIE "DEALER" MACHINE

I don't need it is all. I kicked it.

"NIFTY LOUIE" FOMOROWSKI

Oh, kicked it. One of them.

FRANKIE "DEALER" MACHINE

I mean it.

"NIFTY LOUIE" FOMOROWSKI

Sure. I'll be around.

FRANKIE goes and sits down to SPARROW, who has gone back to combing the schnauzer.

SPARROW

Frankie, don't do it. Don't start up with that peddler again.

FRANKIE "DEALER" MACHINE

Me, I'd rather chop my arm off before I let him touch it. This Dr. Lennox who took care of me down at the hospital, he was a good guy. He told me at least 10 times. He said, "Frankie, when you get out of here, you take even one fix, you're hooked again." Don't worry about me, buddy boy, let's get out of here.

SPARROW goes over to the bar and hands over the schnauzer to YANTEK.

SPARROW

Yantek, take care of this asset for me. I got a customer coming to get it.

YANTEK

Okay, Sparrow.

FRANKIE and SPARROW leave. We see NIFTY LOUIE looking off thoughtfully, smiling cagily.

FRANKIE and SPARROW are now outside on the street, walking.

SPARROW

Don't let him give you no gas.

FRANKIE "DEALER" MACHINE

Him? I'm not going to be around here long enough to let him bother me. I'm going to get me a job in a big-name band.

SPARROW

You're kidding.

FRANKIE "DEALER" MACHINE

What do you think I'm strengthening my wrist for, Buddy-o? The guy who teaches me drumming down there says that I'm a natural. Can't miss, he says; arms made of pure gold.

SPARROW

You mean a job winding these drums?

FRANKIE "DEALER" MACHINE

I got everything planned too. Going to call myself Jack Duvall.

SPARROW

Probably I ain't going to see you around so much then, huh?

FRANKIE "DEALER" MACHINE

Yeah, maybe I can set something up for you. Carrying around instruments or something.

SPARROW

Wow!

They reach the stoop of FRANKIE's apartment building and climb up the stairs.

FRANKIE "DEALER" MACHINE

Traveling around the country, high-type nightclubs. How's that sound to you, punk?

SPARROW

When is it going to be? When?

FRANKIE "DEALER" MACHINE

Right away, today. I'm the kind of guy, boy, when I move, watch my smoke. But I'm going to need some good clothes though.

SPARROW

Oh, well you go on up, I'm going to find you something.

FRANKIE "DEALER" MACHINE

Yeah. Size 39.

SPARROW

39.

FRANKIE "DEALER" MACHINE

Stripes.

SPARROW

Stripes.

FRANKIE "DEALER" MACHINE

Something nice.

SPARROW goes off. FRANKIE goes into the apartment building and up the stairs. From a second-floor apartment comes a loud clangor.

PROPRIETOR

(*off-camera*)

You stop that noise, you and your husband, or I throw you both out. You hear?

VI

(*off-camera*)

I'll make all the noise I want.

PROPRIETOR

Who is landlord? Me. You do like I say.

FRANKIE comes up the stairs to see the proprietor, a middle-aged man with an Eastern European accent, and VI, a scrawny middle-aged woman.

VI

(*to Proprietor*)

Your mother's eye socks, I do like you say.

VI sees FRANKIE.

VI

Frankie Machine. Oh, you look great. How you feeling, Frankie? I mean . . . ?

FRANKIE "DEALER" MACHINE

Fine, Vi. Just fine. Hi, landlord.

PROPRIETOR

She and husband fight all the time, holler, throw things.

FRANKIE "DEALER" MACHINE

Nothing changes.

PROPRIETOR
This is a respectable house, and I am respectable man.

VI
Respectable, my eye. Come on, get out, you're late for the parole board.

FRANKIE takes his gear up to the third floor. He sets it down hesitantly on the landing, then picks it up again and goes to the door of an apartment. He opens the door and goes in. His wife, ZOSH, a beautiful young blonde woman in a nightgown, is sitting in a wheelchair. There is a crudely written sign, "Welcome home FRANKIE" hanging on the wall.

SOPHIA "ZOSH" MACHINE
Oh. Frankie, you're home!

FRANKIE and ZOSH embrace.

SOPHIA "ZOSH" MACHINE
Oh, Frankie, I love you so much! Oh! I missed you so.

She clutches him and kisses him eagerly.

SOPHIA "ZOSH" MACHINE
I've been so lonely, Frankie, without you. I'm so lonely.

FRANKIE "DEALER" MACHINE
Zosh, stop crying. Zosh, let me look at you.

SOPHIA "ZOSH" MACHINE
My eyes are going to be all red.

FRANKIE "DEALER" MACHINE
Naw, you look fine, Zosh.

SOPHIA "ZOSH" MACHINE
You promise? Is the cold sore gone?

FRANKIE "DEALER" MACHINE
Yeah, you look real good.

FRANKIE takes off his hat and closes the apartment door.

SOPHIA "ZOSH" MACHINE
I had this cold, and I wanted to look real nice for you when you came back and I was afraid it wouldn't be gone. So I put this goofy salve on to dry it. Oh, Frankie.

FRANKIE "DEALER" MACHINE
Oh Zosh, everything's going to be all right.

SOPHIA "ZOSH" MACHINE

Oh, you didn't see.

She points to a cake sitting on a side table below the sign.

SOPHIA "ZOSH" MACHINE

Look, Vi got the cake by the bakery, but the sign I made, it's sort of like for a welcome home.

FRANKIE "DEALER" MACHINE

Geez. It's like a real party or something.

FRANKIE picks up the cake and tastes the frosting.

FRANKIE "DEALER" MACHINE

It's real nice, Zosh.

SOPHIA "ZOSH" MACHINE

How are you, Frankie?

FRANKIE "DEALER" MACHINE

I'm clean.

SOPHIA "ZOSH" MACHINE

You sure?

FRANKIE "DEALER" MACHINE

I kicked it for keeps.

SOPHIA "ZOSH" MACHINE

Did it hurt? How was it there for you?

FRANKIE "DEALER" MACHINE

Oh, they treated me fine down there. There was this doctor, this Dr. Lennox, he was really good to me.

FRANKIE moves his drum case across the room. ZOSH wheels her wheelchair back toward him.

SOPHIA "ZOSH" MACHINE

Frankie, Frankie, did you miss me?

FRANKIE "DEALER" MACHINE

Of course, I missed you, Zosh. What kind of silly question is that? Of course I missed you. Honest, no kidding.

He moves his suitcase over.

SOPHIA "ZOSH" MACHINE

What do you have there?

FRANKIE "DEALER" MACHINE
You'll see. Oh, I brought you something.

He takes out a metallic necklace made out of tinfoil and hands it to her.

SOPHIA "ZOSH" MACHINE
Oh, it's an exquisite thing.

FRANKIE "DEALER" MACHINE
You like it? I made it myself out of cigarette wrappers.

SOPHIA "ZOSH" MACHINE
It's just an exquisite thing is all. You made it?

FRANKIE "DEALER" MACHINE
Yeah. For a hobby like. See, part of the cure is to keep yourself busy doing things you enjoy. Like for instance, I wanted to learn the drum and music and Dr. Lennox got them to help me do it. During the day, I was kept busy enough, but sometimes at night, I'd get restless. I wanted to keep my mind off the craving, I made that.

SOPHIA "ZOSH" MACHINE
There's something important I got to tell you.

FRANKIE "DEALER" MACHINE
What?

SOPHIA "ZOSH" MACHINE
Well, I forget right now.

ZOSH produces a whistle, which is hanging on her neck, and blows it.

FRANKIE "DEALER" MACHINE
A whistle?

SOPHIA "ZOSH" MACHINE
Oh, I was scared sometimes being alone. So Vi got it for me. I should blow for her when I wanted her. Go on, you were telling me.

FRANKIE takes out his drums and starts setting them up.

FRANKIE "DEALER" MACHINE
Oh, well, the first thing you do when you get there, you talk to a doctor for about two hours.

SOPHIA "ZOSH" MACHINE
Oh, I know. I know what it is. I know what I had to tell you. Vi took me to this movie. And the girl's kid brother had a friend in it. Now who do you think he looked like?

FRANKIE "DEALER" MACHINE

Who?

SOPHIA "ZOSH" MACHINE

You! That was a good movie. The stage show was really good too. We owe Vi 80 cents for the movie. I was broke, and we owe her for the cake too.

FRANKIE "DEALER" MACHINE

How come you didn't have any money? Schwiefka didn't kick in regular?

SOPHIA "ZOSH" MACHINE

No.

FRANKIE "DEALER" MACHINE

He was supposed to! It was his joint they raided, not mine. I was just the dealer. I kept my mouth shut and took the rap. If he didn't send 50 a month regular, how much did he?

SOPHIA "ZOSH" MACHINE

Well, he sent 50, but not regular. You see, Vi had to kick in for me sometimes.

FRANKIE "DEALER" MACHINE

She took good care of you? You have fun with her?

FRANKIE turns on the radio. Swing music is playing.

SOPHIA "ZOSH" MACHINE

Yeah, but not like when you're here. It was terrible being alone, Frankie, and my legs, when they hurt, she don't massage like you.

FRANKIE "DEALER" MACHINE

What do they say by the clinic, Zosh?

SOPHIA "ZOSH" MACHINE

I stopped going by that goofy clinic.

FRANKIE "DEALER" MACHINE

The clinic must know what's right, Zosh. You gotta start the clinic again; you gotta get well.

SOPHIA "ZOSH" MACHINE

I dreamed that this new doctor around the corner, he cured me. I'd have gone to him already, but he ain't free like the clinic. But now you're back making money again by Schwiefka, I'll go.

FRANKIE "DEALER" MACHINE

I'm finished with Schwiefka; I don't deal for him no more.

SOPHIA "ZOSH" MACHINE

But you always deal. You're a dealer. You're the best dealer in the business.

FRANKIE "DEALER" MACHINE

No more. I'm a drummer now.

SOPHIA "ZOSH" MACHINE

Don't make jokes, Frankie. I never know when you're making jokes.

FRANKIE "DEALER" MACHINE

Who's joking, Zosh? Listen.

FRANKIE starts playing his drums, accompanying the music on the radio.

FRANKIE "DEALER" MACHINE

Nice, huh? This Dr. Lennox, I told him my whole life story from what I was born almost, and about you and me. But he told me that if I lived when I got out like I lived before I went in there, chances are I would be hooked again in no time. So that's why I want to get with a band.

FRANKIE drums.

FRANKIE "DEALER" MACHINE

Listen, how's that?

SOPHIA "ZOSH" MACHINE

Cute. What did you tell him about me, this doctor?

FRANKIE "DEALER" MACHINE

I told him about getting some money and getting you well, and he said getting with a band was a good way to go at it. He even gave me the name of a guy in town right here to get a job.

SOPHIA "ZOSH" MACHINE

That's nice. I mean, if this man with a job ever heard of this great doctor. Most times these things just don't come through.

FRANKIE "DEALER" MACHINE

I got this.

FRANKIE pulls a letter out of his jacket.

SOPHIA "ZOSH" MACHINE

What is it?

FRANKIE "DEALER" MACHINE
It's a letter from Doc. I think I'll go call him now.

SOPHIA "ZOSH" MACHINE
Now? Let's talk about it tomorrow.

FRANKIE "DEALER" MACHINE
I'll be right up, Zosh.

SOPHIA "ZOSH" MACHINE
You haven't even tasted the cake.

FRANKIE "DEALER" MACHINE
It'll only be a minute! I'll be right up.

SOPHIA "ZOSH" MACHINE
No, now, Frankie. First, just a piece of nice—cake.

She lights a candle on the cake, but FRANKIE is out the door before she finishes.

Down on the first floor, FRANKIE goes to the pay phone and makes a call while DRUNKIE JOHN, a disreputable-looking man in a sport coat and tie, is standing at the front door, waiting for MOLLY, who is off camera.

DRUNKIE JOHN
Hey, you coming, baby?

MOLLY NOVOTNY
(*off camera*)
Yeah, Yeah, I'm coming, John.

DRUNKIE JOHN
Hey, Molly?

MOLLY NOVOTNY
(*off camera*)
Yeah. Good.

FRANKIE is talking on the phone.

FRANKIE "DEALER" MACHINE
I want to talk to Mr. Harry Lane, please.

DRUNKIE JOHN
(*to* MOLLY)
How about it? Huh?

FRANKIE "DEALER" MACHINE

Machine. Frankie Machine. Yeah, I got a letter of introduction for him, from Dr. Lennox.

MOLLY NOVOTNY, a beautiful blonde, comes out of the apartment. She talks to FRANKIE while he is still on the phone.

MOLLY NOVOTNY

Hello, Frankie.

FRANKIE "DEALER" MACHINE

Dr. Martin Lennox.

(*turning to* MOLLY, *putting his hand on the receiver*)

How you been, Molly?

MOLLY comes up very close to FRANKIE.

MOLLY NOVOTNY

All right.

DRUNKIE JOHN

Come on, baby, let's go.

MOLLY NOVOTNY

(*to* FRANKIE)

A guy I met when you were away.

FRANKIE is talking into the phone.

FRANKIE "DEALER" MACHINE

Mr. Lane, I got a letter for you.

DRUNKIE JOHN

(*to* MOLLY)

Come on. Yeah, come on. What do you say, kid?

DRUNKIE JOHN and MOLLY go out.

FRANKIE

(into the phone)

This afternoon? Huh? Would you? I sure do appreciate it, Mr. Lane. Thank you so much. Okay, bye-bye.

SPARROW runs into the hallway carrying a new suit under his coat. He rushes up the stairs but halts when he sees FRANKIE on the phone. He shows FRANKIE the suit.

SPARROW

Frankie! A new thing by Brax department store! No salesgirls. Just help yourself. It's what they call a honor system. What's the matter, Frankie?

SPARROW shows him the suit.

SPARROW

Feel that material, and I figured as long as I'm there . . .

SPARROW pulls a new shirt out from under his own shirt. FRANKIE looks pensive.

SPARROW

Nice, huh? Are you all right? Frankie?

FRANKIE "DEALER" MACHINE

I got the drumming job.

SPARROW

Already! Wow!

FRANKIE "DEALER" MACHINE

When I move, I move like a streak, punk.

Back in the apartment, FRANKIE is putting on the suit while ZOSH is brushing her hair.

FRANKIE

Think it looks all right, Zosh?

SOPHIA "ZOSH" MACHINE

How come you ask me all of a sudden?

FRANKIE "DEALER" MACHINE

I just want to know if it looks all right, Zosh.

SOPHIA "ZOSH" MACHINE

And my name ain't Zosh, it's Sophia.

FRANKIE "DEALER" MACHINE

What's the matter?

SOPHIA "ZOSH" MACHINE

Nothing's the matter, except how would you feel if your spine was hurting?

FRANKIE "DEALER" MACHINE

Why didn't you say so?

SOPHIA "ZOSH" MACHINE
On account of your first day back, I just didn't want you should worry.

FRANKIE "DEALER" MACHINE
Don't be like that, Zosh. Is it bad?

He starts massaging her back. SPARROW, who has been there below, helping FRANKIE into his suit, pops up and helps FRANKIE into his jacket.

SOPHIA "ZOSH" MACHINE
Well, maybe the new doctor will do me some good. Huh?

FRANKIE "DEALER" MACHINE
We'll go see him when I get back.

SOPHIA "ZOSH" MACHINE
Oh, take me now, Frankie!

FRANKIE "DEALER" MACHINE
Zosh, I got this appointment. You know how much it means to me. Huh? We'll go as soon as I get back.

SOPHIA "ZOSH" MACHINE
Please, Frankie.

FRANKIE "DEALER" MACHINE
I'll hurry.

SOPHIA "ZOSH" MACHINE
Frankie, well, give me a little more massage then, first, huh?

FRANKIE "DEALER" MACHINE
Zosh, I'm doing this for you to get some money so you can get a good doctor.

SOPHIA "ZOSH" MACHINE
Oh, please, Frankie?

FRANKIE "DEALER" MACHINE
Look, I'll get you a dog too. How's that? Huh?
(*to* SPARROW)
Get her a dog, will you?

SPARROW
I'll give the matter my personal attention. Just have confidence in the management.

FRANKIE "DEALER" MACHINE
Wish me luck, Zosh.

FRANKIE kisses her. He and SPARROW leave the apartment.

SOPHIA "ZOSH" MACHINE

Oh, Frankie. Wait, wait, Frankie.

She opens the door and starts to blow her whistle feebly, but she stops. Then she locks the front door, gets up from the wheelchair, and goes to the window to look out at him.

Out on the street. FRANKIE is nattily dressed in his new suit and a bow tie. He walks down the street with SPARROW.

FRANKIE "DEALER" MACHINE

I can't be in two places at once. What could I do?

SPARROW

Yeah. She just don't realize . . .

FRANKIE "DEALER" MACHINE

Oh, shut up, punk. You just don't realize. How would you like to be nailed to a chair?

They pass by the bar. ZERO SCHWIEFKA, a tough-looking man smoking a cigar (as he always is), looks out the bar window at him. He raps on the window, beckoning FRANKIE in. FRANKIE and SPARROW go into the bar.

ZERO SCHWIEFKA

Frankie, Frankie, how are you? Well, it didn't do you no harm, did it, Frankie? Oh, you look good.

FRANKIE "DEALER" MACHINE

That's right, Schwiefka, it was a real country club.

SCHWIEFKA, FRANKIE, and SPARROW go over to the bar. YANTEK pours him a whiskey. FRANKIE sees MOLLY and DRUNKEN JOHN at a table nearby in the background. The bartender pours drinks for FRANKIE and SCHWIEFKA. SCHWIEFKA fingers FRANKIE's suit.

ZERO SCHWIEFKA

Hmm? They give you this when they let you out?

SPARROW

Give him, nothing! I borrow by Brax.

ZERO SCHWIEFKA

You know, I came as soon as I heard you were out. I figured, he's worried about getting his job again. Tell him don't worry, Schwiefka don't forget so quick. Job's waiting.

FRANKIE "DEALER" MACHINE

You need a dealer, you say?

ZERO SCHWIEFKA

Me? No. I've been dealing myself and, man, I built up a game like nobody's business. I have a great following. The play is bigger than ever.

FRANKIE "DEALER" MACHINE

I hear you wasn't doing so good

ZERO SCHWIEFKA

From who? When I say great, I don't mean a lot—a few, but loaded.

FRANKIE "DEALER" MACHINE

So what do you want me for?

ZERO SCHWIEFKA

Like I'm telling you, I take care of my friends.

SPARROW

Can I polish your halo, Schwiefka? Only a quarter.

ZERO SCHWIEFKA

Knock it off, punk. Look, I've been doing all right, but I don't say that the customers like me better than they like you. The dealer makes the house. I know that. What do you say?

FRANKIE "DEALER" MACHINE

No.

ZERO SCHWIEFKA

You're dealing for some other joint?

FRANKIE "DEALER" MACHINE

I ain't dealing for nobody. I ain't dealing for nobody no more.

ZERO SCHWIEFKA

Is that the way you repay me? Didn't I send money to Zosh? I've gone and tell all my friends that you'll be working for me again. What am I supposed to do?

FRANKIE "DEALER" MACHINE

As far as I'm concerned, you can go back to matching pennies with school kids.

SCHWIEFKA gives FRANKIE a dirty look, throws a dollar on the bar, and leaves.

DRUNKIE JOHN calls the bartender from his table.

DRUNKIE JOHN

Hey, Yantek? Yantek?

FRANKIE "DEALER" MACHINE

(*to* SPARROW)

Who is he?

SPARROW

Drunkie? His name's Johnny something. He's houseman for Gobercheck's poolroom.

FRANKIE gestures toward DRUNKIE JOHN and MOLLY.

FRANKIE "DEALER" MACHINE

Is that a thing with him?

SPARROW

They see each other. You want to meet him?

FRANKIE "DEALER" MACHINE

No. So long, Yantek.

YANTEK

See you, Frankie.

FRANKIE and SPARROW go out into the street. A police car pulls up in front of them immediately. Two policemen, one of them OFFICER PARKER, beefy and middle-aged, get out.

OFFICER PARKER

Hey, you. Get in, dealer.

FRANKIE "DEALER" MACHINE

Who? Me? What for?

SPARROW tries to go off, but the other policeman grabs him.

OFFICER PARKER

You too, punk.

FRANKIE "DEALER" MACHINE

I didn't do nothing. Oh, wait a minute, Parker. Listen, I'm on my way to get a job. It's important to me. You can pick me up some other time. I just need an hour. Be a good guy, will you?

OFFICER PARKER

Shut up.

The policemen push FRANKIE and SPARROW into the car.

The scene changes to police captain BEDNAR's office, like the other officers tough and middle-aged but wearing street clothes. He is seated at his desk, shaving himself with an electric razor.

OFFICER PARKER brings in FRANKIE and SPARROW.

SPARROW
What are you walking talking for? Are you looking to get sued for libel or something? I could sue you right now.

CAPTAIN BEDNAR
You're looking good, dealer, really good. When they let you out?

FRANKIE "DEALER" MACHINE
Monday they let me out. What's the charge, Parker?

POLICEMAN
Shoplifting from Brax the suit.

SPARROW
Who told you a thing like that?

POLICEMAN
A little bird.

FRANKIE "DEALER" MACHINE
A little bird with a cigar.

SPARROW
Schwiefka.

CAPTAIN BEDNAR
I thought you could stay out of trouble. Two days. Dealer, dealer.

FRANKIE "DEALER" MACHINE
Listen, Bednar, I got a chance for a job playing with a band. Honest. If you don't believe me, call the guy on the phone. He'll tell you. Well, just give me a half hour, please.

OFFICER PARKER
Sure, you can wear my badge too.

CAPTAIN BEDNAR
Book him and hold his suit.

FRANKIE "DEALER" MACHINE
A guy needs a half hour. Give me a break, will you?

CAPTAIN BEDNAR
I don't make the rules, dealer.

FRANKIE and SPARROW are being led downstairs into a jail cell by OFFICER PARKER, who is handling SPARROW roughly.

SPARROW

Now, I tell you, you can't hold me, I'm incapable. I ain't smart enough to be running around, but I'm too goofy to be locked up.

The policeman has SPARROW by the neck.

SPARROW

The neck, will you let go the neck? I got a complaint. Let go the neck.

FRANKIE and SPARROW are led into a cell. There are two junkies there.

JUNKIE 1

(*To* OFFICER PARKER)

Hey you. I'm talking to you. Oh, the old silent treatment, huh? All right, let's have your number, fella. I'll show you, you can't give me the business. Your goose is cooked, copper.

FRANKIE sits down, next to a second junkie, who yawns with a tormented look on his face. FRANKIE moves away. SPARROW sits next to him.

SPARROW

Frankie, you got a cigarette? Do a cigarette trick? You know, just to break the dirty monotony.

FRANKIE puts the cigarette through his fingers. Then he opens his hand. The cigarette is missing. FRANKIE opens both his hands. They are both empty. Then he pulls the cigarette out from behind SPARROW's ear.

SPARROW

Wow!

SCHWIEFKA appears in front of the jail cell.

ZERO SCHWIEFKA

Dealer.

FRANKIE and SPARROW go up to the bars.

ZERO SCHWIEFKA

Hello, dealer. I come running as soon as I heard. You want I should get you out, dealer?

FRANKIE "DEALER" MACHINE

You fink.

ZERO SCHWIEFKA

The store will drop the charges, but 37 bucks is a lot of dough. How do I know you'd pay me back?

FRANKIE "DEALER" MACHINE

You fink.

ZERO SCHWIEFKA

It'd be different if you was dealing for me. If you want to deal for me, I can get you out.

FRANKIE grabs SCHWIEFKA by the lapels through the bars of the cell.

FRANKIE "DEALER" MACHINE

Dirty, lousy stool pigeon.

ZERO SCHWIEFKA

I don't know what you mean. Just trying to do you a favor. Yes or no?

FRANKIE "DEALER" MACHINE

Okay.

SCWIEFKA strides off.

SPARROW

He took off like a whipped dog. He's scared of you, Frankie.

FRANKIE "DEALER" MACHINE

Nobody's ever been scared of me.

SPARROW

Them Krauts was scared of you. You was a big man in the army.

FRANKIE "DEALER" MACHINE

Big man. I was the guy picked the fly spots out of the black pepper.

JUNKIE 2 flings himself in a panic against the bars.

JUNKIE 2

Get me out! I can't take it! Get me out!

Two guards go into the cell. Junkie 2 falls on the floor in panic.

JUNKIE 2

I want a fix! I want a fix! A fix! Give me a fix. Can you gimme a fix? I want a fix!

The two guards haul off JUNKIE 2. We see FRANKIE pressing his face against the bars in despair, his eyes in tears as we hear the howls of Junkie 2 in the distance.

We are now in SCHWIEFKA's poker room. FRANKIE is dealing.

FRANKIE "DEALER" MACHINE
Check what? Let say a buck. Big aces, and here we go, down and dirty.

We see SPARROW escorting a losing gambler out.

SPARROW
Better luck next time, friend.

SPARROW opens the door for him and locks it again when the man is out. SPARROW goes over to where a game is going on, with several men around a table, FRANKIE dealing. BARFLY 1 and NIFTY LOUIE are among the players. SCHWIEFKA is supervising.

FRANKIE "DEALER" MACHINE
Check what? Man with a hammer bumps a buck. Jack calls. Bucket of paint all red.

SCHWIEFKA
Coffee.

SPARROW goes to get some coffee.

FRANKIE "DEALER" MACHINE
Doesn't mean a thing if you haven't got the king. Winner every hand. You bet more, you get more. Slip a hand, make me laugh.

"NIFTY LOUIE" FOMOROWSKI
You still take tips, dealer, or don't they pay so good in the music game? What happened to that big job you had lined up? You stink up the joint? Give us a fresh deck.

FRANKIE "DEALER" MACHINE
I decide when we need a fresh deck at this table.

SPARROW
Hey, Louie, borrow me a dirty dollar?

"NIFTY LOUIE" FOMOROWSKI
Get back to the door, lamebrain.

SPARROW
I take orders only from Frankie.

"NIFTY LOUIE" FOMOROWSKI
Don't give me your lip, you cheap little hustler.

SPARROW

Hustler, smushler. I'm legit compared to some. Ain't no 14-year-old junkies waiting around to see me.

NIFTY LOUIE jumps up and grabs SPARROW by the lapels.

"NIFTY LOUIE" FOMOROWSKI

You want to die?

FRANKIE continues the game.

FRANKIE "DEALER" MACHINE

And here we go, down and dirty.

NIFTY LOUIE lets go of SPARROW and sits back down at the game.

At the table, FRANKIE, dealing, slips up and deals one card up.

"NIFTY LOUIE" FOMOROWSKI

Hey.

FRANKIE "DEALER" MACHINE

I'll deal the next one down. Sorry.

"NIFTY LOUIE" FOMOROWSKI

What's it a sign of when a dealer's hands begin to shake?

FRANKIE "DEALER" MACHINE

Schwiefka, could you take the slot for a while, will you?

FRANKIE gets up from the table. SCHWIEFKA sits down in his place.

ZERO SCHWIEFKA

All right, man, new deal. Okay, men, here we go, down and dirty. Ace, 7.

FRANKIE leaves. We see him going down the stairs outside. He stops and lights a cigarette nervously. NIFTY LOUIE comes out and follows him down the stairs.

"NIFTY LOUIE" FOMOROWSKI

You know what's eating at you? You shot off your mouth about kicking it for keeps. So now you're ashamed of even thinking—well what you're thinking, ain't that right? You know I don't talk about my customers. So who'll be the wiser? Why fight it, dealer? For who? For what? Come over my place. What do you say?

FRANKIE goes off. "NIFTY LOUIE" Fomorowski whistles behind him.

"NIFTY LOUIE" FOMOROWSKI

I'll be around.

FRANKIE goes down the street to a nightclub called Club Safari. He goes in. There is a floor show going on, with strippers and a band. FRANKIE goes over to the bar and sees MOLLY, who is at a stand, clerking for a gambling game.

FRANKIE "DEALER" MACHINE

They told me you were working here and I was passing by and I thought I'd come in and have a drink.

MOLLY NOVOTNY

Well, I've been here a while.

FRANKIE "DEALER" MACHINE

Doing any good?

MOLLY NOVOTNY

All right. Small cut of the game, usual cut of the drinks.

A waiter comes up to the two of them.

BARTENDER

I ain't got all night, Jack.

FRANKIE "DEALER" MACHINE

Right, have something.

MOLLY NOVOTNY

Rye.

FRANKIE "DEALER" MACHINE

Two doubles.

The waiter goes off.

MOLLY NOVOTNY

You didn't have to do that, Frankie.

FRANKIE "DEALER" MACHINE

No reason you should go losing money by wasting your time talking to me.

MOLLY NOVOTNY

You know you're no waste. I've been hoping you'd come see me.

FRANKIE "DEALER" MACHINE

You know how it is, Molly.

MOLLY NOVOTNY

Sure. So busy now.

The waiter brings over two large drinks. FRANKIE gives him a dollar.

FRANKIE "DEALER" MACHINE
Here's to it Molly-O.

MOLLY NOVOTNY
Molly-O. I ain't heard that since you went away. You're looking good, Frankie.

FRANKIE "DEALER" MACHINE
Feel good.

MOLLY NOVOTNY
They tell me you're going to be a drummer now.

FRANKIE "DEALER" MACHINE
Yeah, I got an appointment with a man tomorrow.

MOLLY NOVOTNY
Oh, that's swell.

FRANKIE "DEALER" MACHINE
Yeah. Probably I won't get the job though.

MOLLY NOVOTNY
Sure, you will.

FRANKIE "DEALER" MACHINE
Probably I don't play good enough.

MOLLY NOVOTNY
I bet you play fine. You was always whistling and drumming on tables and things, real good too.

FRANKIE "DEALER" MACHINE
Ah.

MOLLY NOVOTNY
I mean it. You got a natural rhythm.

FRANKIE "DEALER" MACHINE
I was thinking maybe I'd take a stage name. Jack Duvall.

MOLLY NOVOTNY
Jack Duvall. Yeah, that's real class.

FRANKIE "DEALER" MACHINE
It is, ain't it?

MOLLY NOVOTNY
That's a swell name; just fits you, Frankie.

FRANKIE "DEALER" MACHINE

This guy I'm going to see tomorrow, he books all the big bands. If I get in with him, boy, I wear a tux.

MOLLY NOVOTNY

You'd look swell in a tux.

FRANKIE "DEALER" MACHINE

I already got the drums.

DRUNKIE JOHN comes up to them.

DRUNKIE JOHN

I need a buck; ante up, kid, huh?

MOLLY opens her purse and gives him a dollar. DRUNKIE JOHN goes away furtively.

MOLLY NOVOTNY

I got lonely. I needed somebody. And he's a poor beat guy who needs somebody too.

FRANKIE "DEALER" MACHINE

Everybody needs somebody, but you can do better than him.

MOLLY NOVOTNY

Can I, Frankie?

FRANKIE "DEALER" MACHINE

Molly, I thought a lot about you while I was away, about you and me and Zosh. It would never work out between you and me as long as she was upstairs sitting in that chair. It'd be different if she didn't love me and she wasn't so helpless. You can't make a fool of somebody who loves you and they're so helpless. That's why I didn't come around sooner. And that's why I ain't coming around no more. You understand?

MOLLY NOVOTNY

Sure. Sure, I understand.

FRANKIE strokes MOLLY's bare shoulder.

FRANKIE "DEALER" MACHINE

You're a good girl, Molly.

MOLLY NOVOTNY

Sure. Real good.

FRANKIE makes to leave.

MOLLY NOVOTNY

Frankie, good luck with that fella tomorrow.

We now see the front of an enormous building: the Lane Building. Then we see FRANKIE in Mr. Lane's large, well-appointed office. Mr. Lane, a man in late middle age in a double-breasted suit and smoking a cigar, looks at a letter.

MR. LANE

You are not the first to come to me with a letter from Dr. Lennox. I've taken care of a lot of you people.

FRANKIE "DEALER" MACHINE

The doc, he told me.

MR. LANE

I like doing it, understand. So don't feel that this is charity or anything like that. Now, have you played professionally before?

FRANKIE "DEALER" MACHINE

Only down at Lexington.

MR. LANE

I see. Well, then, you wouldn't mind auditioning. I mean I know some bandleaders who might have an opening, but they'd have to be sure that you could play.

FRANKIE "DEALER" MACHINE

Oh sure, sure.

MR. LANE

All right then. There's only one thing, Frankie. You see, a good many people like yourself—well, they mean well, but they're, well, they're weak. They let me down. I mean, I go to all this trouble, vouch for them; they go back on the habit. It makes me look bad.

FRANKIE "DEALER" MACHINE

Well, I wouldn't, honest.

MR. LANE

All right. I'm telling you this because, well, once a man lets me down, I'm done with him. He comes back on his knees, and don't think that some of them haven't.

FRANKIE "DEALER" MACHINE

I wouldn't let you down, Mr. Lane.

MR. LANE

Good. I'll call you, let me see, a week from Friday, about noon. All right?

Mr. Lane hands the letter back to FRANKIE.

FRANKIE "DEALER" MACHINE

Fine. I sure do appreciate it.

MR. LANE

Oh, forget it.

FRANKIE "DEALER" MACHINE

Bye.

MR. LANE

Goodbye.

Back in the apartment, FRANKIE is massaging ZOSH's leg while she brushes her hair and looks in a mirror.

SOPHIA "ZOSH" MACHINE

You like my hair better this way or up swept, Frankie? Huh? Well, you can at least tell me. It ain't my fault he don't phone. What did I say? Just don't hold your breath until you hear from that guy. That's what I said. He told you noon. It's almost six o'clock already. So how could you still think he'll phone? Honest, I'm surprised that you . . .

FRANKIE gets up and goes sulkily to the other end of the room.

SOPHIA "ZOSH" MACHINE

I just don't want you to eat your heart out is all. Forget the whole thing, Frankie. I bet he has. You think he got nothing better to do than worry about you? You think he don't sleep nights on account of Frankie Machine? Bet he don't get no rest . . .

The phone rings downstairs. FRANKIE rushes out to get it. ZOSH follows him in her wheelchair, looking over the railing.

FRANKIE, going downstairs, passes Dr. Dominowski, a foreign-looking quack, going up

DR. DOMINOWSKI

Excuse me.

FRANKIE answers the phone downstairs.

FRANKIE "DEALER" MACHINE

Hello?

The proprietor comes up behind him.

FRANKIE "DEALER" MACHINE

Oh, just a minute. For you.

PROPRIETOR

(*picking up the phone*)

Hello?

Dr. Dominowski comes up to the second floor and sees ZOSH still in the hallway.

SOPHIA "ZOSH" MACHINE

Are you Dr. Dominowski?

DR. DOMINOWSKI

Yes. I came as soon as I could.

They go in the apartment, FRANKIE following.

DR. DOMINOWSKI

Well, how are you feeling, little lady?

SOPHIA "ZOSH" MACHINE

See, the doc asks, how am I feeling?

DR. DOMINOWSKI

Ah, I'll have you feeling fine in 1, 2, 3.

The doctor has a large electronic device.

FRANKIE "DEALER" MACHINE

What is this?

DR. DOMINOWSKI

It happens, friend, to be an electric blood reverser and spine manipulator. It helps to reverse the blood.

FRANKIE "DEALER" MACHINE

What's the gimmick?

DR. DOMINOWSKI

Gimmick? It happens so, brother, that I am a member of the American Association of Medical Hydrology, Psychology, and Divine Healing. Where is the socket?

Dr. Dominowski hands him a plug. FRANKIE plugs in the machine. The doctor feels ZOSH's hand.

DR. DOMINOWSKI

Cold hands, poor circulation. Eat lots of hot things. Chili peppers, hot sauces.

SOPHIA "ZOSH" MACHINE

Pickles.

DR. DOMINOWSKI

No more than three a day. Now lean forward and we'll vibrate the vertebraes.

He applies a hand-held electrical device to ZOSH's spine.

SOPHIA "ZOSH" MACHINE

You know how I got like how I am? My spine was hurt.

DR. DOMINOWSKI

Oh, I can see that. The ligaments and the vertebrae is locked together.

SOPHIA "ZOSH" MACHINE

In a car accident, I was hurt, three years ago, May 11th. Maybe you read about it in the papers, huh?

ZOSH pulls out a scrapbook and shows him a picture. FRANKIE starts pacing around the room. Dr. Dominowski's machine buzzes.

SOPHIA "ZOSH" MACHINE

This is the car it happened in. That's me laying there. My husband was the one driving the car, and he was drunk.

DR. DOMINOWSKI

Drunk, eh?

The doctor looks at FRANKIE accusingly.

SOPHIA "ZOSH" MACHINE

He got me in this accident and smashed me up good, so that I can't walk no more, or dance no more, nothing. And he married me right here, in the hospital chapel.

FRANKIE "DEALER" MACHINE

Zosh!

FRANKIE takes his coat and dashes out of the apartment.

DR. DOMINOWSKI

Feeling a little better?

ZOSH strokes the scrapbook affectionately. Dr. Dominowski continues to apply his device to her back.

SOPHIA "ZOSH" MACHINE

Uh-huh. Much better.

FRANKIE goes into YANTEK's bar next door, where SPARROW has a dog sitting on a table near the entrance. NIFTY LOUIE is sitting at the bar. He sees FRANKIE in the mirror.

SPARROW

Help yourself. Hey Frankie, guess what? I got that dog for Zosh. Free spirit! Every claw and hair of him is a champion.

SPARROW pours some beer into a glass for the dog.

FRANKIE "DEALER" MACHINE

Champion or what?

SPARROW

Retrieving. He brings back empties. Hey, I'll show you.

SPARROW rolls the empty beer bottle on the floor. The dog jumps down, picks it up in his mouth, and brings it back.

SPARROW

Come on, beauty, here. Get up, beauty. He's all dog. You can make money out of him, Frankie. See what he's good at is catching them squirrels in the park and shaking the dirty peanuts out of them, know what I mean? Only thing, he's trained to chase only one kind of squirrel, and they're getting kind of rare in Chicago on account of the climate's changing. You know what I mean? So he's just hanging around waiting for the climate to change back a little. He's got a real fighting heart. He's dizzy, but he's still in there trying.

NIFTY LOUIE goes to the bar entrance, looks significantly at FRANKIE, and walks off.

FRANKIE "DEALER" MACHINE

Take the dog up to Zosh.

SPARROW

Frankie, can I go with you?

FRANKIE "DEALER" MACHINE

No.

FRANKIE follows NIFTY LOUIE up into his building across the street.

Inside his apartment, NIFTY LOUIE takes off his shoe and removes some small packets of powder.

"NIFTY LOUIE" FOMOROWSKI

In a minute, dealer.

He wipes the shoe off and carefully puts it in a closet. NIFTY LOUIE opens the door for FRANKIE, who comes in, takes off his jacket, and starts rolling up his sleeve. NIFTY LOUIE pulls out a syringe, and FRANKIE wraps a necktie around his arm.

"NIFTY LOUIE" FOMOROWSKI

Five bucks.

FRANKIE "DEALER" MACHINE

Last time it was two.

"NIFTY LOUIE" FOMOROWSKI

That was more than six months ago, before you went away. They keep raising the price on me.

NIFTY LOUIE takes out a needle and prepares the heroin. FRANKIE pulls out the money and puts it on the bureau.

FRANKIE "DEALER" MACHINE

They keep doing that, I'll have to find something to take its place.

"NIFTY LOUIE" FOMOROWSKI

The monkey is never dead, dealer. The monkey never dies.

NIFTY LOUIE fills a needle with heroin.

"NIFTY LOUIE" FOMOROWSKI:

When you kick him off, he just hides in a corner waiting for his turn.

NIFTY LOUIE shoots up FRANKIE.

FRANKIE "DEALER" MACHINE

And the monkey will die waiting. He ain't climbing up on my back no more. Never again, and I mean it.

"NIFTY LOUIE" FOMOROWSKI

Sure, sure.

FRANKIE takes the necktie off from around his arm and lies down. FRANKIE's eyes grow dim as the drug takes effect.

Now we are back in FRANKIE's apartment. ZOSH is holding the dog and giving him some beer in a cup. FRANKIE is in the background.

SOPHIA "ZOSH" MACHINE

Look, Frankie, look how he drinks it. Oh, isn't that cute? Oh, he's got a thirst like a barfly.

FRANKIE hears the phone ring downstairs and goes to the door. He hears the proprietor answer.

PROPRIETOR
(off camera)
Hello?

SOPHIA "ZOSH" MACHINE
You still expecting that connection to call? For your own peace of mind, forget him.

FRANKIE "DEALER" MACHINE
The doc said I could count on Mr. Lane, and the doc doesn't lie.

SOPHIA "ZOSH" MACHINE
Doc. Look at me. A doc told you I'd be up around in no time, and am I?

He sees some money on a shelf and picks it up.

FRANKIE "DEALER" MACHINE
Have you seen my sticks? See my drumsticks anywhere?

SOPHIA "ZOSH" MACHINE
You know what I'm going to get for this little dog? A little raincoat like for when it rains. Plaid maybe, or maybe all yellow. Huh?

FRANKIE puts down the money and starts to look for his drumsticks.

FRANKIE "DEALER" MACHINE
Where are my drumsticks, Zosh?

He finds them on top of a high bureau.

FRANKIE "DEALER" MACHINE
How'd they get up here?

SOPHIA "ZOSH" MACHINE
(to the dog)
You liked that, didn't you?

FRANKIE "DEALER" MACHINE
Zosh? I never keep 'em way up here.

SOPHIA "ZOSH" MACHINE
(to the dog)
Drank it all up, didn't you?

FRANKIE "DEALER" MACHINE
Zosh!

ZOSH wheels her wheelchair over to FRANKIE.

SOPHIA "ZOSH" MACHINE

I put 'em there. I stood right up, I walked right over, and I put 'em there, all right?

FRANKIE "DEALER" MACHINE

No? No kidding. How did . . .

SOPHIA "ZOSH" MACHINE

Maybe Vi, when she was straightening up for me. I don't know. Stop picking on me.

FRANKIE goes over to his drum set and sits down with his drumsticks.

SOPHIA "ZOSH" MACHINE

Frankie, you can't keep stoning yourself about that. There must be a million drummers who play better than you do who can't get jobs. Just remember that, you're going to feel better.

FRANKIE "DEALER" MACHINE

Yeah, sure I will.

FRANKIE sits down at his drum set and drums on the cymbals.

SOPHIA "ZOSH" MACHINE

Can the noise.

FRANKIE gets up and picks up the money from the shelf.

FRANKIE "DEALER" MACHINE

What's this for, Zosh?

SOPHIA "ZOSH" MACHINE

What? Oh, Vi. She laid out for groceries. We owe her even more. You got any?

FRANKIE "DEALER" MACHINE

No.

SOPHIA "ZOSH" MACHINE

I don't know what we're doing with all our money.

FRANKIE picks up a deck of cards and shuffles through them, about to do a trick for ZOSH.

SOPHIA "ZOSH" MACHINE

Don't you get enough cards by Schwiefka?

FRANKIE "DEALER" MACHINE
I just do it to kill the pastime. That's all.

SOPHIA "ZOSH" MACHINE
What about my pastime?

FRANKIE picks up the money again.

FRANKIE "DEALER" MACHINE
What did you say this is for?

SOPHIA "ZOSH" MACHINE
Sick here all the time, you don't even talk to me. We got any more beer? I'd like some.

FRANKIE "DEALER" MACHINE
Beer bloats, Zosh, when you can't exercise.

He fans the deck out in front of her.

FRANKIE "DEALER" MACHINE
Here, pick a card.

SOPHIA "ZOSH" MACHINE
Everything's no good for me. I'm only 25, and it's like I'm a old lady already. Is it my fault I can't exercise?

FRANKIE "DEALER" MACHINE
You want to pick a card, or don't you want to pick a card?

SOPHIA "ZOSH" MACHINE
No, I don't want to pick a card. All I want is just a little . . .

FRANKIE "DEALER" MACHINE
A little what?

SOPHIA "ZOSH" MACHINE
Oh, just a little . . . a little beer, a little fun, a little anything. I can't dance no more. I can't swim, I can't even drink beer. I don't even know what kinds they got here. What other kinds they got these days, Frankie? All right, pretend like I ain't here. It's what you are all the time wishing anyway, like I was killed that night.

FRANKIE "DEALER" MACHINE
I don't wish any such thing. If I don't talk, you get mad; if I say anything, you bite my head off. I don't know whether I'm coming or going anymore, Zosh.

He practices on his drums.

SOPHIA "ZOSH" MACHINE

I told you it gives me headaches.

FRANKIE "DEALER" MACHINE

Well, I gotta practice sometimes, Zosh. When the job comes along, I want to be ready.

SOPHIA "ZOSH" MACHINE

The job, the job. Take them down to your girlfriend, if you gotta practice.

FRANKIE gets up and goes to her.

FRANKIE "DEALER" MACHINE

What?

SOPHIA "ZOSH" MACHINE

Take them down and give her the headache.

FRANKIE "DEALER" MACHINE

Do you know what you're saying, Zosh? You know what you're talking about?

SOPHIA "ZOSH" MACHINE

Don't give me that innocent look.

FRANKIE "DEALER" MACHINE

I ain't said two words to her since I come back.

SOPHIA "ZOSH" MACHINE

Because I sit here, you think I don't know what goes on.

FRANKIE "DEALER" MACHINE

Not two words.

SOPHIA "ZOSH" MACHINE

I know plenty.

FRANKIE "DEALER" MACHINE

Cut it out, will you, Zosh? Cut it out.

SOPHIA "ZOSH" MACHINE

Take them down to that tramp if you want to make noise. Go on, take them down to her. Why don't you?

FRANKIE "DEALER" MACHINE

All right, I will.

He opens the door and makes to leave. Then he comes back and takes the money.

SOPHIA "ZOSH" MACHINE

Frankie, Frankie, I didn't mean . . .

We are now back in YANTEK's bar. A TV is showing a baseball game.

TELEVISION ANNOUNCER

It's a long drive to right field. It's going, going, it's gone. It's a home run.

SPARROW and VI are sitting at the bar, drinking beer. A blind man comes up to them. We see MOLLY sitting at a table in the background.

BLIND MAN

I have 12 cents to a beer. If I had 15, I'd be all right.

SPARROW

I've got 6 cents here.

SPARROW and VI put some coins into his cap.

BLIND MAN

Thanks.

VI

I ain't going to stand for it much longer. The heartaches my old man gives me. You know what he likes to do most? Tear the dates off the calendar. Watching him, that's supposed to be my big Saturday night pleasure. Sometimes he loses all control. Tears off a whole week at once, bleating like a belly goat.

SPARROW

You know what would fill up that empty spot in your life?

VI

Yeah?

SPARROW

A dog.

FRANKIE comes into the bar and passes behind them.

SPARROW

Ask a satisfied customer. Frankie, that dog I got you makes a big difference in your life, don't it?

FRANKIE "DEALER" MACHINE

Yeah, big.

FRANKIE goes up to NIFTY LOUIE, who is sitting at the other end of the bar.

FRANKIE "DEALER" MACHINE

I want to see you. I want to see you.

"NIFTY LOUIE" FOMOROWSKI

After the inning.

ZERO SCHWIEFKA is sitting at the bar, to LOUIE's left. He is looking at the TV screen.

ZERO SCHWIEFKA

I'll still bet you six to five.

TELEVISION ANNOUNCER

There's the pitch, and it's a strike. Strike one. London's getting set again, there's the pitch. London swings, and it's a high foul. Roberts trying to get it. It may go into the stands. He's going to try. It's going to be close. Roberts makes a tremendous leap. And he's got it.

FRANKIE goes over to a table in front of MOLLY, whom he does not even notice. He stares ahead of him, at NIFTY LOUIE. MOLLY comes up to him from behind.

MOLLY NOVOTNY

How are you, Frankie? You make out all right with the fellow with the job?

FRANKIE "DEALER" MACHINE

Oh, the drumming job? Yeah, fine, fine. Well, not so fine. He sort of tapped out on me. He promised to call me, but . . .

MOLLY NOVOTNY

It's too bad.

FRANKIE "DEALER" MACHINE

There are a million drummers in the world. How do I rate?

MOLLY NOVOTNY

Maybe he lost your number. It happens. Maybe he's just wishing that you'd keep in touch.

FRANKIE "DEALER" MACHINE

He'd think I was a pest.

MOLLY NOVOTNY

Sure. A good drummer, that's something that don't turn up every day. Go on, Frankie, call him. Come on, Frankie.

FRANKIE thinks, pulls out a piece of paper, and goes over to the phone. DRUNKIE JOHN comes over to MOLLY and pours himself some beer out of a bottle on the table.

DRUNKIE JOHN
Come on, Molly, watch the game, huh?

MOLLY NOVOTNY
I don't feel like it, Johnny. Why don't you go ahead? I'll wait for you.

DRUNKIE JOHN goes off.

FRANKIE takes a piece of paper out of his jacket and goes over to the pay phone in the bar.

FRANKIE "DEALER" MACHINE
Yeah, studio B, Monday morning. Fine. Thank you, Mr. Lane. Bye.

FRANKIE goes over to MOLLY.

FRANKIE "DEALER" MACHINE
Monday, I got an audition for Monday. Me! Yeah. He told me to join the union, and be ready to work.

MOLLY NOVOTNY
Oh, that's swell, Frankie.

FRANKIE "DEALER" MACHINE
Well, thank you. You know, he did lose my phone number. He'd been trying to find me all week long. Here I was, ready to forget the whole thing. Gee, if you hadn't opened your mouth, I wouldn't have called him.

MOLLY NOVOTNY
Sure you would.

FRANKIE "DEALER" MACHINE
I've got an audition with a big band. Me on TV!

MOLLY NOVOTNY
You practice a lot, right?

FRANKIE "DEALER" MACHINE
Practice. I'll beat those heads to a shred. Only I gotta find a place where. Zosh can't stand the noise. Molly, you suppose maybe I could put the drums in your place and sort of drop in once in a while?

MOLLY shakes her head.

FRANKIE
Why not? Molly, why not?

MOLLY NOVOTNY
Oh, Johnny wouldn't understand.

FRANKIE "DEALER" MACHINE

So what could he do?

MOLLY NOVOTNY

It isn't a question of what he could do, Frankie. It's like Johnny can't do much about anything. It's a question of what it does to him. I'm all he has in the world. I don't want to hurt him.

FRANKIE "DEALER" MACHINE

Molly, for crying out loud.

MOLLY NOVOTNY

Oh, you don't know, Frankie. A fella like him, sometimes when we're alone . . .

FRANKIE "DEALER" MACHINE

What does he do? Cry? He's a lush, Molly. He's a hundred percent habitual drunk.

MOLLY NOVOTNY

Look, everybody's habitual something. With him, it's liquor.

FRANKIE "DEALER" MACHINE

Please, Molly. Molly-O.

MOLLY NOVOTNY

It isn't just that, Frankie. I don't want us to start with each other again. Look, what you said about us not being good, it was the truth. Even before you went away, I tried to, it just doesn't add up. It never did, it never can.

FRANKIE "DEALER" MACHINE

Well, give it a chance. I told you it would one day.

MOLLY NOVOTNY

All my life has been one day. On and on and on.

FRANKIE "DEALER" MACHINE

I got drums. I'm headed for a good job. Is that so on and on and on? I make some money, make Zosh well. What's so on, and on about that? Don't shut me out, Molly. I'm trying.

"NIFTY LOUIE" Fomorowski comes over to FRANKIE and MOLLY.

"NIFTY LOUIE" FOMOROWSKI

You want to see me?

FRANKIE "DEALER" MACHINE

No.

"NIFTY LOUIE" FOMOROWSKI

What do you mean, no?

FRANKIE goes over to VI at the bar and hands her some money.

FRANKIE "DEALER" MACHINE

Vi, here. What we owe.

NIFTY LOUIE follows and watches him, glaring.

SPARROW

Frankie, Vi says, can she trust me? Tell her, tell her, Frankie, what an honest hustler I am.

FRANKIE goes off past MOLLY at her table.

MOLLY NOVOTNY

Frankie, I guess maybe you could drop in once in a while.

FRANKIE "DEALER" MACHINE

Thanks, Molly-O.

Outside the Safari Club, men and women in formal dress are coming out. MOLLY is among them. The waiter comes out behind.

WAITER

See you tonight.

MOLLY goes back to her building down the street and goes up the stoop. She hears jazz music coming out of her apartment, with FRANKIE's accompaniment on drums.

She goes into her apartment and sees FRANKIE playing.

FRANKIE "DEALER" MACHINE

How's that?

MOLLY NOVOTNY

Real nice.

MOLLY draws down the shade and takes off her shoes. She takes a dressing gown and goes behind a screen to change.

FRANKIE "DEALER" MACHINE

Should have heard what I did with "Perdido" a little while ago.

MOLLY NOVOTNY

Good, huh? I hope the neighbors liked it too.

FRANKIE "DEALER" MACHINE

I'm very big with the neighbors. They keep banging on the pipes to let me know how much they appreciate it. I won't let it go to my head, though.

MOLLY NOVOTNY

Okay. Keep playing drums at 5:00 a.m., you'll see what goes to your head.

FRANKIE stops drumming and turns off the radio, which he has been accompanying.

FRANKIE "DEALER" MACHINE

You slip me a smile, and I give you my autograph. You won't have to fight your way through the bobbysoxers to get to me.

MOLLY NOVOTNY

I bet those bobbysoxers go for you at that.

FRANKIE "DEALER" MACHINE

Ah.

MOLLY NOVOTNY

You tired?

She comes over to him. He gives her a glass of milk.

FRANKIE "DEALER" MACHINE

But in a very nice way. I've been feeling good all night. I joined the musicians' union today.

MOLLY NOVOTNY

Schwiefka loan you the money?

FRANKIE "DEALER" MACHINE

Him?

MOLLY NOVOTNY

Who did?

FRANKIE "DEALER" MACHINE

Nobody. I'm going to hock the drums.

He takes out a sandwich and offers her some. She does not take it. He eats from it bit by bit.

MOLLY NOVOTNY

Oh, Frankie, no.

FRANKIE "DEALER" MACHINE
I got it figured out pretty good. When I get a job, I'll take an advance and get the drums out again. Meantime, I'll use a practice pad.

MOLLY NOVOTNY
You should have asked Schwiefka.

FRANKIE "DEALER" MACHINE
I haven't even seen him.

MOLLY NOVOTNY
You didn't go to work?

FRANKIE "DEALER" MACHINE
I've been practicing here all night. I quit the game, Molly.

MOLLY NOVOTNY
It wouldn't hurt you to wait a couple of days, Frank.

FRANKIE "DEALER" MACHINE
I wanted to quit. I'm quitting a couple of things.

MOLLY strokes FRANKIE's chin. He kisses her hand.

MOLLY NOVOTNY
Is it bad?

FRANKIE "DEALER" MACHINE
Not too bad.

MOLLY NOVOTNY
You shouldn't have started again.

FRANKIE "DEALER" MACHINE
Who knows why I started in the first place. I guess in the beginning, you do it only for kicks. Louie gave me my first shot for nothing. I thought I could take it or leave it alone. So I took it and I took it again and again. One day Louie wasn't around. I nearly went crazy until I found him. Oh, I was sick. I was so sick. You can't be that sick and live. That's when I knew I was hooked. There was a 40-pound monkey on my back. The only way to get along with a load like that is to keep leaning on a fix.

MOLLY starts to cry. FRANKIE comes over, strokes her cheek, and wipes her tears away.

FRANKIE "DEALER" MACHINE

Don't. I'm one of the lucky ones, Molly. I kicked it and I'm not too far hooked to kick it again. I've had my last fix. I mean it, Molly. Tell me something, you think those bobbysoxers will really go for me?

MOLLY NOVOTNY

(choking a sob)

You can be such a ham.

FRANKIE "DEALER" MACHINE

Maybe I'll get Sparrow a job with the orchestra. When I can put enough money together, I can get Zosh into a really good hospital so she can walk and dance again. And then maybe . . .

MOLLY has gone to sleep. He goes over to her, takes her glass of milk, puts it on the counter, puts her to bed, and covers her with a couple of wraps. He shuts off the light, sits in an armchair, and covers himself with his jacket.

Back in FRANKIE's apartment, ZOSH is standing at the kitchen sink, making some coffee. There is a knock on the door.

SOPHIA "ZOSH" MACHINE

Who is it?

ZERO SCHWIEFKA

(off camera)

Schwiefka. Open up.

SOPHIA "ZOSH" MACHINE

Just a minute.

ZOSH pushes the dog off the wheelchair, sits down in it, and wheels herself over to the door. SCHWIEFKA barges in, along with NIFTY LOUIE.

ZERO SCHWIEFKA

All right. All right. Where is he?

"NIFTY LOUIE" FOMOROWSKI

Good morning, Ms. Machine.

ZERO SCHWIEFKA

Frankie. Frankie. Where is he?

SOPHIA "ZOSH" MACHINE

What is it? What did he do?

ZERO SCHWIEFKA

What did he do? You know what he did! He quit. No notice, no nothing. He sends word by that mistress that he's through. I had to take the slot myself. Where is he?

He makes to hit her but pulls back. ZOSH cringes.

SOPHIA "ZOSH" MACHINE

He wasn't at the game?

ZERO SCHWIEFKA

Would we have been looking for him all over if he was at the game? He eats my bread, six years he eats my bread. He gets put away, I send you money regular. He gets out, I give his job back . . .

"NIFTY LOUIE" FOMOROWSKI

Shut up.

ZERO SCHWIEFKA

What do you mean . . .

"NIFTY LOUIE" FOMOROWSKI

Shut up. You think it was easy talking fellas like Williams and Markette up to a two-bit game like yours?

ZERO SCHWIEFKA

Louie, Louie.

"NIFTY LOUIE" FOMOROWSKI

I sold them on Frankie.

ZERO SCHWIEFKA

Why are we getting excited?

"NIFTY LOUIE" FOMOROWSKI

They fatten the pocket and they're hungry for action. We finally get a chance to score big—and you lose the deal.

ZERO SCHWIEFKA

Look, Louie, I swear. I swear. When Markette and Williams come, the dealer will be there, or a player just as good.

"NIFTY LOUIE" FOMOROWSKI

There ain't none as good. Why didn't you offer him more money, or a piece of the play?

ZERO SCHWIEFKA

From your end of mine?

"NIFTY LOUIE" FOMOROWSKI

What's the difference whose end? Do you expect me to stand here and argue about pennies?

NIFTY LOUIE strides toward the door.

"NIFTY LOUIE" FOMOROWSKI

***Your* end.**

NIFTY LOUIE goes out.

Outside on a city sidewalk, MOLLY is standing, looking at the sign on the building in front of her: Musicians' Union Building. FRANKIE comes out.

FRANKIE "DEALER" MACHINE

Look, I'm a musician.

MOLLY NOVOTNY

Well, how does it feel?

FRANKIE "DEALER" MACHINE

Well, it feels like you better hang on my arm, or I go up like a balloon. I'm a musician.

MOLLY NOVOTNY

Where are we going?

FRANKIE "DEALER" MACHINE

I don't know, but I want to buy you something.

MOLLY NOVOTNY

Ah, no.

FRANKIE "DEALER" MACHINE

I have to spend some money or I'll bust.

They are walking in front of a dealer's showroom. FRANKIE points out a luxury car.

FRANKIE "DEALER" MACHINE

How about one of those in green?

MOLLY NOVOTNY

Frankie!

They pass in front of a TV store and see one in the window.

FRANKIE "DEALER" MACHINE

Maybe a color TV set; they're pretty.

MOLLY NOVOTNY

Go on.

They move on to another shop window and see an elaborate 1950s kitchen. Two dummies of a husband and wife are also displayed.

FRANKIE "DEALER" MACHINE

Would you look at this production, and only for cooking? Now, who would want a thing like that? Boy, it's goofy, huh?

MOLLY NOVOTNY

It's pretty, huh?

(she points to the male dummy, who is sitting in a chair in a suit, reading a paper)

I wonder what he does for a living.

FRANKIE "DEALER" MACHINE

Him?

MOLLY NOVOTNY

Must make a nice dollar. Look at the way he dresses, a kitchen like that.

FRANKIE "DEALER" MACHINE

I notice he doesn't help her none, though. I bet he never even married the girl. Look at that, she isn't even wearing a ring on her finger.

MOLLY NOVOTNY

She takes it off when she cooks, maybe, and he's tired after hard day's work.

FRANKIE "DEALER" MACHINE

All right, so let him sit there. But at least he could talk to her once in a while. Doesn't have to sit there with his nose buried in the magazine. I would talk to her.

MOLLY NOVOTNY

What would you say?

FRANKIE "DEALER" MACHINE

I'd say, how you been? How did it go today? What's for supper?

MOLLY NOVOTNY

Steak's for supper, and everything went fine today.

FRANKIE "DEALER" MACHINE

Steak. Good. Now how about you and me stepping out tonight after we eat?

MOLLY NOVOTNY

Why don't we just stay home and turn on some music?

FRANKIE "DEALER" MACHINE

Yeah. I like that better. We'll just stay home and turn on some music.

FRANKIE kisses MOLLY on the cheek.

FRANKIE "DEALER" MACHINE

I wish it was Monday already.

FRANKIE comes into FRANKIE and ZOSH's apartment. ZOSH is in a wheelchair, sipping a cup of coffee.

FRANKIE "DEALER" MACHINE

Hi, Zosh.

SOPHIA "ZOSH" MACHINE

Where you been? Schwiefka was here, and said you quit him. Where you been? Why'd you quit him?

FRANKIE "DEALER" MACHINE

I have a tryout on Monday, and if the bandleader likes the way I play, I'm hired.

SOPHIA "ZOSH" MACHINE

Frankie, go tell Schwiefka that you was fooling; you'll deal. Maybe this bandleader won't like how you play.

FRANKIE "DEALER" MACHINE

Zosh, look, I joined the musician's union.

FRANKIE hands her his union card.

SOPHIA "ZOSH" MACHINE

Why do you gotta go around changing things? Why can't it be like always? Why you gotta quit dealing, Frankie? How we gonna live with no money coming in?

FRANKIE "DEALER" MACHINE

It'll start coming in Monday.

SOPHIA "ZOSH" MACHINE

But suppose they call this great tryout off. You can't tell me it's a sure thing, can you? Frankie, deal for Schwiefka like always. Forget this "great" job.

FRANKIE "DEALER" MACHINE
I quit dealing, Zosh, I can't take the chance. Don't you understand? If the joint gets raided and I get picked up again, Mr. Lane would be through with me. And then how would I play with a band?

SOPHIA "ZOSH" MACHINE
How you're going to play if Schwiefka gets your arms broke?

FRANKIE "DEALER" MACHINE
Go on.

SOPHIA "ZOSH" MACHINE
Yeah, right here he said it, and he wanted to slap me around too. Why can't it be like always?

ZOSH starts to tear up the union card. FRANKIE grabs it from her and shakes her as she sobs. Then he lets go and storms out of the apartment. After he has left, ZOSH fingers her whistle anxiously.

In YANTEK's bar, we see NIFTY LOUIE, who eyes FRANKIE as he comes in and goes to the bar. NIFTY LOUIE gives a whistle to SCHWIEFKA, who has been sitting at a booth. They both go over to FRANKIE at the bar.

FRANKIE "DEALER" MACHINE
Yantek.

YANTEK pours FRANKIE a shot of whiskey.

ZERO SCHWIEFKA
You miserable piece of humanity.

FRANKIE "DEALER" MACHINE
I got a right to quit if I want.

ZERO SCHWIEFKA
Markette and Williams are coming tomorrow. Don't you realize the significance?

FRANKIE "DEALER" MACHINE
Leave me alone.

ZERO SCHWIEFKA
I'll leave you alone in the alley with the cats looking.

"NIFTY LOUIE" FOMOROWSKI
That's enough, Schwiefka. He don't want to deal, he don't want to deal.

ZERO SCHWIEFKA
What are you talking about all of a sudden?

"NIFTY LOUIE" FOMOROWSKI

Don't raise your voice to me, you slob. He's not a slave, you can't force him. So what's the use? You had the best of him all these years. Don't be a pig. He just ain't interested, right?

ZERO SCHWIEFKA

All right. All right. Markette and Williams never heard of him. Money, something to blow your nose on. I wash my hands.

SCHWIEFKA storms off and sits at a nearby table. We can see him in the background.

"NIFTY LOUIE" FOMOROWSKI

He's just a pig is all. Still, you can't blame him so much. Letting the big ones get away on account of the best dealer in the business ain't working for you no more. That ain't easy to swallow. You're the best, all right.

FRANKIE "DEALER" MACHINE

You're a squeeze player, Louie.

"NIFTY LOUIE" FOMOROWSKI

Been tried on you before.

FRANKIE "DEALER" MACHINE

I'm new around here.

"NIFTY LOUIE" FOMOROWSKI

Are we really asking so much, dealer? One night.

FRANKIE "DEALER" MACHINE

I'd like to, but ...

"NIFTY LOUIE" FOMOROWSKI

You help us make a bundle, we'll spread a little of that old sunshine around. Couldn't you use a couple of hundred? Maybe 250, huh? 250 pays a lot of doctor bills.

FRANKIE "DEALER" MACHINE

Tomorrow, huh?

SCHWIEFKA comes back to the bar and is about to grab FRANKIE's arm.

ZERO SCHWIEFKA

Frankie...

"NIFTY LOUIE" FOMOROWSKI

Let him make up his mind.

FRANKIE "DEALER" MACHINE
Okay. But for one night, win or lose, sun up, I case the deck.

ZERO SCHWIEFKA
Sure. You're the dealer. What a load off! Now I can sleep. Take care of that arm.

SCHWIEFKA goes off.

"NIFTY LOUIE" FOMOROWSKI
The character, huh? Were you jacking up the price just now or do you really have this music job?

FRANKIE "DEALER" MACHINE
If they like what they hear.

"NIFTY LOUIE" FOMOROWSKI
Chancy, eh? Nervous? So what are we waiting for?

FRANKIE "DEALER" MACHINE
Don't talk about it. It's tough enough.

"NIFTY LOUIE" FOMOROWSKI
I know, I know. I put down a craving once. No candy, sweets. I used to be eating it all the time. Got examined for the army. They said you gotta sugar in your blood, friend. You gotta give up sweets forever or it's goodbye, Charlie. I had to give up candy.

FRANKIE "DEALER" MACHINE
My gums bleed for you. It's awful.

"NIFTY LOUIE" FOMOROWSKI
It was. That unfinished feeling you got all the time. Well, I don't have to tell you.

FRANKIE "DEALER" MACHINE
So don't.

"NIFTY LOUIE" FOMOROWSKI
I mean you got this one thing on your mind, all the time. Can't stop thinking about it.

FRANKIE "DEALER" MACHINE
You're just a mine of information, aren't you?

"NIFTY LOUIE" FOMOROWSKI
You know what I did? I said to myself, okay, off sweets forever. Well, forever can start tomorrow, but once in my life I'm going to eat all the

candy that I can hold. I bought $18.23 worth of candy, lugged it up to my room. All night long, I ate candy. I was sick, I was sweating. But I kept shoving it in. Ever since then, when I feel like candy, I say to myself, well, you can't complain, brother; you once had it, and had it good. You know what I mean? Huh?

FRANKIE and LOUIE go off together, LOUIE holding FRANKIE's arm, up to and in LOUIE's building across the street.

The scene shifts to the Safari Bar. FRANKIE comes in and goes to MOLLY at her counter.

FRANKIE "DEALER" MACHINE

How is it, Molly-O?

MOLLY NOVOTNY

All right, Frankie, how are you doing?

WAITER

What will you have?

FRANKIE "DEALER" MACHINE

Couple of ryes.

MOLLY NOVOTNY

All day I was expecting you'd be in to practice.

FRANKIE "DEALER" MACHINE

Practice! I'll get down there and knock them dead. It's all in the wrist, and I got the touch, Molly. Look at that. Steady as a rock. It'll do anything I want it to do.

The waiter brings the drinks over. FRANKIE gives him a dollar.

FRANKIE "DEALER" MACHINE

Keep the change, pal.

WAITER

Thanks.

MOLLY NOVOTNY

You got a cigarette, Frankie?

FRANKIE "DEALER" MACHINE

Yeah.

FRANKIE gives her a cigarette and tries to light it, but suddenly his eyes go blank and he blinks in a strange way. He waves the match to put it out.

MOLLY NOVOTNY

You're on it again, Frankie. Why? Why?

FRANKIE "DEALER" MACHINE

No. Listen, Molly, listen.

MOLLY NOVOTNY

Why?

DRUNKIE JOHN comes over and grabs MOLLY by the arm.

DRUNKIE JOHN

Molly? Molly?

FRANKIE "DEALER" MACHINE

Beat it.

DRUNKIE JOHN

Molly, I only want to take a walk . . .

FRANKIE "DEALER" MACHINE

Molly, listen to me. I can explain it.

DRUNKIE JOHN

Molly, I just want to talk to you.

FRANKIE "DEALER" MACHINE

Will you get out of here?

MOLLY NOVOTNY

Stop it.

FRANKIE "DEALER" MACHINE

Molly.

MOLLY NOVOTNY

Please don't hurt him, will you?

FRANKIE "DEALER" MACHINE

Go away.

FRANKIE shoves DRUNKIE JOHN, who falls down on the floor. The manager comes over, irate.

MANAGER

(*to* MOLLY)

You'll lose your job. Can't you manage your customers?

DRUNKIE JOHN stands up.

DRUNKIE JOHN

Molly!

Both DRUNKIE JOHN and FRANKIE grab MOLLY by the arms. She breaks free and rushes out, the strippers onstage in the background dancing.

MOLLY rushes out of the bar and across the street to her building. FRANKIE follows her and runs in front of a car, which screeches to a halt and honks.

MOLLY rushes into her apartment and locks it.

FRANKIE comes into the building and knocks on her front door.

MOLLY hurriedly packs some clothes into a suitcase. She puts on a raincoat and picks up the suitcase and her radio.

FRANKIE "DEALER" MACHINE

Molly. Molly, listen to me. Molly, open the door. Molly, will you open the door? Molly? Let me talk to you. Molly. Molly, Open the door.

MOLLY comes out and storms past FRANKIE in the hallway. They go out down the stoop.

FRANKIE "DEALER" MACHINE

Molly, where you going? Molly? Tell me where you going? Molly!

MOLLY, on the sidewalk, calls for a taxi.

MOLLY NOVOTNY

Taxi.

FRANKIE "DEALER" MACHINE

Will you let me explain? You'll know why I did it.

A taxi pulls up, and MOLLY gets into it. The taxi goes off, leaving FRANKIE behind.

FRANKIE "DEALER" MACHINE

(*calling after the taxi*)

Molly, listen. Will you please let me tell you what happened? Where you going, Molly? Tell me where you going? No, Molly, Molly!

The taxi drives off. FRANKIE is left standing on the sidewalk, looking stunned. Then, in a zombie-like manner, he crosses the street and goes into NIFTY LOUIE's building. In the window, we can see him in LOUIE's apartment, taking off his jacket and rolling up his sleeves. The shade is pulled down.

In SCHWIEFKA's poker room, we see Schiefka, SPARROW, and FRANKIE, seated at the poker table.

ZERO SCHWIEFKA

Don't forget to clean out the kaboon.

SPARROW

I already cleaned it. And say please when you talk to me, or I'll buy a kaboon and go into business for myself. How's that, Frankie? Nothing, huh? Well . . .

FRANKIE "DEALER" MACHINE

I'm reminding you, Schwiefka, I get two, two and a half, maybe more.

ZERO SCHWIEFKA

Would I go back on my word?

There is a knock on the door, and SPARROW goes to answer it.

Several gamblers come in, accompanied by NIFTY LOUIE.

"NIFTY LOUIE" FOMOROWSKI

How you feeling, dealer?

BARFLY 1

How are you, Schwiefka?

ZERO SCHWIEFKA

Ah, big night tonight?

Another knock on the door. SPARROW goes to answer it. Outside are two men: WILLIAMS and MARKETTE. WILLIAMS is burly, MARKETTE short, with a pencil moustache.

SPARROW

Yeah?

WILLIAMS

This the place?

SPARROW

I don't know what place you mean, buddy. This is the endless belt and leather company. You want to buy a endless belt?

NIFTY LOUIE comes to the door and pushes SPARROW aside.

"NIFTY LOUIE" FOMOROWSKI

Come right in. We just started. How have you been?

SAM MARKETTE

How are you?

WILLIAMS

Good.

"NIFTY LOUIE" FOMOROWSKI

(*to* SPARROW)

I could handle the door better if I was blind.

SPARROW

Boy, you couldn't heat towels for a scared barber.

"NIFTY LOUIE" FOMOROWSKI

You know Schwiefka?

ZERO SCHWIEFKA

Oh sure. Glad to have you.

SAM MARKETTE

Hi.

WILLIAMS

Hi.

SAM MARKETTE

Are you Machine? Man with the golden arm, huh?

WILLIAMS holds out a roll of bills.

WILLIAMS

Let's see you try and take this away.

The men sit down at the poker table, and FRANKIE begins to deal.

FRANKIE "DEALER" MACHINE

Here we go down and dirty.

We see VI coming up the alley outside the poker room. She goes up the stairs and knocks on the door. SPARROW answers.

SPARROW

No ladies allowed. You know that, Vi.

VI

Is Frankie in there?

SPARROW

What's the matter?

VI

Zosh, I can't get her to sleep. She and Frankie had an argument and she's almost out of her mind. Is he in there?

SPARROW

Well, I can't call him now.

VI

Well, I just want to know if he's here. I've been bouncing around Clark Street like a pool ball.

SPARROW

He's here. He's here. I gotta get back in.

VI

But I'd tell him she's worried, if you get a chance.

SPARROW

Yeah.

SPARROW goes back in and closes the door. VI goes off.

Back in the poker room:

FRANKIE "DEALER" MACHINE

Three aces, two pairs. Possible straight flush, aces.

WILLIAMS

200.

SAM MARKETTE

I call it 200, and I'll raise it two.

FRANKIE "DEALER" MACHINE

I'll have a look for 400, and the house bumps you 300 more. Up to you. Ace.

WILLIAMS

I don't know. I just don't know.

SAM MARKETTE

You got three aces; show him.

WILLIAMS

He's got a possible straight flush to the queens showing.

SAM MARKETTE

I tell you, he's bluffing.

WILLIAMS

I think he bluffed me out of a couple tonight. You wouldn't be a jerk enough to try it again, would you?

FRANKIE "DEALER" MACHINE

Bet, and find out.

SAM MARKETTE

Oh, bet, bet. I tell you he is a bluff artist.

WILLIAMS

Call.

SAM MARKETTE

I call it, and I raise it 500 more.

WILLIAMS

Sammy.

SAM MARKETTE

I know what I'm doing.

FRANKIE "DEALER" MACHINE

I'll have a look, and the house bumps you 500 more.

WILLIAMS

I told you. I told you he had it.

SAM MARKETTE

Shut up. Will you let me think?

FRANKIE "DEALER" MACHINE

It's up to you.

SAM MARKETTE

What's the rush, I want to know?

FRANKIE "DEALER" MACHINE

Your bet, two pairs.

SAM MARKETTE

I heard you. I heard you. What is this? A force joint or something? A man's got a right to study his hand.

FRANKIE "DEALER" MACHINE

Bet or fold.

Sammy pulls some more money out of his pocket.

WILLIAMS

Use your head, Sammy. I tell you, he's got it. Don't throw good money after bad.

SAM MARKETTE

I know what I'm doing.

SAM MARKETTE is about to put some more money down, but he sees FRANKIE clearing the bets off the table.

SAM MARKETTE

What'd you have?

FRANKIE "DEALER" MACHINE

You didn't pay to find out.

SAM MARKETTE grabs FRANKIE's cards and looks at them.

WILLIAMS

Nothing. Two lousy nines. You let him bluff you out of a full house with a lousy two nines.

FRANKIE "DEALER" MACHINE

You do that again at this table and you'll through.

ZERO SCHWIEFKA

Ah, forget it, this once, dealer. He paid plenty for it.

(*Laughter*)

WILLIAMS

You are good, dealer, maybe too good.

FRANKIE "DEALER" MACHINE

What do you mean by that?

ZERO SCHWIEFKA

Cut the talk. Deal, deal.

"NIFTY LOUIE" FOMOROWSKI

Punk, get some of this smoke out of here.

SPARROW goes over to the window, pulls up the shade, and opens the window. Daylight streams in.

FRANKIE "DEALER" MACHINE

What do you mean, too good?

WILLIAMS

If the shoe fits, brother.

FRANKIE "DEALER" MACHINE
I'm casing the deck, it's daylight.

WILLIAMS
What?

SAM MARKETTE
Tell him to sit down and deal.

ZERO SCHWIEFKA
Well, we always break up around now.

SAM MARKETTE
One more round.

FRANKIE "DEALER" MACHINE
How about my money?

SAM MARKETTE
Put some more back on the slot.

ZERO SCHWIEFKA
Frankie, how about it?

FRANKIE "DEALER" MACHINE
Nope. Just give me what's coming to me.

"NIFTY LOUIE" FOMOROWSKI
One more hour, huh?

ZERO SCHWIEFKA
I'll deal.

SAM MARKETTE
You? We want to play Machine.

ZERO SCHWIEFKA
Oh, you think I can't show you a thing or two, huh? Sit down, we'll get going.

FRANKIE "DEALER" MACHINE
How about my dough?

"NIFTY LOUIE" FOMOROWSKI
As soon as we break.

FRANKIE "DEALER" MACHINE
Now.

"NIFTY LOUIE" FOMOROWSKI
Give us a chance to count it at least. Go home. You'll get it later.

ZERO SCHWIEFKA
Okay. Ante up, here we go. A hundred it is.

WILLIAMS
Yeah, a hundred. Okay, here we go.

FRANKIE comes out of the building, tired and groggy. We see him go down the alley, then follow him as he goes up the stoop of his own building. VI, wearing a hat, gloves, and a purse, comes down the stoop at the same time.

VI
Good morning, Frankie.

We follow her as she goes down the street.

FRANKIE, tired and unshaven, goes into his apartment. He takes off his jacket. We see ZOSH asleep on the bed. FRANKIE stretches. ZOSH does not move. FRANKIE yawns, taking off his shoes. Then he gets up, puts his jacket back on, and leaves the apartment. We see him go down the stairs, outside, and down the stoop. He runs back to the poker room. SPARROW lets him in.

SPARROW
Frankie.

FRANKIE "DEALER" MACHINE
Louie is still here?

SPARROW
He's having an apoplexy, but they're doing a sweep in there.

NIFTY LOUIE comes out.

"NIFTY LOUIE" FOMOROWSKI
We're getting murdered. You'll have to take the slot.

FRANKIE "DEALER" MACHINE
I am not here for dealing.

FRANKIE shows his shaking hands to LOUIE.

FRANKIE "DEALER" MACHINE
Look, Louie, you have to make it stop.

"NIFTY LOUIE" FOMOROWSKI
No deal, no fix.

FRANKIE "DEALER" MACHINE
Well, give me my money and I'll go see somebody else.

"NIFTY LOUIE" FOMOROWSKI
I can't give you any money now. The house needs every cent.

FRANKIE "DEALER" MACHINE
You owe it to me.

"NIFTY LOUIE" FOMOROWSKI
Take me to court.

FRANKIE "DEALER" MACHINE
Please, Louie, you gotta make it stop.

"NIFTY LOUIE" FOMOROWSKI
I'll take care of you. Just work a few hours.

FRANKIE "DEALER" MACHINE
I have to get some sleep. I gotta be fresh tomorrow.

"NIFTY LOUIE" FOMOROWSKI
You work a few hours. Do us a favor. I'll guarantee you'll feel like a week in the country.

FRANKIE "DEALER" MACHINE
Please, Louie, please, now.

"NIFTY LOUIE" FOMOROWSKI
Drop dead.

FRANKIE "DEALER" MACHINE
Wait a second. Okay.

They go in.

The scene switches to YANTEK's bar. SPARROW comes in and goes to the blind man sitting at the bar, drinking a beer.

SPARROW
Louie says you got money for him. Give me. He's waiting.

BLIND MAN
Sparrow?

SPARROW
Yeah, yeah.

BLIND MAN

Yeah, I know he's waiting. So I've seen this one and that one. And they all say the same thing. Tell Louie like he tells us nothing for nothing.

SPARROW

Not a penny?

BLIND MAN

No.

DRUNKIE JOHN

Hey, how is it up there?

SPARROW

What a game. Schwiefka's melting away like a dirty candle.

DRUNKIE JOHN

The dealer's losing, huh? What's happened to that golden arm?

SPARROW

Don't worry about the dealer. The game's just going on a day and a half. He'll come through.

DRUNKIE JOHN

Why not? With those educated fingers. Now you sec it, now you don't.

SPARROW

You keep your dirty mouth off the dealer. Frankie runs a clean game. There ain't nothing in the world that would make him change that. Arggh!

SPARROW storms off.

DRUNKIE JOHN

Hey, Yantek?

Back in the poker room, the game is going. SCHWIEFKA is on the phone.

FRANKIE "DEALER" MACHINE

Piece of hearts, eight of spades.

ZERO SCHWIEFKA

All right. All right.

FRANKIE "DEALER" MACHINE

Six of hearts.

ZERO SCHWIEFKA

Can you let me have a thousand? How about 500? I know it's Sunday night. I didn't call you up to find what day it is.

FRANKIE "DEALER" MACHINE

House checks to you?

WILLIAMS

Hold it a minute.

FRANKIE "DEALER" MACHINE

Yeah. Hold it.

WILLIAMS goes over to the side and pours some water from a pitcher over his head.

SAM MARKETTE

Give me some of that.

WILLIAMS pours some water on MARKETTE's head.

FRANKIE "DEALER" MACHINE

I gotta get out of here, Louie. I'm dead. I ain't slept in almost two days.

"NIFTY LOUIE" FOMOROWSKI

Just a little while now.

FRANKIE "DEALER" MACHINE

It ain't doing any good, the house is still losing.

"NIFTY LOUIE" FOMOROWSKI

Stay with it, dealer. The class is beginning to tell. Just stay with it.

FRANKIE "DEALER" MACHINE

I just can't. My head won't work no more.

ZERO SCHWIEFKA

Louie, Louie, I'm running out of guys to call.

"NIFTY LOUIE" FOMOROWSKI

Lippy.

ZERO SCHWIEFKA

I can't find him.

"NIFTY LOUIE" FOMOROWSKI

I'll find him. He's loaded.

FRANKIE "DEALER" MACHINE

I'm getting out of here.

"NIFTY LOUIE" FOMOROWSKI

Just a little longer while I make a call and I'll take you over to my place.

WILLIAMS and MARKETTE go back to the table. The game resumes.

WILLIAMS
Ah, where were we? You patch.

FRANKIE "DEALER" MACHINE
I'll check you.

WILLIAMS
Okay, I bet one hundred.

In the alley outside the building with the poker game, we see SPARROW approaching holding two full paper bags. He climbs up the stairs and is let into the poker room.

MALE SPEAKER
Coffee?

SPARROW
Good and black.

Cheers from the gamblers. A knock on the door. SPARROW lets in NIFTY LOUIE, who approaches SCHWIEFKA.

"NIFTY LOUIE" FOMOROWSKI
I can't raise another cent. How's it going?

ZERO SCHWIEFKA
They're slugging us with their money, every pot almost. They're raising and raising until we're forced out.

FRANKIE "DEALER" MACHINE
What day is it?

"NIFTY LOUIE" FOMOROWSKI
Can't you think of anybody we can tap for a few thousand?

FRANKIE "DEALER" MACHINE
What day is it? Is it Monday yet?

"NIFTY LOUIE" FOMOROWSKI
Listen to me. You listen to me.

FRANKIE "DEALER" MACHINE
Why? Why?

"NIFTY LOUIE" FOMOROWSKI
Listen to me, I said. The next big pot they try to force out with their raising, you gotta stay with them.

FRANKIE "DEALER" MACHINE
Schwiefka don't let me. He keeps nudging me to fold.

"NIFTY LOUIE" FOMOROWSKI
That's because he ain't sure you'll win.

FRANKIE "DEALER" MACHINE
You can't be sure.

"NIFTY LOUIE" FOMOROWSKI
There's a way you can be sure, all right. You can do anything you want with those cards.

FRANKIE "DEALER" MACHINE
That's only for fun. I haven't got enough to do it for real.

"NIFTY LOUIE" FOMOROWSKI
You want to get out of here, don't you?

FRANKIE "DEALER" MACHINE
What?

"NIFTY LOUIE" FOMOROWSKI
You want to get to that tryout in good condition, don't you?

FRANKIE "DEALER" MACHINE
Yeah. I want to get that feeling good.

"NIFTY LOUIE" FOMOROWSKI
Well, then, make sure. You know what I mean.

WILLIAMS
Let's get on with the game. Let's get on with the game. I feel hot.

The gamblers sit down at the table. FRANKIE sits down and starts to deal, looking dazed.

MARKETTE
I'm in.

WILLIAMS
I'm in.

FRANKIE "DEALER" MACHINE
(laying out cards)
Three, King, Jack.

SAM MARKETTE
King bets.

WILLIAMS

Call.

FRANKIE "DEALER" MACHINE

A pair of trays, King, 10, Jack, 7. A pair of trays.

WILLIAMS

I'll bet 200.

SAM MARKETTE

I call the 2.

FRANKIE "DEALER" MACHINE

House bets two, coming out. Pair of trays, pair of Kings, pair of Jacks.

SAM MARKETTE

I'm back with 500.

FRANKIE "DEALER" MACHINE

(*yawns*)

House sees.

WILLIAMS

Call.

FRANKIE "DEALER" MACHINE

Coming up. Three trays. Kings, Jacks. Three trays,

WILLIAMS

Three little trays bet 500 bucks.

We see FRANKIE doing something tricky when shuffling the cards. WILLIAMS grabs him by the wrists, exposing two cards. He pulls FRANKIE up and slaps him. SPARROW tries to interfere. SAM MARKETTE grabs SPARROW and tries to pull off his glasses.

SAM MARKETTE

Take off your glasses. Take them off.

SAM MARKETTE takes SPARROW's glasses off and slaps him around while WILLIAMS slaps FRANKIE.

ZERO SCHWIEFKA

I didn't know! I didn't know!

WILLIAMS

I'll get to you in a second.

ZERO SCHWIEFKA

I didn't know! This never happened to me before. Eleven years I've been running this game. Ask anybody.

(*Spits on* FRANKIE)

You don't deal for me no more.

(*to Sam* MARKETTE)

You want him?

SAM MARKETTE

I wouldn't dirty my hands.

ZERO SCHWIEFKA

How was I to know? You fellas know that I've been running an honest game. Tell them, tell them.

The gamblers collect their money and storm out of the room. SPARROW puts his glasses back on and walks over on his knees to FRANKIE. SPARROW pulls him up off the floor.

SPARROW

Frankie. Everything's all right now, Frankie. Hey, Frankie, what's a little cuffing around, huh? Nothing. Am I right? You'll see. And now we'll be in Yantek's, just laughing about it. You should have seen Schwiefka's face when Williams said he'd get to him in a minute. He went white. It was so funny!

FRANKIE "DEALER" MACHINE

Cut it out, you hear?

SPARROW

You was the best sport I knew my whole life.

FRANKIE "DEALER" MACHINE

You hear me?

SPARROW helps FRANKIE up. FRANKIE slaps him off.

FRANKIE "DEALER" MACHINE:

Stay away from me, punk.

FRANKIE knocks SPARROW down, kicks over a chair, and stumbles out of the room.

Back in NIFTY LOUIE's apartment, a tired LOUIE opens his vest and draws down the shade. A knock on the door. LOUIE opens the door. It is FRANKIE.

FRANKIE "DEALER" MACHINE

Hurry, quick!

"NIFTY LOUIE" FOMOROWSKI
Oh, I wanna get to sleep.

FRANKIE "DEALER" MACHINE
Please. Quick.

FRANKIE barges in.

"NIFTY LOUIE" FOMOROWSKI
Beginning to wear off quick for you, isn't it? You're a graduating student; you're going to have to step it up.

FRANKIE "DEALER" MACHINE
Anything, but please hurry.

"NIFTY LOUIE" FOMOROWSKI
All right. Let's see your money.

FRANKIE "DEALER" MACHINE
Later. Later.

"NIFTY LOUIE" FOMOROWSKI
Right now.

FRANKIE "DEALER" MACHINE
Trust me this once, will you?

"NIFTY LOUIE" FOMOROWSKI
No, I don't do that.

FRANKIE "DEALER" MACHINE
I'll pay you twice as much later. But I gotta do something right now.

"NIFTY LOUIE" FOMOROWSKI
Beat it.

FRANKIE "DEALER" MACHINE
I'll even push for you, Louie. Hurry.

"NIFTY LOUIE" FOMOROWSKI
A flipping junkie always says that.

FRANKIE "DEALER" MACHINE
Please, please, please, Louie.

FRANKIE grabs at LOUIE, who fights him off.

"NIFTY LOUIE" FOMOROWSKI
Get your dirty hands off me.

FRANKIE smashes a chair over LOUIE's head and back, knocking him out. FRANKIE starts to rifle the cabinets and closets. But he cannot find anything. SPARROW comes into the room.

SPARROW

Frankie.

FRANKIE shakes and throttles the unconscious LOUIE.

FRANKIE "DEALER" MACHINE
(*shaking* LOUIE)

Wake up. Get up.

SPARROW tries to get FRANKIE off LOUIE.

SPARROW

No.

FRANKIE "DEALER" MACHINE
(*to Louie*)

Where did you put it?

SPARROW

Frankie, no.

FRANKIE "DEALER" MACHINE

Where did you put it?

SPARROW

Let go, Frankie.

FRANKIE "DEALER" MACHINE

I can't find it. I can't find it.

SPARROW

Let me take you home, Frankie. Frankie, please let me take you home. Frankie. Frankie, please.

FRANKIE grabs an alarm clock, which reads 9:55.

FRANKIE "DEALER" MACHINE

I gotta be on time. I gotta be on time.

He clips on his bow tie, grabs his jacket, and runs out.

We're now in SHORTY ROGERS' rehearsal room. The band is playing swing.

FRANKIE, wearing a suit and tie but unshaven, comes in goes up to a secretary at the door, who brings him up to SHORTY ROGERS. SHORTY ROGERS calls the music to a halt.

SHORTY ROGERS
(*to the band*)
Wow. What's the matter? Come on. Let's try to really cook it.

SECRETARY
Mr. Machine.

FRANKIE "DEALER" MACHINE
Mr. Lane.

SHORTY ROGERS
Okay, can you read music?

FRANKIE "DEALER" MACHINE
Yes.

SHORTY ROGERS
Shelly, let Mr. Machine sit in on this one.

SHELLY MANNE
Number 37. It's right in front of you.

SHORTY ROGERS
You know it, Mr. Machine? Okay, let's try it. 1, 2, 3, 4.

FRANKIE does nothing.

SHORTY ROGERS
Mr. Machine, the first four bars is all you. Come on, let's try it again. 1, 2, 3, 4.

FRANKIE drops his drumsticks and picks them up.

FRANKIE "DEALER" MACHINE
I'm sorry.

SHORTY ROGERS
Are you all set? Once again. 1, 2, 3, 4. Okay, Shelly, let's go.

This time, FRANKIE starts and does well until he starts drumming uncontrollably on the cymbals. Embarrassed and in shock, he walks out.

We now see FRANKIE going into his building. LOUIE watches him from the window of his apartment across the street. He has a bandage around his neck from FRANKIE's throttling. LOUIE puts on his hat, takes his cane, and goes out.

FRANKIE rushes into his apartment. ZOSH is there.

FRANKIE "DEALER" MACHINE
Zosh, do we have any money? I need some money.

SOPHIA "ZOSH" MACHINE

No. What's the matter?

FRANKIE "DEALER" MACHINE

Some was around here yesterday, wasn't there? I need some money, Zosh.

SOPHIA "ZOSH" MACHINE

Oh, there ain't any. What is it? Frankie? What is it?

FRANKIE runs out and downstairs. ZOSH gets out of her wheelchair to look out the window.

Downstairs at the main entrance, FRANKIE is about to run out but through the window in the door, he sees NIFTY LOUIE coming up the steps. FRANKIE rushes into MOLLY's apartment. NIFTY LOUIE shifts a heavy and menacing ring from the finger of his left hand to the finger of the right and goes upstairs. FRANKIE goes out of MOLLY's apartment and out the door.

NIFTY LOUIE walks into FRANKIE's apartment. ZOSH is standing in her bathrobe. Startled, she draws a blanket in front of her.

"NIFTY LOUIE" FOMOROWSKI

You can walk! Since when? What? What's the angle? What are you and Frankie trying to pull? Come on, tell me, one hustler to another, huh? Come on, let me in on it, or I'll croon for it, you hear? I'll tell everybody you can walk. You always could. I'll tell them all, you can walk; you are a phony.

He goes out of the apartment, ZOSH following him. They grapple at the head of the stairs.

SOPHIA "ZOSH" MACHINE

No, Louie, Louie, no, you can't do that. You can't tell anybody. Please, Louie.

"NIFTY LOUIE" FOMOROWSKI

Let me be.

SOPHIA "ZOSH" MACHINE

Please, Louie.

"NIFTY LOUIE" FOMOROWSKI

Take your hands off.

LOUIE fights ZOSH off, but she pushes him down the stairs. She rushes back into her apartment and sits down in her wheelchair, terrified. We hear:

MALE SPEAKER
(off camera)
Don't touch him. Call the police.

MALE SPEAKER
(off camera)
Did he fall? Was he pushed?

FRANKIE is walking down a street where construction is going on. He looks at a piece of paper and goes up the stoop of a building.

In front of a hotel door, FRANKIE knocks on a room where he knows MOLLY is staying.

FRANKIE "DEALER" MACHINE
Molly, Molly, Molly.

But there is no answer. He sits down in the hallway to wait for her.

CAPTAIN BEDNAR is interrogating ZOSH in her apartment.

CAPTAIN BEDNAR
Ain't that the way it happened? They had a fight; next thing anyone knew, Louie was falling. Come on, level, Zosh. Don't try to outthink me. You'll only get tangled.

SOPHIA "ZOSH" MACHINE
I don't know anything about a fight. I was sleeping all morning right here in this chair

CAPTAIN BEDNAR
Then for all you know, it did happen that way. While you were sleeping, Frankie shoved him over.

SOPHIA "ZOSH" MACHINE
He didn't.

CAPTAIN BEDNAR
How do you know, if you were sleeping?

SOPHIA "ZOSH" MACHINE
It wasn't like I was sleeping, it was more like I was dozing, kind of. I'd have heard a fight if there was one. Frankie didn't do it. He wasn't even here.

CAPTAIN BEDNAR
When wasn't he here?

SOPHIA "ZOSH" MACHINE

When it happened.

CAPTAIN BEDNAR

How can you be sure if you was dozing?

SOPHIA "ZOSH" MACHINE

I was up when he left. That's how I'm sure. I saw him go.

CAPTAIN BEDNAR

And he went home this morning?

SOPHIA "ZOSH" MACHINE

But only a second, honest. He didn't get in a fight. He was here only a second.

CAPTAIN BEDNAR

Why didn't he stick around? Was somebody after him?

SOPHIA "ZOSH" MACHINE

Nobody was after him, nobody. He just wanted some money is all.

CAPTAIN BEDNAR

What for?

SOPHIA "ZOSH" MACHINE

I don't know what for.

CAPTAIN BEDNAR

A fix. He wanted it for a fix from Louie.

SOPHIA "ZOSH" MACHINE

It had nothing to do with Louie.

CAPTAIN BEDNAR

How do you know?

SOPHIA "ZOSH" MACHINE

Because there was no money. Why would he want to see Louie for a fix if he didn't have no money?

CAPTAIN BEDNAR

To try and get one without money. Okay. I can wait; wherever he is, sooner or later he is, he's gotta come out for a fix.

FRANKIE is waiting on the landing in front of MOLLY's room. Finally she comes up the stairs.

FRANKIE "DEALER" MACHINE

Molly. Molly, wait, please.

MOLLY NOVOTNY

It's finished, Frankie, like I told you.

FRANKIE "DEALER" MACHINE

But I gotta talk to you, Molly, please.

MOLLY NOVOTNY

No, once and for all.

She opens the door and goes into her apartment. She tries to shut him out, but he pushes his way in.

FRANKIE "DEALER" MACHINE

I have to talk to you. Got any money, Molly? I need a few dollars. $10 would do it. I'd get it back to you in a few days or $5 even. Five would be fine. Please. I feel so sick, Molly. I hurt all over. I feel so bad. Don't say no. Please don't say no. Why not, Molly? Why not?

MOLLY NOVOTNY

Jump off a roof if you're going to kill yourself, but don't ask me to help you.

FRANKIE "DEALER" MACHINE

I'll do anything for you, Molly, but right now you have to help me. I need a shot.

MOLLY NOVOTNY

No.

FRANKIE "DEALER" MACHINE

Five would do it, or four, three, or two even. But please hurry.

MOLLY NOVOTNY

You mustn't take that dirty stuff no more.

FRANKIE "DEALER" MACHINE

I know, I know you're right, and I promise, but right now I need a fix, just one fix to help me stop hurting, and then I promise you I'll kick it for good. Just a few hours, Molly. Please.

A knock on the door. MOLLY opens it partway. It's DRUNKIE JOHN.

DRUNKIE JOHN

Hello, Molly. I just wanted to come say hello. Ain't you going to let me in?

MOLLY NOVOTNY

I asked you please not to bother me no more.

While DRUNKIE JOHN and MOLLY are talking, FRANKIE is rifling through her purse behind the door.

DRUNKIE JOHN

I miss you.

MOLLY NOVOTNY

Look, I'm awfully tired, Johnny.

DRUNKIE JOHN

I'll stay only a few minutes.

MOLLY NOVOTNY

No.

DRUNKIE JOHN hears FRANKIE inside.

DRUNKIE JOHN

Who's in there with you?

MOLLY NOVOTNY

Go away, Johnny, and don't come back.

DRUNKIE JOHN

Who is it? Not the dealer. You ain't hiding him, are you? You wouldn't be dumb enough to be an accessory, would you?

MOLLY NOVOTNY

What do you mean, accessory?

DRUNKIE JOHN

He killed Louie. Cops are looking for him this minute.

MOLLY NOVOTNY

Frankie Machine?

DRUNKIE JOHN

Is he in there?

MOLLY NOVOTNY

No.

DRUNKIE JOHN

I'm coming in.

MOLLY NOVOTNY

Not if you ever want to see me again.

DRUNKIE JOHN

Will you meet me tomorrow?

MOLLY NOVOTNY
Yeah. Yeah. I'll be around Yantek's. Maybe not tomorrow, but soon.

DRUNKIE JOHN
I miss you.

She closes the door on DRUNKIE JOHN and confronts FRANKIE.

FRANKIE "DEALER" MACHINE
Honestly, I didn't. What am I going to do?

MOLLY NOVOTNY
Go tell Bednar it wasn't you.

FRANKIE "DEALER" MACHINE
I couldn't. I couldn't stand up to the cops the way I am. Look at me. I'd say anything they want me to say, just for a shot.

MOLLY NOVOTNY
Then get cured first.

FRANKIE "DEALER" MACHINE
What are you talking about? How am I supposed to get cured?

MOLLY NOVOTNY
You did it once.

FRANKIE "DEALER" MACHINE
That was with help and medicine and doctors. I can't go applying to Lexington with a murder hanging over my head.

MOLLY NOVOTNY
Couldn't you do it without going there?

FRANKIE "DEALER" MACHINE
You mean just stop, cold turkey? You don't understand the pain.

MOLLY NOVOTNY
What else can you do?

FRANKIE "DEALER" MACHINE
All I need is one shot, just one.

MOLLY NOVOTNY
All right.

She goes to her purse and takes out money.

MOLLY NOVOTNY

Take it. Go on and take it all, because all that you're going to need after that one shot is another and then another, and then another. Take it. Take it. Why should you hurt, like other people hurt?

Yes, so you had a dog's life with never a break. Why try to face it like most people do? No. Just roll up all your pains into one big hurt and then flatten it with a fix. What do you think you'll find just outside that door? Don't you think that Bednar knows what you are and what you need, just to get through that next hour? Don't you know he's just waiting for you to come and get it? Go on, let him kill you. Let him kill you. It'll be quicker and better than doing it your way.

FRANKIE "DEALER" MACHINE

No, no. I won't let him kill me. No. And I won't run into no grave. But kicking it, a guy can't do it by himself.

MOLLY NOVOTNY

I'll help.

FRANKIE "DEALER" MACHINE

You know what you're letting yourself in for? It ain't pretty. And it could be dangerous.

MOLLY NOVOTNY

If they find you here, then they find you, is all.

FRANKIE "DEALER" MACHINE

I don't mean dangerous from Bednar. I mean dangerous from me. Sometimes a junkie will kill to get away from the treatment, understand? So if you got any knives or scissors in the house, you gotta put them away for a while and don't let me out of the room no matter what I say, or promise, or how much I beg, because if I get out, it'll only be to go out and find a fix. That's the way it is, you understand? Just lock me in the room and if I try to make a break for it, stop me any way you know how, and no matter how much you see it hurting me, don't try to help me with pills or dope or anything else like that. You think you can handle it?

MOLLY takes out her key and locks the front door. FRANKIE takes off his jacket and rubs his arm.

FRANKIE "DEALER" MACHINE

Here we go, down and dirty.

OFFICER PARKER drags SPARROW into BEDNAR's office.

SPARROW
You can't hold me. You are committing double jeopardy or something.

CAPTAIN BEDNAR
Sit down.

SPARROW
You can't hold me. I ain't got all my marbles. You know that, Captain.

CAPTAIN BEDNAR
Write down the cases, Sparrow, and quit horsing around.

SPARROW
I didn't do nothing.

CAPTAIN BEDNAR
But Frankie did something, all right, and I want you to tell me about it.

SPARROW
Whoever killed that peddler should get a ticker tape parade.

CAPTAIN BEDNAR
Yeah, and maybe I'd lead the band. I still want you to tell me about it. Listen to me, Sparrow, when we catch him, he stands trial, whether you talk or whether you don't. The only question is, do I ticket you as an accessory?

SPARROW
Bednar, don't nail me to the cross. He's the only guy I ever had for a friend.

CAPTAIN BEDNAR
He's nobody's friend anymore. He'd mash you with a steamroller if you got between him and a pop in the arm. Come on, talk, Sparrow.

SPARROW stares resolutely ahead of him in silence.

CAPTAIN BEDNAR
Okay, beat it.

SPARROW runs out of BEDNAR's office.

In MOLLY's apartment, FRANKIE is thrashing about madly. He tries to pull open the locked door. He drinks some water from a cup and then from a pot that he fills from the tap. He is doubled over in pain. Then he ties his arm, pulls a sharp black object from a drawer, and tries to inject himself with it, but it is useless. He tears into the bathroom and runs back out clutching a towel.

He throws himself down on the bed and thrashes around with severe cramps. He rolls off the bed. He yanks at the door but cannot open it.

FRANKIE "DEALER" MACHINE

Lemme out!

FRANKIE smashes a chair against the door, but it still does not open, and he collapses with severe tetany.

Now we see MOLLY coming up the stairs of FRANKIE's building. She knocks on FRANKIE's apartment door.

SOPHIA "ZOSH" MACHINE
(*inside*)

Yes?

MOLLY goes into the apartment and finds MOLLY in her wheelchair, pasting clippings into a scrapbook.

MOLLY NOVOTNY

I thought I'd come see how you've been, Zosh.

SOPHIA "ZOSH" MACHINE

Alone, that's how I've been.

MOLLY hands her a small package.

MOLLY NOVOTNY

Something to eat, sausage.

ZOSH grabs the package rudely.

SOPHIA "ZOSH" MACHINE

Alone and worried sick. Where is he? You know where he is? Did he go to you? What do you want, anyway?

MOLLY NOVOTNY

Zosh, what you told Bednar? You've seen the papers. You see how bad it makes Frankie look, what you said.

SOPHIA "ZOSH" MACHINE

I didn't tell Bednar nothing. The papers, they twist everything all up.

MOLLY NOVOTNY

They wouldn't be able to if you didn't let them.

SOPHIA "ZOSH" MACHINE

I can't help what they do. What do you expect me to do sitting here?

MOLLY NOVOTNY

Just tell Bednar that Frankie wasn't here when it happened. That he didn't do it.

SOPHIA "ZOSH" MACHINE

I never said he did.

MOLLY NOVOTNY

But that's how it sounds, if he was the only one around at the time, and you know it was somebody else.

SOPHIA "ZOSH" MACHINE

What do you mean? Who?

MOLLY NOVOTNY

I don't know. But maybe Bednar could figure it out if he didn't think it was Frankie.

SOPHIA "ZOSH" MACHINE

What business is it of yours, anyway?

MOLLY NOVOTNY

I just want to help him.

SOPHIA "ZOSH" MACHINE

Who are you kidding? You think I don't know what you really want? You think I don't know what you and him have been up to behind my back while I had to sit here all these years, had to sit here all these years!

MOLLY NOVOTNY

Oh, Zosh, you got it wrong.

SOPHIA "ZOSH" MACHINE

No, you got it wrong, because you'll never get him. He put me in this chair, and as long as I sit here, he'll never leave me. He knows he belongs to me.

MOLLY NOVOTNY

Zosh, I come only to help.

SOPHIA "ZOSH" MACHINE

I wouldn't want to live if he left me. And I'd rather see him dead too than have him go to you.

MOLLY NOVOTNY

Zosh, please . . .

SOPHIA "ZOSH" MACHINE

Yes, get out of here. Get out of here, you lousy tramp. Get out.

MOLLY goes out. ZOSH throws a newspaper at her. When MOLLY is gone, ZOSH begins to sob.

Back in MOLLY's apartment, FRANKIE is walking around, rubbing his arms. He is very cold. He tries to open the door again but fails. He opens the window and is about to jump out when MOLLY comes in and stops him.

MOLLY NOVOTNY

Frankie, no.

FRANKIE "DEALER" MACHINE

I can't stand it any longer

MOLLY NOVOTNY

Just a little longer.

FRANKIE "DEALER" MACHINE

Please help me. Keep me warm. I can't stand it. I gotta get out and get a fix. Open the door. Molly, do like I say, open the door. I'll kill you, I'll kill you.

He lifts a chair and raises it over his head.

MOLLY NOVOTNY

Listen, if you really can't . . .

FRANKIE "DEALER" MACHINE

I can't, I can't.

MOLLY NOVOTNY

Well, then, I do have something put away to make it stop.

FRANKIE "DEALER" MACHINE

Give me quick. Give me, quick. Where? I'll get it.

She leads him into her closet, rushes out, and locks him in.

FRANKIE "DEALER" MACHINE

Molly, Molly, open the door. Let me out, now, now! Molly, open the door.

He keeps beating on the door. MOLLY puts some loud music on the radio. Then he stops.

MOLLY NOVOTNY

Frankie, answer me. Are you all right? Don't think you can fool me into opening this door, because I'm not going to. Are you all right? Frankie, please answer me.

She turns off the music and opens the door. FRANKIE has been leaning against it and collapses on the floor outside.

FRANKIE "DEALER" MACHINE

Molly, if you love me, kill me, please. Oh, I'm so cold. I'm so cold, so cold. Molly, make me warm, please. Oh, please warm me. Molly, please make me warm. Oh, Molly, I am so cold, make me warm.

MOLLY covers him with blankets and rubs his hands.

MOLLY NOVOTNY

God. God.

FRANKIE "DEALER" MACHINE

Please make me warm, Molly. I'm so cold. I'm so cold.

MOLLY lies over him, hugging and kissing him.

The next day, DRUNKIE JOHN shows up at MOLLY's apartment and knocks on the door. Inside, MOLLY is asleep on her bed and FRANKIE is lying on the floor. He stirs. MOLLY answers the door partway.

DRUNKIE JOHN

I waited for you at Yantek's last night.

MOLLY NOVOTNY

I told you it might not be right away.

DRUNKIE JOHN

I thought maybe you were sick or something. I just want to tell you don't look for me in Yantek's no more. He threw me out last night. We had a little argument. So make it the Safari, huh?

MOLLY NOVOTNY

Yeah, sure, Johnny, sure.

She closes the door on him.

FRANKIE gets up, looking weak but better. His hands are no longer shaking.

FRANKIE "DEALER" MACHINE

Pretty good, huh? Molly.

MOLLY NOVOTNY

Take it slow.

FRANKIE "DEALER" MACHINE

Oh, I'm all right. Just a little rocky.

They go to the window and both look out.

Below, on the street, DRUNKIE JOHN stops to light a cigarette. He sees the two of them looking out the window.

Back in MOLLY's room:

FRANKIE "DEALER" MACHINE
The most gorgeous day I ever saw. I think it's the first day I ever saw. I got a craving for something sweet. You got anything sweet?

MOLLY NOVOTNY
Sugar.

FRANKIE "DEALER" MACHINE
Give me.

She pours sugar into his hands. He gobbles it up.

FRANKIE "DEALER" MACHINE
More.

MOLLY NOVOTNY
Oh, how can you, Frankie?

FRANKIE "DEALER" MACHINE
Oh, I never felt as good in my life. I feel like all the things inside me have settled into place. Thanks, Molly. Molly-O.

She kisses him.

FRANKIE "DEALER" MACHINE
Oh, God, you'll scrape your face off.

MOLLY NOVOTNY
I don't care.

FRANKIE "DEALER" MACHINE
You got a razor I can use?

MOLLY NOVOTNY
Can I trust you with one?

FRANKIE "DEALER" MACHINE
Cross my heart.

She takes a sack and empties it of kitchenware and other sundries. They see the pile and laugh. He sees a razor and picks it up.

CAPTAIN BEDNAR's car pulls up to MOLLY's building. DRUNKIE JOHN and another policeman are riding with him. In the car:

CAPTAIN BEDNAR

Is this the place?

DRUNKIE JOHN

Yeah.

CAPTAIN BEDNAR

Okay, come on.

DRUNKIE JOHN

No, please. You don't need me up there.

The two policemen go into the building. DRUNKIE JOHN flees.

Inside MOLLY's apartment, she is polishing a saucepan. She hears a knock on the door. She opens it and CAPTAIN BEDNAR and the policeman barge in.

CAPTAIN BEDNAR

Where is he, Molly?

MOLLY NOVOTNY

He didn't do it, honest.

CAPTAIN BEDNAR

I'm not a judge. They pay me to bring him in. That's all. If you tell me where he is, I promise he'll get every break a junkie can get.

MOLLY NOVOTNY

He's no junkie either. That's finished.

CAPTAIN BEDNAR

Oh sure, you bet.

MOLLY NOVOTNY

You'll see for yourself. He ain't running away from you.

CAPTAIN BEDNAR

So where is he?

MOLLY NOVOTNY

With Zosh.

CAPTAIN BEDNAR

All right, Molly, let's go see.

FRANKIE goes into his apartment. ZOSH is lying in bed.

FRANKIE "DEALER" MACHINE

Hello, Zosh.

SOPHIA "ZOSH" MACHINE
What are you doing here, Frankie? Don't you know Bednar is looking for you?

FRANKIE "DEALER" MACHINE
Don't worry about it, Zosh. I ain't afraid. I didn't do it, you know that.

SOPHIA "ZOSH" MACHINE
Who—who did then, who?

FRANKIE "DEALER" MACHINE
I come to tell you something, Zosh. I'm leaving here.

SOPHIA "ZOSH" MACHINE
But Bednar will arrest you. He told the newspapers you—what?

FRANKIE "DEALER" MACHINE
I'm leaving. You won't have to worry about money or anything. I'll find a way to send you some regular, and Vi will take good care of you.

SOPHIA "ZOSH" MACHINE
Leaving me!

FRANKIE "DEALER" MACHINE
I'm not leaving you, Zosh, just leaving. You saw what happened since I come back. It's like Dr. Lennox told me. I got in the same old routine and before I knew it, I was on it again.

SOPHIA "ZOSH" MACHINE
But you can't leave me. You gotta stay and take care of me.

FRANKIE "DEALER" MACHINE
I know I'm responsible for how you are, Zosh, but I can't go around the rest of my life stoning myself to death about it. I've been carrying my heart ever since it happened. Even now, it hurts me to think about it, but . . . well, it's not that I want to leave, I gotta leave.

SOPHIA "ZOSH" MACHINE
You mustn't leave, Frankie, you mustn't leave.

She clutches at him. He sits down on the bed next to her.

FRANKIE "DEALER" MACHINE
Zosh, say goodbye to me, Zosh.

SOPHIA "ZOSH" MACHINE
You think you're fooling me? I know what's pulling you away. Molly.

FRANKIE "DEALER" MACHINE

No.

SOPHIA "ZOSH" MACHINE

Yeah. You're going just so you can be with that little tramp. Frankie, no.

FRANKIE "DEALER" MACHINE

Goodbye, Zosh.

SOPHIA "ZOSH" MACHINE

No, Frankie, please don't leave! Frankie, no, don't leave.

She rushes out of her bed and is startled to find FRANKIE with the door open, showing CAPTAIN BEDNAR, OFFICER PARKER, and MOLLY in the background. ZOSH rushes back to her wheelchair pathetically.

CAPTAIN BEDNAR

Get dressed, Zosh.

ZOSH gets up slowly and puts on her slippers. She pulls on a bathrobe. She goes toward the front door, but facing MOLLY, turns and runs out the back door.

FRANKIE "DEALER" MACHINE

Zosh, stop!

ZOSH rushes out onto the back porch, FRANKIE and CAPTAIN BEDNAR following. She stops, blows her whistle, flings herself off, and falls to the ground below.

FRANKIE looks over the railing and sees her body below. He rushes down the stairs, CAPTAIN BEDNAR following. When they reach her, she stirs weakly.

FRANKIE "DEALER" MACHINE

Zosh, stop. Zosh, don't move. Don't try to talk. You're going to be all right.

SOPHIA "ZOSH" MACHINE

Just that I love you so much.

FRANKIE "DEALER" MACHINE

Zosh.

ZOSH dies. An ambulance arrives. An attendant rushes up to her, tries her pulse, and listens to her chest with a stethoscope. He places her arms on her chest as is done with the dead. He and another attendant carry her into the ambulance, her face and body covered.

FRANKIE stands to his feet. SPARROW is there. He and FRANKIE go off.

On the street, we see MOLLY coming down from FRANKIE's building onto the street. Rounding the corner, she sees FRANKIE and SPARROW and goes up to join them. FRANKIE and MOLLY walk together. SPARROW stays behind on the corner. The camera focuses on MOLLY and FRANKIE walking side by side. He has a weary but victorious look on his face.

In the background, we see SPARROW shuffle off and CAPTAIN BEDNAR and OFFICER PARKER get into the police car.

THE STRANGE LOVE OF MARTHA IVERS

• • •

Directed by LEWIS MILESTONE
Written by ROBERT ROSSEN
Based on *Love Lies Bleeding* by JOHN PATRICK
Produced by HAL B. WALLIS

CAST

Barbara Stanwyck .... Martha Ivers
Janis Wilson .... Young Martha Ivers
Van Heflin .... Sam Masterson
Darryl Hickman .... Young Sam Masterson
Lizabeth Scott .... Antonia "Toni" Marachek
Kirk Douglas .... Walter O'Neil
Mickey Kuhn .... Young Walter O'Neil
Judith Anderson .... Mrs. Ivers
Roman Bohnen .... Mr. O'Neil
Ann Doran .... Bobbi St. John
Frank Orth .... Hotel Clerk
James Flavin .... Detective #1
Charles D. Brown .... Detective McCarthy
Blake Edwards .... Sailor (uncredited)
Robert Homans .... Gallagher (uncredited)
Gladden James .... John (uncredited)

The camera shows the legend "Iverstown 1928" above a neon sign that says "E.P. Ivers."

It is night. YOUNG SAM MASTERSON is running down a street, past a POLICEMAN and a DETECTIVE.

Stopping in front of the door of a railcar, YOUNG SAM lets out a whistle. The door opens, and YOUNG MARTHA IVERS lets him in.

YOUNG SAM MASTERSON

Shut the door, quick.

The railcar is very dark. YOUNG SAM MASTERSON lights a candle. Thunder roars. YOUNG MARTHA IVERS runs into his arms.

YOUNG SAM MASTERSON

Scared of thunder?

YOUNG MARTHA IVERS

No, I like it.

YOUNG SAM MASTERSON

That's good, because there's going to be more of it. I brought you food, for the kitten too.

YOUNG MARTHA IVERS

Did you steal it?

YOUNG SAM MASTERSON

No, I bought it.

YOUNG MARTHA IVERS

Oh.

YOUNG SAM MASTERSON

And if we get caught, don't go making up any stories that I did. I'm in enough trouble as it is; you and your kitten.

YOUNG MARTHA IVERS

You want me to go back, Sam?

YOUNG SAM MASTERSON

Shut up.

YOUNG MARTHA IVERS

They looking for me?

YOUNG SAM MASTERSON

Your aunt's got every cop in Iverstown peeping through keyholes.

YOUNG MARTHA IVERS

You won't let them find me.

YOUNG SAM MASTERSON

You always come running to me.

YOUNG MARTHA IVERS

I've got nobody else to run to, Sam.

YOUNG SAM MASTERSON

The circus is leaving town tonight. Their train will go right through here. When it does, you just follow me. You run with all your might, and when you grab on, grab tight.

YOUNG MARTHA IVERS

Don't you worry about me, Sam.

The door rumbles.

YOUNG SAM MASTERSON

Hush, quiet.

YOUNG SAM blows out the candle. The door rumbles open, showing the POLICEMAN and the DETECTIVE.

DETECTIVE #1

There they are. All right, kids. Unless you got wings, you're caught.

YOUNG SAM MASTERSON

All right, Martha, let's go.

YOUNG SAM and YOUNG MARTHA descend from the train car, helped by the POLICEMAN and DETECTIVE. YOUNG SAM MASTERSON runs off.

YOUNG MARTHA IVERS

You'll never catch him; you'll never catch him.

Ignoring YOUNG SAM, the DETECTIVE and the POLICEMAN grab YOUNG MARTHA.

DETECTIVE #1

Don't rough her, you chump. All right, miss, we'll take you on home to your aunt.

The scene changes to show MRS. IVERS in her study, writing. A knock on the door; it opens to show LYNCH, a butler dressed in white tie.

LYNCH

Mr. O'Neil to see you, ma'am.

MRS. IVERS

Show him in.

LYNCH

Mrs. Ivers will see you now.

MR. O'NEIL and YOUNG WALTER O'NEIL enter. They are both correctly dressed in suits and ties; YOUNG WALTER is wearing glasses.

MR. O'NEIL

Good evening, Mrs. Ivers.

MRS. IVERS

Good evening.

YOUNG WALTER O'NEIL

Good evening, Mrs. Ivers.

MR. O'NEIL

I have good news. Martha . . .

MRS. IVERS

What about her?

MR. O'NEIL

Martha has been found.

MRS. IVERS

I know.

MR. O'NEIL

Well, it was Walter who was really responsible for Martha being found. He told the police where she and that boy Sam Masterson usually go. Isn't that so, Walter?

YOUNG WALTER O'NEIL

Yes, Father.

MRS. IVERS

The boy will be rewarded.

MR. O'NEIL

Well, he's a good boy and he's bright. If I could afford it, I'd send him . . .

MRS. IVERS

Send him to a school like Harvard.

MR. O'NEIL

I guess I've mentioned it before.

MRS. IVERS

Many times.

MRS. IVERS rings a bell, and LYNCH enters.

LYNCH

Yes, madam.

MRS. IVERS

Take the boy to the kitchen, Lynch; give him some ice cream. You may give him a piece of cake too. Go along.

MR. O'NEIL

You must thank Ms. Ivers, boy.

YOUNG WALTER O'NEIL

Thank you, Ms. Ivers.

LYNCH leads YOUNG WALTER O'NEIL out.

MRS. IVERS

You've lost your pupil, Mr. O'Neil. I'm sending her away. I know why you offered to tutor Martha. I know why you've made Walter do his daily lessons with her. I know why you want him to live here. A scholarship for Walter, that's why. But I'm not a foundation, Mr. O'Neil. I don't care whether Walter drives a truck or goes to Harvard. Probably be a lot happier driving a truck.

Thunder rumbles. The scene is now the foyer to the house. LYNCH opens the front door and lets in the POLICEMAN, the DETECTIVE, and YOUNG MARTHA.

LYNCH

You are expected, Miss.

YOUNG MARTHA runs past him.

LYNCH

Oh, just a minute, Miss.

DETECTIVE #1

The name's Lundeen. You tell Mrs. Ivers the name of the detective who caught her is Lundeen.

LYNCH

I tell her.

LYNCH goes up to YOUNG MARTHA, who is holding her cat in her arms.

LYNCH

I'll take your furs, Miss.

YOUNG MARTHA IVERS

No.

LYNCH

You'd better, Miss; you know how she feels about that cat. I'll bring it up to your room. Your aunt is waiting for you.

YOUNG MARTHA opens the door to the study, slowly and cautiously, and enters. MRS. IVERS and MR. O'NEIL are standing in the middle of the room.

MRS. IVERS

Come closer, Martha.

YOUNG MARTHA advances a little.

MRS. IVERS

Closer, Martha.

YOUNG MARTHA goes up to MRS. IVERS.

MRS. IVERS

Look at me. You don't seem very sorry.

YOUNG MARTHA IVERS

I am. I'm sorry I was caught.

MRS. IVERS slaps YOUNG MARTHA in the face.

YOUNG MARTHA IVERS

No matter what you do, I won't cry.

MRS. IVERS

This is the fourth time you've tried to run away. Each time you were brought back here; no matter how far you got, you were brought back here.

YOUNG MARTHA IVERS

You don't own the whole world.

MRS. IVERS

Enough of it to make sure that you'll always be brought back here. Do you understand that? You understand that!

MR. O'NEIL

Your aunt doesn't deserve such an attitude, Martha. There not very many women who would be as patient and as kind, and there aren't very many little girls who would be as ungrateful.

MRS. IVERS

When will you understand that I'm doing all this for you, that I'm trying to wash the dirt and grime off you? Make an Ivers out of you again.

YOUNG MARTHA IVERS

My name is Smith, the same as my father's was.

MRS. IVERS

Your name is Ivers. I've had it changed legally.

YOUNG MARTHA IVERS

I don't care what you've done.

MRS. IVERS

Your name is Ivers: the same as your mother's was before she was stupid enough to marry that . . .

YOUNG MARTHA IVERS

Shut up, shut up.

MRS. IVERS

How dare you? You've still got his foul mouth.

YOUNG MARTHA IVERS

I won't let you talk that way about my father.

MRS. IVERS

Your father was a nobody, a mill hand. The best thing he ever did for you was to die.

YOUNG MARTHA lunges after MRS. IVERS.

YOUNG MARTHA

I'll kill you! I'll kill you!

MR. O'NEIL steps in to intervene.

YOUNG MARTHA IVERS

You get you off . . .

MR. O'NEIL

Martha, stop it.

MRS. IVERS

It's all right, Mr. O'Neil. Go up to your room and get into some dry clothes. After you've had dinner, I want to have a talk with you.

YOUNG MARTHA goes out into the hallway.

MR. O'NEIL

It's late out. I'll go get my son. Goodnight.

MRS. IVERS

Stay. I'm upset. I want someone to talk to.

MR. O'NEIL

Yes, Mrs. Ivers.

We now see the door of YOUNG MARTHA's bedroom open. YOUNG WALTER O'NEIL is there, holding the cat.

YOUNG WALTER O'NEIL

Lynch told me to sneak Bundles to you. I thought you'd be hungry. So I sneaked the milk too.

YOUNG MARTHA IVERS

She hates cats. She hates everything I like.

YOUNG WALTER O'NEIL

A policeman came to my house this morning. He asked me if I had any idea of where you could have gone. My father said it was my duty to tell them.

YOUNG MARTHA IVERS

Your father.

YOUNG WALTER O'NEIL

I didn't say a thing. No matter what my father told your aunt, I didn't say a thing.

YOUNG MARTHA IVERS

I'm cold; I've got to change my clothes. I'll leave the door open so I can hear you.

YOUNG WALTER O'NEIL

My father says you're foolish. My father says that someday you'll have everything in the world. My father says that if we only had one little part of what you'll have, I could go to Harvard.

MARTHA IVERS

You what?

YOUNG WALTER O'NEIL

I could go to Harvard.

Thunder rumbles, and the lights go out.

YOUNG MARTHA IVERS

The lights. What happened to the lights?

YOUNG WALTER O'NEIL

They went out. I think they went out all over the house.

YOUNG MARTHA IVERS

There's a candle and matches on the table, near the wall. Oh, you stand still. I'll do it.

YOUNG MARTHA lights a candle.

Back in the study, MRS. IVERS and MR. O'NEIL sit near the fireplace with a pair of lit candles. They are playing checkers.

MR. O'NEIL

Don't you think I'd better go up and see if Martha's all right?

MRS. IVERS

Martha will be all right, anywhere. Your play.

Back in YOUNG MARTHA's room, the thunder and lightning flash again.

YOUNG MARTHA IVERS

I am afraid of the thunder and lightning. Draw the curtains; I'm going to change.

YOUNG WALTER goes to draw the curtains; he sees the figure of YOUNG SAM, who raps on the window.

YOUNG WALTER O'NEIL

Martha.

YOUNG WALTER opens the window, and YOUNG SAM comes in.

YOUNG SAM MASTERSON

One peep out of you, and I'll break your nose.

YOUNG WALTER O'NEIL

I won't say anything, Martha. Martha will tell you I won't say anything.

YOUNG MARTHA IVERS

What? Sam! You see, Walter, I told you they'd never catch him.

She turns her back to him; her blouse is unbuttoned at the back.

YOUNG MARTHA IVERS

Sam, button me up.

YOUNG SAM buttons her blouse.

YOUNG SAM

I came to say goodbye. I thought it over, Martha; it's better for you here.

YOUNG MARTHA

I won't stay here. I hate her.

YOUNG SAM

All you have to do is play smart with her.

YOUNG MARTHA

I'm going with you.

YOUNG SAM

Now, you listen to me.

YOUNG MARTHA

I don't want to listen.

YOUNG SAM

It's late. I have to go.

YOUNG WALTER

Let him go, Martha. If he's caught here, he'll be sent to reform school. Mrs. Ivers said so.

YOUNG SAM MASTERSON

They have to catch me first.

YOUNG MARTHA IVERS

All right, Sam, if you won't take me, I'll go without you. I'll go off by myself.

YOUNG SAM MASTERSON

OK. Then let's go.

YOUNG MARTHA IVERS

I want to run up to the attic. I want to get a couple of things.

YOUNG MARTHA goes out into the hallway, holding the candle. We hear the meow of a cat.

YOUNG MARTHA IVERS

Sam, quick, Sam. Sam . . .

YOUNG SAM MASTERSON

What?

YOUNG MARTHA IVERS

She's going downstairs. Sam, my aunt!

YOUNG SAM MASTERSON

I'll get her.

YOUNG SAM runs down the stairs in the dark after the cat.

YOUNG SAM MASTERSON

Here, kitty, kitty.

YOUNG MARTHA IVERS

Have you got him? Have you got him, Sam? Hurry, Sam, the old witch will catch us.

MRS. IVERS goes up the stairs. The cat runs up the stairs behind her. Seeing the cat, she grows furious and starts walloping it with her cane. YOUNG O'NEIL and YOUNG MARTHA watch in horror, the scene lit by a candelabra that MARTHA is holding. YOUNG MARTHA goes down a few steps and hits MRS. IVERS with her own cane. MRS. IVERS falls all the way down the stairs.

The lights suddenly go back on, and MARTHA blows out the candles. MR. O'NEIL comes into the hallway and goes up to the fallen MRS. IVERS.

MR. O'NEIL

She's dead.

YOUNG MARTHA

We were upstairs. We heard a noise and we came down. We saw a man, a big man. He was leaving out of that front door. He left. See? It's open. And she was lying there.

YOUNG MARTHA holds out the cane.

YOUNG MARTHA

And this, this was lying there too. I picked it up. Isn't that true, Walter? Isn't it?

MR. O'NEIL

Is it, Walter?

YOUNG WALTER

Yes, father, it is.

MR. O'NEIL

Put it down. Put it exactly where you found it. Both of you better go upstairs. I'll phone the police.

YOUNG WALTER and YOUNG MARTHA are back in YOUNG MARTHA's room.

YOUNG WALTER O'NEIL

You will never get away with it, never.

YOUNG MARTHA IVERS

Your father believes me.

YOUNG WALTER O'NEIL

I don't know. I'm not sure.

YOUNG MARTHA IVERS

You keep your mouth shut.

YOUNG WALTER O'NEIL

But Sam, what about Sam? He was in the house. He saw it.

YOUNG MARTHA IVERS

Sam will never tell.

YOUNG WALTER O'NEIL

Yes, he will. He's scared. That's why he ran away after it happened.

YOUNG MARTHA IVERS

Sam won't ever tell.

YOUNG WALTER O'NEIL

Sam's scared; he ran away. I didn't. I stayed.

YOUNG MARTHA IVERS

No, no, he won't. Not Sam, not Sam.

MR. O'NEIL comes into the room.

MR. O'NEIL

I want to talk to you both. Sit down. Now, when the police come, you will tell them exactly what you told me. Do you understand, Martha?

YOUNG MARTHA IVERS

Yes, Mr. O'Neil.

MR. O'NEIL

And you too, Walter.

YOUNG WALTER O'NEIL

Yes, father.

MR. O'NEIL

You poor child. You'll be all alone in the world now, except for Walter and myself. But you needn't be afraid. We'll always be with you, Walter and I. We'll never leave you.

YOUNG MARTHA IVERS

Thank you, Mr. O'Neil.

The sound of a train signal. The scene shifts outdoors. It is very dark and raining heavily. A large train is passing. YOUNG SAM jumps onto a railcar, under a gaudily painted circus car. The train goes off.

The scene now shifts to Iverstown, 1946.

It is night. A train is passing again. It goes past a railroad crossing at which a car is waiting. The train goes by, and the arm of the barrier goes up. The car drives through.

Inside the car, a radio broadcast is on. SAM MASTERSON is driving, with a SAILOR asleep in the passenger's seat.

RADIO ANNOUNCER

. . . Your competition at the fairground last week. In the handicap Chestnut King looks like an odds-on favorite.

SAM turns off the radio.

SAM MASTERSON

That guy doesn't know what he's talking about. Chestnut King's a dog. He was losing races to cow ponies years ago in Tijuana.

SAM looks ahead at a lit sign that says "*Welcome to Iverstown.*" He turns to the SAILOR.

SAM MASTERSON

Oh, what do you know? What do you know about that? How do you like that, sailor? Leave a place when you're a kid, maybe 17, 18 years ago, and you forget all about it, and all of a sudden you're driving along and smacko! Your own hometown ups and hits you right in the face.

SAM looks at the road and realizes that he is headed straight for a lamppost, which the car hits. He gets out and opens the hood. The SAILOR is still in his seat, asleep.

SAM MASTERSON

End of the line, sailor. Come on, wake up.

SAILOR

Where are we?

SAM MASTERSON

In a small accident.

SAILOR

What happened?

SAM MASTERSON

The road curved, but I didn't. Come on, I've got to put into Iverstown for repairs.

The SAILOR ruefully gets out of the car.

SAILOR

Next time I'll pick me a guy that don't fall asleep.

SAM MASTERSON

Welcome to Iverstown. Well, maybe this time they mean it.

SAM MASTERSON's car pulls into a garage. DEMPSEY, the garage owner, is sitting, smoking, and reading a newspaper.

SAM MASTERSON

You got anybody here to fix this wreck, mister?

DEMPSEY

Roll her in.

The scene shifts to DICE GAMERS shooting craps in the garage.

DICE GAMERS

10 more, you don't make it. 5 more, you don't make it. Fat hot view, 2. Shoot.

Outside, SAM and DEMPSEY are examining the car.

SAM MASTERSON

How long will it take, pop?

DEMPSEY

Can't tell until we look her over. Come back tomorrow.

SAM MASTERSON

Open game?

DEMPSEY

Nope.

DICE GAMERS

Bet. Four. Right back, little Joe. A 1004. You got a bet? Come on, Harry. Make four. Seven, little Joe. Thanks. Shooting 20 and more. 10 ball, you don't make it than I do.

Back in the garage office:

SAM MASTERSON

What will it cost, pop?

DEMPSEY

Won't know until it's done.

SAM MASTERSON

Hey, now look, I want to know now.

DEMPSEY

Take it someplace else.

SAM MASTERSON

Welcome to Iverstown.

A radio broadcast begins.

RADIO ANNOUNCER

We interrupt this program of dinner music to bring you a special broadcast in the interest of the reelection of District Attorney Walter P. O'Neil.

SAM MASTERSON

Hey, no, leave that on, will you, sir.

RADIO ANNOUNCER

Ladies and gentlemen, it is with deep regret that we are forced to announce that Mr. O'Neil will not be able to address this citizen's forum tonight. Mr. O'Neil was suddenly taken ill. But we are fortunate to have the best-loved civic figure of Iverstown, the gracious Mrs. O'Neil, here in the studio tonight to speak for him.

MRS. O'NEIL

(on the radio)

Citizens of Iverstown. The issues in this election are simple.

DEMPSEY

That's enough of that malarkey.

He turns the radio off.

SAM MASTERSON

This Walter P. O'Neil, isn't he the kid that used to live on Sycamore Street? His father used to be a school-teacher.

DEMPSEY

Yeah, that's him. You know him?

SAM MASTERSON

Yeah. I used to; little scared kid on Sycamore Street. Now he's running for the district attorney. What's the odds?

DEMPSEY

On what?

SAM MASTERSON

The election.

DEMPSEY

No odds. No takers. This is a sure bet, mister. Going to be reelected, going to be governor, and I'm making book right now that someday he'll run for president. Yep. Going to be whatever his wife wants him to be.

SAM MASTERSON

Some gal. Who did he marry?

DEMPSEY

You from this town?

SAM MASTERSON

Used to be.

DEMPSEY

You ought to know her, then. Old lady Ivers' niece.

SAM MASTERSON

Martha Ivers?

DEMPSEY

Yep. Came into the whole works after the old lady died.

SAM MASTERSON

Well, what do you know? What do you know about that? Martha Ivers.

He goes over to a political poster that says, "WALTER O'NEIL for District Attorney." He looks up at a picture of the adult WALTER O'NEIL.

SAM MASTERSON

I don't know; you still look like a scared little kid to me.

SAM MASTERSON is now walking down a sidewalk, passing a storefront that says, "*Tailor.*" He passes the POLICEMAN.

SAM MASTERSON

Hello, Gallagher!

POLICEMAN

Hey, wait a minute. Do I know you?

SAM MASTERSON

Sure. I'm the guy who tossed a rock through that window once. You're the guy who chased me.

GALLAGHER

If I chased you, I'll bet I caught you.

SAM MASTERSON

Come to think of it, I believe you did.

As SAM MASTERSON continues to walk along, he sees a house with a sign saying, "Rooms for Young Women."

TONI MARACHEK is walking out the front door. She is smoking a cigarette and carrying a suitcase. She sits down on the stoop. She sees SAM MASTERSON and crosses her legs enticingly.

SAM MASTERSON

Hello?

TONI MARACHEK

Hello.

SAM MASTERSON

You live here?

TONI MARACHEK

Used to.

SAM MASTERSON

Who runs this place?

TONI MARACHEK

A lady by the name of Mrs. Burke. She's not home.

SAM MASTERSON

You waiting for her?

TONI MARACHEK

Just came back to get my things. I've been away for a while. I'm waiting for a taxi.

SAM MASTERSON

I used to live here in this house 17, 18 years ago. I was born here.

TONI MARACHEK

Don't kid me, you're older than that.

SAM MASTERSON

Well, I didn't move right after I was born.

SAM MASTERSON sits down next to her and lights a cigarette.

TONI MARACHEK

Got one to spare?

He gives her a cigarette.

TONI MARACHEK

Got some more matches?

SAM MASTERSON

Here it is.

He lights her cigarette.

TONI MARACHEK

Got the time?

SAM MASTERSON

It's a quarter after 11.

TONI MARACHEK

I hate that. Just dandy. And I've got an 11:30 bus to catch.

SAM MASTERSON

You can still make it.

TONI MARACHEK

If the taxi doesn't show up fast . . .

SAM MASTERSON

You know anybody who lives around here by the name of Masterson?

TONI MARACHEK

No.

SAM MASTERSON

Know anybody in town at all by that name?

TONI MARACHEK

No. I'm from Ridgeville. Is your name Masterson?

SAM MASTERSON

Yeah.

TONI MARACHEK

You mean you're just getting home after 18 years?

SAM MASTERSON

Well, 17 or 18.

TONI MARACHEK

You're just getting around to look up your people?

SAM MASTERSON

Well, not exactly. I just happened to be driving through on my way west and more or less curious, that's all. So good luck.

TONI MARACHEK

What you going to do?

SAM MASTERSON

What do you mean?

TONI MARACHEK

I mean about your people?

SAM MASTERSON

Well, I don't know. Maybe nothing. Maybe tomorrow I'll go down to the courthouse and look up the deaths in the last 18 years.

TONI MARACHEK

Can you do that?

SAM MASTERSON

Yeah, I think so. Good night.

He goes off. A taxi pulls up. TONI leans in and says to the driver:

TONI MARACHEK

The bus terminal. Please hurry. I've got an 11:30 bus to catch.

The taxi drives past and pulls up in front of SAM.

TONI MARACHEK

I thought it was you, Mr. Masterson.

SAM MASTERSON

I'm glad to see you again. I gave you my last match.

TONI MARACHEK

Want a lift to anyplace on the way to the bus station?

SAM MASTERSON

You talked me into it. You got my matches.

He gets into the taxi.

SAM MASTERSON

Got a name?

TONI MARACHEK

"Toni." Antonia. Antonia Marachek. Ain't that a dilly, Mr. Masterson?

SAM MASTERSON

Sam.

TONI MARACHEK

Please hurry.

The cab pulls up to a railroad crossing. The gate is down and a train is passing through.

TAXI DRIVER

The depot's just across the tracks. You still got four minutes. You would've made it if you didn't stop to pick up your gent.

SAM MASTERSON

You might be able to chase it.

TONI MARACHEK

I can get a bus back to Ridgeville tomorrow. Maybe I won't get a bus back to Ridgeville. Maybe I'll go someplace else. Maybe in another direction. Chicago, further west maybe. Have you ever been out west before?

SAM MASTERSON

Yeah.

TONI MARACHEK

I've never. Maybe I will. What's it like?

SAM MASTERSON

Big.

At the Iverstown bus terminal, a bus marked "Iverstown" pulls up. Another bus is just pulling out. The taxi pulls up, and SAM and TONI get out. TONI has missed her bus.

SAM MASTERSON

You want to go back?

TONI MARACHEK
I can't go back there. I have to go someplace else. Do you drink, Sam?

SAM MASTERSON
Yes, I drink.

TONI MARACHEK
I'll buy you one.

SAM MASTERSON
Okay.

A PORTER comes up to them.

PORTER
Too bad. Do you want me to check your bag in the station here?

TONI MARACHEK
I don't know. I guess I wanted a hotel.

SAM MASTERSON
You want me to take you there?

TONI MARACHEK
Do you happen to be at the Gable Hotel?

SAM MASTERSON
Yeah.

TONI MARACHEK
Can I go there?

SAM MASTERSON
It's a public place. Yeah. Tell the clerk that Sam Masterson wants a room for a young lady. She'll register when she gets there.

PORTER
Yes sir.

MASTERSON gives the PORTER a coin.

PORTER
Thanks!

MASTERSON and TONI walk into a bar past a neon sign that says, "*Cocktails.*"

SAM MASTERSON
Classy. Blue lights, music, everything.

TONI MARACHEK
A cafe.

SAM MASTERSON

When I lived in this town, there were nothing but saloons. My father used to live in them.

TONI MARACHEK

Mine too.

SAM MASTERSON

We're related.

They sit down at a table. A WAITER comes up to them.

TONI MARACHEK

I'll have the same thing you have, if you don't mind?

SAM MASTERSON

Scotch. I take a plain water chaser with that if the Scotch isn't so good.

WAITER

Two water chasers.

TONI MARACHEK

Did you drive far?

SAM MASTERSON

About 600 miles since this morning.

TONI MARACHEK

You aren't driving anything tonight?

SAM MASTERSON

No, my Stanley Steamer's in the garage having her face lifted. ***(to the waiter)*** **Better bring us a couple more before curfew.**

TONI MARACHEK

Oh, that's fine.

WAITER

That'll be $2.

SAM MASTERSON

On me.

TONI MARACHEK

Oh, thanks. Maybe you'd like to drink to finding your people.

SAM MASTERSON

Oh, my mother wouldn't approve of that.

TONI MARACHEK

How would you know after all this time?

SAM MASTERSON

After all this time, you probably wouldn't care one way or the other.

TONI MARACHEK

You talk awful cold-blooded about them, don't you?

SAM MASTERSON

That's life.

TONI MARACHEK

Is it a big family?

SAM MASTERSON

No, it wasn't. Besides me, they're just the usual two people necessary to increase the population. Mother left when I was a baby, and my father probably drank himself to death by now.

TONI MARACHEK

Another man I know talks cold like that's my dad. He's the most cold-blooded man in Ridgeville. Once he kicked me. Gee, it made me sick.

SAM MASTERSON

I can guess why you didn't break your neck to catch that bus back to Ridgeville tonight.

TONI MARACHEK

I probably would've got on and got off before it started up. I would've got the jitters the minute I got on. Anyway, it's gone now for tonight, anyhow; there won't be another one until tomorrow night. And now I know for sure I'm not going to make that one either. Not the one to Ridgeville at least. But I'm so glad you came to have a drink with me tonight. I was so lonesome, I like to have died. Have you ever been that lonesome?

SAM MASTERSON

How lonesome is that?

TONI MARACHEK

About as much as you can hold without busting open. Want to know how I got that way?

The bar's lights start to flash.

SAM MASTERSON

Curfew. Shall we go home?

TONI MARACHEK

The reason I picked the hotel, your hotel, is really very . . .

SAM MASTERSON

You read the hotel advertising on that, when you had it.

TONI MARACHEK

You're smart. Maybe you think I've been trying too hard to get acquainted.

SAM MASTERSON

Maybe you have.

TONI MARACHEK

Maybe you think that's wrong.

SAM MASTERSON

Maybe it's too soon to tell.

TONI MARACHEK

I wonder what you're thinking.

SAM MASTERSON

I don't think you'll take up too much room in my Stanley Steamer.

TONI MARACHEK

Maybe you're all right.

SAM MASTERSON

You think you can hold that thought all the way to the coast?

They walk out of the bar. It is raining.

SAM MASTERSON

You'd better wait here for a minute.

They run under the awning of a furniture shop. The window displays a poster saying, "Re-elect WALTER O'NEIL."

SAM MASTERSON

I want to ask you something. Does that guy look like a scared little boy to you?

TONI MARACHEK

He looks like he's going to cry any minute. Let's get away from him.

The scene changes to the exterior of a stately house. A large, expensive car pulls up, and MARTHA gets out. A BUTLER comes to the door.

MRS. O'NEIL

Is Mr. O'Neil in?

BUTLER

No, madam. Not to my knowledge.

MARTHA goes in and climbs up a long flight of stairs. She goes into her bedroom. It is dark. She turns the light on. WALTER is asleep in bed, with his clothes on.

MARTHA O'NEIL

Walter?

WALTER O'NEIL

Hello?

He sits up. She does not reply.

WALTER O'NEIL

No words?

She lights a cigarette.

WALTER O'NEIL

Can I have a cigarette?

She hands him the cigarette that she has just lit.

WALTER O'NEIL

(taking the cigarette) My lady's lips.

MARTHA O'NEIL

I'll ring for some coffee for you.

WALTER O'NEIL

No, thank you. I'll have another drink.

MARTHA O'NEIL

Walter!

WALTER O'NEIL

If there's to be a discussion, I'll need another drink. Otherwise, I shall neither adhere nor be coherent when and if I reply to whatever it is you're about to say.

MARTHA O'NEIL

Did you forget that you were supposed to speak tonight?

WALTER O'NEIL

I didn't forget, I . . . It's nice, your room, I mean. It's been a long time since I've been here.

MARTHA O'NEIL

Where were you?

WALTER O'NEIL

Getting drunk.

MARTHA O'NEIL

Where?

WALTER O'NEIL

I'm still the people's choice. I did not make a public display of myself anywhere.

MARTHA O'NEIL

You realize, of course, that you will one day inevitably.

WALTER O'NEIL

Inevitably.

MARTHA O'NEIL

It's your career. Not mine.

WALTER O'NEIL

What's mine is yours.

MARTHA O'NEIL

Don't you think I'm entitled to an explanation?

WALTER O'NEIL

What do you want me to say?

MARTHA O'NEIL

I don't want to put words in your mouth.

WALTER O'NEIL

I'd prefer that you would.

MARTHA O'NEIL

All right. When did you get drunk? Where did you get drunk? Why did you get drunk?

WALTER O'NEIL

Don't stand over me like that. I'm a sentimental man, Martha. I started to get dressed, and then I realized it was the fourth anniversary of my father's death. I thought it'd be nice if I went to the cemetery and laid a wreath of flowers on his grave. However, I never got there. Sentiment overwhelmed me. I stopped off to have a drink to his sainted memory. As I drank, I thought to myself, it's such a pity that my father isn't alive, to be able to see for himself all his dreams come true. The dreams he worked so hard for. His son, a famous man, married to a beautiful and wealthy woman.

MARTHA O'NEIL
All right. Now tell me why you got drunk.

WALTER O'NEIL
Because I couldn't get up and speak before people.

MARTHA O'NEIL
Walter, listen to me, what's done is done.

WALTER O'NEIL
The deed's done, not the thought.

MARTHA O'NEIL
You've got a life to live.

WALTER O'NEIL
I don't know. I'm not sure.

MARTHA O'NEIL
A brilliant career.

WALTER O'NEIL
My father always said . . .

MARTHA O'NEIL
Your father was right.

WALTER O'NEIL
He was never right about anything. From the day he walked in and found your aunt on the floor.

MARTHA O'NEIL
I told you I never want that mentioned.

WALTER O'NEIL
The day he sat beside you in the courtroom as the public prosecutor demanded that the state take the life of a man for the brutal murder of Mrs. Ivers. My father said nothing. I looked at him, but he said nothing.

MARTHA O'NEIL
Your father was a realistic man.

WALTER O'NEIL

My father, may he rest in peace, was a greedy man.

MARTHA O'NEIL

The man they executed was a criminal. If he hadn't hanged for that, he would've hanged for something else.

WALTER O'NEIL

The man was a man. Justice is justice. That's the way it is. I can't get up and speak before people. The words stick in my throat. I had rather get drunk. I do get drunk. I did get drunk.

MARTHA O'NEIL

Walter, dear, listen to me. If you carry a thing in your mind, it makes you sick. I want you well. Tomorrow...

WALTER O'NEIL

It'll be like today.

MARTHA O'NEIL

You will leave on a trip for your health for a few weeks.

WALTER O'NEIL

Will you go with me?

MARTHA O'NEIL

No. I'll stay here.

WALTER O'NEIL

And I'll stay here too.

MARTHA O'NEIL

What do you want to do, give everything up? Is that what you want to do?

WALTER O'NEIL

You wouldn't let me do that, would you, Martha?

MARTHA O'NEIL

Do you want to?

WALTER O'NEIL

I don't know, Martha. I ask myself that question all the time. If my father were alive, I could ask him. Only I know what his answer would be. He'd say to me, keep what you have, and make her live up to it. Make her live up to her bargain. That's what he'd say.

MARTHA O'NEIL

I am living up to it, Walter.

He kisses her passionately. He picks up a liquor bottle on a table.

WALTER O'NEIL

There's another drink left, might as well have it.

He pours himself a drink.

WALTER O'NEIL

The bottle's empty now. Good night, Martha. Tell me, Martha, what should I do about my love? You tell me, Martha, why I don't abandon all this. Why don't I just throw it back in your face?

MARTHA O'NEIL

You tell me, Walter.

He leaves the room dejectedly.

SAM and TONI go up to the desk at the Gable Hotel. The CLERK is not in sight.

SAM MASTERSON

Now this is it. Not good, not bad.

HOTEL CLERK'S VOICE

With bath?

SAM MASTERSON

With bath, and come out, come out, wherever you are.

The HOTEL CLERK comes out.

HOTEL CLERK

With bath, hey. There are half as many beds as there are rooms. Half the rooms has baths and half hasn't. That's one way of looking at it. Another is for each two rooms, one has a bath in the middle and the other hasn't, or you might say there's a half a bath to each of two rooms.

SAM MASTERSON

How is that, again?

HOTEL CLERK

Now, there are half as many beds as there is rooms. And if the two . . .

SAM MASTERSON

Sorry.

HOTEL CLERK

I've already sent the boy with those bags up to your room, Mr. Masterson.

SAM MASTERSON

Oh, well, they belong to Miss Marachek here. They came in my name because she wasn't registered yet.

TONI MARACHEK

I missed my bus to Ridgeville.

HOTEL CLERK

Oh, that's too bad. The boy went off at 12. You'll have to manage yourselves. I can't leave the board.

SAM MASTERSON

Thanks.

The CLERK hands a key to SAM MASTERSON.

HOTEL CLERK

Good night. Sweet dreams.

SAM MASTERSON

Good night, cupid.

SAM and TONI go off. The CLERK looks at his hand. He hasn't gotten a tip.

SAM and TONI are in the hotel corridor.

SAM MASTERSON

25, your room number's 25. I'm 23. Makes us neighbors.

In the hotel room, the doors between their rooms through the bathroom are open. SAM goes into TONI's room and sets down her bags as she takes off her coat.

SAM MASTERSON

Why did you buy a ticket to Ridgeville if you didn't want to go back home?

TONI MARACHEK

I didn't. I didn't buy the ticket. I got it, but I didn't buy it.

SAM goes back toward his own room. TONI starts to sob.

SAM MASTERSON

You all right?

TONI MARACHEK

I'm a little cold, maybe.

SAM MASTERSON

You better get out of these wet clothes. I've started your bath for you. Hurry up now, I'm next.

SAM goes back into his room and closes the door.

TONI MARACHEK

Thanks.

We see TONI remove her dress. She is in her slip and has a huge smile on her face. We see her in the shower, with the same smile.

Then the scene changes to show TONI in her bathrobe after her shower. She is hanging up her dress. Then she knocks on SAM's door. He is lying fully dressed on his bed.

SAM MASTERSON

Okay?

TONI enters SAM's room.

TONI MARACHEK

I will loan you a book for a couple of cigarettes, if you don't mind what kind of a book it is.

SAM gets up and approaches TONI.

TONI MARACHEK

That pine soap makes you tingle all over.

SAM MASTERSON

That's something very personal about soap. It's almost as personal as a toothbrush.

TONI MARACHEK

I won't use your toothbrush.

SAM MASTERSON

Where's your book now?

TONI MARACHEK

You don't care what kind of a book it is?

SAM MASTERSON

Suspense is killing me.

TONI MARACHEK

It isn't my book. Somebody here before forgot and left it.

TONI holds up a Gideon Bible.

TONI MARACHEK

I warned you.

SAM MASTERSON

There's one in every room of the hotel. One in practically every room of every hotel in the world. It tells all about it there in the first page or so.

TONI MARACHEK

Well, what do you know?

TONI sits down on the bed and opens the Bible. She is about to get up.

SAM MASTERSON

Oh, no, no, no, don't get up. I want to look at you a minute.

SAM sits down in an armchair and looks at her admiringly.

SAM

That's really a picture.

TONI beams appreciatively.

TONI MARACHEK

Throw me a match. So you're leaving tomorrow?

SAM MASTERSON

Yeah, we're leaving tomorrow. That is, if the car is fixed.

TONI MARACHEK

Sure. You won't mind me being a passenger?

SAM MASTERSON

No, no. Glad of the company.

TONI MARACHEK

Are you going to stay in the west?

SAM MASTERSON

Maybe, maybe not. You might get lonesome again.

TONI MARACHEK

I've been lonesome before. I was so lonesome tonight. I like to have died.

SAM MASTERSON

I know you mentioned that.

TONI MARACHEK

But I tried to tell you why.

SAM MASTERSON

Look, I'm going to take a shower.

TONI MARACHEK

I just got out of jail. I just got out tonight.

SAM MASTERSON

Like I said, we leave tomorrow.

He opens up the Bible and sets it down on the bed next to her.

SAM MASTERSON

I think you'd like that.

TONI picks up the Bible and starts to read. He goes in to take a shower.

Then we see him come out after the shower, in his bathrobe. He sees TONI asleep on his bed. He looks at her tenderly, takes the Bible out from under her, and puts a cigarette in his mouth. Then he covers her with a blanket, takes a bottle of liquor, and goes into the other room.

The next morning, we see a newspaper shoved under SAM's hotel door. It has a huge headline, partly obscured by a sticker for the Gable Hotel, so that we read, *"DISTRICT ATTORNEY PROMISES UP VICE IN IVERSTOWN ON REELECTION."*

Outside, we hear a DETECTIVE's voice:

DETECTIVE

Open up, sonny.

The key clicks in the lock and the door opens. A BELLHOP lets in two DETECTIVES.

We see two DETECTIVES in TONI's room. She is not there. It is dark. They go into the room where TONI fell asleep, but she is not there. One DETECTIVE picks up a piece of paper on the bureau and says to the other:

DETECTIVE

Try that door.

They go through the bathroom into Sam's room. The room is dark. SAM is sleeping. One DETECTIVE rolls up the shade, making a loud noise and waking up SAM MASTERSON, who jumps up, startled.

DETECTIVE #2

Good morning, Mr. Masterson.

SAM MASTERSON

You don't have to show me who you are. I can tell by the smell.

DETECTIVE #2

My nose isn't that big. I want to see. The chief sent us up here to ask you a couple of questions.

One of the DETECTIVES starts going through SAM's wallet.

DETECTIVE #3

Sergeant Masterson.

SAM MASTERSON

The suspense is killing me. What do you want to know?

DETECTIVE #3

You've been around. Look at that. Africa, Anzio, and Normandy. Why don't you wear that button in your coat?

SAM MASTERSON

The same reason you don't wear your badge. I like it incognito. Now what else do you want to know?

DETECTIVE #2

What we wanted to know, this layout told us. There ain't nothing you can add to it.

DETECTIVE #2 shows the note he found in the other room to SAM. The note says, ***"Dear Sam, Gone to the bus station to cash in my ticket to Ridgeville — Back soon, Toni."***

SAM MASTERSON

She didn't get in an accident, did she?

DETECTIVE #2

She's in the can for a nice long stretch.

SAM MASTERSON

What's the charge?

DETECTIVE #2

Violation of probation.

SAM MASTERSON

Probation for what?

DETECTIVE #2

Theft. Terms of her probation when she was released yesterday was that she returned to her home in Ridgeville. An hour ago, we picked her up at the depot when she tried to cash the ticket.

SAM MASTERSON

Well, maybe she wanted to go by train. Maybe she wanted to walk. There's no law that says she . . .

DETECTIVE #2

That's not the reason she gave, wise guy.

SAM MASTERSON

No?

DETECTIVE #2

No. The reason she gave was that she'd got a job, said you were her employer.

SAM MASTERSON

Well, what's wrong with that?

DETECTIVE #2

Nothing, if you can prove it. But take a tip from me, bud. Don't try it. Jake and me don't like to waste our time testifying in court, but we will. So long

DETECTIVE #2 picks up TONI's suitcase, and the two make to leave.

DETECTIVE #2

Exhibit A, bud, in case you get stubborn.

SAM MASTERSON

Now wait a minute, copper. All right, leave her things alone.

DETECTIVE #2

Do you want to come along, soldier?

The two DETECTIVES look at each other and leave.

SAM picks up the newspaper that had been shoved under the door. He looks at a picture captioned, "Walter P. O'Neil," above a headline that says, "Prosecutor Promises Iverstown Will Be Safe and Clean City."

SAM MASTERSON

A little scared boy.

SAM flings the paper aside.

SAM MASTERSON

You're just about to do your old pal a great big favor.

SAM MASTERSON enters the law offices of WALTER O'NEIL. He removes his hat for BOBBI ST. JOHN, the secretary who is typing at the desk.

SAM MASTERSON

How do you like the way the election's going this beautiful morning?

BOBBI ST. JOHN

The election's going good every morning.

SAM MASTERSON

Look, honey. Miss . . .

BOBBI ST. JOHN

St. John.

SAM MASTERSON

St. John.

BOBBI ST. JOHN

Bobbi.

SAM MASTERSON

Better still.

BOBBI ST. JOHN

What can I do for you?

SAM MASTERSON

In?

BOBBI ST. JOHN

In, but not yet ready to face the world. Won't you sit down?

SAM MASTERSON

Look honey, I'm in kind of a hurry here. Would you take a note in for me?

BOBBI ST. JOHN

When he buzzes.

She hands him a pencil.

BOBBI ST. JOHN

Here.

Inside WALTER's office, WALTER calls BOBBI on the intercom.

WALTER O'NEIL

I'll take calls now.

He goes to the liquor cabinet, pours himself a quick drink, and puts a breath mint in his mouth.

WALTER O'NEIL

Come in.

BOBBI comes in.

BOBBI ST. JOHN

There's a gentleman to see you. He says it's very important.

BOBBI hands WALTER a note. He glances over it.

WALTER O'NEIL

Tell him I don't want to . . . wait a minute. Never mind. I'll tell him myself.

WALTER braces himself, grins, and goes into the front office, where SAM is waiting.

WALTER O'NEIL

Sammy! Sammy Masterson!

SAM MASTERSON

Little Walter O'Neil.

WALTER O'NEIL

We were kids together, Miss St. John. I wouldn't have known you, Sam.

SAM MASTERSON

Oh, I wouldn't have known you either, Walter. Only I saw your picture.

WALTER O'NEIL

My picture. Oh, yes, yes, of course. ***(turns to BOBBI)***

I don't want to be disturbed unless it's very important.

BOBBI ST. JOHN

Yes. Mr. O'Neil.

WALTER and SAM go into WALTER's office.

WALTER O'NEIL

How long has it been?

SAM MASTERSON

Oh, 17, 18 years. Something like that.

WALTER O'NEIL

That long.

SAM MASTERSON

We were just kids. You remember, the three of us?

WALTER O'NEIL

Yeah, the three of us.

WALTER lights SAM's cigarette.

SAM MASTERSON

Thanks. What's she like, Walter?

WALTER O'NEIL

Beautiful. I married her.

SAM MASTERSON

I know, I know. You've done all right.

WALTER O'NEIL

I guess so. And you? What have you done?

SAM MASTERSON

Oh, knocked around. Seen a lot, I guess. You know, had some fun, maybe.

WALTER O'NEIL

What have you done mostly?

SAM MASTERSON

Lately or mostly?

WALTER O'NEIL

Mostly.

SAM MASTERSON

Gamble.

WALTER O'NEIL

You mean, gamble?

SAM MASTERSON

Sure, sure. That's my business.

WALTER O'NEIL

Perhaps this is where I should remark that all life is a gamble.

SAM MASTERSON

You don't need to bother. I know it. Some win, some don't.

WALTER O'NEIL

You needn't have made that point. Sorry, Sam. This has been a stuffy conversation. Oh, would you like a drink?

SAM MASTERSON

Isn't it a little early in the morning? I haven't even stopped for breakfast yet.

WALTER O'NEIL

The occasion.

SAM MASTERSON

You talked me into it. Fine, fine.

WALTER pours SAM a drink.

WALTER O'NEIL

Nice of you to look me up, Sam.

SAM MASTERSON

Well, I wouldn't have bothered you Walter, only I met a girl, and you can help.

WALTER O'NEIL

You don't look like you need help with any girl.

SAM MASTERSON

Well, this trip out, I do. This kid's in jail.

WALTER O'NEIL

What's the charge?

SAM MASTERSON

Violation of probation; name is Toni Marachek.

WALTER O'NEIL

That's not easy to square, Sam.

SAM MASTERSON

Oh, you can do it, and you will, for old time's sake.

SAM and WALTER raise their glasses.

WALTER O'NEIL

For old time's sake.

WALTER knocks back his whole drink at once.

WALTER O'NEIL

Thanks.

The intercom buzzes.

WALTER O'NEIL

Excuse me.

BOBBI ST. JOHN'S VOICE
(on the intercom)
Mrs. O'Neil is here to see you.

WALTER O'NEIL
Please have her wait. She usually drops in on her way downtown.

SAM MASTERSON
Oh, I'd like to see her.

WALTER O'NEIL
(to the intercom) Have Mrs. O'Neil come in.

BOBBI ST. JOHN
Yes, sir.

MARTHA enters, sees SAM, and then halts.

MARTHA O'NEIL
Oh, I'm sorry. I didn't know you were busy. I'll wait.

SAM MASTERSON
Hello?

MARTHA O'NEIL
Hello.

SAM MASTERSON
My name is Masterson, Sam Masterson.

MARTHA O'NEIL
I'm sorry . . . Sammy Masterson!

MARTHA runs and gives SAM a hug.

MARTHA O'NEIL
Oh, hello!

SAM MASTERSON
Well, I'll do that again. Hello!

They hug again.

MARTHA O'NEIL
You should have called me.

SAM MASTERSON
I just came in.

MARTHA O'NEIL
Well, you've grown to be a big boy, Sam.

SAM MASTERSON
Well, I always was big for my age. You remember?

MARTHA O'NEIL
Yes, I remember.

SAM MASTERSON
Anything else you remember?

MARTHA O'NEIL
Oh, well, there are, there are lots of things.

SAM MASTERSON
I never figured that a skinny little mutt would grow up so beautiful.

WALTER O'NEIL
I thank you for my wife.

SAM MASTERSON
It sounds funny.

WALTER O'NEIL
What does?

SAM MASTERSON
Well, your saying, "My wife."

WALTER O'NEIL
Does it?

SAM MASTERSON
Oh, so, don't get so, Walter. I mean, well, I've always thought of Martha as . . . Well, you know how it is. You keep something in your mind since the time you're a kid.

MARTHA O'NEIL
How long are you staying, Sam?

SAM MASTERSON
That all depends on our district attorney.

MARTHA O'NEIL
Oh.

SAM MASTERSON
Yeah. I may have to pull out in a couple of hours.

MARTHA O'NEIL
Oh, that's too bad.

SAM MASTERSON

That's the way things are.

The intercom rings again.

WALTER O'NEIL

(to the intercom)

I don't want to be disturbed.

SAM MASTERSON

That's all right, Walter. You're a busy man, so I'll blow, and thanks. Thanks for everything. So long, Martha. Aren't you glad now you missed that circus train?

MARTHA IVERS

I don't know.

WALTER O'NEIL

Where can I reach you, Sam?

SAM MASTERSON

Oh, the Gable Hotel. And you will do that for me, won't you, Walter?

WALTER O'NEIL

I'll try my best.

SAM MASTERSON

You do that. And here's hoping you win that election.

WALTER O'NEIL

Thanks. I will.

SAM MASTERSON

What? Sure thing?

WALTER O'NEIL

Ask Martha.

MARTHA IVERS

Sure, sure thing.

SAM MASTERSON

What odds are you giving it?

MARTHA IVERS

Sure thing is never a gamble.

SAM MASTERSON

No. What odds will you give that that's a fact?

SAM leaves and closes the office door behind him.

WALTER O'NEIL

Breezy character, Sam.

MARTHA IVERS

Thank you.

WALTER O'NEIL

Very sure of himself.

MARTHA IVERS

He always was.

WALTER O'NEIL

This is the first time I've ever seen you off balance.

MARTHA IVERS

I wasn't aware of it.

WALTER O'NEIL

I was.

MARTHA IVERS

It came as a shock.

WALTER O'NEIL

Yes, it did to me too. "Sam will never tell," I'll never forget you saying that.

MARTHA IVERS

What makes you think he will?

WALTER O'NEIL

What makes you think he won't?

MARTHA IVERS

How long has he been here?

WALTER O'NEIL

He came in last night.

MARTHA IVERS

Did he tell you much about himself? Where he has been, what he's been doing?

WALTER O'NEIL

I thought you'd ask what he wanted.

MARTHA IVERS

What does he want?

WALTER O'NEIL

He's playing it smart.

MARTHA IVERS

Sam was always a smart boy.

WALTER O'NEIL

All he wanted was for me to get his girl out of jail.

MARTHA IVERS

His girl?

WALTER O'NEIL

That's what he said he wanted.

MARTHA IVERS

What do you think he wants?

WALTER O'NEIL

What he can get. He's a gambler, a sharp shooter, an angle boy. They come through my office by the hundreds. Couldn't you see blackmail in his eyes?

MARTHA IVERS

I haven't your experience with criminals.

WALTER O'NEIL

You will, when Sammy starts to shake you down.

MARTHA IVERS

Release the girl; maybe he'll just take off and leave.

WALTER O'NEIL

Leave? Do you think he'll leave a touch worth millions?

MARTHA IVERS

There's only one way you'll find out. Release the girl. (to the intercom) Goodbye, Miss St. John.

MARTHA leaves. WALTER goes to the intercom.

BOBBI ST. JOHN'S VOICE

(on the intercom)

Yes, Mr. O'Neil.

WALTER O'NEIL

I want a routine check on a Samuel Masterson, nonresident, registered Gable Hotel. Miss St. John, close the door!

BOBBI comes into WALTER's office and closes the door.

WALTER O'NEIL

(to BOBBI*)*

Stay here, please.

(into the phone)

I want a routine check of all garages. One of them has his car. Stay here, please. I want to check up on all local banks. Get that private detective McCarthy, and tell him to come right over.

The scene changes to the O'NEILS' house. MARTHA comes down to the stairs to find SAM in the library, perusing a book.

SAM MASTERSON

I thought I might improve my mind while I waited.

MARTHA looks at the book.

MARTHA IVERS

Boswell's Life of Johnson? Surely you didn't expect to wait that long.

SAM MASTERSON

I was just going to look at the pictures. I found your message when I got back to the hotel.

MARTHA IVERS

I asked you to phone.

SAM MASTERSON

I figured you wouldn't mind if I came in person.

MARTHA IVERS

I figured you would.

SAM MASTERSON

Why?

MARTHA IVERS

You impressed me this morning as a man who would bet on anything,

SAM MASTERSON

Almost anything, depending on the odds.

MARTHA IVERS

I bet you'd like to hear the story of my life.

SAM MASTERSON

What do you bet?

MARTHA IVERS

My story against yours?

SAM MASTERSON

You got a bet.

MARTHA IVERS

Well, let's see. You left here September 27, 1928. We'll start from there.

SAM MASTERSON

Exact date. How come that's so clear in your mind?

MARTHA IVERS

Why shouldn't it be?

SAM looks appreciatively around the room.

SAM MASTERSON

You know, I used to think this was the swellest spot in the world, but you've really made it just that.

MARTHA IVERS

It used to be so dark and ugly when she . . . I hate it. Come on, I'll show you what I've done with the rest of the house.

They get up and go to the library door.

SAM MASTERSON

Okay, fine. I haven't been on a rubberneck tour in years.

MARTHA IVERS

Soon after my aunt died, the executors of the estate wanted to close the house and send me to school, but Mr. O'Neil . . .

SAM MASTERSON

Mister! You're kind of formal about your husband, aren't you?

MARTHA IVERS

No. I was speaking about his father. Mr. O'Neil was my tutor. You remember him?

SAM MASTERSON

Oh, yeah.

MARTHA IVERS

After my aunt died, he and Walter lived here.

SAM MASTERSON

Hmm. That was cozy.

They walk down a corridor of the house.

MARTHA IVERS

This is Walter's room.

They go in.

SAM MASTERSON

Rich. Very rich. Well, you lived here all the time then, huh?

MARTHA IVERS

Except for the few years I went to college. Mr. O'Neil, Walter's father, thought it would be good for me to get away for a while.

SAM MASTERSON

Mr. O'Neil, Walter's father, he sort of took care of everything, didn't he?

MARTHA IVERS

Yes. Yes. He took care of everything.

SAM MASTERSON

You didn't like that?

MARTHA IVERS

Let's talk about something else.

SAM MASTERSON

What do you want to talk about?

MARTHA IVERS

Pick a subject.

They go into the dining room.

MARTHA IVERS

This is the dining room.

SAM MASTERSON

Isn't it kind of crowded? All right, I pick Walter as my subject. When did you marry him?

MARTHA IVERS

When or why?

SAM MASTERSON

I asked when.

MARTHA IVERS

When I finished school.

SAM MASTERSON

All right, now, why did you marry him?

MARTHA IVERS

Pick another subject.

SAM MASTERSON

It's your turn.

MARTHA IVERS

You.

SAM MASTERSON

An open book. I went out of this town with a circus. The one you were supposed to go with. Made friends with the animals and lived happily ever after, almost.

MARTHA IVERS

Almost?

SAM MASTERSON

I got ambitious in that tour, but good. It got so I wasn't satisfied just being friendly with the animals, I got so I wanted to own the animals. So I bought some animals. Well, my lion got the mange and gave it to the monkeys. The animals became a responsibility and a liability. I lost all my hard-earned cash and ran like a thief out of there with a great yen to become friendly with people. Now on that, I had some success. Me being a gambler and people being what they are. Well, that brings us up to my 21st year, when I became a man, officially.

MARTHA IVERS

How did it feel to become a man officially?

SAM MASTERSON

I felt I'd been there before. How did you feel about becoming a woman, officially?

MARTHA IVERS

I felt I'd been there too.

They go into MARTHA's old room.

SAM MASTERSON

Why, this is the room that you . . .

MARTHA IVERS

Do you remember, Sam?

SAM MASTERSON

Do I?

MARTHA IVERS

It's the only room I didn't change.

SAM MASTERSON

It seems that only yesterday I came through that window. We were going to run away together that night.

MARTHA IVERS

You do remember?

SAM MASTERSON

Yeah. And it was Walter who let me in.

MARTHA IVERS

I come here often, Sam.

SAM sits down at the window seat and picks up a doll.

SAM MASTERSON

Little girls grow up. They never get through playing with dolls.

MARTHA IVERS

There was a storm that night, thunder and lightning. I was afraid of the thunder.

SAM MASTERSON

Why, in the freight car that night, you told me you weren't.

MARTHA IVERS

I didn't want you to know. I wanted to be like you, never afraid of anything. You remember that too, don't you, Sam?

SAM MASTERSON

Things come back to you.

MARTHA IVERS

Don't say it like that, Sam, not to make me feel good, but because it's true.

SAM MASTERSON

All right, it's true. We were just a couple of kids.

MARTHA IVERS

We are not kids now.

SAM MASTERSON

No, Martha. We're not kids. No time for dreams.

MARTHA IVERS

Only one dream, Sam. And it came true. You're here.

SAM MASTERSON

So is Walter.

MARTHA IVERS

About Walter and myself . . .

SAM MASTERSON

Don't tell me.

MARTHA IVERS

I want you to understand.

SAM MASTERSON

I understand, Martha. I understood when I saw both of you together in the office. I watched the way he looked at you.

MARTHA IVERS

Sam, if you stay in Iverstown . . .

SAM MASTERSON

Well, I'm not staying in Iverstown.

MARTHA IVERS

I'm sorry, sorry that you ever left here.

MARTHA puts her arms around SAM'S neck.

MARTHA IVERS

Sam, for old time's sake?

SAM MASTERSON

Yeah. Sure. For old time's sake.

They kiss. Then SAM draws away slowly and goes to the door.

SAM MASTERSON

Bye. Martha.

The scene moves to DEMPSEY's garage. DEMPSEY goes into the garage office. The DETECTIVE, MCCARTHY, follows him. The phone rings. DEMPSEY answers.

MR. DEMPSEY

Dempsey's garage. Oh yes, Mrs. O'Neil.

DETECTIVE MCCARTHY

Mrs. Walter O'Neil?

MR. DEMPSEY

Yes, ma'am. Well, it was a rush job anyway, and I'm rushed enough as it is. Don't mention it. Glad to be of service, Mrs. O'Neil.

DEMPSEY hangs up the phone and addresses DETECTIVE MCCARTHY:

DEMPSEY

You can add this to your report. Ms. O'Neil don't like this guy to go—not yet.

DETECTIVE MCCARTHY

All right, Dempsey. Thanks.

We now go back to WALTER's office. DETECTIVE MCCARTHY enters as WALTER pours himself a drink.

WALTER O'NEIL

Drink?

MCCARTHY

Thanks.

WALTER gives him the drink, pours himself another, and drinks it down in one gulp.

DETECTIVE MCCARTHY

There's not much to report on him locally. The out of town reports are still coming in. You'll have a complete file on him in a couple of hours.

WALTER O'NEIL

What's he look like so far?

DETECTIVE MCCARTHY

Big-shot gambler, broke many times, but always turns up with a new bankroll. The police in every state have tried to find the source of his money, but no dice. Many arrests, no convictions; beat a murder rap in Frisco: self-defense; has a war record few can equal.

WALTER O'NEIL

The car in Dempsey's garage . . .

DETECTIVE MCCARTHY

The ownership certificate says he owns it.

WALTER O'NEIL

What's wrong with it?

DETECTIVE MCCARTHY

Smashed radiator.

WALTER O'NEIL

How long will it take to fix it? Well...?

DETECTIVE MCCARTHY hands WALTER a note.

WALTER O'NEIL

Who did Dempsey get this call from? Didn't you check that?

DETECTIVE MCCARTHY

Yes, I checked it.

WALTER O'NEIL

And who was it?

DETECTIVE MCCARTHY

Mrs. O'Neil.

WALTER O'NEIL

That's all.

MCCARTHY leaves. WALTER clicks on the intercom.

BOBBI ST. JOHN'S VOICE

Yes, Mr. O'Neil.

WALTER O'NEIL

Get me the county jail. I want the superintendent of the women's division.

The intercom clicks again, almost immediately.

WALTER O'NEIL

Yes?

BOBBI ST. JOHN

I have the county jail for you. Mr. O'Neil. Deputy Elizabeth Baker is on.

WALTER O'NEIL

Hello? That girl, the one I called you about before? Yes. Bring her out here at eight. I want to talk to her.

In front of the county jail entrance, it is night. SAM and another MAN are standing there.

MALE SPEAKER

You got the time, bud?

SAM MASTERSON
Yeah, it's five after eight.

MALE SPEAKER
Thanks. I'm expecting my friend out in a few minutes. Say, I ain't seen your face around here before?

SAM MASTERSON
No, I'm a stranger.

MALE SPEAKER
Then you ain't waiting for anybody, huh?

SAM MASTERSON
Oh, she's a stranger too.

MALE SPEAKER
Oh.

SAM MASTERSON
She was due out a couple of hours ago.

The two men continue their wait.

In WALTER's office, TONI is sitting in front of WALTER, who is at his desk. DETECTIVE MCCARTHY is looking on.

WALTER O'NEIL
You are in a lot of trouble, Miss Marachek. The law is very specific on violation of probation.

TONI MARACHEK
It's specific about everything.

WALTER O'NEIL
You're serving a five-year sentence.

TONI MARACHEK
So I was told once before.

WALTER O'NEIL
You lied when you were picked up. You told the police you were employed by Sam Masterson.

TONI MARACHEK
You'd think they would've believed me if I had told the truth?

WALTER O'NEIL
Did he cook up that story between you?

TONI MARACHEK

He had nothing to do with it.

WALTER O'NEIL

You're very fond of him, aren't you? You wouldn't want anything to happen to him. Does he feel the same about you? You wouldn't want to serve out that five-year sentence, would you?

TONI MARACHEK

What are you getting at?

WALTER O'NEIL

Remember, five years, and this time you'll have to serve every day of it. You don't have to.

TONI MARACHEK

All right. Get down to it. What do I have to do?

WALTER moves away from her. TONI stands up. DETECTIVE MCCARTHY approaches her to do the explaining.

In front of the county jail entrance, TONI is descending the steps.

SAM MASTERSON

Toni? Toni? Toni?

TONI almost walks past him. She stops and looks down on the ground.

TONI MARACHEK

Hello, Sam.

SAM MASTERSON

O'Neil phoned me, told me you'd be out at six.

TONI MARACHEK

O'Neil?

SAM MASTERSON

Yeah. Sure. The district attorney is an old friend of mine. I asked him to do me a favor and here you are. You're late, but free.

TONI MARACHEK

There was a mix-up; they lost some papers.

SAM MASTERSON

Oh, I got worried about you. What's the matter kid?

TONI walks along, staring uncomfortably at the ground.

SAM MASTERSON

Toni! Look at me!

TONI MARACHEK

I'd like a drink.

SAM MASTERSON

Ah, you're a cinch. I'll buy a dozen.

SAM waves to a taxi.

HEY, TAXI!

SAM MASTERSON

I'm going to toss you a real coming out party. Hey, taxi!

SAM and TONI enter an Italian restaurant. Then we see them seated. A WAITER sets a plate of spaghetti before TONI.

SAM MASTERSON

Spaghetti.

The WAITER sets another plate of spaghetti in front of SAM.

SAM MASTERSON

Hmm, that looks wonderful.

WAITER

I think you'll like it.

SAM digs into his dinner. TONI does not touch hers.

SAM MASTERSON

Go ahead, eat.

TONI MARACHEK

Guess I'm not hungry. My stomach's in a knot.

SAM passes TONI her glass of wine.

SAM MASTERSON

Here, this ought to help.

TONI MARACHEK

I'd have died if I had to stay on in jail.

SAM MASTERSON

Forget it; now you're out.

TONI MARACHEK

If you'd ever been in, you'd know what I mean.

SAM MASTERSON

I know what you mean.

TONI MARACHEK

A couple of times last night I tried to tell you why I did time; you wouldn't listen.

SAM MASTERSON

I don't want to now.

TONI MARACHEK

Oh, now you've got to, please?

SAM MASTERSON

All right, if it will make you feel any better.

TONI MARACHEK

I want to be sure you understand. One to five, they gave me; one to five years, that is.

SAM MASTERSON

That's a long jolt.

TONI MARACHEK

It's forever. I did three months before I came to trial.

SAM MASTERSON

It can happen to the best of people.

TONI MARACHEK

I'm not the best of people. I'm just Toni Marachek. "Where'd you get the fur coat, Toni?" the judge asked me. "I met a guy," I told him. "He said he was in love with me. He gave me the coat." "A likely story," he said. I said, "But it's true, every word of it. I tried to pawn it because I needed the money." "Where is the man?" he asked. "I don't know." I said. "He took a powder. He blew, he flew to the moon." "You don't fly, Toni," the judge says. The charge is theft; you do one to five."

SAM MASTERSON

Well, how come they gave you probation?

TONI MARACHEK

First offense. You know what probation is?

SAM MASTERSON

Yeah, sure. A knife sticking in your back.

TONI looks behind her uneasily.

SAM MASTERSON

Still looking out for the cops? Relax. Now you're free.

TONI MARACHEK

I don't feel so good.

SAM MASTERSON

You want me to take you back to the hotel?

TONI MARACHEK

Oh no, no. Please let me sit here a while.

SAM MASTERSON

Yeah.

JOE, a disreputable-looking man in a suit and smoking a cigarette, approaches their table.

JOE

(*to* TONI)

Get your coat on.

SAM MASTERSON

What's the gag?

JOE

Get your coat.

TONI MARACHEK

All right, Joe.

JOE

I was up to your hotel. Nice layout you got there. Double rooms, connecting doors, and tall glasses. What did this guy tell you he'd give you when he picked you up?

TONI MARACHEK

All right, Joe, there don't have to be any trouble, forget it.

JOE

She's my wife.

SAM MASTERSON

Brother, you can have her, in spades. Now, beat it. You, too.

JOE

I just want to make sure.

TONI MARACHEK

Joe, there don't have to be no trouble.

SAM MASTERSON

No, there don't have to be no trouble.

JOE

There's got to be. Certain wise guys have to be taught a lesson. Certain wise guys have to be . . .

SAM MASTERSON

Where do you want it, here or outside?

JOE

Outside will do me fine. There's an alley through the kitchen door.

TONI MARACHEK

Sam.

SAM MASTERSON

Shut up.

JOE

(*to* TONI)

Stay here.

JOE leaves, gesturing to three men, who follow him out the door with SAM.

Back at the table, TONI collapses in sobs. DETECTIVE MCCARTHY approaches her table and sits down.

DETECTIVE MCCARTHY

OK, sister, you did a swell job. Now blow.

TONI MARACHEK

Yes, sir.

TONI picks up her coat and leaves dejectedly. She goes out and sees SAM across the street in a car, being beaten up by the MEN. The car pulls away.

We now see a wooden rail fence with a sign pointing to "***Sunny Grove, Midbury, Iverstown.***" Then we see SAM gripping onto the rails of the fence, helping himself up painfully. He climbs over the fence. He has something in his mouth. He spits it out. He opens his hand and finds a badge that says, "***Private Detective.***"

A bus is passing by, and SAM waves it down. He gets into the bus, looking very beat-up.

BUS DRIVER

What happened to you?

SAM MASTERSON

Not a thing. I'm just made up for Halloween.

We now go to the Iverstown bus stop. SAM and some other passengers come out. SAM puts his hand to his mouth in pain. He moves away from the bus. Then he spies TONI headed for the bus. He pulls aside so she does not see him.

As TONI is getting into the bus, SAM pull her aside and says to the driver:

SAM

Go ahead, bud, she'll catch the next one.

The bus drives off. SAM takes TONI aside into an alley.

SAM MASTERSON

Cut that; crying is not going to get you anywhere.

TONI MARACHEK

I'll stop.

SAM MASTERSON

I ought to beat it out of you.

TONI MARACHEK

I think maybe I got it coming.

SAM MASTERSON

Why, why, why?

TONI MARACHEK

Last night in the restaurant, I kept trying to tell.

SAM MASTERSON

Come on, get down to it.

TONI MARACHEK

Before they let me out, they took me to the DA's office.

SAM MASTERSON

O'Neil, his name's Walter O'Neil.

TONI MARACHEK

Yeah, that's right. That's his name.

SAM MASTERSON

All right. They took you to his office.

TONI MARACHEK

He asked me a lot of questions, mostly about you.

SAM MASTERSON

About me?

TONI MARACHEK

About you and me.

SAM MASTERSON

Huh?

TONI MARACHEK

He kept asking me if I knew why you came here. He asked me that a couple of times.

SAM MASTERSON

What else?

TONI MARACHEK

Oh, a lot of questions. I forget.

SAM MASTERSON

Remember.

TONI MARACHEK

My head's mixed up.

SAM MASTERSON

Well, the goons, the ones who worked me over?

TONI MARACHEK

They just wanted to scare you. O'Neil doesn't want you in town. They said if I didn't play with them, I'd go back to jail.

SAM MASTERSON

Who said that? O'Neil?

TONI MARACHEK

No, no, the other man, Mr. O'Neil wasn't there by then.

SAM MASTERSON

You're kidding.

TONI MARACHEK

They said they wouldn't hurt you.

SAM MASTERSON

Much.

TONI MARACHEK

No more parole, they said, if I went for it. I'd do the whole five, they said, if I didn't. I went for it. Go ahead and hit me, Sam. I've got it coming.

SAM MASTERSON

The only thing you got coming, kid, is a break. I'm going back to town.

TONI MARACHEK

They don't want you here, Sam. I don't know what it is. But they don't want you here.

SAM MASTERSON

Like it or not, they got me.

TONI MARACHEK

Next time it'll be worse.

SAM MASTERSON

Look, I don't like to get pushed around. I don't like people I like to be pushed around. I don't like anybody to get pushed around. Kid, I'll tell you what you do. You grab the next bus out, and I'll meet you, wherever you say.

TONI MARACHEK

I'll go back with you.

SAM MASTERSON

Good. I wanted you to say that.

They walk off into the night.

The next morning, at the O'NEILS' mansion, JOHN, the butler, goes to the front door and finds SAM, still disheveled, standing there.

JOHN

Just a moment, sir.

SAM grabs JOHN by the arm and twists it behind his back.

SAM MASTERSON

Take me to Mr. O'Neil and you won't get hurt.

SAM grabs JOHN by the arm and pushes him in front of him.

JOHN

Yes, Mr. Masterson. I hardly recognized you, sir.

They go into WALTER's study and find him there.

SAM MASTERSON

Tell your man to ask Martha to come down here.

WALTER O'NEIL

Tell Mrs. O'Neil that, John.

SAM MASTERSON

I thought we ought to have a little talk. Who'll kick off first, your team or mine?

WALTER O'NEIL

You look terrible, Sam. Have a drink.

SAM MASTERSON

Thanks.

As SAM pours the drink, WALTER reaches into an open drawer for a pistol. SAM slams the drawer shut on WALTER's hand and punches him in the face. SAM collapses unconscious. SAM puts the gun in his pocket, pours two drinks, and sees a folder on the desk.

SAM MASTERSON

A report on Sam Masterson!

He drinks his drink and takes the other one over to WALTER, who is slowly recovering consciousness.

SAM MASTERSON

Here, take this. I'm two up on you.

SAM hands WALTER the drink.

WALTER O'NEIL

Thanks.

SAM MASTERSON

You're out of shape. Walter. For a minute there, I thought you were dead.

WALTER O'NEIL

I was—I wasn't going to shoot.

SAM MASTERSON

I wasn't going to wait and see. Come on. I took a gander on this while you were out. I could have given you a much more detailed picture on Sam Masterson. I didn't know you cared.

WALTER O'NEIL

You know it now.

MARTHA enters in an elegant white, ankle-length coat.

SAM MASTERSON
Now I'll let Martha give it to you.

MARTHA IVERS
Give him what, Sam?

SAM MASTERSON
The facts concerning a guy called Sam Masterson and his attitudes towards life and love. Walter's got the wrong ideas.

MARTHA IVERS
Sam, you're hurt.

SAM MASTERSON
You ought to see the other guy.

MARTHA IVERS
What happened?

SAM MASTERSON
This.

SAM pulls out the Private Detective badge.

SAM MASTERSON
It fell out of a guy's pocket and hit me in the face. Private dicks. What's the trouble, Walter? Don't you trust your own cops?

WALTER O'NEIL
You're right, Sam. I hired the man who worked you over. The idea was mine. I thought it might scare you into not coming back. It hasn't. We're ready to listen to the current quotation on blackmail.

MARTHA IVERS
Walter!

SAM MASTERSON
Blackmail.

WALTER O'NEIL
I said blackmail. Now what is the price? Remember, you're dealing with two old friends.

SAM MASTERSON
Well, which one of you do I deal with?

MARTHA IVERS
With me. Be at my office at the plant at 3.

SAM MASTERSON

Okay.

SAM takes the drink from WALTER's hand, holds it up, and drinks it.

SAM MASTERSON

May the deal be profitable to all of us.

WALTER O'NEIL

Whatever the price is, that's it, Sam, don't try this again. What happened last night can happen again, and worse.

SAM MASTERSON

Don't try it, sweetheart.

SAM hands WALTER his own gun.

SAM MASTERSON

I'll make this a flat statement. I'll kill you.

The scene changes to a bathroom in the O'NEIL mansion.

MARTHA IVERS

Hold your hand under the water.

MARTHA helps WALTER wash his hurt hand.

MARTHA IVERS

Dry your hand. This will hurt.

MARTHA dabs iodine on the wound where SAM slammed the door on WALTER's hand.

WALTER O'NEIL

Even pain at your hands!

MARTHA IVERS

You were lucky.

WALTER O'NEIL

Yes. I'm a very lucky man.

MARTHA IVERS

And a stupid one. Yesterday afternoon, he told me he didn't want anything, but he was going away. Let me handle it.

WALTER O'NEIL

I didn't like what you had in mind. It's quite a thing in a small city like this to be a district attorney; you get to feel like God. You know everything down to the smallest detail. Even a call to Dempsey's garage. Sam's leaving Iverstown today.

MARTHA IVERS

That's what he said.

SAM MASTERSON

Want to hear you say it.

MARTHA IVERS

It's up to him.

WALTER O'NEIL

No, it's up to you. I know you, Martha. You are my life's work. I've studied you all these years. A little girl in a cage waiting for someone to let her out. And along comes Sam. Do you know what's on my mind, Martha, about Sam, I mean?

MARTHA IVERS

I think I do. And that's where it will stay: on your mind. Unless of course I tell you differently.

We are now at a lunch counter, where TONI is sitting. SAM sits down next to her.

TONI MARACHEK

What did O'Neil say? Do you think he'll make trouble?

SAM MASTERSON

No. No. I had him figured out, right? He's still just a scared little kid.

A WAITRESS approaches.

SAM MASTERSON

Coffee, please, black. No. Martha's the one I can't dope out.

TONI MARACHEK

Martha.

SAM MASTERSON

Mrs. O'Neil? The three of us grew up together. I told you about it, remember?

(to the WAITRESS, *who sets down the coffee in front of him)*

Thanks. She's beautiful. That's why I can't figure it out. Why should a beautiful, rich girl stay married to a guy she's not in love with?

TONI MARACHEK

How do you know that?

SAM MASTERSON

I know.

TONI MARACHEK

You sound like you're in love with her.

SAM MASTERSON

You sound like you're jealous.

TONI MARACHEK

Could be. When are we leaving?

SAM MASTERSON

This evening if the car's ready.

TONI MARACHEK

Well, what are we doing until then? I know. Why don't we find out what happened to your people?

SAM MASTERSON

Yeah. That ought to be simple. Now I know I left town September 27th, 1928.

TONI MARACHEK

It's the exact date. How come you remember it?

SAM MASTERSON

Wouldn't you remember a date, the exact date about something that happened that long ago?

TONI MARACHEK

No. Not unless something terrific happened that day.

SAM MASTERSON

Yeah. Come on, let's finish your coffee; we'll go down to the newspaper morgue.

TONI MARACHEK

The morgue?

SAM MASTERSON

Yeah. I think I can find out about my people down there. Afterwards, I'll take you shopping.

At the offices of the Iverstown Register, SAM is sitting at a desk. The IVERSTOWN REGISTER MAN brings over a large folio volume.

IVERSTOWN REGISTER

That was a strange case. It went unsolved for years. Then one day they picked up a guy who stuck up a garage or something. Someone who used to work at Old Lady Ivers' house. Came out at the trial and he was the one that knocked the old lady off. It's my favorite case. The picture of the guy.

SAM MASTERSON

Doesn't looked like very much, does he?

IVERSTOWN REGISTER

Yeah. Kind of a scared little rabbit. I watched him all through the trial. Never had a chance. O'Neil really did a job on him.

SAM MASTERSON

Is that Walter O'Neil?

IVERSTOWN REGISTRY

Yep. Same guy. It's kind of dramatic, though, him being engaged to the niece of the murdered woman. Sure did a job. Jury was unanimous.

SAM MASTERSON

What happened to him?

IVERSTOWN REGISTRY

Oh, they hung him. Interesting, eh? Solving a murder after all those years. It's all in the files there. Go ahead and read it.

SAM MASTERSON

Oh, thanks, I will.

MARTHA O'NEIL is in her office at the plant. The intercom rings.

MARTHA IVERS

Yes.

FEMALE VOICE

Mr. Masterson, by appointment.

MARTHA IVERS

Send him in, please.

SAM comes in.

SAM MASTERSON

Three o'clock, on the nose.

MARTHA IVERS

On the nose. Come in, Sam.

SAM MASTERSON

You should have kept me waiting. Big executives always keep people waiting. Didn't you know that?

MARTHA IVERS

Good executives don't.

SAM MASTERSON

I bet you're good.

MARTHA IVERS

I am.

They both look at a large, incomprehensible picture.

MARTHA IVERS

It catches it, doesn't it? The feeling of a factory?

SAM MASTERSON

When your aunt owned this place, I couldn't get past the gate; now I'm a guest, or am I?

MARTHA IVERS

I invited you here.

SAM MASTERSON

Martha, did your aunt leave you everything?

MARTHA IVERS

I was her only heir.

SAM MASTERSON

I'll never forget the way she looked that night, standing in the doorway, leaning on her cane.

MARTHA IVERS

I don't want to talk about it.

SAM MASTERSON

Okay. Okay.

MARTHA IVERS

You look different than you did this morning. Clean and fresh.

SAM MASTERSON

Yeah. Well, it's the perfume I use that makes me smell so nice. I bet I smell as nice as you and Walter put together.

MARTHA IVERS

What do you want?

SAM MASTERSON

I think I've got what I want. I think I've got a gimmick. A gimmick is an angle that works for you to keep you from working too hard for yourself. Simple.

MARTHA IVERS

Specifically, what is your angle?

SAM MASTERSON

Specifically, half.

MARTHA IVERS

Half of what?

SAM MASTERSON

You tell me.

MARTHA IVERS

All right, Sam, come here.

They go to the window and see a view of the mill and the town.

MARTHA IVERS

My father used to work here as a mill hand.

SAM MASTERSON

So did my father, when he was sober.

MARTHA IVERS

Now I own it.

SAM MASTERSON

Now you're even.

MARTHA IVERS

Now I'm even. I was 21 when I took it over. It had 3,000 workers then, it's got 30,000 now. Ran as far as that gate. Now it goes down to the edge of the river. And I did it all by myself. Without Walter, without his father, all by myself.

SAM MASTERSON

Half of this should make quite a score.

MARTHA IVERS

Half would make you my partner.

SAM MASTERSON

That's what I had in mind.

MARTHA IVERS

You went out of here a dirty little kid once before; that can happen again. I don't have to give you anything if I don't want to.

SAM MASTERSON

But you do want to.

Back at the Gable Hotel, SAM rushes into his room.

SAM MASTERSON

Hey, Toni, come in here, quick.

TONI comes in the room from her own, wearing a sun suit.

TONI MARACHEK

Yes, Sam.

SAM MASTERSON

Make a wish.

TONI MARACHEK

I went shopping.

SAM grabs TONI in his arms.

SAM MASTERSON

Any wish. You make it, you got it.

TONI MARACHEK

You feel good?

SAM MASTERSON

Yeah. I'm high. I had a drink.

TONI MARACHEK

What was in it?

SAM MASTERSON

A bucket of gold. The dice came up 7. Toni, you bring me luck. I'm going to wear you like a charm.

TONI MARACHEK

You really think so, Sam; you really think I bring you luck?

SAM MASTERSON

I know so, and that's an asset for a guy in my business.

TONI MARACHEK

Toni Marachek, asset.

SAM MASTERSON
Toni Marachek, good kid. You stick around, Toni Marachek.

TONI MARACHEK
Now I've got all the luck. I'm funny that way. I say what's on my mind.

SAM MASTERSON
You walk down the street, and a girl asks you for a cigarette . . .

TONI MARACHEK
And a match and the time. Life is funny.

SAM MASTERSON
That's philosophy.

TONI MARACHEK
It's good too. You want to know how it is with me, Sam?

SAM MASTERSON
No. Tell me.

TONI MARACHEK
I've told you, and even if it's over, quick . . .

SAM MASTERSON
Look: what you don't know, don't talk about.

SAM and TONI kiss passionately.

TONI MARACHEK
I bought a new outfit; I want to show you.

SAM MASTERSON
Well, let's take a look at it.

TONI stands back so SAM can admire her sun suit.

TONI MARACHEK
$8.95. How do you like it?

TONI removes the skirt.

SAM MASTERSON
With you in it, it . . .

The door opens, and MARTHA comes in.

MARTHA IVERS
Hello, Sam.

SAM MASTERSON

Toni.

TONI MARACHEK

Yes, Sam.

MARTHA IVERS

I heard you talking.

SAM MASTERSON

Well, even a crummy hotel like this has a switchboard.

MARTHA IVERS

I have special privileges in this hotel, Sam. I own it.

SAM MASTERSON

It's Mrs. O'Neil, Toni.

MARTHA IVERS

Hello. So this is the girl?

TONI MARACHEK

Toni's my name, Antonia Marachek.

MARTHA IVERS

The sun suit looks very well on her. Sam, she's got just the figure for it. She's a very pretty girl.

TONI MARACHEK

I give another show at eight o'clock

MARTHA IVERS

In your room or here?

TONI is about to storm off.

SAM MASTERSON

Toni.

TONI MARACHEK

Yes.

SAM MASTERSON

Ms. O'Neil is sorry she said that.

TONI stops.

MARTHA IVERS

I'm sorry I said that.

TONI MARACHEK

Okay, forget it.

SAM MASTERSON

Toni.

TONI MARACHEK

Yes.

SAM MASTERSON

I'm going out with Ms. O'Neil on business. That's why you came here, isn't it?

MARTHA IVERS

Yes.

SAM MASTERSON

I'll be back after a little while.

TONI MARACHEK

I've got no place to go. I'll be here.

TONI goes into her room and closes the door.

SAM MASTERSON

I didn't like that.

MARTHA IVERS

I apologized.

SAM MASTERSON

There was ice on your tongue.

MARTHA IVERS

If you want me to say anything else to her . . .

SAM MASTERSON

You spoke your piece. Let's get out of here.

MARTHA IVERS

I've never been in a hotel room like this before.

SAM MASTERSON

I've been in too many.

MARTHA IVERS

Just the way you read about it in books. Window shade. Scotch on the dresser. Let's stay here, Sam.

SAM MASTERSON

No.

MARTHA IVERS

Why not? We can order our dinner here.

SAM MASTERSON

I don't like room service.

MARTHA IVERS

All right, Sam.

SAM MASTERSON

Come on, let's go.

SAM and MARTHA are dancing together in a crowded nightclub.

MARTHA IVERS

What's your Toni Marachek really like?

SAM MASTERSON

That's what she asked me about you.

MARTHA IVERS

What are your plans for her?

SAM MASTERSON

Oh, she's very independent.

MARTHA IVERS

Hardly. How did you meet her?

SAM MASTERSON

We lived in the same house.

MARTHA IVERS

In Iverstown?

SAM MASTERSON

Yeah.

MARTHA IVERS

When?

SAM MASTERSON

Now . . . now and then.

The nightclub orchestra stops playing, and the audience applauds.

SAM MASTERSON

Well, let's go back to our drinks.

SAM and MARTHA go back to their table. The orchestra strikes up again.

MARTHA IVERS

To continue with your Antonia Marachek, have you other things in common?

SAM MASTERSON

Taxi cabs, hotels, and Bibles. And we don't like some of the same people and places.

MARTHA IVERS

All sounds like a very substantial beginning. How long have you known her, really?

SAM MASTERSON

Since the day before yesterday.

MARTHA IVERS

How long have you known me?

SAM MASTERSON

Martha, I'm not sure that I've ever known you. What do you say? Let's get down to business.

MARTHA IVERS

Let's get out of here.

SAM MASTERSON

Waiter?

WAITER

Yes, sir.

SAM MASTERSON

Check, please.

WAITER

Yes, sir.

At the bar, we see JOE.

JOE

Whiskey and soda.

SAM pays the WAITER.

BARTENDER

Thank you, sir.

SAM sees JOE.

SAM MASTERSON

Wait outside.

MARTHA IVERS

Sam, what is it?

SAM MASTERSON

Wait outside.

SAM steals upon JOE from behind, grabs him and punches him several times. He takes away JOE's gun.

WAITER

Beautiful, beautiful, beautiful.

SAM MASTERSON

Give that back to him when he sobers up. Tell him I run an honest book. I always pay off.

SAM and MARTHA are at the nightclub entrance.

SAM MASTERSON

I thought I told you to wait outside.

MARTHA IVERS

I wanted to see.

SAM MASTERSON

You saw.

MARTHA IVERS

You wanted to kill him, didn't you?

SAM MASTERSON

Yes, I did.

Now SAM is driving MARTHA in her convertible. She is wearing a kerchief over her head. They stop at a place that has a panoramic view of Iverstown.

SAM

That's the spot?

MARTHA IVERS

Yes.

SAM MASTERSON

I like your car. You know what happened to Lot's wife when she looked back, don't you?

MARTHA IVERS

What?

SAM MASTERSON

She was turned into a pillar of salt.

MARTHA IVERS

What happened to Lot?

SAM MASTERSON

Well, he got away. He didn't look back.

MARTHA IVERS

You know your Bible.

SAM MASTERSON

You would too, if you spent as much time as I did in hotel rooms.

MARTHA IVERS

I'll take it up. Come on, let's get out of here. I love to watch the city from this spot.

The two of them get out of the car.

SAM MASTERSON

From up here, it doesn't even look real, is it?

MARTHA IVERS

It's real, very real. Owning it gives you a sense of power. You'd know what I meant if you had it.

SAM MASTERSON

Ivers, Ivers, Ivers.

MARTHA IVERS

If anyone asked me my name now, I'd say it was Martha Smith.

SAM MASTERSON

I smell smoke.

SAM turns around.

SAM MASTERSON

Better take a look.

Behind them, we see smoke. SAM goes over and finds a fire burning. He tries to put it out.

SAM MASTERSON

Must have been some kids up here.

MARTHA IVERS

Sam, don't, let it burn. We used to come up here when we were kids and build a fire.

SAM MASTERSON

Ah.

MARTHA sits down by the fire and takes off the kerchief.

MARTHA IVERS

Let it burn, Sam. In those days, we used to think that this was real and that, that didn't even exist.

SAM MASTERSON

Just now you look like Martha Smith.

MARTHA IVERS

If only you hadn't run away.

SAM MASTERSON

Well, I waited for you. I remember I waited a long time in the rain, but you didn't show.

MARTHA IVERS

Give me a cigarette, Sam. If only you hadn't left town. I had no one to turn to.

SAM leans over to light his cigarette from the fire and lets out a garbled sound.

MARTHA

What did you say, Sam?

SAM MASTERSON

Nothing. I didn't say anything.

MARTHA IVERS

When I found out, it was too late. Much too late. One thing led to another.

SAM MASTERSON

Another what?

MARTHA IVERS

I don't want to talk about it anymore.

SAM MASTERSON

No, go ahead, Martha. It'll do you good. Another what?

MARTHA IVERS

Where was I?

SAM MASTERSON

One thing led to another?

MARTHA IVERS

It would've been so different if you hadn't run away. Would've been you instead of Walter, or if you had stopped me when I lifted the cane . . . why didn't you stop me? You knew how much I hated her. Why didn't you stop me?

SAM MASTERSON

I wasn't there, Martha.

MARTHA IVERS

And then I stood there afterwards . . . you—you weren't there?

SAM MASTERSON

No, Martha. I wasn't there. I left when your aunt came into the hallway. I didn't want to stick around. I was in enough trouble as it was. I never saw what happened. I never knew until tonight about your aunt or that man, the one they hung; a man that you and Walter killed.

MARTHA picks up a flaming stick from the fire and goes to strike SAM, but he holds her off. He holds her arm behind her back and starts kissing her passionately as she sobs. We see her arm move to wrap around his shoulder as they both kiss. SAM throws the flaming stick back into the fire.

Later, the fire burns down into smoldering ashes.

MARTHA

(crying)

Sam, help me. Help me.

SAM MASTERSON

All right. Martha, tell me. Talk.

MARTHA

All right, Sam. I never imagined anyone could die so quickly. I'd always supposed that wherever I went, she would be with me. That she would never die. But it wasn't like that. I expected to find her when I went back to my room. Later I became frightened. The coroner and the police were sympathetic, the doctor very attentive. They believed my story, the one I told Walter's father. That night, I slept heavily, peacefully.

SAM MASTERSON

How did you sleep the night after they hung that man?

SAM MASTERSON

It wasn't long when I found out why Walter's father believed my story. It was as if my aunt had never died. He took her place. He wanted to make something of his son, and I was tied to them both from that time on. It became so unbearable that I wanted to tell the truth. But he had deliberately given me such a sense of guilt and had painted such a picture of what would happen to me that I was crazy with fear. He used that fear well. To increase it, he made me part of another crime. My testimony sent an innocent man to the gallows, and he used that to make me marry Walter. Sam, you're not going to go away again. I want you here, Sam. I've lived so much inside of myself, so choked off, wanting something else that lives and breathes, so desperate for air and room to breathe it in. Oh, Sam, please, please stay.

They kiss passionately.

MARTHA's car stops in front of the Gable Hotel. TONI is looking out the window. She sees SAM and MARTHA kiss.

SAM MASTERSON

Bye, Martha.

SAM gets out, and the car drives off. TONI looks distraught. We see an ashtray filled with burnt cigarette stubs.

In the hotel, SAM knocks on TONI's door.

SAM MASTERSON

Toni, you still up? Toni?

TONI MARACHEK

Yes.

SAM MASTERSON

It's me. It's Sam. Can I come in?

TONI MARACHEK

Yes, Sam.

SAM MASTERSON

Mind if I put your light on?

TONI MARACHEK

In a little while. I was sound asleep, I've got a headache.

SAM MASTERSON

Okay. I've got something to tell you, Toni.

TONI MARACHEK

Yes, Sam.

SAM MASTERSON

Toni, you're crying. You're crying because you saw. You were at the window there when we drove up. Well, that's what I came in to tell you about, Toni: Martha and me.

TONI MARACHEK

You didn't have to, Sam; no strings on this deal.

SAM MASTERSON

Well, that's why I wanted to. See, it started a long way back. I don't know yet how it's going to finish.

TONI MARACHEK

What do you want me to say?

SAM MASTERSON

I don't know.

TONI MARACHEK

What do you want me to do?

SAM MASTERSON

I don't know.

TONI MARACHEK

All you had to do is tell me the truth.

SAM MASTERSON

Like you did when those goons worked me over.

TONI MARACHEK

Now we are even: now I'm beat up.

SAM MASTERSON

I'm sorry I said that, Toni. Look, kid, I'm sore at myself, not at you.

TONI MARACHEK

Do you want me to leave?

SAM MASTERSON

Do you want to leave?

TONI MARACHEK

That's up to you, Sam. I'm here on a rain check.

SAM MASTERSON

Well, now don't put it that way. You're here because that's the way we wanted it.

TONI MARACHEK

And now?

SAM MASTERSON

I'm not sure. I'm just not sure.

SAM goes out of the room.

In the O'NEIL mansion, MARTHA enters the office. As she does, she hears WALTER on the phone.

WALTER O'NEIL

Hello, Gable Hotel? I want to speak to Sam Masterson.

MARTHA IVERS

Put that phone down.

WALTER O'NEIL

Hello, Sam. This is Walter. I know I'm not disturbing you. Martha just came in.

SAM MASTERSON
(ON THE PHONE)

Well, what do you want?

WALTER O'NEIL

I want you to come up here, now, right now.

MARTHA IVERS

Are you crazy? The servants . . .

WALTER O'NEIL

I gave them the night off.

MARTHA IVERS

You're drunk.

WALTER O'NEIL

I had a lot to drink, but I'm not drunk. I suppose it would be stupid to ask where you were.

MARTHA IVERS

Yes, it would.

WALTER O'NEIL

Sam's not leaving, is he?

MARTHA IVERS

Ask him when he gets here.

WALTER O'NEIL

I just got my answer.

MARTHA IVERS

Then there are no more questions.

WALTER O'NEIL

No, I know what I need to know. Sam, the superman. Sam, the dirty little boy from the other side of the tracks.

MARTHA IVERS

I'll go and change. I wouldn't want him to see me in the same dress twice.

At the hotel, SAM knocks on TONI's door.

TONI MARACHEK

Come in.

SAM comes into TONI's room.

SAM MASTERSON

Toni.

SAM sees TONI putting on her coat.

SAM MASTERSON

You're leaving, huh?

TONI MARACHEK

There's a bus out in about an hour.

SAM MASTERSON

Toni.

TONI MARACHEK

Sam, it's, it's better this way.

SAM MASTERSON

Look . . .

TONI MARACHEK

Sam, I came back here with you because you said you didn't like to be pushed around. I liked you when you said that; you were looking for trouble, but it was a good kind of trouble. And now . . .

SAM MASTERSON

Now what?

TONI MARACHEK

Sam, I saw her. You're going to get hurt. Leave her, Sam, leave this town, even without me, but leave.

SAM MASTERSON

I can't, at least not just yet. You're going to need some money.

TONI MARACHEK

No, thanks. Let's break clean.

SAM MASTERSON

See you around.

TONI MARACHEK

Yeah. Around.

Back at the O'Neil mansion, SAM is at the front door. WALTER answers.

SAM MASTERSON

Where's Martha?

WALTER O'NEIL

Upstairs, getting dressed for the occasion.

SAM MASTERSON

We'll go upstairs.

WALTER lets SAM in. They go upstairs.

SAM MASTERSON

Why did you call me?

WALTER O'NEIL

Got a riddle, Sam, maybe you can help me solve it. It's a little riddle called, "What's to be done about me, Martha, and you?" Sounds just like a poem. If it rhymed, it would rhyme with murder.

They go into MARTHA's room. She is there.

MARTHA IVERS

He's drunk. He's been sitting here drinking all night.

WALTER O'NEIL

Draw a chalk line and I'll walk it, or I'll take a mental test. Any question like . . . what is my object in life?

MARTHA IVERS
I tried to stop him from calling you.

WALTER O'NEIL
You're a wise egg, an angle boy. You know all the answers, don't you? How are you on dreams?

MARTHA IVERS
Then I was glad he called you. I was frightened of him, Sam.

WALTER O'NEIL
She was frightened of me! I had a dream, Sam. It was about you. In my dream, you were not a handsome corpse.

SAM MASTERSON
Maybe there was some other guy.

WALTER O'NEIL
In other dreams, there were.

MARTHA IVERS
I told you he's drunk.

SAM MASTERSON
Did you say others?

WALTER O'NEIL
Oh, little Martha. Life was so empty. Is that what she told you, Sam?

MARTHA IVERS
I don't want him in here, Sam. Make him get out.

WALTER O'NEIL
Now, you're all of them, Sam. Every one of them rolled into one.

MARTHA IVERS
Sam, make him . . .

SAM MASTERSON
Keep talking. I'm all of them rolled into one.

WALTER O'NEIL
Yes. You're a gymnasium instructor in Philadelphia with a muscle for a brain and a tendency to insipid verse. You're a guy, just a guy named Pete in Erie, who smells of fish and sings. You're last year's greatest fullback and you flunk your bar exam, but you wanted to be an industrial engineer. You're a guy who came along to fix a tire so well, you

became a city paid inspector, and you're a lot of others, but worst of all, you're the one and only man who shares with me the only claim I have on her. Ask her, Sam, say to her, "Martha, is all this true?"

SAM MASTERSON

What if it is? What did you expect? She never wanted to marry you. If you had any self-respect . . .

WALTER O'NEIL

She married me because she felt that way I would never tell.

SAM MASTERSON

That's a lie. Your old man forced her. How long do you expect her to go on paying off?

WALTER O'NEIL

Forever.

SAM MASTERSON

Whatever happens to you, you've got coming.

WALTER O'NEIL

What can happen, Sam? Shall I tell you? She'll try to get you to kill me. Like she got me to send an innocent man to the gallows.

MARTHA IVERS

I told you the way it was. It was his father's idea. He made . . .

WALTER O'NEIL

Did she tell you how she stood up in the police station? How she looked at the man without batting an eye? How she said, "Yes, that's the man. He's the one who came into the house that night. He's the man who killed my aunt." That even stuck in the throat of my father. My poor, dear, departed, greedy father. But he went right on, and so did I.

MARTHA IVERS

He's lying. You believe me, don't you, Sam?

WALTER O'NEIL

You believe her, Sam? Martha, at least tell the truth now. Tell how much you were afraid of an unsolved murder. Tell what a threat it was to the power and the riches that you'd learned to love so much—and that I'd learned to love too. Tell why I became district attorney. Tell why you made me hang that man. Tell the truth!

MARTHA IVERS

I told the truth. They were like leeches, both of them. They wanted everything.

WALTER O'NEIL
All I ever wanted was you.

MARTHA IVERS
Everything you want, everything you had I gave you.

WALTER O'NEIL
You gave me nothing.

MARTHA IVERS
Let that go.

WALTER O'NEIL
You're insane. You're out of your mind. Me too. You see, Sam, how close we really are to each other. Don't break up our happy home. It'll have to be you or me. And unless you do it now, it'll be you.

WALTER finishes his drink and walks unsteadily toward the door, clutching onto an armchair to keep from falling over.

WALTER O'NEIL
You mustn't think I'm drunk. I'm not. It's just that I'm sick; inside of me, I'm sick.

WALTER goes to the doorway and has to steady himself on the doorposts.

WALTER O'NEIL
Martha, help me, please.

WALTER walks out into the hallway. MARTHA puts her arms around SAM.

MARTHA IVERS
Sam, you believe me, don't you?

They hear the sound of WALTER falling down the stairs. They go out to find him unconscious and go down to examine him. Halfway down the stairs, MARTHA clutches at SAM.

MARTHA IVERS
Now, Sam, do it now. Set me free. Set both of us free. He fell down the stairs and fractured his skull. That's how he died. Everybody knows what a heavy drinker he was. Oh, Sam, it can be so easy.

SAM draws away from her and walks down the stairs to WALTER. MARTHA looks on eagerly. SAM stands over WALTER. We see MARTHA's face, with its look of cruel but triumphant expectation. But this look turns to dismay.

SAM picks up the unconscious WALTER and carries him onto a chaise longue in the office. MARTHA follows. She sees SAM preparing a poultice for WALTER.

MARTHA IVERS

I thought you loved me.

SAM MASTERSON

I thought I did too.

MARTHA IVERS

Now you hate me.

SAM MASTERSON

Now I'm sorry for you.

MARTHA IVERS

And I dreamed about you coming back.

SAM MASTERSON

Your whole life has been a dream.

MARTHA IVERS

I thought you'd be the Sam I knew as a child.

SAM MASTERSON

Martha, you're sick.

MARTHA IVERS

I could run to you when I was in trouble.

SAM MASTERSON

In your mind, I mean, that's where you're sick.

MARTHA IVERS

And you'd help me.

SAM MASTERSON

So sick that you don't even know the difference between right and wrong anymore.

SAM pours a drink.

MARTHA IVERS

You've killed; it says so in your record.

SAM MASTERSON

I've never murdered.

SAM sees WALTER coming to. He gives him the drink.

SAM

Are you all right now?

WALTER O'NEIL

All right.

SAM MASTERSON

You fell down the stairs.

WALTER O'NEIL

I remember. You carried me in here?

SAM MASTERSON

Yeah.

WALTER O'NEIL

You had your chance, Sam.

MARTHA picks up the pistol from the drawer and holds it behind her back.

WALTER O'NEIL

It's a thin line, the one between life and death.

MARTHA IVERS

You said I didn't know the difference between right and wrong. What's right for Walter and myself—for us to tell the truth?

SAM MASTERSON

I think so. Yes.

MARTHA IVERS

And hang for it?

SAM MASTERSON

You wouldn't hang for it, not if you confessed; you'd do time, sure.

MARTHA IVERS

Sure, I'll rot in prison for the rest of my life. And for what? What am I guilty of?

SAM MASTERSON

Murder.

MARTHA IVERS

What were their lives compared to mine? What was she?

SAM MASTERSON

A human being?

MARTHA IVERS

A mean, vicious, hateful old woman who never did anything for anybody. Look what I've done with what she's left me. I've given to charity, built schools, hospitals, given thousands of people work. What was he?

SAM MASTERSON

Another human being . . .

MARTHA IVERS

A thief, a drunk, someone who would've died in the gutter, anyway. Neither one of them had any right to live.

SAM MASTERSON

You didn't think Walter had either. Bye, Martha.

SAM moves to leave, but MARTHA draws the gun on him.

MARTHA IVERS

Sam. Sam's going away. Did you hear what I said, Walter?

WALTER O'NEIL

Yes, I heard you.

MARTHA IVERS

We can't let him go, can we?

SAM MASTERSON

Martha's waiting for your answer, Walter.

MARTHA IVERS

We'd always be afraid of him. We couldn't live that way. We'd be fools to let him go, knowing so much about us.

SAM MASTERSON

You may have a little trouble squaring this one.

MARTHA IVERS

You broke into the house, you demanded money; you tried to attack me, and I shot you in self-defense. I have a right to kill in self-defense. That's what the law says, doesn't it, Walter? Isn't that what the law says, Walter?

WALTER smiles gleefully.

SAM MASTERSON

It'll hold up, Walter. A man with a police record. It's a perfect case, if you can get Walter to be your witness. Do you want to bet?

Turning his back on them, SAM walks toward the door. MARTHA points the gun at him.

SAM MASTERSON

I feel sorry for you, both of you.

SAM walks out. MARTHA lowers the gun. MARTHA rushes to the window to watch him go.

WALTER O'NEIL

You love him.

MARTHA IVERS

I hate him.

WALTER O'NEIL

That's why you dropped the gun.

MARTHA IVERS

I was afraid. For the first time in my life I was afraid. I felt you'd no longer stand by me. That you'd leave me.

WALTER O'NEIL

No, Martha, I believe you. I love you. Don't cry, Martha. It's not your fault.

MARTHA IVERS

It isn't, is it, Walter?

WALTER O'NEIL

No, nor mine. Not my father's, not your auntie's.

MARTHA IVERS

It's not anyone's fault.

WALTER O'NEIL

It's just the way things are. It's what people want and how hard they want it; how hard it is for them to get it.

MARTHA IVERS

He's near the gate. I'm glad he's going.

WALTER O'NEIL

He'll always be . . .

MARTHA IVERS

No, he won't, Walter, he won't. And he'll never tell. You needn't be afraid, and you'll see: things will be different now between you and me. Just like . . . just like nothing ever happened.

WALTER O'NEIL

Just like nothing ever happened. Will you kiss me, Martha?

They kiss.

MARTHA IVERS

You believe me?

We see WALTER draw the gun out of his pocket. MARTHA sees him and puts her hand on the gun, startling WALTER. MARTHA's hand pulls it toward her, and she fires it.

SAM'S VOICE

(in her head)

Ivers, Ivers, Ivers.

MARTHA IVERS

No, Martha Smith.

She falls to the ground dead.

Outside, SAM hears the gunshot and runs back towared the house. He sees WALTER at the window, holding MARTHA's dead body. Seeing this, SAM walks away.

Back in his hotel room, SAM starts packing. The door opens, and he sees TONI.

TONI MARACHEK

I missed a bus once, and I was lucky. I wanted to see if I could be lucky twice.

We are now passing a sign saying, "You Are Now Leaving Iverstown: America's Fastest Growing Industrial City."

SAM is driving his convertible, and TONI is in the passenger's seat. She looks back at the sign.

SAM MASTERSON

Don't look back baby, don't ever look back. You know what happened to Lot's wife, don't you?

TONI MARACHEK

Whose wife?

SAM MASTERSON

Sam's wife.

TONI MARACHEK

Sam's wife.

ABOUT THE FILM

Film noir is a genre that reached its peak in the 1940s and 1950s. Characterized by dark lighting and inspired by crime fiction, it often features characters such as a tough-guy hero, mysterious beauties who may or may not be on the level, and prominent people with crimes to hide.

The Strange Love of Martha Ivers (1946) is a beloved film noir classic.

Itinerant gambler and war hero Sam Masterson (played by Van Heflin) comes back to his hometown after seventeen years, restarting a drama that left off when he ran away to the circus as a boy.

Sam encounters old acquaintances: Martha Ivers (played by Barbara Stanwyck), then a rebellious girl, now a beautiful and formidable businesswoman, and her husband, Walter O'Neil (Kirk Douglas, in an early role), a hard-drinking district attorney tormented by shadows from his past.

Sam also meets Toni Marachek (Lizabeth Scott), a deep-voiced beauty just paroled from prison, whom he rescues and befriends.

Sam's encounters with Martha, Toni, and Walter start a game in which characters vie to assess and manipulate one another's motives. The film unravels a series of events that dredge up unwholesome secrets from the past and plunge the characters into a passionate melodrama with a bloody ending.

Sam struggles between his newfound attraction to Toni, whom he alternately trusts and distrusts, and his childhood love for Martha, who almost ran away with him when they were young.

Martha Ivers also displays other traits from the film noir genre: settings perfumed with whiskey and cigarette smoke; a tension between cynicism and decency; threats of blackmail; and a tight, well-constructed plot that hinges on its characters' strengths and weaknesses.

The Rotten Tomatoes film review site rates *Martha Ivers* at 100 percent on its Tomatometer. Comments by reviewers: "a gripping film noir, all the more effective for being staged... as a steamy romantic melodrama"; "a brilliant film noir with fantastic performances"; "films don't get much better." *The Strange Love of Martha Ivers* will enthrall longtime fans of film noir as well as newcomers to the genre.

REBECCA

* * *

Directed by ALFRED HITCHCOCK
Produced by DAVID O. SELZNICK
Screenplay by ROBERT E. SHERWOOD and JOAN HARRISON
Based on the novel by DAPHNE DU MAURIER
Adapted by PHILIP MACDONALD and MICHAEL HOGAN

CAST

Maxim de Winter .... Lawrence Olivier
Mrs. de Winter .... Joan Fontaine
Jack Flavell .... George Sanders
Mrs. Danvers .... Judith Anderson
Giles .... Nigel Bruce
Frank Crawley .... Reginald Denny
Colonel Julyan .... C. Aubrey Smith
Beatrice .... Gladys Cooper
Mrs. Van Hopper .... Florence Bates
The Coroner .... Melville Cooper
Dr. Baker .... Leo C. Carroll
Ben .... Leonard Carey
Tabb .... Lumsden Hare
Frith .... Edward Fielding
Robert .... Philip Winter
Charlcroft .... Forrester Harvey

Beneath the blackened stonework is a once fine old English house of early Tudor style. Above the window frames, gaping holes tell us that the building is nothing but a burnt-out shell. The once magnificent gardens are an overgrown mass of weeds. At the end of the driveway, the growth is jungle-like.

"I'S" VOICE

Last night I dreamt I went to Manderley again. It seemed to me I stood by the iron gate leading to the drive, and for a while I could not enter, for the way was barred to me. Then, like all dreamers, I was possessed of a sudden with supernatural powers and passed like a spirit through the barrier before me. The drive wound away in front of me, twisting and turning as it had always done. But as I advanced, I was aware that a change had come upon it. Nature had come into her own again and little by little had encroached upon the drive with long tenacious fingers. On and on wound the poor thread that had once been our drive. And finally there was Manderley. Manderley, secretive and silent. Time could not mar the perfect symmetry of those walls. Moonlight can play odd tricks upon the fancy and suddenly it seemed to me that light came from the windows. And then a cloud came upon the moon and hovered an instant like a dark hand before a face. The illusion went with it. I looked upon a desolate shell with no whisper of the past about its staring walls. We can never go back to Manderley again, that much is certain. But sometimes, in my dreams, I do go back to the strange days of my life which began for me in the south of France.

Manderley was the most beautiful house I ever saw—a thing of grace, exquisite and faultless. Its clean grey stone had been mellowed by the centuries. Time could not harm the perfect symmetry of these walls. Its shining mullioned windows looked down upon bright gardens and trim velvet lawns which swept in terrace after terrace to the sea... We can never go back there again. The past is still too close to us. But sometimes in my dreams I do go back...

(*pause*)

... to the strange days of my life which began, for me, on the top of a cliff, in the South of France...

In the South of France, MAXIM, with an agonized look on his face, is standing upon a precipice, watching the angry sea dashing itself against some rocks.

He is almost about to take a fatal step. Suddenly there is a tiny scream behind him.

"I"

No! Stop!

MAXIM's head turns quickly, and, as though just passing, is a young girl of twenty: "I." He commences to stride towards her.

SEMI CLOSE UP

MAXIM

Who are you? What the devil are you staring at?

"I"

I'm sorry, I didn't mean to stare. Only I thought . . .

MAXIM

Oh, you're English, are you! What are you doing here?

"I"

I was only walking . . . I . . .

MAXIM

Well, get on with your walking—don't hang about here screaming.

The girl hastens away.

LONG SHOT—INT.—EARLY EVENING

In the lounge of the Hotel de Paris, it is evening. MRS. VAN HOPPER, an upper-class middle-aged English snob, is surveying the assemblage through her lorgnette and indicating acute distaste. "I" is sitting next to her.

MRS. VAN HOPPER

I'll never come to Monte Carlo out of season again. There isn't a single well-known personality in the hotel.

MRS. VAN HOPPER sips her coffee, and makes a face.

MRS. VAN HOPPER

Stone cold!

As a WAITER passes by, she calls after him.

MRS. VAN HOPPER

Waiter. Garçon. Call him. Tell him to get me some—

MRS. VAN HOPPER's expression changes as she looks across the lounge and sees MAXIM DE WINTER, the man who was at the top of the cliff. MRS. VAN HOPPER'S expression shows that she is preparing to greet an old friend gushingly.

MRS. VAN HOPPER

Why! It's Max de Winter.

As MAXIM comes nearer to them, we see that "I" is awed by his approach. She starts to rise from her armchair, her hands gripping the arms. But MAXIM looks straight through "I" as though he had never seen her before and steers himself through the furniture to pass them. MRS. VAN HOPPER smiles eagerly and inclines her head.

MRS. VAN HOPPER

Mr. de Winter! How do you *do*?!

MAXIM looks at her. He is not sure where or when he met her, or what her name is. He is only sure that he doesn't want to see her now.

MAXIM

(uncertainly)

How do you do.

MRS. VAN HOPPER

I'm Edith Van Hopper. It's *so* nice to run into you here, just when I was beginning to *despair* of finding any old friends in Monte . . . But do sit down and have some coffee.

MRS. VAN HOPPER turns to "I."

Mr. de Winter is having coffee with me. Go and ask that stupid waiter for another cup.

MAXIM

I'm afraid I must contradict you. You are both having coffee with me. Garçon!

MRS. VAN HOPPER

You know, I recognized you just as soon as you walked into the restaurant. Even though I haven't seen you since that night at the Casino in Palm Beach.

(provocatively)

But perhaps you don't remember an old woman like me . . . Are you playing the tables much here at Monte?

MAXIM

No. I'm afraid that sort of thing ceased to amuse me years ago.

MRS. VAN HOPPER

I can well understand it. As for me, if I had a home like Manderley, I'd certainly never come to Monte. I hear it's one of the biggest places in that part of the country and that you just can't beat it for beauty.

MAXIM does not answer, but turns to "I."

MAXIM

And what do you think of Monte Carlo? Or don't you think of it at all?

"I"

(embarrassed and tremblingly)

I—I'm afraid I find it rather artificial . . . I . . .

MRS. VAN HOPPER

(annoyed, interrupting)

She's spoilt, Mr. de Winter. That's her trouble. Most girls would give their eyes for the chance to see Monte.

MAXIM

Wouldn't that rather defeat the purpose?

MRS. VAN HOPPER

(impervious to the dig)

Now that we've found each other again, I hope I shall see something of you. You must come and have a drink in my suite . . . I hope they've given you a good room? The place is empty, so if you're uncomfortable, mind you make a fuss. Your valet has unpacked for you, I suppose?

MAXIM

I'm afraid I don't possess one. Perhaps you'd like to do it for me?

MRS. VAN HOPPER

(at last embarrassed)

Well—I hardly think—

MRS. VAN HOPPER turns to "I."

MRS. VAN HOPPER

Perhaps you can make yourself useful to Mr. de Winter if he wants anything done. You're a capable child in many ways.

MAXIM

(with a faint sardonic smile)

That's a charming suggestion. But I'm afraid I cling to the old motto: "He travels fastest who travels alone." Perhaps you've not heard of it.

MAXIM rises, bows, and exits.

MRS. VAN HOPPER

What do you make of that! Do you suppose that sudden departure was intended to be funny?

MRS. VAN HOPPER says to "I":

Come. Don't sit there gawking. Have you got the key? Let's go upstairs.

"I" and MRS. VAN HOPPER cross the lobby toward the elevator.

MRS. VAN HOPPER

(without stopping)

I remember when I was younger, there was a well-known writer who used to dart down the back way whenever he saw me coming. I suppose he was in love with me and wasn't sure of himself... Well, c'est la vie!

MRS. VAN HOPPER turns to "I."

By the way, my dear, don't think I mean to be unkind, but you were just a teeny-weeny bit forward with Mr. de Winter. Your effort to enter the conversation quite embarrassed me, as I'm sure it did him. Men loathe that sort of thing.

"I" shrivels at this attack.

MRS. VAN HOPPER

Oh come, don't sulk. After all, I am responsible for your behavior here.

They are now nearly at the elevator.

MRS. VAN HOPPER

Perhaps he didn't notice it.

As they enter the elevator, MRS. VAN HOPPER says,

Poor thing, I suppose he just can't get over his wife's death.

As "I" turns around from entering the lift, she looks at MRS. VAN HOPPER but doesn't answer.

MRS. VAN HOPPER

They say he simply adored her.

The next day at lunchtime, "I," carrying a portfolio of her sketching paraphernalia, comes into the dining room. The HEADWAITER comes forward. He turns her over to a subordinate to take her to her table across the enormous, almost empty room. Two or three tables away is MAXIM, alone. She is embarrassed and self-conscious as she walks toward her table.

In unfolding her napkin, she awkwardly knocks over a small vase of flowers. The waiter comes in quickly to take away the vase and the sprawling flowers.

"I"

(to waiter)

How awkward! Please don't bother. It doesn't matter.

MAXIM comes up to them.

MAXIM

(to waiter)

Leave that—and set another place at my table. Mademoiselle will have lunch with me.

"I"

Oh, no—I couldn't possibly.

MAXIM

Why not?

"I"

Please don't be polite. It's very kind of you, but I shall be all right if the waiter just changes the cloth.

MAXIM

But I'm not being polite. I'd have asked you to have luncheon with me even if you hadn't knocked over that vase so clumsily. We needn't talk to each other unless we feel like it.

"I"

Thank you very much.

She rises, and they seat themselves at MAXIM'S table. MAXIM'S luncheon is already on the table. The headwaiter comes to the table and hands a menu to "I."

"I"

(to the waiter)

I'll just have some scrambled eggs, please.

WAITER

Oui, Mademoiselle.

The WAITER exits with the menu.

MAXIM

What's happened to your friend?

"I"

She's ill in bed with a cold.

MAXIM

I'm sorry I was so rude to you yesterday. The only excuse I can make is that I've become boorish through living alone . . .

"I"

Oh, you weren't, really. You simply wanted to be alone, and—

MAXIM

Tell me: is Mrs. Van Hopper a friend of yours? Or just a relation?

"I"

No, she's my employer. I'm what is known as a paid companion.

MAXIM

I didn't know that companionship could be bought.

"I"

(with a smile)

I once looked up the word "companion" in the dictionary. It said "a friend of the bosom."

MAXIM

I don't envy you the privilege.

"I"

She's very kind, really, and—and—I have to earn my living.

MAXIM

Haven't you any family?

"I"

No, my mother died years and years ago, and then there was only my father. He died last summer. And then I took this job.

MAXIM

How rotten for you.

"I"

Yes, it was, you see, because we got on so well together.

MAXIM

You and your father?

"I"

Yes—a lovely person. Very unusual.

MAXIM

What was he?

"I"

A painter.

MAXIM

Ah, was he a good one?

"I"

Well, I thought so. But people didn't understand.

MAXIM

Well, that's often the trouble.

"I"

He painted trees. At least it was one tree.

MAXIM

You mean he painted the same tree over and over again?

"I"

Yes, you see, he had a theory that if you should find one perfect thing or place or person, you should stick to it. Do you think that's very silly?

MAXIM

No, not at all. I feel very much like that myself. And what did you find to do with yourself while he was painting his tree?

"I"

I sat for him, and I sketched a little. I don't do it very well, though.

MAXIM sees "I"'s sketching portfolio.

Oh, you're going sketching this afternoon? Where?

"I"

(embarrassed)

Well. I hadn't made up my mind.

MAXIM

I'll drive you somewhere in the car.

"I"

Oh, but really, I didn't mean to . . .

MAXIM

(interrupting)

Nonsense. Finish up that mess and we'll get along.

During this, "I" has not touched her eggs at all.

"I"

Oh, thank you . . . It's very kind of you . . . but I'm not very hungry.

MAXIM

Come on—eat it up like a good girl.

"I" shyly, rather embarrassed, lifts a forkful of egg to her mouth, keeping her eyes on MAXIM.

On a terrace balcony overlooking Monte Carlo is a long flight of steps, with a terrace, leading down to the sea. At the top of the stairs is MAXIM's car.

"I" is seated on the terrace, apparently sketching the view. MAXIM leans over the railing of the balcony, gazing at the bay. Then he glances over towards "I."

MAXIM

You're taking a long time with that sketch. I shall expect a really fine work of art.

"I" begins feverishly to rub out, as she protests:

"I"

Oh, no, don't look at it . . . it's not nearly good enough.

MAXIM

(getting to his feet)

It can't be as bad as all that. Let me see before it's all rubbed out.

As MAXIM comes over and stands behind her, "I" tries to cover up her sketch with her hands to prevent him seeing it.

"I"

It's the perspective. I never *can* get it right.

MAXIM's expression as he looks at the sketch changes to one of comic surprise. It is a badly done, childish drawing of himself.

MAXIM

(interrupting with mock gravity)

Do you think it's the perspective that makes my nose take such a bend in the middle?

Seeing that he is only amused and in no way offended, "I" takes her cue from his mood, and smiles back happily at him, as she answers in her own defense.

"I"

You're not a very easy subject—your expression keeps changing all the time.

MAXIM

(pointing out to sea)

Does it? I'd concentrate on the view instead, if I were you—much more worthwhile. Rather reminds me of our coastline at home.

"I" follows him, and they sit facing each other on the railing.

MAXIM

(suddenly)

Do you know Cornwall at all?

"I"

Yes, I was there once with my father on holiday. I was in a shop once, and I saw a postcard with a beautiful house on it right by the sea. I asked what house it was, and the old woman said, "That's Manderley." I felt ashamed for not knowing.

MAXIM

Manderley is beautiful. To me, it's just the place where I was born, I've lived in all my life. Now I don't suppose I shall ever see it again.

MAXIM doesn't answer. He is lost in thought, looking out to sea. There is a silence while "I" thinks of something to say. She looks around for inspiration down toward the shore. Then turning back to her companion, with a great effort she starts to chat.

"I"

We're lucky to be away from home during the bad weather, aren't we? I can't ever remember being able to enjoy swimming in England till about June, can you?

MAXIM fails to react to her efforts. He remains silent.

"I"

The water's so warm here—I could stay in all day. Though there's a dangerous undertow—a man was drowned here last year... I've never had any fear of drowning, have you?

There is still no response from her companion. She turns to look at him. MAXIM is no longer seated beside her. He is standing at the other end of the stone balcony, motionless, staring out to sea. After a moment he swings round and comes forward with a grim expression. "I" is still looking at MAXIM unhappily, unable to understand what she has said to upset him. She gives a little shiver, half of apprehension, half of cold.

MAXIM

Come, I'll take you home.

Back in the hotel, "I" hurries up to the door of MRS. VAN HOPPER's suite. She pauses a moment outside, then goes in. MRS. VAN HOPPER is propped up in bed. Standing beside the bed, a nurse is measuring out some medicine.

MRS. VAN HOPPER

Oh, yes, I knew Mr. de Winter well. I knew his wife too. Before she married she was the beautiful Rebecca Hildreth, you know. She was drowned, poor dear... while she was sailing... near Manderley. He never talks about it, of course, but he's a broken man.

The NURSE gives MRS. VAN HOPPER some medicine, which she swallows.

MRS. VAN HOPPER

Wretched stuff! Give me a chocolate, quick!

To "I," MRS. VAN HOPPER says,

MRS. VAN HOPPER

Oh, *there* you are. And it's about time. Hurry up, I want to play some rummy.

FADE OUT.

FADE IN: INT. "I'S" BEDROOM—CLOSE SHOT—NIGHT

"I" is asleep in bed. The moonlight streams across her. Her head shirts with a faint movement now and again. As she tosses and turns, we hear MRS. VAN HOPPER'S voice.

MRS. VAN HOPPER

She was the beautiful Rebecca Hildreth, you know... They say he simply adored her... She was the beautiful Rebecca Hildreth, you know... I suppose he just can't get over his wife's death. She was the beautiful Rebecca Hildreth, you know... but he's a broken man...

FADE IN: INT. MRS. VAN HOPPER'S SUITE—SEMI CLOSE UP—DAY

MRS. VAN HOPPER is still propped up in bed. "I" comes in, brightly, with a tennis racket.

MRS. VAN HOPPER

Well, where are you going?

"I"

I thought I'd take a tennis lesson.

MRS. VAN HOPPER

I see. I suppose you had a look at the pro, and he's desperately handsome, and you've conceived a schoolgirl crush on him? All right, go ahead, make the most of it!

As "I" walks through the lobby toward the main door, she stops short at the sound of MAXIM's voice.

MAXIM

Off duty?

"I"

Yes, Mrs. Van Hopper's cold has turned to flu, so she's got a trained nurse.

MAXIM

I'm sorry for the nurse . . . Are you keen on tennis?

"I"

Not particularly, but—

MAXIM

(taking the racket from her)

Good! We'll go for a drive.

MAXIM puts the racket behind a potted palm and, taking her arm, leads her towards the revolving door.

We see MAXIM and "I," driving contentedly but in silence along a country road.

DISSOLVE TO: INT. MRS. VAN HOPPER'S ROOM—SEMI CLOSE UP—DAY

Back in the hotel, "I" enters MRS. VAN HILDRETH's room, with her tennis racket, beaming. MRS. VAN HOPPER is still in bed.

MRS. VAN HOPPER

You've been gone for *hours*! You got on rather well with him, didn't you?

"I" is startled by this question. She doesn't know how to reply.

MRS. VAN HOPPER

That pro must have been teaching you other things than tennis . . . Now hurry up. I want you to make some calls.

MRS. VAN HOPPER puts out her cigarette in a jar of cleansing cream.

MRS. VAN HOPPER

I wonder if Mr. de Winter is still in the hotel.

We see a close-up of a handwritten letter:

Dear Mr. de Winter:

Why don't you return my calls, you naughty man!

As soon as I get over this nasty old cold, I promise to keep you from being bored here in Monte. Because I know that's just what you must be—bored, bored, bored!

In fond friendship, Edythe Van Hopper

The scene then turns to a formal outdoor dance on the patio, both "I" and MAXIM dancing in evening wear. "I" looks at MAXIM longingly and happily—and he at her.

DISSOLVE TO: INT. MRS. VAN HOPPER'S SUITE—DAY

The next day, in her suite, MRS. VAN HOPPER is seated in a chair, wearing a rather loud dressing gown while her bed is being made. The door opens, and "I" comes in, dressed in spotless white.

"I"

May I go now?

MRS. VAN HOPPER

For the number of lessons you've had, you ought to be ready for Wimbledon. But this will be your last . . . so make the most of it. The trouble is, with me laid up like this, you haven't had enough to do. But I'm getting rid of that nurse today, and from now on you'll stick to your job.

"I's"expression becomes slightly desperate.

"I"

Yes, Mrs. Van Hopper.

She turns and goes.

MRS. VAN HOPPER

Nurse?

NURSE

Yes?

MRS. VAN HOPPER

Are you absolutely *sure* you left those messages for Mr. de Winter?

NURSE

Why, yes, Madame.

MRS. VAN HOPPER

I simply can't believe it. He would most certainly have called me back. Oh, well, poor boy, I simply hate to see him so alone.

DISSOLVE TO: PICTURESQUE SECTION OF CORNICHE ROAD—LONG SHOT—DAY

On the corniche road, MAXIM's car is running at a comfortable pace. MAXIM has an expression of calm contentment. "I" looks at him shyly, wistfully.

"I"

I wish there could be an invention that bottled up a memory, like perfume. And it never faded, and it never got stale. And I could uncork the bottle any time I pleased, and live the moment all over again.

MAXIM

And what particular moment in your young life would you want to keep?

"I"

(embarrassed)

Oh, all of them—from these past few days. I think I've collected a whole shelf full of bottles.

MAXIM

(gravely)

Sometimes, you know, those little bottles contain demons that pop out at you just when you're trying most desperately to forget.

"I" is considerably let down, having gone so far as to practically declare her love. MAXIM turns and looks at her, sees that she is depressed and that her mood is changed.

He looks away and steps on the gas. The car gathers speed. There is a few moments' silence. "I" looks at him nervously out of the corner of her eyes and starts biting her nails.

MAXIM

(looking at her)

Stop biting your nails!

There is another moment's silence while "I" broods, embarrassed, and then she blurts out:

"I"

I wish I were a woman of thirty-six, dressed in black satin, with a string of pearls.

MAXIM

You wouldn't be here with me if you were.

She puts her hands in her lap. She seems close to tears. Suddenly she turns and speaks sharply:

"I"

(passionately)

Will you please tell me, Mr. de Winter . . . why do you ask me to come out with you? Oh—it's obvious that you want to be kind—but why choose me for your charity?

MAXIM stops the car and turns on her.

MAXIM

I asked you to come out with me because I wanted your company. You've blotted out the past for me more than all the bright lights of Monte Carlo. But if you think I'm just being charitable or kind, you can leave the car now and find your own way home! Go on, open the door and get out!

He looks at her. Her face is averted. Tears have started from her eyes. He looks back ahead. Suddenly he reaches in his pocket, pulls out his handkerchief, tosses it into her lap.

MAXIM

Here. Blow your nose.

She uses the handkerchief, blowing her nose hard.

MAXIM

Please don't call me Mr. de Winter. I have a very impressive array of first names—George Fortescue Maximilian. You needn't bother with all of them at once. My family call me Maxim.

She looks at him. He is certainly the most unpredictable person she has ever encountered.

MAXIM

And another thing—I want you to promise me never to wear black satin, or pearls, or to be thirty-six years old.

"I"
(smiles)
Yes—MAXIM . . .

MAXIM kisses his finger and places it affectionately on her forehead.

FADE IN: INT. "I'S" BEDROOM—MORNING

We see a flower box on a table, with a note saying "Thank you for yesterday—MAXIM." "I" is humming happily, arranging MAXIM's white flowers in a vase on the same table.

Suddenly, she hears MRS. VAN HOPPER let out a scream.

MRS. VAN HOPPER
For the love of Pete! Come here!

"I" hurries into the next room.

INT. MRS. VAN HOPPER'S ROOM

MRS. VAN HOPPER is in bed, smoking a cigarette, an open cable in her hand as "I" comes in. Her breakfast tray is still by her bed.

MRS. VAN HOPPER
What do you think! My daughter's engaged to be married!

"I"
Really? I'm so glad.

MRS. VAN HOPPER jumps out of bed and slips into her robe.

MRS. VAN HOPPER
We must leave for New York at once. Get reservations on the *Aquitania*, and we'll take the 12:30 train for Cherbourg. Hurry up!

"I" is crestfallen. MRS. VAN HOPPER, now putting on her slippers, notices her look.

MRS. VAN HOPPER
Hurry up! We have no time to waste, and don't dawdle! Hurry up and got a maid in to help us with the packing! We've no time to waste. Go on—and don't dawdle!

"I" goes swiftly from the room and turns into the door to her own room. "I" comes to the bedside telephone and, lifting the receiver hurriedly, speaks quickly and quietly:

"I"

Mr. de Winter, please.

Her face falls.

"I"

He's gone out and won't be back till noon? Oh. Give me the porter, please.

DISSOLVE TO: INT. MRS. VAN HOPPER'S SUITE—SEMI LONG SHOT—DAY

A close-up of a clock that is about to strike twelve o'clock. Then, in MRS. VAN HOPPER's suite, we see "I," dressed in her hat and coat, with her bag in one hand, standing apart from MRS. VAN HOPPER, looking very miserable. She turns suddenly to her employer.

"I"

I'll go and see if anything's left in my room.

She hurries out of the door.

INT. "I'S" BEDROOM—SEMI CLOSE UP—DAY

"I" hurries into the room and over to the telephone, saying very quietly:

"I"

Has Mr. de Winter come in yet? Oh, he has? Would you connect me, please?

INT. MRS. VAN HOPPER'S SUITE—SEMI LONG SHOT—DAY

MRS. VAN HOPPER looks around impatiently, then comes out into the lobby and toward "I"'s room.

INT. "I'S" BEDROOM—SEMI LONG SHOT—DAY

As MRS. VAN HOPPER enters the room, "I" springs away from the phone guiltily. MRS. VAN HOPPER looks at her suspiciously.

"I"

I'm trying to find a book—I must have packed it.

MRS. VAN HOPPER

Well, come on . . . the car's waiting at the door.

She turns to go, and "I" follows unwillingly. As she leaves, the phone starts to ring, unheard.

DISSOLVE TO: EXT. HOTEL DE PARIS—SEMI CLOSE UP—DAY

Outside the hotel the hand luggage is being loaded into a car.

EXT. HOTEL DE PARIS—SEMI CLOSE UP

"I" gives a final despairing look back into the hotel. Then with sudden decision, she turns to MRS. VAN HOPPER:

"I"

I want to leave a forwarding address—in case they happen to find that book.

She has leapt up the steps almost before she has finished speaking. MRS. VAN HOPPER opens her mouth to speak angrily, but the girl is gone.

INT. HOTEL DESK—SEMI CLOSE UP—DAY

"I" is speaking to the CONCIERGE.

"I"

Would you ring Mr. de Winter, please?

CONCIERGE

Oui, Madame.

(*into the phone*)

Cent quarante-deux.

INT. MAXIM'S BEDROOM—SEMI LONG SHOT—DAY

In MAXIM's room, the telephone starts to ring. There is the loud sound of running water from the bathroom. We can hear MAXIM splashing and singing in the bathroom, sufficiently loud to make him fail to hear the telephone.

INT. HOTEL DESK

"I" waiting nervously while the CONCIERGE listens at the telephone. He puts down the phone and shakes his head.

CONCIERGE

There isn't any answer.

"I" turns away.

EXT. HOTEL DE PARIS—SEMI CLOSE UP—DAY

MRS. VAN HOPPER in the car, expostulating with the PORTER.

MRS. VAN HOPPER

Tell her to hurry up!

PORTER

Yes, Madame.

INT. HOTEL LOBBY & DINING ROOM

"I" hurries across the lobby toward the dining room. She looks in, then quickly turns back into the lobby.

"I"

I'm looking for Mr. de Winter.

WAITER

Mr. de Winter just ordered breakfast in his room, Madame.

EXT. MAXIM'S SUITE—CORRIDOR (3)—
SEMI CLOSE UP—DAY

"I" breathlessly arriving at the door of MAXIM's room. She knocks.

MAXIM'S VOICE

Come in.

She opens the door and is in the little foyer leading to the sitting room. (Beyond are MAXIM's bedroom and bathroom.)

INT. MAXIM'S BEDROOM—SEMI CLOSE UP—DAY

MAXIM stands in the half-open door of the bathroom, attired in trousers and dressing gown, his face still lathered from shaving. He looks in astonishment as he sees who it is and comes toward "I."

MAXIM

(wiping the remaining lather from his face)

Hello. What are you doing here? Anything the matter?

SEMI LONG SHOT—SITTING ROOM

"I" advances further into the sitting room and stands awkwardly.

"I"

I've come to say good-bye . . . We're going away.

MAXIM

What on earth are you talking about?

"I"

(COMING TO HIM)

It's true. We're going now. I was afraid I wouldn't see you again.

MAXIM

Where's she taking you to?

"I"

New York—and I don't want to go. I shall hate it. I shall be miserable.

MAXIM turns to go back into the bathroom, picking up his clothes from a nearby chair.

MAXIM

I'll dress in here. I shan't be long.

He goes back to the bathroom, leaving the door half open.

SEMI LONG SHOT

"I" stands a lonely figure in the middle of the room. There is a pause. Then we hear MAXIM's voice from the bathroom.

MAXIM'S VOICE

Which would you prefer, New York or Manderley?

"I"

(calling back appealingly)

Please don't joke about it . . . Mrs. Van Hopper's waiting . . . I'd better say good-bye now.

(*she looks around nervously, worried about the time*)

MAXIM'S VOICE

I'll repeat what I said—either you go to America with Mrs. Van Hopper or you come home to Manderley with me.

"I"

You mean you want a secretary or something?

MAXIM'S VOICE

I'm asking you to marry me, you little fool.

At this moment there is a knock on the outer door. MAXIM, his shirt now on, puts his head out of the bathroom door beyond and calls:

MAXIM

Come in.

The waiter enters, wheeling the table and breakfast.

MAXIM

Is that my food? I'm famished. I haven't had any breakfast.

There is a long silence while he lays the breakfast out and pulls up a chair. Eventually he goes out of the room. "I" still stands helplessly in the middle of the room. The bathroom door opens, and MAXIM emerges, putting on his coat. He comes through the bedroom and toward the table.

SEMI CLOSE UP

MAXIM sits at the table and motions "I" to a seat. He starts to spread butter on a piece of toast, and as he proceeds to eat it, speaks:

MAXIM

My suggestion doesn't seem to have gone at all well—I'm sorry.

"I"

But you don't understand . . . I'm not the sort of person men marry.

MAXIM

What on earth do you mean?

"I"

I don't belong in your sort of world, for one thing.

MAXIM

(laughs a little)

What *is* my sort of world?

"I"

Well—Manderley—you know what I mean.

MAXIM

I'm the best judge of whether you belong there or not. Of course, if you don't love me, that's different. A fine blow to my conceit, that's all.

"I"

(desperately)

Oh, I do love you! I love you most dreadfully. I've been crying all morning because I thought I'd never see you again.

He laughs and stretches a hand out across the table to her.

MAXIM

Bless you for that . . . I'll remind you of this one day. You won't believe me. It's a pity you have to grow up.

He starts to eat again, talks between mouthfuls of toast and sips of coffee.

MAXIM

(continuing)

Now that's settled, you may pour me some more coffee. I take two lumps of sugar and milk. The same with my tea. Don't forget.

As "I" pours out the coffee, he continues:

MAXIM

Who's I going to break the news to Mrs. Van Hopper? Shall you, or shall I?

"I"

(still scarcely believing it)

You—you tell her—she'll be so angry.

He pushes his plate away.

MAXIM

What's the number of her room?

"I"

She's not there. She's downstairs in the car.

He stretches out to the desk nearby and picks up the telephone.

MAXIM

Give me the desk, please.

(slight pause)

You'll find Mrs. Van Hopper waiting at the front entrance. Would ask her very kindly with my compliments if she could come up to see me in my room. Yes, in my room.

EXT. HOTEL DE PARIS—SEMI LONG SHOT—DAY

INT. CAR—CLOSE UP—DAY

Outside the Hotel de Paris, the CONCIERGE comes up to MRS. VAN HOPPER's car.

CONCIERGE

Mr. de Winter asks you to come up to his room.

MRS. VAN HOPPER

Mr. de Winter? . . . Why certainly . . .

She starts to clamber out, assisted by the COMMISSIONAIRE and CLERK.

INT. MAXIM'S SITTING ROOM—SEMI CLOSE UP—DAY

Back in MAXIM's room, he bends over "I" and with a hand on her shoulder says:

MAXIM

This isn't your idea of a proposal, is it? It ought to be in a conservatory—you in a white frock with a rose in your hand, and a violin playing in the distance—and I should be making violent love to you behind a palm tree.

"I" looks up at him a trifle self-consciously.

MAXIM

Poor darling—never mind.

"I"

(smiling happily)

I *don't* mind.

There is a knock at the door.

MAXIM

Don't worry, don't worry. You won't have to say a word.

SEMI CLOSE UP

MAXIM holds open the door as MRS. VAN HOPPER comes in. Her face is wreathed in smiles. She is chattering rapidly.

MRS. VAN HOPPER

I'm so glad you called me, Mr. de Winter. I was making *such* a hasty departure. It was rude of me not to let you know, but a cable came this morning announcing that my daughter is engaged to be married . . .

MAXIM comes up beside her. "I" is in the background near the door.

MAXIM

That's rather a coincidence, Mrs. Van Hopper. I asked you up here in order to tell you of *my* engagement.

MRS. VAN HOPPER

You don't mean it! Well, how perfectly wonderful! How romantic. Who *is* the lucky lady?

MAXIM merely gestures toward "I." MRS. VAN HOPPER turns and looks. Her face presents a pretty picture of utter bewilderment.

MAXIM

I have to apologize for depriving you of your companion in this abrupt way. I hope it doesn't inconvenience you too greatly.

MRS. VAN HOPPER

When did all this happen?

"I"

Just now, Mrs. Van Hopper. Only a few minutes ago.

MRS. VAN HOPPER

I simply can't believe it!

(*roguishly*)

And I suppose I ought to scold you for not having breathed a word of this to me. What am I thinking of? I should give you both my congratulations and my blessings. I'm so *very* happy for you both! When and where is the wedding to be?

MAXIM

Here. As soon as possible.

MRS. VAN HOPPER

Whirlwind romance! Splendid! I can easily postpone my sailing for a week. This poor child has no mother, so I shall take responsibility for all the arrangements—the trousseau, the reception, everything! And I'll give the bride away.

But—my luggage!

(*she wheels on "I" by force of habit*)

Go down and tell the porter to take everything out of the car.

"I" seems about to obey, but MAXIM intervenes.

MAXIM

We're most grateful to you, Mrs. Van Hopper—but I think we both prefer to have it all as quiet as possible. I couldn't possibly allow you to change your sailing plans.

MRS. VAN HOPPER

But—

MAXIM

I'll have your luggage brought back.

"I"

Thank you, MAXIM. I'll be right down.

He looks into her eyes, sees she is no longer afraid to face MRS. VAN HOPPER, and goes. MRS. VAN HOPPER turns on "I" the minute MAXIM has gone, dropping all pretense.

MRS. VAN HOPPER

So this is what has been happening during my illness! Tennis lessons my foot!

(*she goes close to* "I")

I suppose I've to hand it to you for a fast worker. How did you manage it? Still waters certainly run deep! Tell me: have you been doing anything you shouldn't?

"I"

I don't know what you mean.

MRS. VAN HOPPER

Oh, well—never mind. I always did say that Englishmen have strange tastes. But you'll certainly have your work cut out as mistress of Manderley. To be perfectly frank with you, my dear, I can't see you doing it. You haven't the experience, you haven't the faintest idea what it means to be a great lady. Of course, you know why he's marrying you, don't you? You haven't flattered yourself that he's in love with you. The fact is, that empty house got on his nerves to such an extent he nearly went off his head. He just couldn't go on living alone.

"I"

You'd better leave, Mrs. Van Hopper. You'll miss your train.

MRS. VAN HOPPER turns and faces "I." A queer twisted smile crosses her face.

MRS. VAN HOPPER

(*with withering sarcasm*)

Mrs. de Winter.

(*with a sour laugh*)

Good-bye, my dear, and *good luck*.

FADE OUT.

FADE IN: EXT. MONTE CARLO STREET—LONG SHOT—DAY

In the foreground of a Monte Carlo street stands MAXIM's car—empty. It is a fairly busy market street. A flight of steps leads up to a stone building. A sign on the building says, "*MAIRIE: SALLE DES MARIAGES*" ("Mayoralty: room for marriages.")

From the entrance come MAXIM and "I." They walk down the steps. The MAYOR leans out of one window and calls, excitedly:

MAYOR

Monsieur! Vous avez oublié votre carnet de mariage!

"I"

What is he saying?

MAXIM

(laughing)

I forgot the proof that we're married!

The MAYOR lets the certificate fly, and it flutters down to MAXIM.

EXT. MONTE CARLO STREET—SEMI LONG SHOT—DAY

MAXIM

Ahh. Somebody else had the same idea.

Near the foot of the steps, where MAXIM and "I" are standing, a noisy crowd of children and townspeople run into the picture, followed by a wedding group. The bride is in white and carries a sheaf of lilies. MAXIM and "I" look at the new wedding party.

"I"

(wistfully)

Isn't she sweet?

MAXIM

(giving her a quick look)

You'd have liked a bridal veil, or at least a bouquet, wouldn't you!

"I" doesn't answer. MAXIM looks at her and realizes he has been right. MAXIM goes over to the flower seller, and pulling a handful of notes from his pocket, takes a huge bouquet, which he presents to "I."

"I"

Oh, Max, how lovely! How perfectly lovely!

DISSOLVE TO: EXT. FRENCH STREET—
SEMI LONG SHOT—DAY

We see the car speed away up the long, rising, cobbled street.

FADE OUT.

FADE IN: EXT. MANDERIEY GATES—CLOSE UP—DAY

Worked into the wrought-iron scroll work of a pair of big gates, is the word, "*MANDERLEY*."

EXT. LARGE GATES—SEMI LONG SHOT—DAY

MAXIM and "I," seated in an open car, drive up to the opening gates of Manderley. The car slows down and continues through a Gothic arch. The car rounds the bend. Ahead is a long, gloomy stretch and another bend.

TWO SHOT—"I" & MAXIM IN THE CAR PLATE ALREADY SHOT

"I" is looking ahead, nervously. She suddenly shivers with a strange apprehension. MAXIM looks at her.

MAXIM

Cold, darling?

"I"

(with a tremulous smile)

Yes. Just a little bit.

MAXIM

No need to be frightened, you know. You've only got to be yourself and they'll all adore you. And you don't have to worry about the house—Mrs. Danvers is the housekeeper. Just leave it to her.

The length of this drive is oppressive. "I" thinks that beyond each bend she will see the house. MAXIM, with a slight frown, looks up at the sky.

MAXIM

Hello . . . started to rain.

Big raindrops begin to descend. "I" pulls a mackintosh from the back. The rain increases.

MAXIM

We'd better hurry up.

We hear the car increase in speed.

EXT. DRIVE (2D UNIT)—LONG SHOT & ANGLE OVER BONNET OF CAR—RAIN

Over their shoulders we see the hood of the car approaching another bend, and then another. At length the car turns a sharp bend and there, suddenly, is the house. The rain is now falling in torrents, but it cannot conceal the imposing building.

CLOSE TWO SHOT—"I" AND MAXIM IN CAR—
RAIN PLATE ALREADY SHOT

MAXIM turns to "I," smiles, and waves his hand toward the house.

MAXIM

That's it! That's Manderley!

As the car comes to a standstill in front of the house, we see a butler and footman waiting on the steps.

EXT. MANDERLEY—SEMI LONG SHOT—DAY

FRITH, the butler, comes running down the steps with an umbrella. MAXIM and "I" rush out under the umbrella held by FRITH.

EXT. MANDERLEY—SEMI CLOSE UP—DAY

As they mount the steps, MAXIM says:

MAXIM

Here we are, Frith. Everyone well?

FRITH

Yes, sir. Thank you, sir. I'm glad to see you home, sir. I hope you've been keeping well.

MAXIM

This is Mrs. de Winter, Frith.

"I," with wet wisps of hair hanging down her face, shyly puts out her hand to FRITH.

"I"

How do you do?

FRITH gives a little bow, then sees the outstretched hand, and takes it.

INT. HALL—SEMI LONG SHOT—
DAY SHOT FROM BEHIND THEM.

As they enter the hall and FRITH removes the umbrella, MAXIM stops. Beyond them we see about twenty servants lined up in a semicircle.

MAXIM

(annoyed)

I didn't expect the whole staff to be in attendance.

During this "I" has been pulling the mackintosh from her head. Her hair has been flattened by it, and wisps of hair have got wet and hang down her face. FRITH replies to MAXIM in a low voice.

FRITH

Mrs. Danvers' orders, sir.

MAXIM

(without expression)

Oh.

He turns to "I," from whom FRITH is taking the mackintosh.

MAXIM

I'm sorry about this, but it won't take long.

They turn towards the group of waiting servants and start to go towards them.

LONG SHOT

We get the impression of a tableau with MAXIM guiding "I" towards the group. The hall is vast, with its minstrel gallery and broad sweeping staircase.

SEMI CLOSE UP

"I" goes towards the group; rain still drips down her cheeks from the front of her hair. "I" is piloted towards the group of waiting servants by MAXIM. We see the shyness overcoming her as she advances.

Almost as though from nowhere, the figure of a tall, gaunt woman steps into the side of the picture and advances.

MAXIM

This is Mrs. Danvers.

MRS. DANVERS

(coldly to "I")

How do you do, Madam. I have everything in readiness for you.

"I"

Oh, . . . that's good of you, I'm sure. I didn't expect . . . anything.

She is playing with her glove in her nervousness and drops it.

MAXIM

We'd like some tea, Frith.

FRITH

It's ready in the library, sir.

MRS. DANVERS stoops to pick up "I"'s glove. She hands it to her with the faintest trace of a smile of scorn. "I" is very unhappy. MRS. DANVERS looks her straight in the eye. "I" cannot bear her look and lowers her eyes.

MAXIM

Come along, darling.

As "I" steals a look at MRS. DANVERS and turns away, the scorn on MRS. DANVERS' face increases slightly.

FADE OUT.

FADE IN: INT. "I'S" SUITE—LATE EVENING TWILIGHT

In "I"'s bedroom, thin streaks of light coming in from outside.

CLOSE SHOT

ALICE, the maid, is rather distastefully handling "I's" wet clothes.

"I" is seated at the dressing table, trying to do something with her lank hair. "I," furtively watching ALICE in the mirror, wishes she'd go. There is a knock at the door. "I" looks up eagerly.

"I"

Oh, MAXIM? Come in!

MED. SHOT—DOOR

The door opens and in comes MRS. DANVERS.

"I'S" VOICE

(disappointed)

Oh. Good evening, Mrs. Danvers.

MRS. DANVERS

Good evening, Madam.

MRS. DANVERS moves into the room. She glances at ALICE—a glance of dismissal. ALICE puts "I's" wet clothes over her arm, looks at Mrs. Danvers as much as to say "look at these rags," and goes.

MRS. DANVERS

I hope that Alice has been satisfactory, Madam?

"I"

Oh, yes, thank you—perfectly.

MRS. DANVERS

She's the parlor maid. She'll have to look after you until your own maid arrives.

"I"

But I haven't a maid. I'm sure Alice will do very nicely.

MRS. DANVERS

(coldly)

I'm afraid that would not do for very long, Madam. It's usual for ladies in your position to have a personal maid.

CLOSE UP

"I" looking at MRS. DANVERS. She is unable to stand the steady, freezing gaze of this woman, and turns away, pretending to be busy with her face powder.

SEMI LONG SHOT

MRS. DANVERS goes over to inspect the arrangement of the beds.

MRS. DANVERS

I hope you approve the new decoration of these rooms, Madam.

"I"

Oh, I didn't know they'd been changed. I hope you didn't have to go to too much trouble.

MRS. DANVERS

I only followed Mr. de Winter's instructions.

"I"

What did it look like before?

MRS. DANVERS

It had an old paper and different hangings. It was never used much, except for occasional visitors.

"I"

Then it wasn't Mr. de Winter's room originally?

MRS. DANVERS

No, Madam. He has never used the *east* wing before. Of course, there is no view of the sea from here.

"I" is looking toward MRS. DANVERS.

MRS. DANVERS

The only good view of the sea is from the *west* wing.

"I"

The room is very charming, and I'm sure I shall be comfortable.

There is a moment's silence. "I" doesn't know what to do with herself, picks up her brushes again.

SEMI LONG SHOT

MRS. DANVERS turning from window and coming back to "I."

MRS. DANVERS

If there is anything you want done, Madam, you have only to tell me.

"I"

I suppose you've been at Manderley for many years—longer than anyone else?

MRS. DANVERS

Not so long as Frith. He was here when the old gentleman was living—when Mr. de Winter was a boy.

"I"

And you didn't come until after that?

MRS. DANVERS

I came here when the first Mrs. de Winter was a bride.

CLOSE UP

"I" looks away sharply. For a second we see the effect of the words on her face; then with an effort she summons her courage and swinging round in her chair, faces MRS. DANVERS directly.

"I"

Mrs. Danvers, I hope we shall be friends. You must be patient with me. This sort of life is new to me. And I do want to make a success of it and make Mr. de Winter happy. I know I can leave all the household arrangements to you.

MRS. DANVERS
(coldly)
Very well. I hope I shall do everything to your satisfaction, Madam. I've managed the house since Mrs. de Winter's death, and Mr. de Winter has never complained.

MRS. DANVERS turns to leave but stops at the door and glares back at "I."

"I"
I—I think I'll go downstairs now.

INT. HALL—SEMI LONG SHOT

Along the long passage, MRS. DANVERS and "I" go toward the stairs.

SEMI CLOSE UP

As they reach the top of the stairs, MRS. DANVERS pauses and points to a door along the broad passage on the other side of the stairs.

MRS. DANVERS
The room in the west wing I was telling you about is there—through that door. It's not used now. It's the most beautiful room in the house—the only one that looks down across the lawns to the sea. *It was Mrs. de Winter's room.*

"I" hesitates while looking at the door. She turns and sees MRS. DANVERS' eyes fixed on her. MRS. DANVERS turns and moves swiftly out of picture. "I" glances back toward the door.

SEMI LONG SHOT

Over "I's" shoulder we see the mysterious door. Then we see lying against the foot of it, Rebecca's dog, JASPER.

FADE OUT.

FADE IN: INT. DINING ROOM—NIGHT

CentEred in the foreground, on a place setting, is a napkin bearing the monogram: "R de W." Then we see "I" removing it and placing it on her lap. Then we see the whole dining table, with MAXIM at the head, unfolding his napkin, with FRITH and ROBERT, the footman, removing the service plates and preparing to serve the soup.

FADE OUT.

FADE IN: EXT. MANDERLEY—LONG SHOT—DAY

A long view of Manderley in the early morning. It is a beautiful, sunny, peaceful day.

DISSOLVE TO: INT. DINING ROOM—LONG SHOT—DAY

"I" comes into the dining room carrying her handbag, just as she did in the hotel. She is surprised to see a stranger seated at the table, near MAXIM's place. It is FRANK CRAWLEY. He has a great many letters and papers before him, which he is sorting out. He jumps to his feet as he sees "I."

FRANK
(awkwardly and shyly)
Good morning.

"I"
Good morning.

FRANK
You're Mrs. de Winter, aren't you?

"I"
Yes.

FRANK
(embarrassed)
My name is Crawley. I manage the estate for Maxim.
(pause)
I'm awfully glad to meet you.

Fearful lot of stuff piled up while Maxim was away.

"I"
Yes, I'm sure there must have been.
(Another embarrassed pause)
I do wish I could help with some of it.

SEMI CLOSE UP—DINING ROOM DOOR

MAXIM has come in, carrying some letters. He has heard "I's" remark.

MAXIM
Oh, no. Frank won't allow anyone to help him. He's like an old mother hen with all his bills and rents and taxes. Well, come on, Frank. We must go over these estimates.

FRANK

I'll get my papers.

FRANK goes out of scene to gather up the papers.

SEMI CLOSE UP

MAXIM

You'll find quantities of breakfast over there, on the sideboard. You must eat it all, or cook will be mortally offended.

"I"

(smiling)

I'll do my best, MAXIM.

MAXIM

I have to go over the place with Frank to make sure he hasn't lost any of it. But you'll be all right, won't you? Getting acquainted with your new home.

MAXIM gives her a quick, perfunctory kiss on the forehead and turns and goes.

MAXIM

Have a look at *The Times*. There's a thrilling article on what's the matter with English cricket.

MEDIUM SHOT

As MAXIM and FRANK go to the door, MAXIM turns.

MAXIM

Oh—I forgot to tell you—my sister, Beatrice, and her husband, Giles Lacy, have invited themselves over for lunch.

"I"

Today?

SEMI CLOSE UP

MAXIM

Yes. I suppose the old girl can't wait to look you over. You'll find her very direct. If she doesn't like you, she'll probably tell you so to your face.

Don't worry, darling—I'll be back in time to protect you from her. Good-bye, darling.

"I"

Goodbye, Maxim.

SEMI CLOSE UP

"I" lifts the lids of the numerous covered dishes on the sideboard. There are eggs, bacon, sausages, kedgeree, kippers, haddock, kidneys, oatmeal—and great sides of cold meats. The sight of so much food destroys whatever appetite she may have had. She pours herself a cup of tea and takes it to her lonely place at the end of the great table.

MED. SHOT—SCREEN BEFORE PANTRY DOOR

FRITH and ROBERT enter. ROBERT goes to the sideboard, FRITH to "I."

FRITH

Good morning, Madam.

"I"

Good morning, Frith.

FRITH crosses to the side table, glances at the covered dishes, undisturbed, then turns again to "I."

FRITH

Isn't there anything I could get for you, Madam?

"I" is drinking her tea.

"I"

No thank you. Really, I'm not hungry.

"I" puts down her cup, rises, and starts to go.

FRITH

The papers, Madam.

ROBERT has picked them up and handed them to her.

"I"

Oh—thank you.

She takes the papers and starts to the door. As she comes near it, she slips on the polished floor, almost falls.

MEDIUM SHOT

FRITH rushes forward to catch her. The camera swings with them as they come up to her.

"I"
(lamely)
I—I slipped.

She goes into the great hall. FRITH steadies her for a few steps, guiding her by the arm.

"I"
Thank you, Frith.

She looks about the hall.

"I"
It's very big, isn't it?

FRITH
Yes, madam—Manderley *is* a big place. This was the banquet hall in the old days. It's still used on great occasions, such as a big dinner or ball, and the public is admitted here, you know, once a week.

"I"
That's nice.

She walks on, unable to think of anything better to say.

INT. LIBRARY—SEMI LONG SHOT—DAY

In the library, the windows are wide open and the curtains blowing. "I" enters and gives a shiver. She crosses to the windows, looks out. Masses of clouds are blowing up from over the sea, covering the sun. She closes the windows, goes to the fireplace, looks about for matches.

LIBRARY DOOR

FRITH appears in the doorway.

FRITH
I beg pardon, madam.

CLOSE UP

"I" turns quickly, guiltily. She feels she's been caught doing something she shouldn't.

FRITH
I wished to say, madam, that the fire is not usually lit in the library until the afternoon.

But you will find one in the morning room. Of course, if you wish this fire lit now, madam . . .

"I"

Oh, no—I wouldn't dream of it. Thank you, Frith.

FRITH

Mrs. de Winter—(he hesitates, fearing that he has been tactless)—I mean, the late Mrs. de Winter—always did her correspondence and telephoning in the morning room after breakfast.

"I"

Thank you, Frith.

She turns and goes back towards the hall.

INT. HALL—DAY—SEMI CLOSE UP

Outside the dining room door, she takes a few steps, then pauses awkwardly.

FRITH

Is there anything wrong, madam?

"I"

(hesitating)

No. Which way is the morning room?

FRITH

It's that door there, on the left.

SEMI LONG SHOT

FRITH in the foreground, "I's" small figure crosses the large hall.

INT. MORNING ROOM—LONG SHOT—DAY

"I" comes into the small morning room. It is a bright and cheerful room, exquisitely furnished and obviously a woman's room by the quantities of flowers in it. There is a blazing fire, in front of which JASPER is lying. "I" shyly inspects the room.

SEMI CLOSE UP

JASPER gets up from before the fire and ambles out the room.

SEMI CLOSE UP

"I" does not notice the dog has gone. She behaves almost as though she were an intruder. She crosses to the writing desk, and begins to examine its contents, which include an address book, guest book, and menu book. She looks almost furtively about her. A slight sound from outside makes her start guiltily away, but after a moment she turns back.

CLOSE UP

She picks up an address book, and we see the initials "R de W." "I" lowers herself into the chair. Suddenly we hear a telephone ring.

"I" starts, and with her eyes still fixed on the open book, lifts the telephone hurriedly. She puts the receiver to her ear. She listens for a moment, and then apparently repeats what was said to her.

"I"

Mrs. de Winter? I'm afraid you've made a mistake. Mrs. de Winter has been dead for over a year.

As she starts to replace the receiver, she suddenly realizes her faux pas and exclaims:

"I"

Oh, I mean . . .

There is a slight sound behind her; she turns quickly and looks upwards.

MRS. DANVERS stands behind her chair, regarding her with expressionless eyes.

MRS. DANVERS

That was the house telephone, Madam. Probably the head gardener, wishing instructions.

"I"

(lamely)

Did you want to see me, Mrs. Danvers?

MRS. DANVERS

Mr. de Winter has informed me that his sister, Beatrice Lacey, and Major Lacey are expected for luncheon. I'd like to know if you approve of the menu.

She bends over "I" and, picking up a menu from the desk, proffers it to her.

"I"

(without looking at it)

Oh, I'm sure they're very suitable—very nice, indeed.

MRS. DANVERS

You will notice, Madam, that I left a blank space for the sauce. Mrs. de Winter was always most particular about sauces.

"I"

Oh... let's have whatever you think Mrs. de Winter would have ordered.

MRS. DANVERS prepares to withdraw. She looks steadily at "I" as she says:

MRS. DANVERS

Thank you, Madam. (as she goes she adds) When you have finished your letters, Madam, Robert will take them to the post.

"I"

My letters? Oh, yes, of course, Mrs. Danvers.

"I," feeling it incumbent on her to do some correspondence, hesitates, looks around, then opens the drawer at the left of the writing table. She takes out a sheet of the expensive note paper, puts it down on the desk and sits. She opens Rebecca's address book.

CLOSE UP

We see a page of address book from over "I's" shoulder. In Rebecca's handwriting we see several names:

Duchess of Atherton
12 Wingate Place
Sir Nigel Armbruster
412 Landsdowne Road
Marquis of Armingham
3 Palace Court Lane

"I" knocks over a china cupid on the desk. It falls to the floor and smashes. She hastily gathers up the pieces and stuffs them in the back of a desk drawer. Then she settles down again despondently in her chair.

FADE OUT.

INT. HALL—LONG SHOT—DAY

In the hall, GILES and BEATRICE are entering. FRITH is taking GILES' hat and BEATRICE 's cape.

BEATRICE

Hello, Frith.

FRITH

Good morning, Mrs. Lacy.

BEATRICE

Where's Mr. de Winter?

FRITH

I believe he went down to the farm with Mr. Crawley.

BEATRICE

How tiresome of him not to be here when we arrive—and how typical!

During this we see "I" in foreground at the head of the stairs, shrinking back into the shadows out of view as FRITH shows GILES and BEATRICE into the library. JASPER looks up at her and whines.

HALL LEADING TO LIBRARY—MEDIUM SHOT AT DOOR

"I" comes into the scene and stops a few feet from the library door, which is partially open. She stops to adjust her clothes a little and gives a few frantic pats to her hair. She hears voices from the library.

BEATRICE'S VOICE

I must say that old Danvers does keep the house looking lovely. She certainly learned that trick of arranging flowers from Rebecca.

GILES' VOICE

I wonder how she likes it now—being ordered about by an ex-chorus girl.

BEATRICE'S VOICE

Now—where on earth did you get the idea she's an ex-chorus girl?

GILES' VOICE

He picked her up in the South of France, didn't he?

BEATRICE'S VOICE

What if he did?

GILES' VOICE

Well—I mean to say—there you are.

"I" pushes open the door and goes in. GILES and BEATRICE stand up.

"I"
(timidly)
How do you do—I'm MAXIM's wife.

For a moment they both stare at her, both obviously surprised, then BEATRICE starts forward.

BEATRICE
(murmuring as she approaches)
How do you do?

SEMI CLOSE UP

BEATRICE goes close to "I" and subjects her to close scrutiny.

BEATRICE
Well—I must say—you're quite different from what I expected!

CLOSE UP

"I," upset as well as taken aback by BEATRICE's remark, shyly shakes the hand BEATRICE is holding out to her, as GILES adds an embarrassed—

GILES
(palpably lying)
Don't be silly. She's exactly what I told you she'd be.

He also holds out his hand and shakes very firmly with "I," as he continues:

GILES
Well—er—er—how d'you like Manderley?

"I"
It's very beautiful, isn't it?

BEATRICE
And how are you getting along with Mrs. Danvers?

"I"
Well, I've never met anyone quite like her before. She's—er—

GILES
You mean she scares you—she's not exactly an oil painting, is she? (he laughs uproariously at his own joke)

BEATRICE
Giles, you're very much in the way here. Go somewhere else.

GILES
(coughing)
I'll try to find Maxim, shall I?

GILES lingers.

BEATRICE
Giles . . .

GILES goes out.

"I"
(shyly)
I—I—didn't mean to say anything against Mrs. Danvers.

BEATRICE
Oh, there's no need to be frightened of her. But I shouldn't have any more to do with her than you can help. Shall we sit down?

"I"
Oh, yes, yes—please.

BEATRICE
You see, she's bound to be insanely jealous at first and she must resent you bitterly.

"I"
(astonished)
But why should she?

BEATRICE
Don't you know? I should have thought Maxim would have told you. She simply adored Rebecca!

We see "I" reacting to BEATRICE's statement.

DISSOLVE TO: LONG SHOT

DINING ROOM

In the dining room, BEATRICE is on MAXIM's right, FRANK on his left. GILES is on "I"'s right.

ROBERT is offering a platter of meat and vegetables to BEATRICE. She puts some on her plate.

BEATRICE
How are you, Robert?

ROBERT

Quite well, thank you, Madam.

BEATRICE

Still having trouble with your teeth?

ROBERT

(embarrassed)

Unfortunately yes, Madam.

BEATRICE

You must have them out—all of them! Wretched nuisances—teeth.

ROBERT

Thank you, Madam.

With a great air of cheeriness, GILES is making conversation with "I."

GILES

Do you hunt?

"I"

No—I'm afraid, I don't even ride.

GILES

Have to ride down here. We all do. Which do you ride—side-saddle or astride? Oh, I forgot—you don't, do you? You must! Nothing else to do down here.

BEATRICE

Maxim, When will you start having parties here like the old days?

MAXIM

(grimly)

Haven't thought about it.

BEATRICE

But everyone's dying to see you and—

(she looks off toward "I"*).*

MAXIM

I can imagine.

BEATRICE

What about having the masquerade ball again this summer?

BEATRICE calls down to "I."

BEATRICE

My dear, are you fond of dancing?

SEMI CLOSE UP—"I" AND GILES

"I"

I love it. But I'm not very good at it.

GILES

Do you rhumba?

"I"

I've never tried.

GILES

You must teach me.

(he turns to MAXIM)

I say, old boy—I've been trying to find out what your wife *does* do.

MAXIM

(smiles)

She sketches a little.

GILES

Sketches! Not this modern stuff, oh? You know, picture of a lamp-shade upside down to represent a soul in torment.

You don't—uh—you don't sail, do you?

"I"

(in a strained voice)

No—I don't.

GILES

Thank goodness for that!

There is general consternation about the table. MAXIM stares grimly into space. BEATRICE glares at GILES as though she would slay him. GILES slaps his hand over his mouth.

Slowly the significance of what GILES has said begins to show on "I's" face. She flushes with embarrassment and looks down at her plate.

FADE OUT.

FADE IN: INT. "I'S" BEDROOM—SEMI CLOSE UP—DAY

In "I"'s bedroom, BEATRICE is adjusting her hat before the mirror. "I" is beside her.

BEATRICE

You're very much in love with Maxim, aren't you?

"I"

Why?

BEATRICE

I can see that you are . . . Don't mind my saying so, but why don't you do something about your hair? Why don't you have it cut . . . or sweep it back behind your ears?

"I" holds her hair back behind her ears, turning her head for BEATRICE's inspection. The latter looks at her critically.

BEATRICE

No, that's worse. What does MAXIM say about it . . . Does he like it like that?

"I"

I don't know—he's never mentioned it.

BEATRICE

Oh, well—don't go by me. I can tell by the way you dress you don't care a hoot how you look. But I wonder Maxim hasn't been at you. He's so particular about clothes.

"I"

I don't believe he ever notices what I wear.

BEATRICE

(as they start out)

He must have changed a lot, then . . .

INT. UPPER CORRIDOR—DAY

During this scene BEATRICE and "I" go to the stairs and down them, reaching a point in the lower hall near the large table.

BEATRICE

You mustn't worry about old Maxim—and his moods. One never knows what's going on in that quiet mind of his. Off he gets into a terrible rage—and when he *does!* But—I don't suppose he'll lose his temper with you. You seem such a placid little thing.

GILES' VOICE

(from the front door)

Come *along*, old girl. We're supposed to be on the first tee at three o'clock.

BEATRICE

All right. I'm coming!

As they go out the front door, GILES says:

GILES

Goodbye, Maxim, old boy!

MAXIM

Goodbye, Giles. Thanks for coming, old boy.

EXT. MANDERLEY—SEMI LONG SHOT—DAY

On the steps of the front entrance, MAXIM, "I," GILES, and BEATRICE emerge onto the steps. ROBERT stands near the door in the background. JASPER comes out too.

BEATRICE kisses "I" on the cheek.

BEATRICE

Well, goodbye, my dear. Forgive me for asking so many rude questions. We both really hope you'll be very happy.

"I"

(almost emotional in her hunger for kindness)

Oh, thank you, Beatrice, thank you very much!

BEATRICE

And I must congratulate you on the way Maxim looks. We were all very worried about him this time last year. But, of course, you know the whole story.

DISSOLVE TO:

GILES and BEATRICE are just pulling away in a car, waving good-bye. It disappears out of the picture for a moment and then sweeps around the wide drive, away into the distance.

SEMI CLOSE UP

MAXIM takes a step or two down and looks up into the sky.

MAXIM

Thank heavens they're gone! Now, at last, we can have a walk about the place. It looks like we might have a shower—but you won't mind that, will you?

"I"

(happily)

Of course not, Maxim. I'll go upstairs and get a coat.

MAXIM

There's a heap of mackintoshes in the flower room.

MAXIM goes up and steps inside the front door, calling inside.

MAXIM

Robert! Run and get a coat from the flower room for Mrs. de Winter.

MAXIM comes back to "I."

What did you think of Beatrice?

"I"

I liked her very much. But she kept saying that I was quite different from what she expected.

MAXIM

What the devil *did* she expect?

"I"

Someone much smarter, more sophisticated, I suppose.

(*she pauses*)

Do you like my hair?

MAXIM looks at her in astonishment.

MAXIM

Your hair? Of course I do. What's the matter with it?

"I"

Oh, nothing. I just wondered.

MAXIM

(*looking at her*)

How funny you are.

ROBERT comes out from the house, carrying an oilskin coat.

"I"

Do I have to put it on?

MAXIM

Yes, certainly, certainly, certainly. Can't be too careful with children.

MAXIM helps "I" into it, then says to JASPER:

Come on, you lazy little beggar, and take some of that fat off.

SEMI LONG SHOT

They descend the steps and set out, arm in arm, across the lawn, JASPER following at MAXIM's heels.

CLOSE UP—JASPER

As he follows behind them.

DISSOLVE TO: 2ND UNIT AS SHOT—
EXT. MANDERLEY—LONG SHOT—DAY

"I" and MAXIM are walking over the grounds away from the house, JASPER with them.

EXT. LAWN—LONG SHOT. 2ND UNIT (L.S. AS SHOT)

EXT. NEAR TOP OF CLIFF—WITH SEA BELOW

As they walk along, they come to a fork in the paths leading down to the sea, and JASPER unhesitatingly runs ahead and disappears down the path farthest to the right.

MAXIM

Jasper! Not that way! Come here!

JASPER starts to scamper down stairs which lead to the beach.

CLOSE SHOT—MAXIM AND "I"
(AGAINST PLATE AS SHOT)

"I"

Where does that lead to?

MAXIM
(briefly)
It leads to a small cove where we used to keep a boat.

"I"

Let's go down there.

MAXIM
(irritably)
Well, no, It's just a dull and uninteresting stretch of sand—just like any other.

"I"

Oh, please . . .

MAXIM

(seeing her look of disappointment)

All right . . . We'll walk down and take a look if you really want to.

2ND UNIT AS SHOT LONG SHOT

"I" and MAXIM start forward again.

2ND UNIT AS SHOT LONG SHOT

"I" and MAXIM turn from the top of the palisades down onto the stairs leading to the beach, and walking down. JASPER runs ahead, barking.

"I" and MAXIM come down onto the beach. JASPER has disappeared, but they hear his bark from the other side of the rocks.

"I"

(pointing)

That's Jasper!

(worried)

There may be something wrong—perhaps he's hurt himself.

MAXIM

He's all right. Leave him alone.

"I"

Don't you think I'd better go and see?

MAXIM

(angrily)

Don't bother about him, I tell you. He can't come to any harm. He'll find his own way back.

But "I" has already left the picture. She starts clambering over rocks, calling out:

"I"

Jasper, Jasper! Oh, there you are!

"I" has reached the other side of the rocks and is now on a stretch of beach in a cove, hidden from MAXIM's view. This is a seminatural harbor created by the rocks jutting out into the sea. A mooring buoy is a little way out from the shore.

Shaded by the trees, which come down very nearly to the water's edge, is a small cottage. "I" stands a moment as she sees the reason for JASPER's barking.

JASPER is barking and leaping at the front door of the cottage, then lies down.

"I" comes up to him and crouches down.

"I"

Come on. What do you want in there? Let's go home. Jasper, Jasper!

The door of the cottage slowly opens, revealing BEN, a man dressed like a fisherman, with the face of an idiot. He peers fearfully at "I," then looks down at JASPER.

"I"

I didn't know that there was anybody . . .

BEN

I know that dog. He comes from the 'ouse. He ain't your'n.

"I"

No. He's Mr. de Winter's dog. Have you anything I could tie him with?

BEN gapes open-mouthed at her. Suppressing her exasperation, she goes into the boathouse.

INT. INNER BOATHOUSE

In the boathouse, "I" enters a room completely furnished with bookshelves, table, chairs, bed sofa, and a blanket with the monogram "R de W." There are also ropes, sails, pots of paint, and other paraphernalia. "I" looks round and finds a short piece of thin rope. She picks it up and hurries out with it.

Outside, "I" ties up JASPER. In front of the cottage, BEN is standing in a shadow in a corner.

BEN

Don't tell anyone you saw me in there, will you?

"I"

Don't you belong on the estate?

BEN

I wasn't doing nothin'. I was just putting me shells away.

She's gone in the sea, ain't she? She'll never come back no more.

CLOSE TWO SHOT—"I" AND BEN

"I"

No, she'll never come back. Come on, Jasper.

"I" climbs back onto the other section of beach toward where she had left MAXIM, with JASPER on his makeshift leash, to find it empty of MAXIM. She hurries, JASPER running ahead of her, to the stairs and up.

MAXIM sees "I" approach, turns and goes off. "I" runs into scene, breathless, calling after him.

"I"

Maxim! What's the matter? Maxim?

She starts out after, trying desperately to catch up with him.

"I"

I'm sorry I was such a time, but I had to find a rope for Jasper.

MAXIM strides forward silently at a still faster pace. The dog lags behind, delaying "I." MAXIM turns to look down at him.

MAXIM

Hurry up, Jasper, for heaven's sake!

"I"

Please wait for me. You look so angry!

MAXIM

You knew I didn't want you to go there—but you deliberately went.

"I"

Why not? There was only a cottage down there—and a strange man who was—

MAXIM

You didn't go *into* the cottage, did you?

"I"

Yes.

MAXIM

(interrupting)

Don't go in there again! Do you hear?

"I"

Why not?

MAXIM

Because I hate the place—and if you had my memories, you wouldn't go there or talk about it or even think about it!

"I"

MAXIM, what's the matter? I'm sorry, darling! Please!

MAXIM

We ought to have stayed away. We should never have come back to Manderley! What a fool I was!

"I"

I've made you unhappy. Somehow I've hurt you. I can't bear to see you like this, because I love you so much.

MAXIM

(tensely, searching her face; takes her in his arms)

Do you? Do you?

He kisses her, then relaxes his hold.

Ah, I've made you cry . . . Forgive me—I sometimes seem to fly off the handle for no reason at all, don't I. Come: we'll go up and have some tea and forget all about it.

She smiles up at him through her tears.

"I"

Yes, let's forget all about it.

MAXIM

Here—let me have Jasper.

As she hands the leash to MAXIM, "I" automatically puts her hand in the pocket of the mackintosh, pulls out a handkerchief, and puts it to her eyes. She glances down at the handkerchief as she starts to return it to her pocket. The handkerchief is marked in the corner with a large embroidered initial "R." "I" stares down at the initial with a faraway look.

FADE OUT.

FADE IN: INT. HALL—SEMI CLOSE UP—DAY

In the large hall, "I" seated with her legs curled under her on one of the window seats, looking thoughtfully out.

EXT. MANDERLEY—SEMI LONG SHOT—DAY

INT. HALL—SEMI CLOSE UP—DAY

"I" looks very disturbed. She turns away from the window, thinking hard.

SEMI CLOSE UP

"I" suddenly jumps to her feet and with a determined air crosses to the library.

INT. LIBRARY—SEMI LONG SHOT—DAY

As she comes into the library, she sees FRANK CRAWLEY seated at a desk, immersed in his work.

INT. OFFICE—SEMI LONG SHOT—DAY

As he sees "I" come in, FRANK stands up.

FRANK

Oh, hello, come in.

"I"

(as he rises)

No, please don't get up, Mr. Crawley. I was wondering if you really meant what you said the other day about showing me the run of things?

FRANK

Of course I did.

"I"

What are you doing now?

FRANK

Notifying all the tenants that in celebration of Maxim's return with his bride, this week's rent will be free.

"I"

(greatly pleased)

Was that Maxim's idea?

FRANK

Oh, yes! All the servants get an extra week's wages, too.

"I"

He didn't tell me. Can't I help you? I could at least lick the stamps.

FRANK

(weakly)

That's terribly nice of you. Won't you sit down?

"I"

Oh, yes, thank you.

"I" sits down. He starts handing her envelopes as he addresses them. She licks the stamps and applies them as they talk.

"I"

(assuming a much too casual tone)

I was down at the cottage on the beach the other day. There was a man there—a queer sort of person. Jasper kept barking at him.

FRANK

It must have been Ben. He's quite harmless. We give him odd jobs now and then.

"I"

That cottage place down there seemed to be going to rack and ruin. Why isn't something done about it?

FRANK

I think if Maxim wanted anything done about it, he'd tell me.

"I"

Are those all Rebecca's things down there?

FRANK

Yes, yes, they are.

"I"

What did she use the cottage for?

FRANK

The boat used to be moored near there.

"I"

What boat? What happened to it? Was that the boat she was sailing in when she was drowned?

FRANK

Yes, it capsized and sank. She was washed overboard.

"I"

Wasn't she afraid to go out like that alone?

FRANK

She wasn't afraid of anything.

"I"

Where did they find her?

FRANK

Near Edgecoombe, about forty miles up channel—about two months afterwards. Maxim went up to identify her. It was horrible for him.

"I"

Yes, it must have been. Mr. Crawley, please don't think me too morbidly curious. It's just that I always feel myself at such a disadvantage—all the time. Whenever I meet anyone—Maxim's sister—even the servants—I know they're all thinking the same thing: they're all comparing me with—(she can't get the name out)—with—her—with Rebecca.

FRANK turns to her, very much concerned.

FRANK

You mustn't think that! For my part, I can't tell you how delighted I am that you married Maxim. It's going to make all the difference to his life . . . And from my point of view, it's very refreshing to find someone like yourself who is not entirely—in tune, shall we say, with Manderley.

"I"

(her eyes lowered)

That's very sweet of you. I daresay I've been stupid, but every day, I realize the things that she had that I lack. Beauty and wit and intelligence and all the things that are so important.

FRANK

But you have qualities that are just as important—more important, if I may say so. Kindliness, sincerity, and—if you'll forgive me—modesty mean more to a husband than all the wit and beauty in the world. We none of us want to live in the past, Maxim least of all. It's up to you, you know, to lead us away from it.

"I"

I promise you I won't bring this up again, but before we leave this conversation, would you answer just one more question?

FRANK

If it's something I'm able to answer, I'll do my best.

"I"

Tell me. What was Rebecca really like?

FRANK

(looks ahead reflectively and answers slowly)

I suppose—I suppose she was the most beautiful creature I ever saw.

FADE OUT

CLOSE UP

We see a close-up of a fashion magazine: *Beauty: The Magazine for Smart Women*. As the pages turn, they stop on a black gown with roses adorning the front, with the caption "For the Gala Evening."

FADE IN: INT. MANDERLEY HALL—NIGHT

In the hall, "I" is clad in the same gown that we have just seen in the magazine. She is very conscious of her clothes and appearance, rather excited by them, but very nervous. She goes into the library.

"I"

Good evening, Maxim.

CLOSE SHOT—MAXIM—HIS BACK TO CAMERA

MAXIM

(without turning)

Hello... The films of the honeymoon have arrived at last. Have we time for them before dinner?

On his last words, he turns and gradually is aware of her appearance. He looks at her. She walks in, affected and nervous.

MAXIM

What on earth have you done to yourself?

"I"

(casually)

Oh, nothing... I just ordered a new dress from London... I hope you don't mind.

MAXIM

Oh, no. But do you think that sort of thing is right for you? It doesn't seem your type at all.

"I"

(very let down)

Oh... I thought you'd like it.

MAXIM

(the cruel male!)

And what have you done to your hair?

"I" doesn't answer. MAXIM sees he has hurt her, puts his arm around her.

Oh, I see, I see, I see... Oh, dear, well . . . never mind . . . You look lovely—lovely. It's very nice—for a change . . .

(dismissing the whole thing)

Shall we see these pictures?

"I"

(very let down)

Yes, I'd love to see them.

MAXIM goes over and turns out the lights. The room is now lit only by the one lamp and the light from the projector. MAXIM is more or less lost in darkness. They watch the films with delight.

MAXIM

Look! Look! Look at you!

"I"

Wasn't that wonderful, darling? Can't we go back there sometime?

MAXIM

Yes, yes, of course! Ahh, look at you! There! Won't our grandchildren be delighted when they see how lovely you were!

"I"

Oh, look at you! Oh, I like that! Oh, remember that! Oh, I wish our honeymoon could have lasted forever, Maxim!

The film suddenly comes off the sprockets and breaks.

MAXIM

Oh, dash it! Oh, hang it! Threaded it up wrong as usual or something!

By this time the lights in the room are on. FRITH enters.

MAXIM

Yes, Frith, what is it?

FRITH

Excuse me, sir. May I have a word with you?

MAXIM

Yes, come in!

FRITH

It's about Robert, sir. There's been a slight unpleasantness between him and Mrs. Danvers.

MAXIM

Oh, dear.

FRITH

Robert is very upset.

MAXIM

Well, this *is* trouble! What is it?

FRITH

(with a nervous cough)

It appears that Mrs. Danvers has accused Robert of stealing a valuable ornament from the morning room. Robert denies the accusation most emphatically, sir.

MAXIM

What was the thing, anyway?

FRITH

The china cupid, sir.

MAXIM

Oh, dear, that's one of our treasures, isn't it? Well, tell Mrs. Danvers to get at the bottom of it, but tell her I'm sure that it wasn't Robert.

FRITH

(relieved)

Very good, sir.

He exits. As soon as he has gone, MAXIM walks over toward the machine.

MAXIM

Why do they come to me with these things? That's your job, sweetheart.

"I"

Maxim . . . I wanted to tell you, but . . . but well, I forgot. The fact is . . . *I* broke the china cupid.

MAXIM

(very surprised)

You broke it? Now why on earth didn't you say something about it when Frith was here?

"I"

I don't know. I didn't like to. I was afraid he would think me a fool.

MAXIM

He'll think you much more of a fool now. You'll have to explain to him and Mrs. Danvers.

"I"

Oh, no, Maxim! You do it! I'll go upstairs.

MAXIM

(very annoyed)

Don't be such a little idiot, darling. Anyone would think you were afraid of them.

FRITH enters, ushering in MRS. DANVERS, who is obviously very angry.

MAXIM

(interrupting and obviously very annoyed with the whole thing)

It's all a mistake, Mrs. Danvers. Apparently Mrs. de Winter broke the cupid herself and forgot to say anything about it.

"I"

I'm so sorry. I never thought that I would get Robert would get into trouble.

MRS. DANVERS

Is it possible to repair the ornament, Madam?

"I"

No, I'm afraid it isn't. It smashed in pieces.

MAXIM

What did you do with the pieces?

"I"

I put them at the back of one of the drawers in the writing desk.

MAXIM

It looks as though Mrs. de Winter were afraid you were going to put her in prison, doesn't it, Mrs. Danvers? Well, never mind. Do what you can to find the pieces, see if they can be mended, and above all, tell Robert to dry his tears.

MRS. DANVERS

I will apologize to Robert, of course. Perhaps if such a thing happens again, Mrs. de Winter will tell me personally . . .

MAXIM

(interrupting impatiently)

Yes, yes, all right, thank you, Mrs. Danvers...

MRS. DANVERS leaves the room. MAXIM goes about the business of repairing the film or of taking off the reel and putting in another, the scene continuing the while.

MAXIM

Well, I suppose that clip will hold all right, I don't know...

"I"

I'm awfully sorry, darling. It was very careless of me. Mrs. Danvers must be furious with me.

MAXIM

Hang Mrs. Danvers! Why on earth should you be frightened of her? You behave more like an upstairs maid or something, not like the mistress of the house at all.

"I"

I know I do. But I feel so uncomfortable... I try my best every day, but it's very difficult with people looking me up and down as if I were a prize cow.

MAXIM

(putting the film into the projector)

What does it matter if they do? You must remember that life at Manderley is the only thing that interests anybody down here.

"I"

What a slap in the eye I must have been to them, then... I suppose that's why you married me... You knew I was dull and gauche and inexperienced, so there could never be any gossip about me.

MAXIM

Gossip! What do you mean?

"I"

I—I don't know. It was just something to say. Don't look at me like that! What's the matter? What have I said?

MAXIM turns off the projector.

MAXIM

It wasn't a very attractive thing to say, was it?

"I"

No. It was rude, hateful.

MAXIM

(coldly)

I wonder if I did a very selfish thing in marrying you.

"I"

(her voice almost a hoarse whisper, with fright)

How do you mean?

MAXIM

I'm not much of a companion to you, am I? You don't get much fun, do you? You ought to have married a boy, someone of your own age . . .

"I"

(interrupting)

Oh, MAXIM, why do you say this? Of course we're companions.

MAXIM

Are we? I don't know. I'm very difficult to live with.

"I"

(eagerly)

You're not difficult! You're easy, very easy. Our marriage is a success, isn't it—a great success!

He doesn't answer. She continues, pleading, desperate.

We're happy, aren't we? Terribly happy?

He still doesn't answer, and his failure to answer is a terrible blow to "I." She goes to him.

"I"

If you don't think we are happy, it would be much better if you didn't pretend. I'll go away. Why don't you answer me?

MAXIM

How can I answer you when I don't know the answer myself? If you say we're happy, let's leave it at that. Happiness is something I know nothing about.

MAXIM starts the projector. On the screen appear some films of the happy smiling faces of MAXIM and "I."

MAXIM'S VOICE

Look. There's the one when I left the camera on the tripod. Remember?

We see on the screen MAXIM's and "I"'s laughing faces.

FADE OUT.

FADE IN:

Close-up of a letter that reads: "Have gone up to London on some business of the estate. I shall return before evening, and certainly this brief holiday from me should be welcome. Maxim."

DISSOLVE TO: INT. MORNING ROOM—
SEMI CLOSE UP—DAY

"I" is standing gazing unhappily at a glass case of china. Her mind is obviously occupied with thoughts of Rebecca. She has been crying, and we can still see traces of her tears. HILDA, the parlour maid, enters bringing in afternoon tea.

HILDA

Pardon me, Madam. Is there anything I can do for you?

"I"

I'm all right. Thank you very much.

HILDA

I'll bring the sandwiches immediately, Madam.

HILDA leaves. "I" goes to the window and looks out. She sees the west wing, with the figure of MRS. DANVERS moving about, closing a window.

HILDA reenters.

"I"

Hilda. The west wing. Nobody ever uses it anymore, do they?

HILDA

No. Madam. Not since the death of Mrs. de Winter.

"I" goes out into the main hall and hears voices above. JASPER comes running.

MRS. DANVERS' VOICE

Come along, Mr. Jack, or someone may see you.

FAVELL'S VOICE

Well, Danny, old harpy, it's been good to see you again. Makes me feel so breathless to pick up all the news.

JASPER starts to bark.

MRS. DANVERS' VOICE

I really don't think it's wise for you to come here, Mr. Jack.

JASPER continues to bark.

"I"

Jasper, come here!

FAVELL'S VOICE

Nonsense, nonsense. It's just like coming back home.

MRS. DANVERS' VOICE

Why, Mr. Jack . . .

FAVELL'S VOICE

Yes, and we must be careful not to shock Cinderella, mustn't we?

MRS. DANVERS' VOICE

If you leave through the garden door, she won't see you.

FAVELL'S VOICE

I must say I feel a little like a poor relation, sneaking around through back doors. Well, toodle-oo, Danny.

MRS. DANVERS' VOICE

Goodbye, Mr. Jack. And please be careful.

JASPER starts to whine.

"I"

Jasper, be quiet, be quiet.

FAVELL

Looking for me?

"I" turns around and is startled to see FAVELL through a wide-open window.

FAVELL

Hope I didn't make you jump, did I?

"I"

No, no, of course not. I didn't quite know who it was.

JASPER leaps up to the window, wagging his tail at FAVELL, who pats him affectionately.

FAVELL

Yes, you're pleased to see me, old boy. I'm glad there's someone in the family to welcome me back to Manderley. And how is dear old Max?

"I"

Very well, thank you.

FAVELL

I hear he went up to London, leaving his little bride all alone. Too bad. Isn't he rather afraid that someone might come down and carry you off?

MRS. DANVERS suddenly enters, looking extremely severe.

FAVELL

Danny, all your precautions were in vain. The mistress of the house was hiding behind the door. Oh, what about presenting me to the bride?

MRS. DANVERS

This is Mr. Favell, Madam.

"I"

How do you do?

FAVELL leaps through the window into the room and grasps "I" eagerly by the hand.

FAVELL

How do you do?

"I"

Won't you have some tea or something?

FAVELL

Well, now, isn't that a charming invitation? I've been asked to stay to tea, Danny, and I have a mind to accept.

MRS. DANVERS glares at FAVELL.

FAVELL

Oh, well, perhaps you're right. It's a pity, just when we were getting on so nicely. We mustn't lead the young bride astray, must we, Jasper?

JASPER looks up at FAVELL, wagging his tail.

FAVELL

Goodbye. It's been fun meeting you. Oh, and by the way, it would be very decent of you if you didn't mention this little visit to your revered husband. He doesn't exactly approve of me.

"I"

Very well.

FAVELL

That's very sporting of you. I wish I had a young bride of three months waiting for me at home. I'm just a lonely old bachelor. Fare thee well—ook!

FAVELL leaps awkwardly out the window.

FAVELL

Oh, and I know what was wrong with that introduction. Danny didn't tell you, did she? I am Rebecca's favorite cousin. Toodle-oo!

THE EMPTY ROOM—FROM "I'S" VIEWPOINT

MRS. DANVERS has disappeared.

CLOSE UP

"I" comes to a sudden decision. She determinedly starts out of the room into the hall.

INT. HALL—SEMI LONG SHOT—DAY

"I" starts to ascend the stairs.

INT. CORRIDOR—SEMI LONG SHOT—DAY

"I" goes directly toward the door of Rebecca's big room.

SEMI CLOSE UP

She glances round almost furtively as she starts to turn the handle. She holds herself in a tense attitude when the wood makes a sound of crackling as it swings on its hinges. Opening it the minimum amount of space, she almost sidles in.

INT. REBECCA'S ROOM—LONG SHOT—DAY

Inside the room it is practically dark. Just the vague shapes of furniture can be seen lit from the slightly open door through which "I" has come. We see her figure cross toward the window. She raises her hand and with sudden resolve pulls the cord which parts the curtains.

The flood of daylight reveals an astonishing scene. "I" swings round amazed, as she sees a most elegantly furnished room, expressed in the lightest possible tones—white predominates nearly everywhere. The four-poster bed is very regal on its double-stepped dais. The bed is made up with the coverlet folded back. A large spray of lovely fresh white flowers is set in a prominent position. There is also an ornate dressing table complete with brushes, combs, mirrors, and elaborate bottles of perfume. "I" approaches it, but is startled to see a large photo of MAXIM. She moves one of the brushes.

CLOSE UP

"I" gazes spellbound as her eyes begin to take in more details of the room.

SEMI CLOSE UP

Suddenly there is a sharp rap as the window blows open.

The window slams open.

MRS. DANVERS' VOICE

Do you wish anything, Madam?

She looks up as MRS. DANVERS comes through the doorway. MRS. DANVERS stops short as she sees "I." There is a flash in her eyes—a flash of triumph. "I" stands by the bed, entirely confused. She puts a hand behind her back almost like a guilty child and half lowers her eyes. Then looking up she swallows slightly and says timidly:

"I"

I—I didn't expect to see you, Mrs. Danvers. I noticed one of the windows wasn't closed and I came up to see if I could fasten it.

MRS. DANVERS

Why did you say that? I closed it before I left the room. You opened it yourself, didn't you?

MRS. DANVERS goes to the open window and, in a business-like way, she closes it, shutting out the sound of the sea. She turns with her back to the windows and faces "I" who has come to the foot of the bed.

MRS. DANVERS

You've always wanted to see this room, haven't you, Madam? Why did you never ask me to show it to you? I was ready to show it to you every day.

MRS. DANVERS comes across and opens a second set of curtains, letting in a great deal of light.

MRS. DANVERS

A lovely room, isn't it? The loveliest room you've ever seen. Everything is kept just as Mrs. de Winter liked it. Nothing has been altered since that last night.

The girl automatically follows MRS. DANVERS as she passes to a small anteroom.

SEMI CLOSE UP

In a small anteroom lined with cupboards MRS. DANVERS suddenly stops. She indicates the cupboards to "I."

MRS. DANVERS

Come, I'll show you her dressing room. This is where I keep all her clothes. You would like to see them, wouldn't you?

"I" nods. As MRS. DANVERS opens the door of one closet, we see it is lined with furs. MRS. DANVERS takes out a chinchilla. She holds it out to "I".

MRS. DANVERS

Feel this. It was a Christmas present from Mr. de Winter. He was always giving her expensive gifts, the whole year round.

CLOSE UP

"I" cannot take her eyes from MRS. DANVERS' face as the chinchilla is held against her cheek.

SEMI CLOSE UP

MRS. DANVERS withdraws it and replaces it among the other furs as she continues:

MRS. DANVERS

(opening another wardrobe)

I keep her underwear on this side. Here are her underclothes in this drawer. They were made specially for her by the nuns in the Convent of St. Claire.

I always used to wait up for her, no matter how late. Sometimes she and Mr. de Winter didn't come home until dawn. While she was undressing she'd tell me about the party she'd been to . . . She knew everyone that mattered—everyone loved her!

When she had finished her bath, she'd go into the bedroom and go over to the dressing table.

She turns and goes towards it—"I" following obediently.

SEMI CLOSE UP

By the dressing table, MRS. DANVERS puts her hands on "I's" shoulders and gently pilots her onto the stool.

MRS. DANVERS

(suddenly)

Oh, you've moved her brush, haven't you?

(she carefully straightens the brushes)

There, that's better, just as she always laid it down.

"Come on, Danny, hair drill," she would say. And I'd stand behind her like this . . .

(she moves behind, taking up a brush)

. . . and brush away for twenty minutes at a time.

And then she would say, "Goodnight, Danny" and step into her bed.

MRS. DANVERS raises "I" from the stool and leads her towards the bed.

SEMI CLOSE UP

She leads her right to the bedside and up the two steps. "I's" breathing becomes heavier and heavier as she nears the breaking point.

MRS. DANVERS lifts up the monogramed nightdress case and carefully takes from it a black chiffon nightdress.

MRS. DANVERS

I embroidered this case for her myself, and I keep it here always.

MRS. DANVERS puts a hand inside the chiffon and spreads open her fingers.

MRS. DANVERS

Did you ever see anything so delicate? Look, you can see my hand through it.

Suddenly "I" breaks away and stumbles blindly towards the door. MRS. DANVERS follows her quietly.

SEMI CLOSE UP

At the door, MRS. DANVERS come a alongside her—saying in a low voice:

MRS. DANVERS

You wouldn't think she had been gone so long, would you? Sometimes when I walk along the corridor, I fancy I hear her just behind me—that quick, light step, I couldn't mistake it anywhere. It's not only in this room—it's in all the rooms in the house. I can almost hear it now.

(she is pleased by the effect of her words on "I")

Do *you* believe the dead come back and watch the living?

"I"

(too vehemently)

NO! NO! I *don't* believe it!

MRS. DANVERS

(whispers)

Sometimes I wonder if she doesn't come back here to Manderley and watch you and Mr. de Winter together. You look tired. Why don't you stay here a while and rest? . . . Listen to the sea . . .

"I" looks wildly about the room.

MRS. DANVERS

It's so soothing . . . Listen to it . . . listen . . . Listen to the sea.

We hear the boom of the distant surf—it grows louder and louder.

FADE OUT.

FADE IN: INT. MORNING ROOM—DUSK

(There is a fire in the fireplace)

CLOSE UP on the monogram on Rebecca's address book, which fills the screen. CAMERA MOVES UP to show "I" staring at it. She has an expression of wild, hysterical despair. Suddenly she turns, looks all about the room, then back at the desk. She turns the book over so that the monogram is hidden. "I's" hand seizes the phone and lifts the receiver.

"I"

(into phone)

Tell Mrs. Danvers I wish to see her immediately!

"I" hangs up the phone, yanks the drawer open, and start pulling out Rebecca's lists and papers. A folded card is revealed at the bottom of the drawer. It is an engraved invitation card that says:

Mr. and Mrs. Maximilian de Winter
request the pleasure of Mr. Jack Favell's
presence at a costume ball
at Manderley
Thursday, June the fifteenth
Ten o'clock

and on it is scrawled:

Rebecca—
I'll be there—and how!
Jack

MRS. DANVERS enters.

MRS. DANVERS

You sent for me, Madam?

"I" looks up as MRS. DANVERS comes in. Her face is grimly set, as though she were ready for a fight.

"I"

Yes, Mrs. Danvers. I want you to get rid of all these things.

MRS. DANVERS looks down toward the desk.

MRS. DANVERS

These are Mrs. de Winter's things.

"I"

(with quiet determination)

I **am Mrs. de Winter now.**

MRS. DANVERS

(with a slight bow)

Very well. I will give the instructions.

The sound of an automobile horn is heard. "I" turns eagerly toward the window. MRS. DANVERS is just about to exit into the hall.

"I'S" VOICE

(coldly)

Just a moment, please.

MRS. DANVERS stops and turns.

CLOSE TWO SHOT

"I"

Mrs. Danvers, I intend to say nothing to Mr. de Winter about Mr. Favell's visit. In fact, I prefer to forget ***everything*** **that happened this afternoon.**

She goes out past MRS. DANVERS, who looks after her grimly.

INT. HALL—LONG SHOT—DUSK

MAXIM comes into the hall from the front door. "I" runs to him, throws her arms about him, and holds him frantically.

"I"
(in his arms)
Oh, Maxim, Maxim! You've been gone all day.

MAXIM
(laughs)
I'm choking! Well, well! What have you been doing with yourself?

"I"
I've been thinking.

MAXIM
(smiling)
What did you want to do that for?

"I"
Come into the library, and I'll tell you.

They walk together into the library.

INT. LIBRARY

"I"
Darling, could we have a costume ball—just as you used to?

MAXIM
(surprised)
Now what put that into your mind? Has Beatrice been at you?

"I"
No! I just feel we ought to *do* something—to make people feel that Manderley is the just the same as it always was. Please, darling, could we?

MAXIM
(trying gently to put her off)
You don't know what it would mean, you know. You'd have to be hostess to hundreds of people—all the county—and a lot of young people would come up from London and turn this house into a nightclub.

"I"
(pleading)
Yes, but I want to, MAXIM. Please. I've never been to a large party—but I can learn what to do. I *promise* you, you wouldn't be ashamed of me.

He looks into her eyes. Her face is so eager, so appealing that he relaxes and takes her in his arms.

MAXIM

(tolerantly)

All right—if you think you'd enjoy it. You'd better get Mrs. Danvers to help you, hadn't you.

"I"

No, no, I don't need Mrs. Danvers to help me. I can do it myself.

MAXIM

All right, my sweet.

(kisses her)

"I"

(while she is being kissed)

Oh, thank you, darling. Thank you. What will you go as?

MAXIM

(smiling at her)

I never dress up. That's the one privilege I claim as the host. And what will you be? Alice in Wonderland—with that ribbon round your hair?

"I"

(happily)

No, I won't tell you. I'll design my own costume and give you the surprise of your life!

CLOSE UP—SKETCH BOOK.

"I" is sketching in her bedroom. "I's" hand is adding a few strokes to a design for a costume. It is a female suit of armor, like that of Joan of Arc. She scratches it out, throws it on to a pile of other rejected sketches, and continues on to another. A knock at the door.

"I"

(preoccupied)

Come in.

MRS. DANVERS enters, holding a few slightly crumpled sketches in her hand.

MRS. DANVERS

Robert found those sketches in the library, Madam. Did you intend throwing them away?

"I"

Yes, Mrs. Danvers, I did. They were just some ideas I was sketching for my costume for the ball.

MRS. DANVERS

Hasn't Mr. de Winter suggested anything?

"I"

(hesitantly)

No. I want to surprise him. I don't want him to know anything about it.

MRS. DANVERS

I merely thought that you might find a costume among the family portraits that would suit you . . .

"I"

(rising)

Do you mean those at the top of the stairs? I'll go and look at them.

She goes out into the hall, followed by MRS. DANVERS.

MOVING SHOT—GALLERY—DAY

"I" and Mrs. MRS. DANVERS walk along the gallery, looking up at the departed de Winters.

MRS. DANVERS

This one, for instance.

She turns and indicates the portrait of Caroline de Winter behind them.

MRS. DANVERS

It might have been designed for you, I'm sure you could have it copied.

Anxious to be convinced, "I" looks back at Mrs. Danvers and then to the picture again, uncertainly.

MRS. DANVERS

I've heard Mr. de Winter say this is his favorite of all the paintings. It's Lady Caroline de Winter, one of his ancestors.

"I" remains gazing at the picture as MRS. DANVERS, after a slight pause, moves silently away. "I," with almost a touch of relief combined with delight, turns spontaneously.

"I"

That's a splendid idea, Mrs. Danvers . . . I'm very grateful.

FADE OUT.

FADE IN: INT. HALL—SEMI LONG SHOT—NIGHT

It is a dark and foggy night. In the hall in Manderley is a long table garlanded and decorated with candles for the ball. On it is set the usual type of buffet supper, served for such an affair. Behind the table stand a couple of men servants and half a dozen maids ready to wait on the guests, when they arrive. FRITH is superintending last final touches to the preparations. FRANK CRAWLEY enters dressed in a mortar board and B.A. gown.

FRANK

Everything under control, Frith?

FRITH

Yes, sir, thank you.

(*pause*)

Excuse me, sir, are you supposed to be a schoolmaster?

FRANK

Not exactly—just my old cap and gown.

FRITH

It certainly makes a very nice costume, sir—and economical too.

FRANK

Yes, that was the idea.

MED. SHOT—INT. LOBBY OF HALL

In the lobby, MAXIM descends the stairs to greet his guests. As ROBERT opens the door, we can see the fog outside. GILES and BEATRICE enter, GILES wearing bowler hat and overcoat, and BEATRICE in a long coat with a handkerchief tied over her headdress.

GILES

(as he divests himself of his coat)

Evening, Robert. Not very good weather for the ball. Very misty on the way. Very chilly.

By this time GILES' coat is off, revealing him dressed in faded white tights with long sleeves and a high neck—over the tights is an imitation tiger skin. Long blonde braids hang down BEATRICE'S back.

BEATRICE

Wig's so blasted tight—they ought to have sent an aspirin with it.

By this time MAXIM has joined the two at the door; he surveys them both.

MAXIM

What's the idea? Adam and Eve?

BEATRICE

Oh, MAXIM, don't be disgusting.

GILES

Strong man, old man. Where's my weight thing?

BEATRICE

You didn't leave it in the car, did you?

At this moment their chauffeur appears, carrying a large pair of imitation spherical weights, joined by a painted wooden bar. The way he holds it shows that it has no weight at all. He hands them to GILES.

GILES

Oh, there it is.

BEATRICE

Are you the only one down? Where's the child?

MAXIM

She's keeping her costume a terrific secret, wouldn't even let me into her room.

BEATRICE

Lovely. I'll go up and give her a hand.

She exits. GILES and MAXIM go to join FRANK in the hall.

GILES

I could do with a drink.

MAXIM

(indicating GILES' *costume)*

Won't you catch cold, in that thing?

GILES

Don't be silly.

(fingering his tights)

Pure wool, old boy.

ROBERT enters the picture carrying the weights.

ROBERT

Pardon me, sir, you forgot this.

ROBERT drops the weights. They are inflated, so they bounce. GILES picks them up with an indignant glance at ROBERT.

INT. CORRIDOR—SEMI CLOSE UP—NIGHT

Outside the door of "I's" room, BEATRICE is knocking. She starts to turn the handle.

BEATRICE

Here I am dear—it's Bee. I've come to give you a hand.

"I"

(calling from inside)

Please don't come in, Beatrice. I don't want anyone to see my costume.

BEATRICE

Oh, well, you won't be long, will you? Because the first people will be arriving any moment.

She moves away from the door.

INT. "I'S" BEDROOM—SEMI CLOSE UP

CLARICE, a very young maid, is kneeling on the ground putting finishing touches to the wide skirt of "I's" fancy dress.

"I"

Now you're sure that's where it should be?

CLARICE

Yes, Madam, just right. Oh, *yes*, Madam. It's *just* right.

"I" is dressed in a copy of the striking costume in the painting of Caroline de Winter. She is admiring herself in the mirror, turning her shoulders this way and that.

"I"

Isn't it exciting!

CLARICE

Indeed it is, Madam. I've always heard about the Manderley ball—and now I'm really going to see one. I'm sure there will be no one there to touch you, Madam!

"I"

Oh, do you really think so? . . . Where's my fan?

While CLARICE fetches the fan, "I" has a last, loving look at herself, then she takes the fan.

"I"

You're sure I look all right?

CLARICE
(reverently)
You look ever so beautiful.

"I"
Well, here goes!

She starts towards the door; CLARICE darts ahead of her to open it.

INT. CORRIDOR—SEMI CLOSE UP—NIGHT

The door of "I'S" room opens and "I" emerges. As she comes along the corridor, she pats her hair, and fusses with parts of her dress. Her pace increases until she comes opposite the picture. She pulls up for a moment to compare herself with the original. Almost preening herself, she adopts the pose of the picture and, changing her pace to a dignified one, starts to move away towards the staircase.

With a light step, she starts to descend the stairs. When she reaches the bottom, she pauses, catches her breath, and starts to move forward towards them across the floor. MAXIM's back is turned toward her.

"I"
Good evening, Mr. de Winter.

MAXIM turns—still laughing and changing to a smile of anticipation on hearing her voice. Slowly the smile begins to fade from his face, and he eyes her up and down. A look of deep anger takes its place. "I's" expression changes from the excited smile to one of crushed bewilderment.

MAXIM takes half a step towards her—and speaks fiercely.

MAXIM
What the devil do you think you're doing?

"I" almost backs away from him. We see the startled faces of FRANK and GILES. BEATRICE is the last one to see her.

BEATRICE's hand flies to her mouth as though she would suppress her own cry of:

BEATRICE
Rebec . . . O . . . Oh . . . no . . .

"I," gazing with petrified eyes at MAXIM, gestures weakly:

"I"
It's—it's the picture —the one in the gallery.

MAXIM does not reply—he stands facing her like stone.

"I"

(desperately)

What is it? What have I done?

MAXIM takes one step towards her and speaks in an icy tone.

MAXIM

Go and take it off! It doesn't matter what else you put on . . . anything will do.

"I" stands motionless—unable to believe what she has heard MAXIM say.

MAXIM

What are you standing there for—didn't you hear what I said?

"I" looks about her desperately—then suddenly she turns and dashes towards the stairs. MAXIM takes a step forward as if he might follow her, but at this moment ROBERT announces in a loud voice:

ROBERT

Sir George and Lady Moore.

(*and then*)

Mr. Dudley Tennant—

(*again*)

Admiral and Lady Burbank.

The first guests are arriving—a flock of about eight. We hear their laughing chatter. MAXIM is forced to turn and play the part of host.

"I" rushes along the corridor until she comes to the picture—then pulls up suddenly. She looks at it, then turning her head towards the west wing, she sees MRS. DANVERS standing there, a smile of supreme triumph on her face. MRS. DANVERS turns and goes through the door. "I" runs after her.

"I" nearly reaches the door of Rebecca's room—it is just closing. She hurries to it and then, bracing herself with courage, pushes the door open and goes in.

MRS. DANVERS

I watched you go down—just as I watched her a year ago. Even in the same dress you couldn't compare.

"I" takes a step nearer to her—she looks down at the dress, then back to MRS. DANVERS.

"I"

You knew it? You knew she wore it and yet you deliberately suggested that *I* wear it!

"I" leans toward MRS. DANVERS.

"I"

(with great intensity)

Why do you hate me? What have I ever done to you that you should hate me so?

MRS. DANVERS

(speaking into the mirror)

You tried to take her place. You let him marry you. I've seen his face, his eyes—they're the same as those first weeks after she died, when he shut himself up in his room. I used to listen to him—walking up and down, up and down, all night long, night after night. Thinking of her—suffering torture, because he'd lost her.

"I"

I don't want to know—I don't want to know.

MRS. DANVERS

You thought you could be Mrs. de Winter—live in her house—walk in her steps—take the things that were hers. But she's too strong for you. *You* can't fight her. No one ever got the better of her—never, never. She was beaten in the end. But it wasn't a man—it wasn't a woman—it was the sea!

"I"

(unable to bear any more)

Stop, stop, I tell you . . .

She throws herself on the bed, breaking into convulsive sobs.

MRS. DANVERS stands looking down at the sobbing figure. A new thought comes into her face.

MRS. DANVERS comes to the window and throws it open. We see a heavy mist outside—there is a slight movement of the curtains. She glances round toward the window. Then turning back again to the bed, she speaks with uncanny calmness.

MRS. DANVERS

You're overwrought, Madam. I've opened a window for you. A little air will do you good.

"I" raises herself from her lying position and moves across toward the window, gasping for breath.

MRS. DANVERS

Why don't you go? . . . Why don't you leave Manderley? He doesn't need you. He's got his memories. He doesn't love you—he wants to be alone again with *her*.

"I's" face looks down to the depths below.

MRS. DANVERS

You've nothing to stay for. You've nothing to live for, really, have you? Look down there. It's easy, isn't it? Why don't you? . . .

"I" stares out, hypnotized, then slowly looks down again. In her eyes we see the growing thought of self-destruction.

MRS. DANVERS

Why don't you? . . . Go on . . . go on . . . Don't be afraid . . .

Suddenly the silence and the mist are shattered by an explosion. Then another, accented by the strident wailing of a siren; then a third. "I" stands frightened and mystified. From below comes the sound of doors being opened. MRS. DANVERS, with regained control, steps back.

Outside, the running figures of the guests emerging from the front and side doors of the house. They are hardly discernible in the mist, but we hear their voices.

MAN'S VOICE

Ship on the rocks!

ANOTHER MAN'S VOICE

Shipwreck!

THIRD MAN'S VOICE

Notify the Coast Guard! She's aground!

MAXIM

Come on, everybody—down to the bay—ship ashore!

"I" hears MAXIM's voice. She cries down to him.

"I"

Maxim! Maxim!

SEMI LONG SHOT

Below, MAXIM half turns as though he heard something. He hesitates for a moment, then runs on, his figure disappearing into the mist. "I" glares at MRS. DANVERS as she leaves the room. MRS. DANVERS turns aside, looking confused and distraught.

FADE IN: EXT. COVE—DAWN—LONG SHOT

In the dim half-light of dawn with shafts of sunlight just beginning to penetrate the blanket of fog, we can vaguely discern the outline of rocks. We hear the pounding of the surf and the scream of gulls. In the distance we hear the shouts of the men who are helping to raise the boat: "They'll never shift 'er, not with that tide." "Diver's gone down again." "Headed for the reef—runs out quite a way." "Lend a hand here." Vague figures, clad for the most part in oilskins, loom out of the mist and go towards the direction of the shouts.

"I" appears scrambling down over the rocks.

Suddenly "I" gives a little scream. In the half light she has stumbled against a figure crouched down beside the breakwater. It is BEN. He scrambles to his feet.

TWO SHOT—BEN AND "I"

"I"
(smiling kindly at him)
Ben, have you seen Mr. de Winter anywhere?

BEN stares at her foolishly, shaking his head—then, suddenly becoming slightly hysterical:

BEN
She won't come back no more, will she? You said so.

"I"
Who, Ben? What do you mean?

BEN
(jerking his thumb towards the sea)
Her. The other one.

"I," realizing she can get nothing out of BEN as to the whereabouts of MAXIM, passes on.

FRANK comes up, bareheaded, and wearing a mackintosh. "I" seizes FRANK's arm.

"I"
Frank, have you seen Maxim anywhere?

FRANK
Not since about half an hour ago. I thought he'd gone up to the house.

"I"
No, he hasn't been home at all, and I'm afraid something might have happened to him.

There is a moment's silence as "I" looks curiously at FRANK, and he shifts a little uncomfortably under her gaze.

"I"

Frank, what's the matter? Is anything wrong? There *is* something wrong.

FRANK

When the diver went down to inspect the bottom of the ship, he found the hull of another boat—a little sailboat . . .

"I"

Frank, is it . . . ?

FRANK

(looking her in the eyes)

Yes . . . it was Rebecca's.

"I" digests this in silence for a moment, then speaks quietly:

"I"

How did they recognize it?

FRANK

He's a local man; he knew it instantly.

"I"

Oh, that's going to be so hard on poor Maxim . . .

FRANK

Yes. It'll bring it all back again, and worse than before.

"I"

Why did they have to find it? Why couldn't they have left it there in peace—at the bottom of the sea?

FRANK

(after a moment, embarrassed)

I'd better get along and arrange some breakfast for the men.

"I"

All right, Frank, I'll go look for Maxim.

FRANK goes off. "I" stands indecisively for a second. We can still hear shouts from the men helping to raise the boat, and the noise of the waves. She starts to walk hesitantly in the direction from which the shouts come.

As "I" scrambles over the rocks and into the cove, she looks across to the cottage.

Suddenly her attention is arrested as she sees a lamp alight in the window of the cottage, and firelight throwing flickering shadows on the windowpane. Determinedly but nervously she hurries toward the cottage and opens the door.

Inside the cottage, she is confronted by the figure of MAXIM, sitting in a corner.

"I"

(in amazement)

MAXIM!

MAXIM

(turning)

Hello—

"I" advances toward him, extremely worried. MAXIM has a disheveled look, but it is more than that: he has the air of a man who has come to the end of his tether.

"I"

(as she gets near him)

Maxim—you haven't had any sleep. Have you forgiven me?

MAXIM

Forgiven you? What have I got to forgive you for?

"I"

For last night—my stupidity about the costume.

MAXIM

Oh, that! . . . I'd forgotten. I was angry with you, wasn't I?

"I"

(shyly)

Mm.

(There is a moment's silence. She looks at him pleadingly)

Maxim, can't we start all over again? I don't ask that you should love me . . . I won't ask impossible things. I'll be your friend, your companion . . . I'll be happy with that.

He looks at her strangely, takes her face between his hands and looks at her, tortured.

MAXIM

You love me very much, don't you? But it's too late, my darling . . . We've lost our little chance of heaven.

"I"

(frantically)

No, Maxim, no!

MAXIM

Yes. It's all over now. The thing's happened—the thing I've dreaded day after day, night after night.

"I"

Maxim, what are you trying to tell me?

MAXIM

Rebecca has won.

"I" looks at him, her worst fears realized: he still loves Rebecca. After a moment, he speaks again.

MAXIM

Her shadow has been between us all the time—keeping us from one another. She knew that this would happen.

"I"

(gazing at him, speaking in stifled voice)

What are you saying?

MAXIM

They sent a diver down. He found another boat—

"I"

(interrupting, comfortingly, but somewhat relieved)

Yes, I know. Frank told me. Rebecca's boat. It's terrible for you,

I'm so sorry.

MAXIM

The diver made another discovery. He broke one of the ports and looked into the cabin. There was a body in there.

"I" reacts sharply to this, bewildered at the tone of utter fatality with which MAXIM speaks.

"I"

Then she wasn't alone. There was someone sailing with her and you have to find out who it was. That's it, isn't it, Maxim?

MAXIM

You don't understand. There was no one with her.

(a moment's pause while she looks at him)

It's Rebecca's body lying there on the cabin floor.

"I"

No, no!

MAXIM

The woman that was washed up at Edgecoombe—the woman that is now embedded in the family crypt—that wasn't Rebecca. It was the body of some unknown woman, unclaimed, belonging nowhere. I identified it, but I knew it wasn't Rebecca. It was all a lie. *I* knew where Rebecca's body was! Lying on that cabin floor, on the bottom of the sea.

"I"

(terrified)

How did you know, Maxim?

MAXIM

Because—I put it there!

Will you look into my eyes and tell me that you love me now?

MAXIM is searching her eyes. He reads there that she is stunned, overwhelmed, horrified by what he has told her. She turns and walks away from him.

MAXIM

You see, I was right. It's too late.

"I" comes into scene toward MAXIM, her heart jumping in quickened, sudden panic.

"I"

No, it's not too late!

(she puts her arms around him)

You're not to say that! I love you more than anything in the world . . . Please, Maxim, kiss me, please!

MAXIM

No. It's no use. It's too late.

"I"

We can't lose each other now! We've got to be together—always! With no secrets, no shadows . . .

MAXIM

We may only have a few days, a few hours.

"I"

(pleadingly)

Oh, Maxim, why didn't you tell me before?

MAXIM

I nearly did several times, but somehow you never seemed close enough.

"I"

(looks at him)

How could we be close when I know you were always thinking of Rebecca? How could I even ask you to love me when I knew you loved Rebecca still?

MAXIM

What are you talking about? What do you mean?

"I"

Whenever you touched me, I knew you were comparing me with Rebecca. Whenever you spoke to me or looked at me, walked with me in the garden, I knew you were thinking, "This I did with Rebecca—and this, and this . . . "

MAXIM stares at her, bewildered, amazed, then turns slightly away.

"I"

(takes a step toward him)

It's true, isn't it?

MAXIM

(whips around)

You thought I loved Rebecca? You thought that? I *hated* her!

"I" is incredulous. MAXIM starts to pace up and down, speaking in an almost quiet, reflective voice.

MAXIM

Oh, I was carried away by her, enchanted by her, as everyone was. And when I was married, I was told I was the luckiest man in the world . . . she was so lovely, so accomplished, so amusing. "She's got the three things that really matter in a wife," everyone told me, "Breeding, brains, and beauty" . . . and I believed her—completely . . . But I never had a moment's happiness with her . . . She was incapable of love, or tenderness, or decency.

There is exultation in "I"'s face as she looks at him.

"I"

(almost to herself)

You didn't love her! You didn't love her!

MAXIM

Do you remember that cliff where you first saw me in Monte Carlo? Well—I when there with Rebecca on our honeymoon . . . That's when I found out about her—four days after we were married . . . She stood there laughing, her black hair blowing in the wind. She told me all about herself—everything . . . things I'll never tell a living soul.

MAXIM moves off abruptly.

MAXIM

I wanted to kill her. It would have been so easy. You remember the precipice? I frightened you, didn't I? You thought I was mad. Perhaps I was. Perhaps I am mad. It wouldn't make for sanity, would it, living with the devil?

"I'll make a bargain with you," she told me. "You'd look rather foolish trying to divorce me now, after four days of marriage. So I'll play the part of a devoted wife, mistress of your precious Manderley. I'll make it the most famous showplace in England, if you like, and people will visit us and envy us and say we're the luckiest, happiest couple in the country. What a grand joke it will be! What a triumph!"

He comes to a halt and swings around to "I." She looks up at him with deep compassion, as he continues, in desperate self-accusation:

MAXIM

I should never have accepted her dirty bargain. But I did. I was younger then—and tremendously conscious of—(contemptuously) "the family honor." The family honor!

She knew I'd sacrifice everything rather than stand in a divorce court and give her away, admit that our marriage was a rotten fraud.

You despise me, don't you, as I despise myself? You can't understand what my feelings were, can you?

"I"

(with infinite tenderness)

Of course I can, darling. Of course I can.

MAXIM

I kept the bargain—and so did she—apparently. Oh, she played the game brilliantly . . . But after a while she began to grow careless. She took a flat in London, and she'd stay away for days at a time . . . Then she started to bring her friends down here. I warned her, but she shrugged her shoulders. "What's it got to do with you?" she said . . .

She even started on Frank, poor faithful Frank... Then there was a cousin of hers—a man named Favell.

"I"

I know him. He came here the day you went to London.

MAXIM

Why didn't you tell me?

"I"

I didn't like to. I thought it would remind you of—Rebecca.

MAXIM

Remind me!

(*with a laugh*)

As if I needed reminding! Favell used to visit her here—in this cottage. I found out about it and I warned her if I found him here again, I'd shoot them both.

One night, when I found she'd come back quietly from London, I thought Favell was with her. And I knew then that I couldn't stand this life of filth and deceit any longer. I decide to come down here and have it out with both of them. But she was alone. She was expecting Favell, but he hadn't come.

She was lying on the divan, a large tray of cigarette stubs beside her. She looked ill—queer. Suddenly she got up, started to walk toward me.

"When I have a child," she said, "neither you nor anyone else could ever prove it wasn't yours. You'd like an heir, wouldn't you, Max, for your beloved Manderley?" And she started to laugh. "How funny... how supremely, wonderfully funny! I'll be the perfect mother—just as I've been the perfect wife. No one will ever know. It ought to give you the thrill of your life, Max, to watch my son grow bigger day by day and to know that when you die—Manderley will be *his*!"

She was face to face with me, one hand in her pocket, the other holding a cigarette. She was smiling. "Well, Max, what are you going to do about it? Aren't you going to kill me?" I suppose I went mad for a moment... I must have struck her. She stood staring at me. She looked—almost triumphant. Then she started toward me again, laughing. Then suddenly she stumbled and fell. When I looked down—ages afterwards, it seemed—she was lying on the floor. She had struck her head on a heavy piece of ship's tackle. I remember wondering why she was still smiling... And then I realized she was dead.

"I"

But you didn't kill her . . . it was an accident!

MAXIM

Who would believe me? I lost my head . . . I just knew I had to do something—anything. I carried her out to the boat. It was very dark. There was no moon. I put her in the cabin. When the boat seemed a safe distance from the shore, I took a spike and drove it again and again through the planking of the hull. I'd opened up the seacocks and the water began to come in fast. I climbed into the dinghy and pulled away. I saw the boat keel over and sink . . . I pulled back to the cove . . . It started raining . . .

"I"

Does anyone else know this?

MAXIM

(shakes his head)

No one—except you and me.

"I" becomes alert, intelligent, mature, taking command of the situation. She is the adult wife concerned with her husband's safety.

"I"

We must explain it. It's got to be the body of someone you've never seen before.

MAXIM

They're bound to know her . . . The bracelets and rings she always wore . . . They'll identify her body, and then they'll remember the other woman—the other woman buried in the crypt.

"I"

(clipping out orders)

If they find out it's Rebecca, you must say simply that you made a mistake about the other body. You must say that when you went to Edgecoombe you were ill, you didn't know what you were doing. Rebecca's dead, that's what we've got to remember! Rebecca's dead. She can't speak—she can't bear witness. She can't harm you anymore. We're the only two people in the world who will ever know, MAXIM—you and I.

MAXIM

I told you once that I'd done a very selfish thing in marrying you. You can understand now what I meant. I've loved you, my darling—I shall always love you—but I've known all along that Rebecca would win in the end!

"I"

No! No! She *hasn't* won! No matter what happens now—she *hasn't* won!

They cling to each other desperately. They are really together for the first time with no secret between them.

Suddenly the phone rings jarringly. MAXIM picks up the phone.

MAXIM

(into phone)

Hello . . .

(pause)

Hello, Frank . . . Who? Colonel Julyan! (pause) Yes, tell him I'll meet him there as soon as I possibly can. What? Well, say we can talk about that when we're sure about the matter.

He hangs up.

"I"

What's happened?

MAXIM

Colonel Julyan called . . . He's the chief constable of the county. He's been asked by the police to go to the mortuary. He wants to know if I could possibly have made a mistake about—that other body.

The two of them stand looking at each other, the girl terrified as to what this may mean. MAXIM steps toward her, puts his arms around her.

FADE OUT.

DISSOLVE IN: MED. SHOT—DAY

Five men, two of them policemen in uniform, are in an interrogation room: MAXIM, COLONEL JULYAN, and FRANK are the others. MAXIM is in the middle of the group, but we can see no faces. After a moment, MAXIM turns slightly and nods to the man on his left. Then he turns completely and walks away from the group, COLONEL JULYAN and FRANK following him.

MAXIM

Well, Colonel Julyan, apparently I did make a mistake about that other body.

FRANK

The mistake was quite natural under the circumstances. Besides, you weren't well at the time.

MAXIM

That's nonsense—I was perfectly well.

JULYAN

Don't let it worry you, Maxim. Nobody can blame you for making a mistake. Pity is, you've got to go through the same thing all over again.

MAXIM

What do you mean?

JULYAN

Well, there'll have to be another inquest, of course. Same formality and red tape. Wish you could be spared the publicity of it, but I'm afraid that's impossible.

MAXIM

Oh yes—the publicity.

JULYAN

I suppose that Mrs. de Winter went below for something, and the squall hit the boat when there was no body at the helm. I imagine that's the solution, don't you, Crawley?

FRANK

Oh, yes. Probably the door jammed, and she couldn't get up on deck again.

JULYAN

Tabb will undoubtedly come to some type of conclusion.

FRANK

Why? What would he know about it?

JULYAN

Well, he's examining the boat now. Purely a matter of routine, you know. I'll be at the inquest tomorrow, Maxim, quite unofficially, you know. We must get together for a game of golf when it's all over, eh? Bye-bye.

FADE OUT.

FADE IN: LONG SHOT—HALL AT MANDERLEY—NIGHT

We see "I" come down the stairs of the Manderley hall. She is simply attired. FRITH is approaching from another direction, two or three newspapers in his hand.

FRITH

I have the evening papers, madam. Would you care to see them?

"I"

No, thank you, Frith, and I'd prefer that Mr. de Winter were not troubled with them either.

FRITH

I understand, Madam... Permit me to say that we're all most distressed outside.

"I"

Thank you, Frith.

FRITH

I'm afraid the news has been a great shock to Mrs. Danvers.

"I"

Yes, I rather expected it would be.

FRITH

(hesitantly)

It seems there's to be a coroner's inquest, Madam?

"I"

Yes, Frith, it's purely a formality.

FRITH

Of course, madam. I wanted to say that if any of us might be required to give evidence, I should be only too pleased to do anything that might help the family.

"I"

(touched)

Thank you, Frith. I'm sure Mr. de Winter will be very happy to hear it. But I don't think anything will be necessary.

She gives him a kindly look and walks off as he bows slightly. "I" strolls into the library.

LIBRARY

In the library, MAXIM is standing at the fireplace, his back to the door, smoking moodily. He turns as the girl comes in and affects cheeriness.

"I"

Max.

MAXIM
(tenderly)
Hello, darling.

"I"
Oh, Maxim, I'm worried about what you'll do at the inquest tomorrow.

MAXIM
What do you mean?

"I"
You won't lose your temper, will you? Promise you won't let them make you angry.

MAXIM
(after a moment)
All right, darling . . . I promise.

"I"
No matter what he asks you, you won't lose your head?

MAXIM
Don't worry, dear.

"I"
They can't do anything at once, can they?

MAXIM
No.

"I"
Then we've a little time left to be together?

MAXIM
Yes.

"I"
I want to go to the inquest with you.

MAXIM
I'd rather you didn't, darling.

"I"
But I can't wait here alone . . . I promise you I won't be any trouble to you . . . I must be near you so that no matter what happens we won't be separated for a moment.

MAXIM

All right. I don't mind this whole thing—except for you. I can't forget what it's done. I've been thinking of nothing also since it happened. . . . (He lifts her chin and looks her in the face.) It's gone forever . . . that funny, young, lost look that I loved. It won't ever come back again. I killed that when I told you about Rebecca. It's gone . . . in a few hours . . . You've grown so much older.

"I"

Maxim . . . Maxim . . .

He takes her in his arms and crushes her to him, and they kiss feverishly, desperately, like guilty lovers who have not kissed before and may never kiss again.

FADE IN: EXT. CORONER'S COURT—DAY

A POLICEMAN is standing in front of the coroner's court, addressing a crowd.

POLICEMAN

Blackjack Bridey was his name. The most important arrest I ever made. It must have been about two years ago now. Course there was no doubt about it. He was 'ung a month after I caught him.

Now wait a minute.

The POLICEMAN opens the courtroom door.

They've got old balmy Ben up now.

BEN is standing in the courtroom as he is being questioned by the CORONER.

CORONER

You remember the late Mrs. de Winter, don't you?

BEN

She's gone.

CORONER

(slightly impatient)

Yes—we know that.

BEN

She went into the sea. The sea got her.

CORONER

That's right. Now—we want you to tell us whether you were at the shore that last night when she went out and didn't come back?

Were you on the shore that last night, when she went out?

When she didn't come back?

BEN

I didn't see nothing. I don't want to go to the asylum! They'm cruel folks there.

CORONER

Now, now—nobody's going to send you to the asylum. All we want you to do is tell us what you saw.

BEN

I didn't see nothing!

CORONER

Come, come. Did you see Mrs. de Winter get into her boat that night?

BEN

I don't know nothing! I don't want to go to the asylum!

CORONER

Very well. You may go.

BEN

Eh?

CORONER

You may go now.

FAVELL, in the court, exchanges looks with MRS. DANVERS.

CORONER

Mr. Tabb, will you come forward?

TABB advances and stands holding the back of the witness chair. He is sworn in by the bailiff.

CORONER

The late Mrs. de Winter used to send her boat to your shipyard for reconditioning?

TABB

That's right, sir.

CORONER

Can you remember any occasion when she had any sort of an accident with the boat?

TABB

No, sir. I often said Mrs. de Winter was a born sailor.

CORONER

When Mrs. de Winter went below, as is supposed, and a sudden gust of wind came down, that would be enough to capsize the boat, wouldn't it?

TABB

Excuse me, sir, but there's a little more to it than that.

CORONER

What do you mean, Mr. Tabb?

TABB

I mean, sir, the seacocks.

CORONER

What are the seacocks?

TABB

The seacocks are the valves to drain out the boat. They're always kept tight closed when you're afloat.

CORONER

Yes?

TABB

Yesterday when I examined the boat, I found that they'd been opened.

CORONER

What could have been the reason for that?

TABB

Just this, sir. That's what flooded the boat and sunk her.

CORONER

(gravely)

Are you implying that boat never capsized at all?

TABB

I know it's a terrible thing to say, sir, but in my opinion she was scuttled. And there's them holes.

CORONER

What holes?

TABB

In her planking.

CORONER

What are you talking about?

TABB

Of course, that boat's been under water for over a year, and the tide's been knocking her against the ridge. But it seemed to me, them holes looked as if she'd made 'em from the *inside.*

MAXIM'S face is almost mask-like in his effort to retain an outward show of imperturbability. The hubbub of excitement from the crowd has grown louder.

CLOSE UP—FRANK

Looking from MAXIM to "I" with extreme concern.

CORONER

And you believe she must have done it deliberately.

TABB

Couldn't have been no accident. Not with her knowledge of boats.

The CORONER leans across to speak in a low tone to COLONEL JULYAN.

CORONER

You knew the former Mrs. de Winter well, I believe?

JULYAN

Oh, yes.

CORONER

Would you have believed her capable of suicide?

JULYAN

No, frankly, I would not. But you never can tell.

CORONER

You may stand down, Mr. Tabb. Mr. de Winter, please.

MAXIM has now reached the witness chair. CORONER turns to him.

CORONER

I'm sorry to drag you back for further questioning, Mr. de Winter. But you've heard the statement from Mr. Tabb. I wonder if you can help us in any way.

MAXIM

I'm afraid not.

CORONER

Can you think of any reason there should have been holes in the planking of the late Mrs. de Winter's boat?

MAXIM

Of course I can't think of any reason.

CORONER

Has anyone ever discussed these holes with you before?

MAXIM

Well, sir, since the boat has been at the bottom of the ocean, I scarcely think that likely.

CORONER

Mr. de Winter, I want you to believe that we all feel very deeply for you in this matter, but you must remember I don't conduct this enquiry for my own amusement.

MAXIM

That's rather obvious, isn't it?

CORONER

I hope it is. Well, since she went sailing alone, are we to believe that she drilled those holes herself?

MAXIM

You may believe what you like.

CORONER

Can you enlighten us as to why Mrs. de Winter would have wanted to end her own life?

MAXIM

I know of no reason whatever.

"I" seems to be losing control. She hears the voices murmuring, which, although loud, are unintelligible, until the CORONER's voice comes through:

CORONER

Mr. de Winter, however painful it may be, I have to ask you a very personal question: were relations between you and the late Mrs. de Winter perfectly happy? *Were the relations between you and the late Mrs. de Winter perfectly happy?*

MAXIM

I won't stand for it any longer, and you might know now!

"I" faints and falls to the floor. There is a slight commotion in the court. MAXIM leaves the witness stand and hastens across to where "I" has fallen to the floor. He helps her up with the aid of FRANK.

CORONER

We'll adjourn until after lunch. Mr. de Winter, I presume you'll be available for us then?

MAXIM nods.

MAXIM is now supporting "I." He has his arm around her shoulder.

MAXIM

(tenderly)

I told you you should have had some breakfast. You're hungry—that's what's the matter with you.

"I" responds to his forced cheerfulness by smiling wanly at him.

DISSOLVE TO: EXT. INN YARD—DAY

Outside the courtroom, the yard is beginning to fill up with people emerging from the schoolroom, which is on the opposite side to the inn. Most of them are making their way toward the bar and dining room. There are three or four cars parked. MAXIM emerges from the schoolroom with "I," who has recovered a little. At this moment a large Rolls-Royce turns into the yard. The CHAUFFEUR pulls up on seeing MAXIM.

CHAUFFEUR

Mr. Frith thought you might like to have some lunch from the house, and sent me with it.

MAXIM

(cheerfully)

That's fine, Mullen.

(indicating)

Can you pull around the corner?

CHAUFFEUR

Yes, very good, sir.

He exits, and MAXIM and "I" start walking, MAXIM guiding her.

"I"

Awfully foolish of me . . . fainting like that.

MAXIM

(tenderly)

Nonsense. If you hadn't fainted like that I'd have *really* lost my temper.

"I"

Darling, *please* be careful.

He gives her arm an affectionate, reassuring little squeeze, and they are at the car, where the CHAUFFEUR is holding the door open.

MAXIM

(as "I" gets in)

Darling, wait here a few moments, I'll see if I can find old Frank.

"I"

Of course, darling. Don't worry about me. I'll be all right.

MAXIM has been opening the basket, and now pulls out a flask of brandy and hands it to her:

MAXIM

Here, try a spot of this. It'll do you good.

She takes it, smiling wanly at him.

MAXIM

Are you all right?

"I"

Yes, of course, darling.

MAXIM

I won't be long.

"I"

Right you are.

He exits.

CLOSE UP OF "I"

(with the brandy, making a wry face)

She looks over and sees FAVELL, who is leaning into the open car window, smiling slyly at her.

FAVELL

Hello, and how does the bride find herself today? I say, marriage with Max is not exactly a bed of roses, is it?

"I"

I think you'd better go before Maxim gets back.

FAVELL

Jealous, is he? Well, I can't say I blame him. But *you* don't think I'm the big bad wolf, do you? I'm not, you know. I'm a perfectly ordinary, harmless bloke. And I think you're behaving splendidly over all this . . . perfectly splendidly. You know, you've grown up a bit since I last saw you last.

"I" does not answer.

FAVELL

Well, it's no wonder . . .

MAXIM enters scene. For a moment FAVELL does not see him. MAXIM is clearly in a rage at finding FAVELL here.

MAXIM

What do you want, Favell?

FAVELL

(coolly)

Hullo, Max. Things are going pretty well for you, aren't they? Better than you ever expected. I was rather worried about you at first. That's why I came to the inquest.

MAXIM

I'm touched by your solicitude, but if you'll excuse me, I'd rather like to have my lunch.

FAVELL, nothing daunted, looks down at the lunch basket. He steps into the car.

FAVELL

Lunch? I say, what a jolly idea! Rather like a picnic, isn't it?

Without being asked he dips into the basket, FAVELL takes a leg of chicken and starts to gnaw at it.

You know, Max, I really feel I ought to talk things over with you.

MAXIM

(sharply)

Talk what things over?

FAVELL

Well, those holes in the planking, for one thing—those holes that were drilled from the *inside*. (he gets a sudden thought, leans back to the driver) Oh, Mullen . . .

CHAUFFEUR

Yes, sir?

FAVELL

I say, would you like a good fellow get my car filled with petrol? It's almost empty.

CHAUFFEUR

Of course, sir.

FAVELL

Oh, and Mullen, close the door, will you?

CHAUFFEUR

Yes, sir.

The CHAUFFEUR closes the car door and exits.

FAVELL

(indicating his cigarette)

Does this bother you?

FAVELL tosses his cigarette out the window.

FAVELL

(resuming his munching)

You know, I've a strong feeling, old boy, that before the day is out, somebody's going to make use of that expressive though rather old-fashioned term, "foul play."

FAVELL picks up the brandy flask and a small glass. He pours himself some brandy.

FAVELL

Am I boring you with all this? No? Good.

(*he sips the brandy*)

You see, Max, I'm finding myself in rather an awkward position.

FAVELL pulls a folded note from his pocket.

You've only got to read this note to understand. It's from Rebecca, and what's more, she had the foresight to put a date it. She wrote it to me on the day she died. Incidentally, I was out at a party that night, so I didn't get the note until the next day.

MAXIM

And what makes you think the note would interest me?

FAVELL

Oh, I'm not going to bother you with the contents now, but I can assure you that it is not the note of a woman who intends to drown herself that same night.

FAVELL finishes chewing on the chicken leg.

FAVELL

By the way, what do you do with old bones? Bury them. However, for the time being . . . (he throws the chicken bone out the window).

You know, Max, I'm getting awfully fed up with my job as a motor car salesman. I don't know if you've experienced the feeling of driving in an expensive car that isn't your own, but it can be very, very exasperating. You know what I mean—you want to own the car yourself.

I've often wondered what it'd be like to retire to the country—have a little place with a few acres of shooting. I've never figured out what it'd cost a year, but I'd like to talk it about it with you, Max. I'd like to have your advice on how to live comfortably without hard work . . .

FRANK appears at the window of the car.

FRANK

(coldly)

Hello, Favell.

(*in a different tone*)

Were you looking for me, Maxim?

MAXIM

Yes. Mr. Favell and I have a little business transaction on hand.

I think it would be better if we conducted it over at the inn.

They may have a private room there.

MAXIM and FAVELL leave the car.

FAVELL raises his hat to "I," looks at her provocatively.

FAVELL

See you later.

MAXIM suddenly leans back into the car and quietly and hastily says to FRANK:

MAXIM

Find Colonel Julyan. Tell him I want to see him immediately.

(*to* FAVELL)

Come on, Favell. Let's go.

INT. INN—DAY

As MAXIM and FAVELL enter the inn, the buzz of conversation dies down when most of the customers see who enters. MAXIM goes over to the PROPRIETOR.

MAXIM

Have you a private room, please?

PROPRIETOR

Of course, sir, there, sir.

He immediately bustles into activity and loads them through a small door into another room. MAXIM and FAVELL enter, as the PROPRIETOR stands, servile, bowing them in.

PROPRIETOR

I hope this will do, Mr. de Winter?

FAVELL

It's splendid, splendid—exactly like the Ritz.

PROPRIETOR

Any orders, gents?

FAVELL

Yes, you might bring me a large brandy and soda. How about you, Max? Have one on me. I feel I can afford to play host.

MAXIM

Thanks. I don't mind if I do.

FAVELL

(turns to proprietor)

Make it two.

PROPRIETOR

Very good, sir.

He exits. At that point, JULYAN, FRANK, and "I" enter.

MAXIM

This is Colonel Julyan, Mr. Favell.

FAVELL

Oh I know Colonel Julyan. We're old friends, aren't we, Colonel?

JULYAN stares at Favell coldly, doesn't reply.

MAXIM

Since you're old friends, I assume you know that he is also head of the police here. I think he might be interested to hear your proposition. Go on, Jack. Tell him all about it.

FAVELL

I don't know what you mean. I merely said I hoped to give up selling motor cars and retire into the country.

MAXIM

Actually he offered to withhold some vital evidence from the inquest if I'd make it worth his while.

FAVELL, looking steadily at MAXIM, switches his eyes to JULYAN and speaks calmly:

FAVELL

I only want to see justice done. That boat builder's evidence suggested certain possible theories concerning Rebecca's death . . .

One of them, of course, is suicide. Now I've a little note here, which I consider puts that possibility quite out of court . . . Read it, Colonel.

JULYAN

(reading)

"Jack darling—I have just seen the doctor and I'm going down to Manderley right away. I shall be at the cottage all this evening, and shall leave the door open for you. I have something terribly important to tell you. —Rebecca."

FAVELL

Now does that look like a note from a woman who had made up her mind to kill herself? And apart from that, Colonel, do you mean to tell me that if you wanted to commit suicide, you'd go to all the trouble of putting out to sea in a boat, and then take a hammer and chisel, and laboriously knock holes through the bottom of it? Come, Colonel—as an officer of the law, don't you feel that there are some slight grounds for *suspicion*?

JULYAN

(gravely)

Of murder?

FAVELL

(interrupting casually)

What else? You've known Max a long time, so you know he's the old-fashioned type who'd die to defend his honor—or who'd kill for it!

FRANK

(steps up hurriedly and furiously)

It's blackmail—blackmail pure and simple.

JULYAN

Blackmail is not so pure, nor so simple. It can bring a lot of trouble to a great many people, and sometimes the blackmailer finds himself in jail at the end of it.

FAVELL

Oh, I see. You're going to hold de Winter's hand through this. Just because he's the big noise around here and he's actually permitted you to dine with him.

JULYAN

Be careful, Favell... You've brought an accusation of murder. Have you any witnesses?

FAVELL

I do have a witness. It's that fellow Ben. If that stupid coroner hadn't been as much of a snob as you are, he'd have seen that halfwit was hiding something.

JULYAN

And why should Ben do that?

FAVELL

Because we caught him once, Rebecca and I, peering at us through the cottage window. Rebecca threatened him with the asylum. *That's* why he was afraid to speak. But he was always hanging about; he must have seen this whole thing...

FRANK

(breaking in)

It's ridiculous even listening to all of this!

FAVELL

You're like a little trades union, all of you, aren't you? And if my guess is right, there's a bit of malice in your soul toward me, isn't there, Crawley? Crawley didn't have much success with Rebecca. But he ought to have more luck this time. The bride will be grateful for your fraternal arm, Crawley, in a week or so—every time she faints, in fact...

Suddenly MAXIM moves forward and strikes FAVELL on the point of the jaw, stopping his words. FAVELL crumples and falls as we hear:

JULYAN

De Winter!

"I"

(screams)

Maxim, please!

(goes to him)

FAVELL

(nursing his jaw, rises, smiling)

That temper of yours will do you in yet, Max.

There is a knock on the door. The PROPRIETOR enters with the drinks, places them before them.

PROPRIETOR

Excuse me, gentlemen. Now is there anything else?

FAVELL

Yes. You might bring Mr. de Winter a sedative.

JULYAN

(shortly to the PROPRIETOR*)*

No, no, nothing at all. Just leave us.

The PROPRIETOR looks strangely around and exits from the room, closing the door. FAVELL reaches for one of the two drinks and drinks it greedily.

JULYAN

And now, Favell, let's get this business over with. Since you have this whole thing worked out so carefully, perhaps you can provide us with a motive?

FAVELL

I knew you were going to bring that up, Colonel. I've read enough detective stories to know there must always be a motive. And if you will all excuse me for a moment, I'll supply that too.

MAXIM looks at "I," sees the great alarm in her face. He tries to give her a reassuring smile.

MAXIM

I wish you'd go home. I don't think you ought to stay through all this.

"I"

(pleadingly)

No, no. Please let me stay, Maxim.

FRANK

Surely, Colonel, you're not going to allow this man to—

Before he can go on, JULYAN puts up a restraining hand.

JULYAN

My opinion of Favell is no higher than yours, Crawley, but in my official capacity, I have no alternative but to pursue his accusation.

As he has been speaking, we have heard the door opening.

FAVELL

I agree with you entirely, Colonel.

FAVELL is standing at the door in an attitude of mock gravity.

FAVELL

In a matter so serious as this we should make sure of every point, explore every avenue, in fact, to coin a phrase, leave no stone unturned.

FAVELL looks past the open door.

Ah, here she is . . . the missing link . . . the witness who will help supply the motive!

As he is saying these words, MRS. DANVERS has stepped into the room, and FAVELL closes the door behind her.

FAVELL

Colonel Julyan—Mrs. Danvers. I believe you know everyone else.

JULYAN

Won't you sit down?

FAVELL pulls out a chair, which MRS. DANVERS ignores.

FAVELL

No offense, Colonel, but I think if *I* put this to Danny she'll understand it more easily.

(he turns back to Mrs. Danvers)

Danny—who was Rebecca's doctor?

MRS. DANVERS

(coldly)

Mr. de Winter always had Dr. McClean from the village.

FAVELL

(urgently)

Now you heard . . . I said *Rebecca's* doctor—in London.

MRS. DANVERS

I don't know anything about that.

FAVELL

Don't give me that, Danny. You knew everything about Rebecca. You knew she was in love with me, didn't you? Surely you haven't forgotten the good times she and I used to have down at the cottage on the beach.

MRS. DANVERS

She had a right to amuse herself, didn't she? Love was a game with her, only a game. It made her laugh, I tell you. She used to sit on her bed and rock with laughter at the lot of you.

JULYAN

Can you think of any reason why Mrs. de Winter should have taken her own life?

MRS. DANVERS

No... No. I refuse to believe it. I knew everything about her, and I *won't* believe it.

FAVELL

There—you see? It's impossible. She knows that as well as I do.

Listen to me, Danny... we know that Rebecca went to a doctor in London on the last day of her life. Who was it?

MRS. DANVERS

I don't know!

FAVELL

I understand, Danny. You think we're asking you to reveal secrets of Rebecca's life. You're trying to defend her. That's what *I'm* doing. I'm trying to clear her name of the suspicion of suicide.

JULYAN

(steps forward)

Mrs. Danvers, it has been suggested that Mrs. de Winter was deliberately murdered.

FAVELL

There you have it in a nutshell, Danny. But there's one more thing you'll want to know—the name of the murderer. It's a lovely name that rolls off the tongue so easily—George Fortescue Maximilian de Winter.

MRS. DANVERS displays a look of horror.

MRS. DANVERS

There was a doctor. Mrs. de Winter sometimes went to him privately. She used to go to him even before she was married.

FAVELL

We don't want reminiscences, Danny. What was his name?

MRS. DANVERS

Dr. Baker—165 Goldhawk Road—Shepherd's Bush . . .

FAVELL

(triumphantly)

There you are, Colonel! There's where you'll find your motive! Go and question Dr. Baker! He'll tell you why Rebecca went to him—to confirm the fact that she was going to have a child—a sweet, curly-headed little child.

MRS. DANVERS

It isn't true! It isn't true! She would have told me!

FAVELL

She told Max about it—Max, who knew *he* wasn't the father! So, like the gentleman of the old school that he is, he killed her!

JULYAN

I'm afraid we shall have to question this Dr. Baker.

FAVELL

Hear! Hear! . . . But for safety's sake, I think I'd like to go along too.

JULYAN

Yes, unfortunately, I suppose you have the right to ask that . . .

(*He starts out*)

I shall see the coroner and arrange for the inquest to be postponed ponding further evidence.

FAVELL

(watching JULYAN *exit)*

Aren't you rather afraid that the—uh—shall we say the prisoner will bolt?

JULYAN

You have *my* word for it that he will not do that.

(*he exits*)

FAVELL

Toodle-oo, Max, old boy . . . Come along Danny . . . Let's leave the unhappy couple to spend their last minutes together alone . . .

He starts to leave—MRS. DANVERS following. She throws a cold glance at MAXIM and exits.

DISSOLVE TO: EXT. INN—DAY

Outside the inn is the big de Winter car. MAXIM is walking with "I" toward the cars, FRANK behind them.

"I"

(concealing all emotion)

Are you sure you don't want me to go with you, Max?

MAXIM

You'd better not, darling. The journey would be very tiring for you . . . I'll be back the very first thing in the morning. I won't even stop to sleep.

"I"

(simply, covering her own feelings completely)

I'll be waiting for you.

She kisses him and gets into the large car. The CHAUFFEUR steps into the scene. MAXIM gives him a nod to leave, which he does. MAXIM closes the door of the car himself, as JULYAN enters.

JULYAN

Ready, Maxim?

MAXIM

Yes.

JULYAN

You two go along ahead. I'll follow along with Favell.

The road is either in the country or somewhere that looks like the suburbs of London. One car is following the other, both speeding.

DISSOLVE

*FADE IN: EXT. GOLDHAWK ROAD—
EXTREME LONG SHOT—(STOCK)—NIGHT*

Goldhawk Road, Shepherd's Bush. A house which has steps leading up to it, rather like a New York brownstone house, the cars of MAXIM and FAVELL are drawn up. MAXIM, JULYAN, CRAWLEY, and FAVELL are going up the steps.

DISSOLVE TO: INT. CONSULTING ROOM—NIGHT

The four men and DR. BAKER are sitting in the doctor's consulting room.

JULYAN

Dr. Baker, you may have seen Mr. de Winter's name in the papers . . .

DR. BAKER

Oh yes . . . yes . . . In connection with the body that was found in a boat . . . My wife was reading all about it. Very sad case . . . My condolences, Mr. de Winter.

FAVELL

This is going to take hours—let me—

JULYAN

(interposes sharply)

Don't bother, Favell . . . I think I can tell Dr. Baker.

(turns back to DR. BAKER)

We're trying to discover certain facts concerning the late Mrs. de Winter's activities on the day of her death, October the twelfth, last year. I want like you to tell me, if you can, whether any one of that name paid you a visit on that date.

DR. BAKER

(worried)

I'm awfully sorry, but I'm afraid I can't help you. I should have remembered the name de Winter. I've never attended a Mrs. de Winter in my life.

FAVELL

(sharply)

How could you possibly tell all your patients' names?

DR. BAKER

I can look it up in my engagement diary if you like.

(picks up engagement book from his desk)

Did you say the twelfth of October?

JULYAN

Yes.

DR. BAKER looks through his engagement book.

DR. BAKER

Ah, here we are . . . No . . . No de Winter.

FAVELL

(disappointed)

Are you sure?

DR. BAKER

Here are all the appointments for that day . . . Ross . . . Campbell . . . Steadall . . . Perrino . . . Danvers . . . Matthews . . .

MAXIM

(suddenly cries out)

Hold on!

FAVELL

Danny! What the devil . . .

JULYAN

Did you say Danvers?

DR. BAKER

Yes, I have Mrs. Danvers for three o'clock.

FAVELL

What did she look like? Can you remember?

DR. BAKER

Yes, I remember her quite well. She was a very beautiful woman—tail, dark, exquisitely dressed.

FRANK

Rebecca!

JULYAN

This lady must have used an assumed name.

DR. BAKER

Is that so? . . . This *is* a surprise! I'd known her for a long time.

FAVELL

What was the matter with her?

DR. BAKER

(interposes protestingly)

My dear sir—there are certain ethics —

FRANK

(interrupting)

Could you supply a reason, Dr. Baker, for Mrs. de Winter's suicide?

FAVELL

(breaking in quickly)

For her *murder*, you mean! She was going to have a kid, wasn't she? Come on—out with it! Tell me, what else would a woman of her class be doing in a dump like this?

DR. BAKER

I assume that the official nature of this visit makes it necessary for me . . .

JULYAN

I assure you that we would not be troubling you if it were *not* necessary.

DR. BAKER

You want to know if I can suggest any motive as to why Mrs. de Winter should have taken her life? Yes, I think I can. The woman who called herself Mrs. Danvers was very seriously ill.

MAXIM

She was not going to have a child?

DR. BAKER

That was what she thought . . . But my diagnosis was different. I sent her to a well-known specialist for an examination and x-rays . . . and on this date, she returned to learn his report . . .

(he speaks gravely. All are listening intently.)

I remember her standing here holding out her hand for the photograph. "I want to know the truth," she said. "I don't want soft words and a bedside manner. If I'm for it, you can tell me right away." I knew that she was not the type to accept a lie. She asked for the truth, and I let her have it . . . She thanked me . . . I never saw her again, so I assumed . . .

MAXIM

What was wrong with her?

DR. BAKER

Cancer. Yes . . . The growth was deep-rooted. An operation would have been no earthly use at all. In a short time, she would have been under morphia. There was *nothing* that could be done for her—except wait.

MAXIM

Did she say anything—when you told her —

DR. BAKER

She smiled in a queer sort of way... Your wife was a wonderful woman, Mr. de Winter... and, oh yes... I remember she said something that struck me as being very peculiar at the time... When I told her it was a matter of months, she said, "Oh no, Doctor, not that long."

JULYAN

You've been very kind, and you have told us all we wanted to know. We shall probably need an official verification...

DR. BAKER

Verification?

JULYAN

Yes—to confirm the verdict of suicide.

DR. BAKER

I understand... Can I offer you gentlemen a glass of sherry?

JULYAN

No, very kind, but I think we ought to be going.

DISSOLVE TO: EXT. DR. BAKER'S—NIGHT

The four come down from the doctor's house and over toward the cars at the curb.

FRANK

Thank Heaven we know the truth!

They have now all reached the cars at the curb.

JULYAN

Dreadful thing—dreadful. A young and lovely woman like that... No wonder.

FAVELL

I never had the remotest idea. Neither did Danny, I'm sure. Wish I had a drink!

FRANK

Will we be needed further at the inquest, Colonel Julyan?

JULYAN

No. I can see to it that Max is not troubled any further.

FAVELL

Are you ready to start, Colonel?

JULYAN

No, thank you. I'm staying in town tonight. And let me tell you, Favell, blackmail is not much of a profession. We know how to deal with it in our part of the world. Strange as it may seem to you.

FAVELL

I'm sure that I don't know what you're talking about! But if you ever need a new car, Colonel, just let me know.

FAVELL goes off.

MAXIM

Impossible to thank you for your kindness to us through all this. You know how I feel without my saying it.

JULYAN

Not at all. Put the whole thing behind you. But let your wife know, or she'll be getting worried.

MAXIM

Yes, of course I'll phone straight her at once, and we'll get straight along to Manderley.

As MAXIM goes off, JULYAN turns to FRANK.

JULYAN

Goodbye, Crawley. Maxim's got a great friend.

As JULYAN goes off, MAXIM returns. FRANK helps him put on his topcoat.

MAXIM

Frank.

FRANK

Yes, Maxim?

MAXIM

There's something you don't know. I didn't kill her, Frank . . .

(FRANK's *face betrays relief*)

But I know now that when she told me about the child, she *wanted* me to kill her . . . She lied on purpose . . . She foresaw the whole thing . . . That's why she stood there laughing when she . . .

FRANK

Don't think about it any more.

MAXIM

Thank you, Frank.

DISSOLVE TO: INT. STREET PHONE BOOTH—NIGHT

FAVELL is at the phone. He hears a reply in the receiver and speaks into the mouthpiece:

FAVELL
(bitterly)
Hello, Danny . . . I just wanted to tell you the news . . . Rebecca held out on both of us . . . She had *cancer!* . . . Yes—suicide . . . And now Max and that dear little bride of his will be about to stay on at Manderley and live happily ever after . . . Bye bye, Danny.

FAVELL comes from the phone booth and walks to his car at the curb, where a POLICEMAN is standing.

POLICEMAN
Is this your car, sir?

FAVELL
Yes.

POLICEMAN
Will you be going soon? This isn't a parking place, you know.

FAVELL
Oh, isn't it? Well, people are entitled to leave their cars outside if they want to. It's a pity some of you fellows haven't anything better to do!

EXT. COUNTRY ROAD—NIGHT—SEMI CLOSE UP

MAXIM and FRANK are driving back to Manderley.

FRANK
When you phoned her, did she say she'd wait up?

MAXIM
Yes—I asked her to go to bed, but she wouldn't hear of it. I wish I could get more speed out of this thing!

FRANK
Is something troubling you, Maxim?

MAXIM
I can't get over the feeling that something's wrong.

EXT. MANLERLEY—LONG SHOT—HIGHT

While heavy clouds pass over the roof of Manderley, we see a strange light passing through the upper windows. The whole of the place is in darkness otherwise.

INT. HALL

From the top of the stairs we see ahead of us a moving light, which traverses the paneled walls and staircase. We follow it down and down until it reaches the open library door. The light passes through into the library and eventually reveals "I" asleep in a chair. The light also includes JASPER, who raises his head. There are a few nearly dead embers in the fireplace, which do not add to the light in the room.

We see the back of MRS. DANVERS' head and shoulders. She is carrying a lighted candle. She looks down at the sleeping "I" and then turns round into the camera, a mysterious, cunning look on her face, which is lit from below by the candle she holds.

EXT. COUNTRY ROAD—LONG SHOT—NIGHT

On the country road, suddenly MAXIM pulls the car up with a jerk.

MAXIM

Frank.

FRANK

What's the matter? . . . why did we stop?

MAXIM

What time is it?

FRANK

This clock's wrong. It must be three or four. Why?

MAXIM

That can't be the dawn breaking over there.

FRANK

It's in the winter you see the Northern Lights, isn't it?

MAXIM

That's not the Northern Lights . . . That's Manderley!

MAXIM starts the car off frantically in a burst of speed.

Finally they come to the lawn in front of Manderley. The whole place is in flames. Furniture has been piled high in front of the house, servants moving about in their night attire.

MAXIM and FRANK get out of the car.

MAXIM

Frith, Frith!

FRITH

I thought I saw her, sir.

MAXIM

Where?

"I" comes, led by JASPER on a leash.

"I"

(rushing toward him)

Maxim! Maxim!

She flies into his arms. He holds her silently and tightly to him, her face pressed against his coat.

"I"

Maxim, Maxim! Thank God you've come back to me!

MAXIM

My darling! Are you all right?

They kiss.

"I"

Mrs. Danvers. She's gone mad. She told me she'd rather destroy Manderley than see us happy here.

A SERVANT

Look! The west wing!

We see flames flashing through a window, and MRS. DANVERS rushing about inside, surrounded by flames. A flaming roof comes down on her head. It is Rebecca's room, and we see her bed and sheets, with the initial "*R*," also in flames.

www.ingramcontent.com/pod-product-compliance
Lightning Source LLC
Chambersburg PA
CBHW070642310726
48982CB00001B/386
* 9 7 9 8 3 5 0 5 0 1 8 1 0 *